MW01486781

RESCUING REBEL

Guardian Hostage Rescue Specialists

ELLIE MASTERS   USA TODAY BESTSELLING AUTHOR

MASTER OF SUSPENSE

JEM Publishing

Editor: Erin Toland

Proofreader: Roxane Leblanc

Published in the United States of America

JEM Publishing

ISBN: 978-1-952625-82-4

Dedication

This book is dedicated to my one and only—my amazing and wonderful husband.

Without your care and support, my writing would not have made it this far.

You pushed me when I needed to be pushed.

You supported me when I felt discouraged.

You believed in me when I didn't believe in myself.

If it weren't for you, this book never would have come to life.

Also by Ellie Masters

The LIGHTER SIDE

Ellie Masters is the lighter side of the Jet & Ellie Masters writing duo! You will find Contemporary Romance, Military Romance, Romantic Suspense, Billionaire Romance, and Rock Star Romance in Ellie's Works.

YOU CAN FIND ELLIE'S BOOKS HERE:

ELLIEMASTERS.COM/BOOKS

Military Romance

Guardian Hostage Rescue Specialists

Rescuing Melissa

(Get a FREE copy of Rescuing Melissa

when you join Ellie's Newsletter)

Alpha Team

Rescuing Zoe

Rescuing Moira

Rescuing Eve

Rescuing Lily

Rescuing Jinx

Rescuing Maria

Bravo Team

Rescuing Angie

Rescuing Isabelle

Rescuing Carmen

Rescuing Rosalie

Rescuing Kaye

Cara's Protector

Rescuing Barbi

Charlie Team

Rescuing Rebel

Rescuing Stitch

Military Romance

Guardian Personal Protection Specialists

Sybil's Protector

Lyra's Protector

The One I Want Series

(Small Town, Military Heroes)

By Jet & Ellie Masters

EACH BOOK IN THIS SERIES CAN BE READ AS A STANDALONE AND IS ABOUT A DIFFERENT COUPLE WITH AN HEA.

Saving Abby

Saving Ariel

Saving Brie

Saving Cate

Saving Dani

Saving Jen

Rockstar Romance

The Angel Fire Rock Romance Series

EACH BOOK IN THIS SERIES CAN BE READ AS A STANDALONE AND IS ABOUT A DIFFERENT COUPLE WITH AN HEA. IT IS RECOMMENDED THEY ARE READ IN ORDER.

Ashes to New (prequel)

Heart's Insanity (book 1)

Heart's Desire (book 2)

Heart's Collide (book 3)

Hearts Divided (book 4)

Hearts Entwined (book5)

Forest's FALL (book 6)

Hearts The Last Beat (book7)

Contemporary Romance

Firestorm

(KRISTY BROMBERG'S EVERYDAY HEROES WORLD)

Billionaire Romance
Billionaire Boys Club

Hawke

Richard

Brody

Contemporary Romance

Cocky Captain

(VI KEELAND & PENELOPE WARD'S COCKY HERO WORLD)

Romantic Suspense

EACH BOOK IS A STANDALONE NOVEL.

The Starling

~AND~

Science Fiction

Ellie Masters writing as L.A. Warren

Vendel Rising: a Science Fiction Serialized Novel

To My Readers

This book is a work of fiction. It does not exist in the real world and should not be construed as reality. As in most romantic fiction, I've taken liberties. I've compressed the romance into a sliver of time. I've allowed these characters to develop strong bonds of trust over a matter of days.

This does not happen in real life where you, my amazing readers, live. Take more time in your romance and learn who you're giving a piece of your heart to. I urge you to move with caution. Always protect yourself.

Grab the First Book in The Guardian Hostage Rescue Specialists Series for Free

ONE

Ethan

"BREACHING IN 3... 2... 1..." MY BOOT SLAMS INTO THE DOOR, splintering it open. The smell hits me first, invading my nostrils. It settles deep into my lungs. Charlie team, my team, pours through the splintered door behind me, weapons sweeping side to side.

The thick, metallic tang of blood overwhelms my senses and hangs heavy in the stale air. Heavy enough to taste as it slithers down the back of my throat. Heavy enough to smell as the acrid scent settles deep into my lungs. Heavy enough to touch as if I could pluck the congealing liquid from the air.

It's a sensory onslaught.

But we're used to such things. Charlie team presses on, under my leadership, boots sliding grotesquely through the carnage.

Following the gruesome trail leads us to a closed door. My heart pounds, my rifle slick in my sweaty grip. We've arrived too late. The intel was bad.

This was a slaughter.

I nod to the team, taking position. Once again, I kick in a door. This time, I reveal a scene from a horror movie. Bodies tangled together, throats slashed, vacant eyes staring.

They killed the evidence and left a mess behind.

A child lays motionless on a blood-soaked mattress. I approach with a sinking dread. I check for a pulse I know won't be there.

"Dead," I call back to command. "They're all dead."

We're too fucking late.

"Push forward, Charlie-One. There are others to save."

I'd like to say the disembodied voice on the other end of my comms is dispassionate and heartless, except it's CJ, lead for the Guardians. He wouldn't have sent us here if there weren't lives to save.

"Copy that." I rely on the intel of our technical team.

I lead Charlie team down a dimly lit hall, assault rifles at the ready.

"Charlie-One, clear left." My voice rasps low over the comms. Footfalls echo off the concrete as my team leapfrogs down the hall.

The resistance we met and destroyed, getting this far, lingers in the acrid stench of gunpowder coating the back of my throat and the sprays of blood congealing on my fatigues.

"Charlie-Two, clear right," Hank's gruff voice responds, relaying his actions to our team and those sitting at Command and Control.

Our boots thud dully on the cold concrete. They echo off the cavernous walls that have borne silent witness to unspeakable evil.

I spot the first cell, a heavy padlock sealing it shut.

"Cutters!" Reaching behind me, I open my hand, waiting. Jeb hurries over and slams the bolt cutters into my palm. I take the tool and snap through the rusty lock. The door swings open with a screech of rusty metal on rustier hinges.

A girl cowers inside the closet-sized cell, bearing the brutal handiwork of our enemy.

I crouch down, keeping my voice gentle. "It's okay, we're getting you out of here."

She flinches when I reach for her but allows me to guide her into the hall. Eyes wide, she takes in my team of Guardians, unsure if we're heroes sent to save her or devils intent on causing further harm.

Down the corridor, on both sides, small cells showcase the devastating impact of Artemus Gonzales's cruelty, a man whose morals put the devil to shame. One by one, we crack the cells, freeing broken souls. Some sob in relief, some stay silent, but the message is clear—freedom is finally here.

I swallow the bile rising in the back of my throat and focus on the mission of freeing these women.

Charlie team moves swiftly with bolt cutters, methodically freeing each captive. With every lock snapped, the haunting images of these girls—cowering, shuddering, their eyes wide with a mixture of terror and hope—will forever be etched in my mind.

The condition we find them in is horrendous. Artemus Gonzales deprived them of the most basic of human dignities. The mats they sit on are soaked with waste because no buckets were provided in the cramped space. Their medical needs are clearly ignored. Each sunken face bears the indelible imprint of Artemus's monstrous cruelty.

Women drained of life gaze out from behind corroded iron bars with empty, tormented eyes. Their gaunt figures resemble mere skeletons, the tragic result of unending terror and deprivation. They appear more spectral than human. I clench my jaw at the rank air and the rags used for bedding. Monstrous men dehumanized these women, but we'll help these poor victims reclaim what was taken from them.

The air grows thick with emotion: the heartrending sound of relief, the silent gratitude in a tight grip, the paralyzing shock evident on faces that have forgotten the feeling of freedom. The degradation these women suffered is palpable in every putrid mat, every untreated wound, and every sunken cheek—a sickening testament to Artemus Gonzalez's inhumanity.

As we reach the last cell, a fiery-haired woman stands out from the others. Fierce intelligence flickers in her gaze, her spirit unbroken despite the condition we find her in. Though her surroundings scream the same degradation, her defiant eyes speak of a resilience that's hard to find. The lock falls away with a clink, but she doesn't wait for my help. She strides out, a beacon of strength amid despair.

"Form up!" My voice rings out, commanding and clear.

Charlie team forms a protective circle around the women, ensuring every step they take is one step closer to freedom. We're not out of the woods yet, but Charlie team will not fail.

Shouts in the distance and the clatter of hurried footsteps grow louder. Armed resistance is imminent. Our pace quickens, the sounds of battle looming as we move, always vigilant, weapons at the ready.

The dimly lit corridor vibrates with tension, and the weight of responsibility for my men and the vulnerable women has never felt heavier. Every corner we turn, every shadow that moves, might signal the start of a confrontation I'm desperate to avoid but am fully prepared to face.

Suddenly, the sharp report of bullets interrupts our cautious progression. A cluster of Artemus Gonzales's henchmen burst forth from a side passage, their weapons aimed and ready. There's no time for diplomacy, no room for hesitation. We react as we've been trained, moving with the precision of a well-oiled machine.

We're death walking.

"Cover and return fire." I signal two of my men to flank our left while the rest shield the rescued women, pushing them to the safety of alcoves and side passages. Our primary focus is ensuring no further harm comes to these traumatized souls.

Though far from the battle-hardened mold of Charlie team, the redhead displays an impressive awareness of her surroundings.

Not one to be sidelined, she aids in ushering the more vulnerable women into protective spots, a whispered word of encouragement or a steadying hand guiding their way.

Bullets ricochet off the stone walls and sparks illuminate dark corners as the firefight intensifies. Charlie team's resolve shines through. Every shot we take is calculated, and each move is strategic. After a tense few minutes, the corridor goes silent, save our rescues' occasional whimper or muffled cries.

Emerging from our defensive positions, we quickly assess the situation. Artemus's men lay defeated, and though we have a few scrapes and bruises, no major injuries are sustained. Every member of my team and every rescue is accounted for.

We navigate our way out of the estate, moving toward the exfil staging site, a small farmer's hut at the edge of the nearest field.

Unfortunately, another sound, a more menacing threat, pulls me up short. Boots on the ground, moving toward us. I raise a hand and make a fist, signaling the group to stop. Using hand gestures, I instruct the women to huddle low and stay silent. We take cover behind a looming concrete divider, the cold of it pressing into my back. I send two of my team ahead to scout the oncoming threat.

Time stretches, every second punctuated by the thumping of my heart. Suddenly, the relative silence is broken by the *pop-pop* of gunfire, tearing through the tranquility of the night. The ambush is quick and intense. My team takes out the desperate and poorly trained gunmen.

Then, suddenly, there is silence.

Hank, Charlie-Two, raises a fist, then spreads his fingers wide. It means the threat's been neutralized.

"Head for the farmer's hut across the field," I bark out the order, pointing to a small, dimly lit structure in the distance.

Our exfil location was chosen for its field where our chopper can land and extricate those we've rescued.

Under the covering fire of Charlie team, the women, driven by a mixture of fear and determination, dash toward the safety of the farmer's hut. Once inside the modest dwelling, they huddle together, some praying, others staring into the void, their faces pale but resolute.

My team and I take defensive positions, prepared to hold our position and defend those we've rescued.

I call in a status update to Command. "Charlie-One to Command, all friendlies secure. Ready for extraction at LZ, over."

The mission is complete now, but the real fight has only begun. Helping these women reclaim what those monsters tried to destroy —their dignity. Their humanity. Their futures—this is where the Guardian Hostage Rescue Specialists truly shine.

"Charlie, hold for exfil," Command and Control calls out through the comms. *"Bravo inbound."*

"Copy that."

Inside the dimly lit farmer's hut, the women murmur quietly in huddled groups, seeking whatever consolation they can find. Their threadbare clothes hang loosely on malnourished frames, and I scan their faces one by one as my team secures the perimeter.

My gaze sticks on one woman—the redhead with fiery locks and stunning aquamarine eyes. She holds herself taller than the others. Something in her manner sets her apart from the hopelessness surrounding her.

Before I can approach the intriguing redhead, Bravo team arrives with their precious cargo—Alec and Barbi.

They're the reason we're here.

Bravo-Six went missing with his woman, Barbi, not too long ago. That rescue mission brought us to Artemus Gonzales's doorstep, where we expected to recover Alec and Barbi.

With a look at the women around me, we did far more than that. Not only have we rescued Alec and Barbi, but we freed a score of women destined for slavery.

Alec and Barbi look rough, tortured, and abused, but they're still fighting strong. Bravo team may have brought them to the safety of the farmer's hut, but Alec embraces Barbi before retreating back to the estate with his team. A true Guardian, he's not done fighting. That man has unfinished business with the monster holding this place.

In their absence, Barbi drifts over to the redhead, introducing herself. The woman bristles at the overture but engages, mentioning the name *"Rebel."*

I file that fact away.

As they talk, I track Rebel's body language. Her questions come sharply, her brow furrowed in concentration as she absorbs every word. Her inquisitiveness catches me off guard.

Why would someone fresh from the horrors of human trafficking be so curious? I find it unusual, making me pause, trying to understand the underlying reasons. Mentally noting her peculiar interest, I shift my focus back to maintaining the safety of this fragile refugee.

We're vulnerable here.

"Hank, Blake." I motion to the north and west windows. "Secure those points. Eyes sharp, I want to know if anyone so much as looks in our direction. Walt, take that door. I need it fortified yesterday. Jeb, Gabe, I want you two outside—perimeter sweep. Stay alert and relay anything suspicious immediately."

Like a well-oiled machine, Charlie team jumps into action. Each move honed by years of training.

The faint roar of an incoming helicopter fills the air, growing louder by the second. It's truly the best sound on Earth. We gather the women and prep them for exfil.

Once the chopper touches the ground, my team guides the women outside and into the waiting aircraft, ensuring they're secured from this hellhole. Barbi and Rebel are the last to board.

As the helicopter lifts off, Rebel sits beside Barbi, gaze fixed on the receding landscape below. Though tempered by the horrors she endured, a formidable spirit radiates from the redhead.

Just then, her head swivels, eyes locking fiercely with mine. In that blistering gaze is a glimpse of the resilient fighter within.

A captive no longer.

I hold her gaze unflinchingly as the helicopter disappears into the sky.

TWO

Ethan

—————

WHEN THE HELICOPTER RETURNS, IT'S CHARLIE TEAM'S TURN FOR extraction. I load my men into the waiting helicopter as Bravo returns from their final act. The expression on Alec's face tells me everything I need to know.

Artemus Gonzales breathes no more.

With the helicopter packed, we head to the airstrip where Guardian HRS's modified passenger plane waits for the final step of our rescue mission.

When I board, the rescued women have already been triaged and seated by the medical team. The medics complete an initial sweep for injuries and explain to the catatonic women what to expect from here on out.

I make my way through the expansive interior of Guardian HRS's customized passenger jet, moving to the back, where I stow my gear for the seven-hour trip back to California.

Up front is the general seating area, plush chairs that fully recline to a flat position. Beyond that is a galley, then a conference room for inflight mission planning. Next, I pass a suite of modified lavatories. In addition to a sink and toilet, they hold full-blown showers, an extravagance for our shell-shocked rescues.

My heart swells with pride with the excellent care shown to these survivors. The shower facilities were installed so they can physically—and emotionally—wash away the vestiges of captivity during the flight back to Guardian HQ.

No detail of their recovery is overlooked.

I spot an area prepared for the women—blankets, clothing, water bottles, and protein bars laid out thoughtfully by the medical team. Counselors speak gently to those who seem ready to talk. Others stare silently ahead, not ready to process their trauma and rescue. When they are, our experts will be there for them.

The entire plane hums with our mission—not just the rescue but rebuilding the lives of victims shattered by trauma. As the newest member of the Guardian HRS team, I'm honored to be part of an organization that works tirelessly to help survivors heal.

My only hope is that I'm equal to the task.

This place—these people—represent more than simple hope to those who need it most. They are Guardians and Saviors, Protectors and Healers, Defenders and Nurturers. Their dedication is unwavering, their commitment unquestionable, and their resolve unshakable.

Every scarred soul that steps through our doors isn't just a life saved but a life ready to be reborn, rebuilt, and renewed.

As I sit among these heroes, I'm filled with a sense of purpose like never before. The weight of my responsibilities as Charlie-One are daunting but also invigorating. On the shoulders of these giants, I'll learn, grow, and hopefully, make a difference.

I'm humbled to be a part of Guardian HRS.

After stowing my gear at the back of the plane, I head to the front and rejoin my team. On the way, Alec thrusts out his hand.

"Name's Alec. Haven't seen you before."

"Ethan Blackwood." I shake his hand. "Took over Charlie team."

My mentor, long-term friend, and former Charlie team leader, Rex, saw my potential amongst the SEAL teams early on, but it was Sam who took a chance and hired me based solely on Rex's word.

Rex convinced Sam I'd be an asset to the team, vouching for my skills honed from years in service to the SEALs and Delta Force. Next thing I knew, I was flying out to interview at their headquarters, getting sized up by Sam, the man in charge of the Guardian Hostage Rescue Specialists, and by Forest Summers, founder of the impressive organization.

Now, I find myself one of the best of the best.

With Rex moving on, I've got some big shoes to fill, taking over as Charlie-One. His wisdom and decades of experience will be sorely missed, but I'm up to the task. Stepping into a new unit, especially as the commander, is always difficult, but leadership is in my blood. Rex saw that early on and knew this would be a good fit for me.

I recall our last conversation as he handed over the reins, clasping my shoulder with his weathered hand. *"Charlie team is yours now. Lead them well. They won't let you down."*

"Ah, Charlie's new commander." Alec gives a solid nod. "Nice to meet you, and thanks for getting me out of that hellhole." Alec turns to his teammate Brady with a burning question. "How did you guys find us? They removed my trackers."

"Mitzy Magic," Brady laughs, leaning back in his chair. "It never ceases to amaze me what that woman can do."

I'm only now getting to know who's who around Guardian HRS. They speak of Mitzy, the talented genius of Guardian HRS's technical team.

As for getting Alec out of that hellhole? Charlie acted in support, never knowing what we would find beneath Artemus Gonzales's estate.

Alec's experience makes me curious about what Artemus was after. I lean forward, eyes intent. "What did he want from you anyway?"

"Get this—Forest, of all people." Alec shakes his head in disbelief.

Forest Summers, along with his foster sister, Skye Summers, are the co-founders of Guardian HRS. A self-made billionaire, Forest's singular vision is to rid the world of men like Artemus Gonzales, men who feed off the suffering of others.

He's the reason I'm here; Forest Summers, not that creep Gonzales.

With takeoff imminent and the rescued women settled into their seats, I take a moment to appreciate what my new employers do for the survivors we rescue. We not only rescue those who've been taken, but we provide a safe haven for them to heal from unimaginable suffering. Guardian HRS helps survivors rebuild their lives. They manage all stages of recovery through counseling, resources, and community.

With well over a dozen traumatized women on board, the medical team makes the rounds, checking on each under their thin blankets. I assist where I can and find myself assigned to escort each woman to the rear of the plane where she can take advantage of the expanded lavatories and shower—if that's what she wants—and change into clean clothes provided for their comfort.

While they take a moment for themselves, my job is to be ready to provide aid however needed and assist without triggering them.

It's a delicate balance.

To be honest, knowing how I look to other women, I can't help but feel I'm not the best person for this job. I'm a big guy—huge—and more likely to intimidate than anything else. Regardless, I trust the process. Guardian HRS knows what they're doing.

I hope.

I mean, let's look at this clinically.

I escort women to the rear of the aircraft from their seats, where I usher them to lavatories to strip and shower while I stand guard outside.

How is that not triggering?

I don't know, but I'm assured my presence is *comforting* to these women.

After escorting a freshly showered woman back to her seat, my attention is drawn to one woman in particular—the redhead named Rebel. Not too surprising, she sits beside Barbi, the two of them deeply engrossed in conversation.

She's one of the last to avail herself of the facilities.

"We have showers if you want to freshen up." I clear my throat to get her attention.

Freshen up?

What the fuck?

Being confined to a cage, starved, and forced to defecate and urinate in that same cage requires far more than a bit of *freshening up*. I sound like an idiot.

Rebel rises, posture rigid, bare shoulders back. Eyes forward, her shoulders tense. Shoeless, her toes curl into the carpet. Everything about her screams *rage*. Without a word to acknowledge me, she strides down the aisle as if it's her decision to *freshen up*.

Freshen up? I smack my forehead and desperately want to bite back those words.

I follow behind her as she makes her way to the lavatory and hope she doesn't stop suddenly to pivot and call me out for being a perv for following her. It's not like I need to stand outside the lavatory while she showers.

Strike that.

That's exactly my job.

I volunteered to escort the women to and from their seats, watching them closely for signs of *decompensation*.

That's code for losing their ever-loving minds.

At the door to the lavatory, I make a sweeping gesture. It's not like I'm going in there with her. I'm just here in case she freaks out. Swallowing my tongue, I shift my stance. One look at the stunning redhead and it's clear freaking out isn't in her vocabulary.

"Take your time. Everything you need is inside, including clean clothes." I shift from foot to foot, feeling like a fool.

Rebel's eyes blaze before she disappears inside. I stand guard, granting her this moment of privacy to wash away the surface grime —and perhaps start rinsing away her deeper scars.

Despite their brief showers, the other women remain curled in on themselves, blankets gripped tight, still processing their shock. There's power in taking some small bit of control back in their lives.

Rebel, however, carries herself apart from the others, seemingly untouched by the trauma surrounding her. When she exits the lavatory, freshly showered and looking radiant, it's all I can do to remember my role and shut my gaping mouth.

The woman is stunning. Jaw-dropping gorgeous.

I clear my throat. "If there's anything you need…"

Rebel bristles, turning sharply. "I'm fine." She shrugs off my concern, her aquamarine eyes flashing with warning.

I hold up my hands apologetically. "Of course. I just wanted to check."

She gives a terse nod and heads back to her seat, bare feet padding whisper-soft on the carpet. We provide them with slippers, but she opts to dangle those from her fingers rather than slip them on her feet. I don't know why, but her standoffishness heightens my curiosity.

It's the kind of interest that is not only unprofessional but dangerous.

I return to my post, pondering the defiance burning behind those flinty eyes. Whatever inner fire fuels Rebel, it's clear the flames won't be extinguished easily. She piques my curiosity in a way no other survivor has before.

Hours pass, but thoughts of Rebel occupy my mind. When she rises, I trail her to the galley. The sleek space looks more like a high-end lounge than an airplane, with plush leather seats, warm mood lighting, and polished wood detailing.

Rebel studies the offerings—healthy foods juxtaposed with luscious dark chocolates. Her fiery hair tumbles down her back in undulating waves, each strand reminiscent of the vibrant dance of flames in a passionate blaze.

"Do you need anything?" I ask gently.

Rebel tenses, not turning. "I'm fine, thanks." Her tone brooks no argument. She's definitely not interested in making conversation.

"Please let me know if there's any way I can help. Anything you need."

She faces me now, eyes sharp. "I don't need your help. I can take care of myself."

I hold up conciliatory hands. "Meant no offense. You can talk to one of our counselors if you need to. You don't have to go through this alone." I take a step back, giving her room.

Her lip curls derisively. "I'm not interested in counseling or spilling my guts. I'm not traumatized; I'm pissed off. I just want my life back."

Her aquamarine eyes flash with warning as she brushes past me, spine straight, chin high. I resist the urge to touch her, to provide false comfort.

I watch her go, equal parts fascinated and curious. She burns bright, an enigma I long to understand, but her healing must unfold at her pace, not mine.

For now, I'll keep my distance and give her the space she needs to heal in her own way.

THREE

Rebel

WE BEGIN OUR DESCENT HOURS AFTER BOARDING THE PLANE. My fingers grip the armrests, and my jaw clenches. While happy to be out of that hellhole—things *did not* go as I intended—this whole rescue means starting over from scratch.

I'm such a fucking idiot!

Too confident. Too desperate. My perfect plan resulted in perfect chaos. Next time, I'll do things differently.

I ignore the huddled women around me and confine my conversation to a woman named Barbi, asking her everything and anything I can about this organization: the Guardian Hostage Rescue Specialists.

They sound like gallant heroes, and they saved Barbi and her beau, Alec, but these arrogant Guardians ripped me away too soon. Years of sacrifice and careful planning are wasted. Now, I'm forced to begin again.

From scratch.

The plane's tires screech as we land, jolting me backward against the seat. My lips press tightly while I ignore the women whispering around me. I refuse to take comfort in the blanket they draped over me like some trembling victim.

The things I've endured would break these sheltered do-gooders, and while I'm thankful the stench of shit and piss from the cells is gone, I've lost much with this unwanted *rescue*.

Speaking of piss and shit, I'm not too cynical that I don't appreciate the delicate aroma of the floral-scented shampoo and being freshly clean. I keep catching myself twirling my fingers in my hair and lifting the loose curls to my nose.

Lavender. It's my favorite scent.

I'd rather sniff my hair than breathe in the stench of testosterone from these modern-day heroes who *rescued* me. Their *maleness* is a thousand times more potent than the lavender citrus from the shampoo. I take another sniff of my hair and close my eyes.

Violet prefers Jasmine.

Preferred.

Not prefers.

Violet's gone.

Nervous energy hangs thick in the cabin air. Unlike the others, I refuse to huddle under the blanket they gave me like some pitiful victim. I survived hell once already, and I'll claw my way back no matter how long it takes.

That may not make sense, but if you know, you know.

Only one Guardian gives me pause—the man who ripped open my cage and freed me from my *misadventure*. He introduced himself to Barbi's man as Ethan Blackwood. It's a conversation I eavesdropped on, among many others, eager to obtain any information about the operation that ruined my hard work and years of delicate planning.

Although my plan—such as it was—completely fell apart.

His steel-blue gaze holds more intelligence and perception than I like, and when he turns that attention to me, I respond to that potent force. The dark unruliness of his hair does nothing to detract from his overwhelming presence. It only *intensifies* it.

Dark hair.

Blue eyes.

Dimples when he grins.

He's got a body that would put Superman to shame. Yeah, his

type is my kryptonite, and I can't stop staring. My lady bits tingle, indulging in fantasies I'm not ready to process.

Focus!

He's no Clark Kent, and I'm no Lois Lane.

But damn, if I don't want to be.

Learning Guardian secrets from him could prove useful and fun.

But *he's* not on my side. In fact, we're on completely opposite sides.

Not quite an enemy, he and his Guardian friends are self-righteous Samaritans who swooped in oblivious to the battle I waged in the shadows. I have to tread carefully. Perhaps, if I can learn their secrets, it might be something I can sell. Or barter? Or use?

I need to get close to him.

Indulging my interest, while unwise, might be necessary. Attachments are dangerous in my world. Yet I can't miss an opportunity to press Ethan Blackwood for details about these Guardians and their operations. It could be fun wrestling that information out of him from the comfort of his bed.

Honestly, it's been too long since I've enjoyed sex. Too long since I've focused on my pleasure.

With my thoughts on him, I miss the moment the wheels touch down. Featherlight, it's the smoothest landing I've ever experienced. The plane slows, and I steel myself for whatever comes next. I survived hell once already. I can do it again. I'll find some way to turn this setback to my advantage.

These Guardians have no clue about the monsters I've faced or the depths I've sunk to in pursuing my goal.

Let's call it what it is. I'm obsessed.

Darkness provides strength if you let it.

And I refuse to fail.

Hours later, after a transfer off the plane to a bus, we arrive at a place they call The Facility.

We're herded like cattle, led from one place to the next without a care for what we want.

Ugh, I'm about ready to pull my hair out. They want me to play the victim—the traumatized, trembling girl who needs their guiding hand to rest, recuperate, and re-integrate into society. Little do they realize I was never a captive.

At least not in the way they assumed. Not until I fucked up.

I paste on a fragile smile as the perky counselor leads me through The Facility, giving me the hard sell about their comprehensive services.

"We'll get you back on your feet in no time. Group therapy, art, yoga—oh, and the grounds! We have gardens and walking trails and the most delightful little pond. Not to mention the cliffs and the beach below. It's not a sandy beach. It's got pebbles and stones instead of sand, but when the tide's out, the tide pools are a wonder to explore. You have free range of the grounds and don't worry. Our security is tighter than Fort Knox. You'll be safe."

With its cozy living spaces and panoramic windows with million-dollar views, The Facility is deceptively pleasant for a glorified prison.

I tune out her bubbly pitch about all the activities that will *"restore my sense of self."* As if a few trust falls and macaroni necklaces can erase what I endured in that squalid compound. What I gave up to get there in the first place—my identity, my dignity, the last shreds of innocence—that's not something they can fix with *woo-woo mumbo-jumbo-magic.*

This place isn't about healing. It's about control. They want to mold us into whatever sympathetic narrative best suits their image, but I refuse to be a character in their PR story.

I'm no one's victim.

As we walk past a common area, women glance up from board games and conversations, their sympathetic eyes following me. My counselor notices. "Oh good! These are some of your fellow survivors. Why don't we stop and chat? We can buddy you up, and they can show you the ropes."

Buddy up?

Um, hell no.

But with a smile fixed on my face, there's no avoiding it. We pause as she waves to the young women. "Ladies, meet our newest arrivals. I know you'll make them feel welcome."

Their assessing eyes crawl over me as we exchange stiff pleasantries. The quicker I extract myself, the better, but the older woman speaks up as I open my mouth to excuse myself.

"You have anger in your eyes." She studies me intently. "You think you're hiding it, but it's plain as day. It'll fester if you don't confront it. Believe me, I know."

How do I tell her I couldn't care less? Like, I'm not here to share sob stories with a stranger. I narrow my eyes, unsettled by her perception. Schooling my features, I force a light laugh.

"I'm just tired. A good night's sleep and I'll be right as rain."

The woman's knowing gaze remains fixed on me a moment longer. Inwardly, I bristle, even as I keep up the façade. I can't afford to have someone see through my act. The counselor makes our goodbyes and steers us toward our assigned rooms, chattering about settling in.

I have to be careful.

Very, very careful.

Before I know it, we're ushered to the dining hall for our first meal at The Facility. The air buzzes with voices and laughter, survivors swapping stories over heaping plates of comfort food. The very picture of a supportive, uplifting environment.

It makes my skin crawl.

A quick glance at the baked chicken and mashed potatoes on my tray leaves me unenthused. My gaze darts around the dining facility, looking for an empty table on the periphery. Spying a small one in the corner by the window, I snag the spot before anyone else approaches.

I'm halfway through forcing down a bite of amazing chicken when a giggle makes me look up. A wisp of a girl, no more than twenty, stands shyly across from me.

"Do you mind if I sit with you? I'm one of the new rescues, too. I'm Daisy."

"I prefer to eat alone, thanks." I fix her with an icy stare. Hell, I'm not here to make friends. Shared trauma does not mean we get to be besties. I shoo her off quickly and focus on the meal I want to hate but secretly love.

I may grab seconds.

Daisy looks stricken. "Oh, um, okay..."

She scurries back to the safety of a crowded table. Part of me feels a twinge of guilt at the kicked-puppy expression on her face, but I force down the unwelcome emotion. I can't afford sympathy or attachment. Those will only compromise my focus.

As I pick at the buttery smooth mound of garlic mashed potatoes, the cafeteria's noise fades into the background.

I feel—trapped.

I don't need their solidarity or sympathy circles. The only allies I trust anymore are my own cunning and a knife in the back. If I'm going to take back what I lost, I have no room for anything as useless as friendship.

Lying awake long past midnight, I finally give up on sleep and slip out of bed. The moonlight paints my spartan room with an eerie indigo glow through the windows. They want us to feel safe, but the armed guards and perimeter fencing give away The Facility's true purpose.

Changing quickly into dark clothes, I open my door and scout the hallway.

Empty.

A night staff member sits at a monitoring station down the hall, head nodding drowsily.

Sloppy.

Hugging the wall, I creep toward the side exit door I passed during intake. The red light on the keypad glows like a taunting eye. No dice there. Moving as silently as a shadow, I head for the main stairwell door. Also securely locked.

Of course.

Frustrated, I sneak back to my room, thoughts churning. I need to find where they keep patient records and files. There must be something useful I can use among those pages, but first, I must figure out a way to slip past their suffocating security.

FOUR

Rebel
———

SLIPPING BACK UNDER THE COVERS, I STARE UP AT THE CEILING. THE Facility may cultivate a tranquil appearance, but it's still a gilded prison. There has to be a way out. I just need to bide my time and probe for weaknesses. A chink in their armor will emerge.

When it does, I'll be ready.

In this way, the days pass until a week's gone by. I take advantage of a lull in the schedule of therapy, art expression, and other useless things. The Facility is located near cliffs looking down on the Pacific Ocean. I go there when I need to think.

When I've had enough nurturing from The Facility's staff.

When I just need to be alone.

I tilt my face to the sun and let its rays warm my skin. A refreshing breeze blows off the ocean and tugs at my hair, carrying the smell of brine and freedom. I can hardly believe I'm standing here after being locked away by Artemus in that cramped cell.

On a clifftop above the Pacific Ocean.

Its vast majesty extends all the way to the horizon, where sea and sky become one.

One week.

Has it been that long?

One week since Ethan Blackwood ripped open my cell door and looked at me like I was worth saving. Now I'm here, on the grounds of The Facility where Guardian HRS brings all its rescued girls, surrounded by high fences and therapy sessions.

It's a safe place, but not where I need to be.

Footsteps approach on the dirt path behind me. Glancing back, I see none other than Ethan Blackwood himself walking toward me as if my thoughts magically conjured him. We make eye contact, and an instinctive spark ignites low in my belly.

Even from a distance, his masculine energy is palpable. His tactical gear accentuates his broad shoulders and muscular build, but his eyes draw me in—intense blue, gazing at me with an unspoken question.

Does he feel this strange magnetism pulling us together, or is it just me?

I offer a small smile in greeting. Ethan comes here to assist in combat training for those of us he and his team rescued. In the week since arriving, I've seen him every other day, and each time, our eyes linger a moment longer than proper. An unspoken tension simmers beneath the surface.

"Getting some air?" His voice is pleasant but neutral as he joins me at the cliff's edge. His unique scent teases my nose. Being near so much raw masculinity makes my skin prickle pleasantly.

"Just appreciating the view." I don't only mean the ocean. From the corner of my eye, I admire the striking lines of Ethan's profile.

I suspect he knows it, too.

We stand in companionable silence for a bit, letting the sound of the waves fill the space between us. A strange peace settles over me, existing beside this man without pressure or expectation. Without words, I know Ethan understands the demons that haunt me. His steady presence gives me hope I can heal.

All too soon, he clears his throat and steps back. "I should head back and get ready for today's lesson. Will I see you at training?"

I nod, offering a small wave as he turns to leave. Our eyes catch and hold for a breathless moment. Something unspoken passes between us before he disappears back down the dirt path. The imprint of his gaze lingers long after he's gone from sight.

Over the next week, Ethan and his team return several times to teach us self-defense. I make sure to partner with him whenever possible, using the exercises as excuses to touch. To graze his arm as if steadying myself or grip his bicep to "break" his hold.

The spark I felt the first day only burns hotter with each interaction. He remains stoic, but I catch his sharp inhale when my fingers linger too long on his arm. See his throat work when I get close. The intensity of our mutual attraction seems to grow with each glance, each touch, and each shared breath.

Despite that attraction, I'm wasting time. I know this, but hope sparks, thinking the Guardians might be able to help me. Before I enlist their aid, I need to know if they'll help rather than hinder. As grateful as I am for being rescued from Artemus's clutches, I've lost valuable ground in my search, and I don't need another rescue getting in my way.

Between mind-numbing art therapy and "sharing circles," I manage to convince a ditzy kitchen staff, Brittany, to let me sneak into the restricted office hall, claiming I need to call someone important to me. I go on about not wanting the Guardians to know.

That they may not approve.

I'm a great actress. Lying comes easily to me.

Brittany laps up the sob story like a puppy. "Oh, you poor thing, they won't judge you."

"I know, but I'd just rather keep this to myself. I don't want them thinking…" I don't finish that sentence.

Truthfully, I have no idea what my lie should be, but fortunately, the human brain is pretty fantastic. It fills in the gaps like a pro, turning my half-stated lie into a full-bodied reality for Brittany. Whatever she pictures, it must be pretty intense because she gestures for me to follow her, eyes darting around, checking to see if the coast is clear.

What a joke.

As soon as she bustles off, I dart through the swinging doors into the administrative corridor. The offices sit dark and empty—perfect for a little unsupervised research. I breeze into the records room, unsurprised to find it securely locked.

That's okay. This is recon. A plan will form when it's ready.

Down the hall, the director's office door stands slightly ajar.

Jackpot.

I slip inside, making a beeline for the file cabinets along the far wall. I hope to find anything on the facility's background, financials, and personnel files—anything potentially useful. Instead of info, all I find are file cabinets stored with junk.

Shit.

I hate the digital age.

It looks like it's time to crack their computer systems.

Easier said than done. I've never seen encryption like this.

Hearing footsteps approach out in the hall, I duck under the desk just as the director himself walks in, oblivious to my presence. I hold my breath, praying he doesn't sit in his chair inches from my face.

Luck is with me. He shuffles some papers on his desk, then departs, locking his office behind him.

I slip out, heart pounding. Another fruitless endeavor, but at least now I know where the administrator's offices are and that they keep nothing on paper. There must be some weakness I can exploit to dig up information on this place. I just have to keep pressing and remain watchful. Sooner or later, they'll make a mistake. And when they do, I'll be there to take full advantage.

Two more weeks of trust falls and art therapy have me ready to lose my ever-loving mind. Fortunately, there's Ethan to distract me.

I join the eager group of women in the gym, snagging a spot up front to increase the chance I'll be paired with Ethan during our self-defense sparring matches.

When he saunters through the doorway with several of his teammates in tow, I arrange my face into a mask of pleasant surprise and give a tentative finger wave. Then, I flutter my fingers over my chest, drawing his eye exactly where I want it to linger. I hate playing the coquettish female, but it works wonders on men.

Always has.

But it doesn't take much to snag a man's attention when you've been gifted with the face of an angel, fiery-red hair, and eyes the color of tropical seas. Beauty is my curse as much as it's a gift.

My point being Artemus Gonzales, who decided I'd be better sold to his clients than working as part of his team. I misjudged that big time.

"Are you settling in all right?" Ethan pauses, his gaze heading exactly where I drew it: my ample bosom. Other than that, he remains frustratingly professional.

"Yes. The staff here is wonderful." Lord, I want to gag on the lie.

Instead, I bat my lashes and simper like a lovestruck fool. He really does look like Superman in the flesh. The only thing missing is the tiny whorl of hair up front.

"I'm happy to hear that." His eyes sweep over me with heightened curiosity.

Good.

Ethan calls for a volunteer, and I eagerly raise my hand. As I join him at the front, he asks me to attack him so he can demonstrate a defensive technique.

I throw a punch aimed at his head. Quick as a viper, he grabs my wrist, pulling me off balance. His other arm wraps around my torso, pinning my free arm to my side as my back presses against his chest.

My pulse spikes at the intimate contact, so much that I barely hear what he says to the class.

"From this position, you can stomp your attacker's foot or throw your head back into their nose." His breath is hot on my ear as he explains.

But I already know how to escape this hold. I deftly snake my foot around his ankle and twist my hips, using leverage to flip our positions until I have Ethan pinned face-first against the wall. A murmur rises from the watching women.

Ethan quickly regains control, but not before his eyes widen in surprise. "Good improvisation." The wheels turn behind his assessing gaze. He knows that wasn't beginner's luck.

Throughout the demonstration, I make sure to engage and ask interested questions, laughing lightly at his lame attempts at humor.

When we pair off to practice maneuvers, I snag him as my partner and smile invitingly, navigating the line between sweet innocence and hungry predator.

Hmm, now that I'm thinking about it. I could eat him alive. Bet he's great in bed. A man like that? With looks like that? He's certainly had plenty of time to practice his moves.

"Let's run through some basic techniques." He clears his throat, and I shake my head, wondering how much of my thoughts were expressed on my face.

As we lightly grapple, I take the opportunity to compliment his strength and finesse. "Could you show me that disarm again? You make it look so easy." I trail a finger along his forearm.

He disengages and clears his throat. "Just remember to keep your stance solid and pivot your hips like I showed you."

I try a few more subtle touches and leading comments, but Ethan remains stubbornly professional, oblivious, or immune to my charms. It's clear he won't be so easily swayed by flirtation alone. His restraint is admirable, if frustrating.

As we lightly tussle, I gain a new appreciation for all those sculpted muscles barely hidden under his shirt.

We continue sparring under the pretense of instruction, but each grapple brings our bodies tight together, limbs tangled in a dangerous dance. My pulse races as our eyes lock again and again. Ethan seems just as affected.

After a slick escape from his hold, he appears determined to test my skills. He forces me into closer contact, and our bodies press tight as we strain against each other.

At one point, he traps me against the wall, his muscular thigh wedged between my legs. Wedged meaning pressed against my lady bits, rubbing said bits. Our heaving chests are inches apart, and his pupils dilate when his gaze drops to my lips.

"Not bad." I can't help but tease him, and I admit to having fun as I slip my tongue out and glide it over my bottom lip. "But never lose focus."

I use the distraction to hook my calf behind his knee, sending us crashing to the mat in a tangle of limbs. We roll until I straddle him, pinning his wrists above his head. I smirk down at his stunned expression.

"You lost focus." I shift my hips and can't help but feel his growing arousal. "That's dangerous."

His jaw tightens, but it's too late. He's aroused. I know it.

And he knows I know it.

Damn, this is fun.

I lean closer, lowering my voice so only he can hear. "Does this frustrate you? Having the woman on top?" He strikes me as the kind of man who never relinquishes control, especially during sex, and I can't be more blatant about what I'm offering.

A grunt is his only reply as he tosses me off and quickly stands. His chest heaves and a light sheen of sweat coats his skin. When he dismisses the class, his frustration is palpable.

I linger as the other women file out and plaster a satisfied smirk on my face. "Thanks for the lesson," I call out sweetly. "I look forward to more *hands-on* training."

Ethan turns away, jaw tight. Oh yes, I got under his skin in more ways than one. Good. The more I disrupt his steely control, the more secrets will spill forth when I finally get him alone.

I'm going to have fun cracking you, Ethan. So much fun.

Over the next few days, I make good on that promise. One day, after class, I fake an ankle injury so he'll walk me back to my room.

"I twisted my ankle. Would you mind helping me back to my room?" I milk it for all it's worth.

With a resigned look, he obliges, letting me lean against his sturdy frame as we move slowly toward the dormitory. When his arm wraps firmly around my waist, my pulse flutters wildly.

At my door, I gaze up through my lashes. "Do you want to come in? I could use some help wrapping my ankle." It's a blatant invitation, and the heat in Ethan's eyes says he knows exactly what I'm offering.

But propriety wins out.

"You should ice it. I'll see you tomorrow."

I grab for any excuse to make him stay. "At least give me your number in case I *need* help."

The corner of his mouth ticks up with amusement. I'm not fooling anyone, but that's the point, right? I'm blatantly inviting him to my room and bed for hot and heavy sex.

"Check with the front office if you need to reach Guardian headquarters." He shakes his head. "And get that ankle checked out if it really is *bothering* you." With that, he pivots sharply and strides away.

He disappears around the corner, leaving me equal parts furious and fascinated. Ethan's discipline is clearly rock-solid.

Seduction and manipulation have failed.

So far.

But…

It's only a matter of finding the right leverage. Once I discover his weakness, I'll exploit it to get what I need. A mind that strong will surely be a goldmine of intel. I just have to keep chiseling away to uncover the cracks.

Until then, I love a good challenge. Ethan will tell me what I need to know, in bed or out.

FIVE

Rebel

IF I HAVE TO TIE-DYE ONE MORE SHIRT, GLAZE ONE MORE CRAPPY mug, or finger-paint another piece of abstract art showing my *feelings*, I'm going to kill myself. Frustrated, I storm out of the art therapy session, an asinine waste of time, and ignore the staff calling out to me, wondering if "I'm *okay.*"

Bloody handprints litter my abandoned canvas. It's a riot of righteous anger and rebellion. Right now, all I want is to feel the warm ocean breeze on my face and taste the salt of the sea.

I need fresh air and space to think.

I head for the coastal trail, where the breeze coming off the ocean whispers through my hair. Down below, the crashing surf booms with the fury of Mother Nature. Its beauty leaves me groping for words I can't seem to find, and its rhythm grounds me, connecting me to the timeless pulse of the earth.

This isn't my first foray to the cliffs since arriving at The Facility. It's the only place that soothes my restless spirit. I'm spinning my wheels and wasting time. I need to get back to what matters, but this place offers an opportunity I can't pass up.

Frustration bubbles up within me, tangling with a myriad of emotions making my chest tighten. I let out a deep breath, tasting the salty tang of the sea and allow myself to gaze out at the endless blue expanse of the ocean.

Seventy feet below me, the waves pummel the rocky shore. Water against stone. Soft against hard. It's a never-ending battle and delivers a powerful message.

Weakness can prevail against great strength. All it takes is perseverance. The raw fury of nature is right there beneath my feet, mimicking how I feel.

A cool breeze carries fine sprays of ocean mist up the cliffs where it grazes my skin and reminds me of the vastness of the world and my place within it.

Talk about feeling small and insignificant.

I squint against the glare of the sun reflecting off the water, taking in the endlessness of the blue horizon. It stretches out before me, vast and infinite. Below me, the rocky beach nestles against the cliffs, constantly shaped and reshaped by the tireless waves.

That's how I feel—constantly reshaped and molded by the forces around me. The sight is both beautiful and haunting, a reminder of how fleeting time can be.

And how much of it I've wasted.

The ocean breeze whips through my hair as I contemplate my next move and stare out at the endless blue expanse. I gather the fiery-red strands into my fist and yank my hair over my shoulder. With my thoughts turning to Ethan, I plait my hair and wonder how best to attack both the problem he presents and the opportunity he offers.

He's proven more disciplined than anticipated. Resistant to my charms. I need to isolate him if I'm going to ratchet up the seduction and extract intel.

Lost in thought, I don't hear him approach until he calls out. "There you are. I heard you stormed out of group and wanted to check on you. Is something wrong?"

I turn, surprise flickering through me. I didn't expect to see him out here, but perhaps fate is on my side.

Perfect timing.

Schooling my features, I arrange my lips into a pleased and somewhat flirtatious smile.

"Fancy running into you here." I keep my voice light and playful.

Ethan moves closer, his brilliant blue eyes roaming my face. "It's a nice spot to get away and think. I come out here myself sometimes."

"You do?" I peer up at him through my lashes.

He nods, hands sliding casually into his pockets. "Yeah, it's a great place to clear your mind."

I sweep my hair over one shoulder, angling my body toward him. "That's exactly what I needed today—fresh air to clear my mind."

Sensing him about to ask again if I'm okay, I hold up one hand to forestall the question. "I'm fine. Just had to get out of 'Art Therapy' and that stuffy room."

Ethan's blue eyes delve into mine, as if trying to decide whether I'm being truthful. He moves even closer, and I'm enveloped by his woodsy scent on the ocean breeze.

Comforting, inviting.

"It helps to talk through what you're feeling. Bottling it up often makes things worse. I've got a willing ear if you need it." He reaches out and touches the tip of my shoulder.

His concern seems so genuine. So real. A small part of me wants to open up and share the real reason that brought me here—the truth, not the lie he knows.

He strikes me as an honest man, a true protector.

Dare I say a hero?

But I force aside that momentary weakness, aiming to steer the conversation to lighter territory. I let out a small, strangled laugh instead.

"I'm not one for deep talks about feelings." I wave a dismissive hand. "I'd much rather enjoy these amazing views... Unless you have something more fun in mind?"

Unable to resist, I reach out and squeeze his bicep in appreciation. Taut muscle flexes under my exploring fingertips. Out of the corner of my eye, his throat works as he swallows.

Men react to touch. It's one tool out of many in my arsenal of seduction.

Hard muscles tense under my fingers.

"Well, uh…" Ethan pauses, gaze dipping briefly to my lips before skittering away. "There's plenty of nature and wildlife to enjoy around here, if you need a distraction."

I perk up, interest piqued. Keeping my voice coy, I take a half step closer, fully in his personal space now. "Oh yeah? What did you have in mind?" I lightly trail my fingertips along his forearm.

Ethan stands his ground, towering over me. This close, I can see his pulse throbbing in his neck. "The tide pools have an amazing little ecosystem if you want to check them out." His voice takes on a deliciously lower octave.

I press close, drawn like a moth to a flame. "That sounds perfect. I'd love for you to show me."

We're now only a breath apart, tension crackling in the scant space between us. His earthy scent surrounds me, the heat of his body calling to me like a siren song. I can almost taste his lips, they're so close…

The world blurs into nothingness, leaving us suspended in a pocket of escalating sexual tension. The crashing waves fade into white noise as we stand in this electric moment.

Ethan's piercing eyes hold mine, our thundering heartbeats seeming to match pace.

After an endless moment, he steps back, breaking the spell. My skin prickles from the sudden absence of his warmth and proximity.

"At low tide, we can explore the tide pools safely down on the beach." Clearing his throat, Ethan gestures to the cliffside path.

Eager for a glimpse of our destination below, I scamper to the very brink of the cliff's edge, but the loose gravel shifts treacherously beneath my feet. Suddenly, I teeter off-balance, tottering far too close to the precipice.

My heart leaps into my throat, but Ethan's strong arm coils

around my waist before panic can take hold. He yanks me back against him, my back crashing against his solid chest.

The abrupt, almost jarring contact with his hard body steals my breath and overwhelms my senses. I gasp, disoriented, my footing still unsteady. Ethan's grip on my waist is the only thing keeping me upright.

Pulse racing, I twist in the cradle of his arms to face him. My hands land reflexively on his rock-hard chest, feeling the thrum of his racing heart beneath my palms. Our faces are mere inches apart.

Looking up, I meet his gaze. He looks genuinely alarmed, his eyes a deep well of untamed concern. The moment stretches; gravity seems to alter, my world narrowing to the space between his eyes and mine.

Still hyped on adrenaline, I whisper, "My hero." The words emerge like a prayer hanging in the suddenly charged air.

Ethan's chest heaves beneath my hands. His eyes bore into me, full of untamed concern and another, more primal emotion. Time seems to slow around us.

His lips part, their magnetic allure a force of nature pulling me in.

My fingers trail up, almost of their own volition, grazing along the coarse terrain of his jawline. I thrill at the contrast of stubbled skin and smooth flesh beneath. Ethan doesn't pull away, his lips parting slightly at my exploratory touch.

We stand balanced on a knife's edge of anticipation, caught in this delicate moment. Then, succumbing to an irresistible pull neither of us can deny, our mouths meet in a fiery kiss.

Everything else fades away.

My eyes flutter closed, senses overwhelmed. The softness of his lips, his intoxicating woodsy taste and scent, the warmth of his skin under my palms—it steals my breath and sets my body ablaze. It's a conflagration of passion, a kiss that's both fierce and tender, consuming and endless.

A low groan rumbles through Ethan's broad chest. His strong arms lock around me like iron bands, crushing me tighter to him.

One hand burrows into my windswept hair, angling my head as he deepens the kiss.

Our tongues meet, tentative and seeking at first. Then growing bolder, both hungry for more. My fingers curl in his shirt, anchoring myself against the onslaught of sensation threatening to sweep me away.

Wave after wave of desire courses through me, burning hotter with every frantic meeting of our mouths. I mold myself to him, awash in the drugging kiss that leaves me dizzy and gasping.

Just when I think I might combust from the scorching heat coiled between us, Ethan breaks the kiss with a ragged gasp.

We stand clutched together, both breathing hard. His pupils are blown wide, lips kiss-swollen. He looks oddly stunned, like a man emerging from a dream.

I laugh breathlessly, trying to cut through the sensual haze fogging my mind. "Maybe I should fall off cliffs more often."

At my joking words, guilt flashes across Ethan's face. He drops his hands from my body as if burned, taking a deliberate step back.

"I'm so sorry. That was completely out of line." He drags a hand through his hair, looking tormented. "I sincerely apologize."

I can't hold back an exaggerated eye roll.

"For kissing me? Men can be so absurdly noble sometimes. I've been trying to get you to notice me for weeks." I poke his chest for emphasis. "Trust me, if I didn't want you to kiss me, you'd currently be writhing on the ground cupping your balls in agony."

Ethan blinks, clearly thrown. I continue before he can respond.

"Second, I'm not made of glass. I won't shatter because someone kisses me." I step closer, looking up into his eyes defiantly. "That just happens to be the best kiss of my life. So don't you dare apologize for it."

Ethan still seems hesitant, so I grab his hand, tracing lazy circles on his palm. His throat bobs. I lean in, dropping my voice. "You promised to show me the tide pools. Who knows what other—fun— might happen down there?"

His chest hitches, and the muscles of his jaw clench. Genuinely confused, I love the way his brows tug together as he tries to remember what he promised.

"Maybe you can think about how professional, or unprofessional, you want that excursion to be." I can't help but tease and be overly suggestive. Ethan's nobility is too strong and is getting in the way. "After a kiss like that, I definitely want to explore what else might happen." I rake my eyes over him suggestively before stepping back.

With a cheeky wave, I sashay away, adding extra sway to my step. His smoldering gaze follows me as I depart. I literally feel the heat of his passion burning a hole through my back.

Let him mull over what he started by that cliff. Next time his noble side rears up, I won't let him pull away so easily. I lick my still-tingling lips as I follow the path back, trying to clear the sensual fog from my mind. Damn, that was an amazing kiss.

He surprises me.

And I can't deny the effect Ethan Blackwood has on me. I didn't anticipate such an intense attraction. Those kisses were blockbuster movie magnificent, straight out of a romance novel, devouring me.

Glancing back, I catch Ethan watching me, eyes simmering with banked heat. Anticipation coils low in my belly. Soon, we'll finish this sensual dance, but letting the tension marinate could make the payoff even sweeter.

Out of sight, I touch my lips, swollen from the fierceness of our kiss. I can't hold back a giddy smile. Playing with fire is risky, but I'm ready to get burned.

Squaring my shoulders, I continue onward, still floating on a hormonal high, but I force myself to refocus. I have my mission. Eyes on what's important. There's far more than a steamy kiss at stake.

Still, maybe mixing a little pleasure into the business wouldn't be so bad. I grin wickedly to myself. Ethan won't know what hit him, and I have a feeling I'm going to thoroughly enjoy every second of letting the anticipation simmer between us.

Time to turn up the heat.

SIX

Rebel

ONLY THE NEXT DAY, CHARLIE TEAM ISN'T THERE TO TEACH US SELF-defense. The men of Alpha team take over. The next month, it's the men of Bravo team. Evidently, Ethan's team is on a training rotation. There's no sign of Charlie team or Ethan for two agonizing months.

I'm about ready to give up when, one morning, I come across Ethan standing alone by the cliffside during my morning stroll.

Drawn by instinct, I approach and touch his arm. He goes very still but doesn't pull away. Slowly, I slide my palm up his shoulder, feeling the hard muscle beneath. Our eyes lock, simmering with unspoken desire.

"Rebel. Don't." My name escapes his lips like a plea.

"Why not?" I press closer, fingers trailing up his neck's strong column. His pulse hammers under my fingertips.

"We can't." Ethan grasps my wandering hand, though he doesn't move away from our charged embrace. "It would be taking advantage."

I shake my head, rising up on tiptoe. "Not if that's what I want," I whisper softly against his lips.

His eyes search mine, looking for any hint of coercion. Finding only willingness, he makes a rough sound and crushes his mouth to mine in a searing kiss.

Warmth spreads through me at the feel of his soft lips. The kiss begins tame, but rapidly deepens, our passion unrestrained now that the gates have opened. I whimper into Ethan's mouth as his tongue strokes mine. His arms yank me flush to his hard chest, leaving no doubt about his desire.

We come up gasping, foreheads pressed together.

"That was..." Ethan struggles for words, his voice rough.

"Perfect." I cradle his face and draw him back to me. With a muffled groan, he gives in, mouth hot and hungry on mine. However this started, we're both falling fast.

We steal what moments we can over the next few weeks, hyper-aware of listening ears and watching eyes. A brush of fingers as we pass in the hall. Stolen kisses in empty rooms. Murmured conversations lasting into the night, laying bare our damaged souls.

Ethan never presses for physical intimacy, letting me set the pace, but the sexual tension between us simmers below the surface. A heated look is enough to convey everything left unspoken between us. I crave his touch, but he seems determined to be a gentleman.

The day comes when Ethan invites me to Guardian HRS head-quarters—my first time leaving The Facility since being rescued. Ethan gives me the grand tour, those piercing eyes monitoring me for any sign of distress.

He's protective to a fault, which I find both endearing and infuriating. I don't need to be handled like something fragile.

At the firing range, I ask if we can go inside. His brows lift, but he puts on a good show, fetching earmuffs and safety glasses. It's been long enough that the weapon feels foreign in my hands, but muscle memory takes over.

I empty the clip in rapid succession, forming a tight cluster over the heart of the human outline.

Lowering the smoking gun, I meet Ethan's stunned expression.

"Beginner's luck?" I quip with forced lightness.

He nods, seeing me in a new light, but I say nothing. He doesn't pry, and for that, I'm grateful.

Everyone has their secrets.

The tour concludes back at The Facility. We wander to the cliff's edge, holding hands, and stare out toward the ocean. The setting sun bathes us in golden rays as we stand close, our shoulders barely touching. A tantalizing contact, hinting at further intimacy to come. My restless hands itch to pull him closer, to feel his body pressed fully against mine.

But Ethan seems content taking things slow.

Too slow. His noble restraint is admirable but also frustrating. Doesn't he feel this urgency between us? This hunger that gets tighter each day we deny it?

Oblivious to my frustration, he takes my hand, stroking his thumb softly over my skin. "Have dinner with me tonight?" His tone holds a new vulnerability. My earlier irritation melts away. This feels like more than satisfying desire.

I lace our fingers together. "I'd love that."

Later that night, I open my door to find Ethan freshly showered, holding a bouquet of wildflowers. The care and hopefulness shining from his eyes melt something inside me. No one has ever looked at me that way.

We enjoy dinner at a cozy restaurant on the waterfront, and conversation flows easily. Laughter comes quickly to my lips for the first time in ages. Away from The Facility and Guardian HRS, we're simply a man and woman sharing an intimate meal.

Exploring a fragile new connection.

Over dessert, Ethan's eyes turn serious. "You're an unexpected breath of fresh air." He brushes his fingers over my wrist.

My throat tightens at his sincerity, but old instincts aren't silenced so easily. The thought of giving someone power over me again chills my blood. Sensing my hesitation, Ethan squeezes my hand. Unspoken words shine from his eyes. He's offering me a choice unlike any I've had before.

That means everything.

In answer, I bring his hand to my lips in a feather-light kiss, pouring all the words I can't yet say into it. The promise of warmth and shelter in his arms calls like a siren song. I'm still afraid, but I believe I can be brave with him.

Outside my room, I tug Ethan into a long, scorching kiss. Trusting him feels terrifying and freeing all at once. When we break apart, there are tears in my eyes.

"Stay with me tonight?" It comes out barely a whisper, and I hold my breath, willing him to say yes.

Ethan's eyes widen fractionally. He understands what I'm asking and what it signifies. Wordlessly, he brushes his lips to my forehead.

"Not yet. I would love nothing better than to spend the night with you, but I don't want to rush things. You need time to process what happened to you. To heal and decide where you want your life to go from here. I don't think it's a good idea for us to take that step just yet."

Disappointment crashes through me. Doesn't he want me in that way? I try to keep the hurt from my eyes.

"Shouldn't I be the one to decide when I'm ready?"

He rushes to explain. "It's only because you mean so much to me. I don't want to rush physical intimacy until you're absolutely certain it's right for you. After what you've been through, it's too soon. I don't want to take advantage of you or have you regret doing something that should be special."

I love how he says *physical intimacy* rather than *sex*. Somehow, it makes it feel as if having sex with him will mean a lot more than simple physical pleasure.

"You're infuriating. I'm literally inviting you to spend the night with me."

"And I'm politely declining." He folds into his strong embrace. "I'm not looking for a one-night stand. I want something real. Something that lasts beyond your stay at The Facility." Leaning back, he pushes the hair back from my face. "Isn't that something worth waiting for?"

"For how long?"

"Until you know without a shadow of a doubt that this is what you want."

"I want this." I try to drag him into my room, but he resists.

"There's tension in your shoulders, a hitch in your breath, and fear in your eyes. We have plenty of time to get to know each other. I'm not going anywhere."

I want to argue more, but the sincerity in his eyes stops me. He's offering to set aside his own desires to protect my heart. That simple act means everything.

I fold my arms across my chest and huff with false indignation. The truth is, I respect Ethan for wanting to take things slow.

My problem is I don't have a lot of time to waste.

More time passes, another couple of weeks. It feels like a dream. Ethan spends all his free time with me, enveloping me in the safety of his world. We cook dinner together and talk late into the night. Make weekend trips up the coast just because. Share a hundred quiet moments I tuck away like jewels.

I know the staff at The Facility whisper about why a man like him is with someone like me. Broken. Damaged goods. But Ethan never tries to change me, even the hardest edges. His quiet faith soothes my jagged pieces until they begin to fit back together again.

Despite the idyllic haze, there's an undercurrent of restlessness in me. A clock ticking at the back of my mind, reminding me this interim period at The Facility can't last.

Leaving will hurt him, but I have no choice other than to continue on my path. I selfishly cling to every moment we share, memorizing the sensation of being cradled in his arms. My time with Ethan has always been a gift I'll treasure for the rest of my life.

But all good things must come to an end.

SEVEN

Ethan

DESPITE THE CLEAR BLUE SKIES AND SERENITY OF THE CALIFORNIAN coastline, a storm brews within me. Everywhere I turn, reminders of Rebel amplify my hunger—a stray redhead in the crowd, the tantalizing scent of Rebel's perfume lingering on the breeze, the soft melody of a tune she always hums. Each one turns simple cravings into visceral pangs of need.

But as much as my body screams for release, my conscience weighs heavily on me. The challenges she faces, the emotional labyrinth she's navigating—her recovery isn't just an obstacle in my path. It's a stark reminder of the care she requires.

She deserves understanding and patience, not the unchecked desires of a madman craving her touch.

When I try to immerse myself in work, her image fills my mind and makes concentration impossible. Whether it's the women's mundane chatter or the ocean's distant roll, every sound around me fades to the background as I remember the echo of her laughter, the promise lingering in her whispered words and the pleasure behind her soft sighs.

Nights are worse. There's no rest in the emptiness of my bed.

The cool sheets do nothing to quell the burning heat that spreads through me when I remember our stolen kisses.

With each night that passes, the divide between what I crave and what seems right widens. I struggle for air, clarity, and control while the beast within me rages for more Rebel.

Yet another beautiful sunny day, I find myself back on The Facility's grounds, getting ready for another training session with the rescues. The quintessential California sun beats down on me, but its warmth pales compared to the fire Rebel ignites when we kiss.

I get to see her today, and lord help me restrain myself.

Three days and three nights have done their worst, dragging out the agony of the desire flowing in my veins. Three restless nights where my sole relief was found in my hand, followed by the fleeting satisfaction of an empty release. What pleasure I experienced was hollow and empty, tainted by my growing frustration.

Each time I close my eyes, Rebel's face, lips, and touch haunt my thoughts. My need becomes a palpable ache clawing at my insides.

I'm a man standing on the edge, teetering dangerously between longing and taking what I want. My hunger for her grows. My desire to taste her lips intensifies. My need to feel her tucked in tight against my body turns dangerous.

But as my desire ignites, I remind myself what brought her here.

There are dangerous lines I shouldn't cross.

The late-midday sunlight streams into the courtyard where we train those we've rescued. My attempts to fill out progress reports on our new students keep getting sidelined when my thoughts drift to Rebel.

Tangled in tactile memories—the warm glide of her skin under my hand, the hungry press of her lips claiming mine—I still feel her curves molded tight around me, our passion cresting like the crashing waves around us.

Even now, my pulse quickens, my body reliving each gasp and desperate plea for more. I shift restlessly, craving her touch, her taste, and her sweet embrace. The woman drives me wild.

I need more.

But there's a line.

A line I can't cross.

With my thoughts in turmoil and not at all focused, Sam, leader of Guardian HRS, makes a surprise appearance. Great, this is exactly what I don't need. I stand at attention as he saunters across the courtyard, his shrewd eyes fixed on me.

His presence, while a surprise, isn't alarming. Sam often pops in unannounced, checking in on his team. It's something he encourages in CJ and Mitzy as a way to enhance teamwork.

"Got a minute?" he asks.

"Just finishing annotating the progress of our trainees. It's time to split them up and work on their strengths."

"Excellent. I'm happy to hear that. I wanted to check in and see how you're acclimating to taking over Charlie team." Sam takes a seat on a low-set wall.

"It's going well. The men have welcomed me. I'm not sensing any friction."

"How's the training going with the women?" Sam's eyes bore into mine.

"I'm impressed by Guardian HRS's dedication to helping those you've rescued to heal."

"You're a part of our team now."

"True, and honored to assist any way I can." I meet his gaze evenly.

"You're fitting right in. My door's always open if any issues arise." Sam smiles and rises. "You seem distracted. Everything okay?"

"Yeah, just tired." I clear my throat, scrambling for composure.

Sam's gaze bores into me. "Well, shake it off. I need you sharp." He claps my shoulder. "Keep your head in the game. Eyes on the prize."

His words couldn't come at a more opportune time. I chose this life of service and sacrifice and won't toss it away, no matter the temptation. Except, no matter what I try, my thoughts turn toward Rebel with her fiery red hair, emerald eyes, and luscious lips.

Closing my eyes, I relive running my hands over the smoothness of her bare skin. Her tiny and delicious gasps and moans stir a reaction in me.

It's an endless loop, making me want her again.

Trying to concentrate and finish my task, I straighten my paperwork and return to work.

That lasts all of thirty seconds.

My problem is I crave her on a cellular level. No matter how much I try to distance myself with work, the ache within me builds. I've tried to remain professional, but the thoughts streaming through my mind are far from professional. Try as I might, they're not going anywhere.

Still, I wrestle for control. Reminding myself she depends on me for safety, not seduction. She's a survivor under my protection, not someone to be touched and tasted so intimately.

Why is that so difficult to remember?

I need to recommit to my duty and keep our relationship professional.

However, when I passed Rebel in the hall this morning, her floral perfume enveloped me. Her whispered words stopped me cold. *I can't stop thinking about you.* Those words keep running through my mind.

It took all my discipline not to pull her into my arms when she said that to me. I groan inwardly, desire simmering in my veins. She's not making restraint easy. I need to resist, but part of me craves more.

Far more.

My thoughts tangle in a battle between duty and reckless want.

Somehow, I make it through my notes before our students arrive.

We're at a point where the women are ready for more focused training according to their strengths and weaknesses. I pair up the women according to their strengths, except for one woman in particular.

When Rebel arrives at practice, she makes a beeline toward me.

"You forgot your promise to show me the tide pools. I've been looking forward to spending time alone with you." She pouts playfully.

I shift on my feet. "Apologies, duty called. We can reschedule when I'm free." I avoid meeting her eyes and hate the brusqueness of my tone. I'm desperately trying to keep things professional while she's constantly trying to seduce me.

"It's an hour to low tide—the perfect time for a stroll on the beach." Stepping close, she trails a finger down my chest. "I want you to take me."

"I don't think we should..." I swallow thickly as her fingertips reach my belt. She loops her finger around the leather and gives a little tug.

"You most definitely should." She gives another, more insistent, tug on my belt. "Unless you think I'm unattractive? Or too *fragile?* Maybe you don't think I can consent, considering why I'm here. Is that the problem?"

She leaves it unspoken how insulting it would be if I think she's too fragile for sex after being rescued from a sex-trafficking ring.

I mean, I get it. Most women would never want to be touched by a man again, but she does. She steps back, giving me room to make up my mind. Why the hell am I being so damn difficult? Others wouldn't think twice and jump on the opportunity for a quick fuck with a willing woman.

Not me.

I'm a valiant warrior with a ridiculous sense of honor.

"You're the most beautiful woman I've ever met, but..."

"I want you to do very bad things to me, Ethan Blackwood, and I'm tired of waiting." Her words are *way* over the top, but they do the trick.

"Maybe after training?" Holy hell, what have I done?

"After training, it is."

She's our most advanced trainee, demonstrating skills far beyond what she openly admits. She's holding back, and I want to know why. It would be great to push her myself, but the last thing I need is more one-on-one time with Rebel.

Before we begin self-defense training, I strategically pair her with

Hank rather than myself. Sam's warning to *Keep my head in the game* runs through my mind.

I intend to do exactly that.

I try to focus on showing Daisy, my student for this session, a proper choke hold, but my eyes keep cutting to Rebel. Hank makes her laugh as they spar and tangle. They're having too much fun, but when she trails a suggestive finger down his arm, leaning in to whisper into his ear, something snaps within me, a simmering jealousy erupting into a full boil.

She meets my stare knowingly. Oh, she's playing with fire, that minx. The beast in me rages to reclaim those smirking lips and erase all traces of another man's touch from her supple skin.

"That hurts." Daisy, my sparring partner, cuts through the red haze.

My grip tightened painfully on her wrist without me realizing it. I release her, clearing my throat, ashamed of my distraction.

"My apologies. You executed that technique well."

Fuck!

I avoid Rebel for the rest of the training session. She stirs a dangerous possessiveness in me, and my lust for her is beyond reason. If I don't get a grip on myself, we'll both end up burned. After training, I don't head to the cliff to meet her as promised.

Instead, I stay late into the afternoon, long after my team leaves, pretending to work, trying in vain to steer my thoughts from Rebel.

Desperately hoping she'll circle back around this way.

I stare blindly at training reports, pen poised in mid-air, my thoughts far from tracking the progress of the women we train.

The memory of Rebel's touch haunts me—her soft curves gliding beneath my palms, her silken hair sliding between my fingers, and her lavender scent flooding my senses.

The woman drives me wild.

I shift in my seat as desire tightens my body, almost painful in its intensity. I can't keep thinking this way. I flip the page in my notebook, and a folded note flutters to the ground. My pulse spikes when I read the hastily scrawled text.

Meet me at the trailhead down to the beach at sunset.
Bring condoms.
~Rebel

My hand shakes as I read Rebel's note for the tenth, twentieth, and thirtieth time. I should throw it away. Toss it in the trash.

I should walk away.

Instead, I bring it to my nose and sniff to see if any trace of her perfume lingers. It does, and a low groan escapes me. This woman... I can't explain her effect on me.

Animalistic hunger tangles with visceral want, turning me into a prowling beast. I pace the courtyard, arguing with myself as the sun dips toward the horizon. The day's heat disappears, swept eastward by the prevailing winds coming off the ocean, but my blood boils with raw, carnal desire.

This is reckless.

Dangerous.

My thoughts of her are madness.

Even though I know I shouldn't, I find myself striding toward the cliffs, my pace quickening the closer I get. Marching like a fool toward disaster. Running to my doom.

Racing toward Rebel.

With plenty of condoms.

EIGHT

Rebel

I MEANDER THROUGH THE BUILDINGS THAT MAKE UP THE FACILITY until finally coming to the raw beauty of windswept grasses that blanket the cliffs of Northern California. The blades of grass bow and dance in the gusts, whispering to the rhythm of an unseen force. To the west, the Pacific Ocean stretches to the horizon, its vastness a weighty presence anchoring me to this moment.

My promise to Violet weighs on me like a silent, heavy thing, dragging me down to the depths. She's everywhere and nowhere—whispers in the wind and echoes in the waves.

It's time to leave. Time to keep my promise. I've lingered here too long.

But first, I pray Ethan will come. Hope pulses through me that he read my note and will come. It's selfish of me to use him, but I can't leave before stealing one night of intimacy—one night where I can get lost in the illusion that everything is okay, even if just for a fleeting moment.

And then it happens.

A subtle change, a softening in the relentless wind. I pivot away from the churning of the ocean, my heart kicking against my ribs.

It's Ethan.

He came.

A wave of relief surges through me, so intense it nearly buckles my knees. There's a flutter in my chest, a rapid dance of anticipation at the sight of him, knowing what his arrival means.

As he nears, there's determination in his approach, a cadence of assurance that thrums through the air. It's in the certainty of his stride, the resolute tilt of his jaw, and the unwavering focus in his eyes.

This man has the power to carry my pain away.

Despite his determined stride, Ethan's pace holds a deceptive calm, an unhurried ease that belies the purpose that drives him. He moves with a tranquility that's out of place in this landscape, a stark contrast to the storm of memories churning within me.

His intense and piercing gaze wraps around me long before he's close enough to speak. When his eyes meet mine, they steady the chaos of my thoughts. Of course, he knows nothing about my past. I hold that close, revealing it to no one.

Nevertheless, I find haven in the depths of his eyes. It's a look that doesn't just see me, but finds me. With just a glance, he offers a lifeline, and in that moment, I'm not just seen—I'm known.

If only I could trust him with my secrets. Instead, I will use him and lose him.

"How is therapy going?" Ethan's words reach out, grounding me back to the present, to life, and to hope.

"Therapy is stupid, and it's the last thing I want to discuss."

"I'm worried about you. If something's bothering you, I'm here."

"You're determined to fix me, aren't you?"

"I'm determined to ensure you're in a good place mentally, emotionally, spiritually, and physically before you're—"

"Released?"

"That's not what—"

"Then you mean to ask if I'm in a good place mentally, emotionally, spiritually, and physically before I consent to sex?" I scoff at him. "Seriously, if I thought it was going to be this hard—"

"That's not a character flaw."

"I don't need to be mentally, emotionally, or spiritually anything. I just need to want it." I pull up short. "Look, if you're not interested, then by all means..." I make a sweeping gesture back the way he came.

"Rebel..." He pauses. "Would you rather me take what I want and not care what you need? That's not the kind of man I am."

"Look, right now, I want to do what men and women do when their chemistry is off the charts hot. I don't want to be reminded I was a victim you saved. There's nothing sexy about that. Stay or go. Chose now. Decide now. But choose me."

"I don't want to take advantage of—"

"If you dare say the words *fragile*, or *survivor*, or any of the things they try to tell us in group, I'm going to scream. I want is to feel *normal*. I want to be with a handsome man, walk on the beach at sunset, look at a few tide pools if we can, then find someplace secluded to be swept off my feet by an amazing kiss, and what I hope to be much more." I stare up at him, watching the play of expressions parade across his face.

He knows what will happen if he follows me to the beach, and I'm tired of waiting. With a puff of breath to push an errant curl out of my eyes, I spin around and march down the rocky path.

Agonizing seconds pass—agony when I think he won't follow— but the crunch of gravel behind me tells me everything I need to know.

Ethan is more than willing to join me down on the beach. As for sex? Who knows? His gallant-knight-on-a-white-stallion-savior-thing might still get in the way.

We descend the cliffside path in silence.

Once on the beach, I take a shaky breath. "It's just—memories of what was done to me are things I don't want to visit. They don't haunt me like they do the others. I'm way more resilient than most people. I don't want to discuss that in therapy, but I listen to what they say. To take back our lives, we need to find a new normal. I don't need *new*. I just need normal, and you feel a whole lot like normal. A man I can get lost in."

Ethan's jaw tightens. "I can't imagine how traumatic that must have been for you. You have such strength. Would it help to share what happened with me? I find the act of discussing trauma is generally a good first step to overcoming it."

I cling to his arm. "Something about you makes me feel safe, but discussing *that* with *you?* It only makes me feel worse about what happened. Maybe later?" I place my palm gently on his chest. His heart pounds rapidly under my touch.

"I'm here if you feel safe to share." Clearly, he needs to hear my sob story before anything between us has a chance of beginning.

I take a breath and share a story that's not mine. It's ridiculous, but he's not going to let this go. The Alpha Hero in him demands he save me from my *trauma* in addition to rescuing me from that hellacious place.

"I met a man at a cafe near my college. He was charming and handsome. Said all the right things to make me believe he cared." This is not my story. It belongs to my sister, but I can't help but get choked up telling it. I describe Violet's abductor wooing me, planting ideas of a future together. "He gained my trust before asking me to meet him at a secluded spot. When I arrived, everything changed." I recount what Violet told me, those few rushed words before her abductor turned hostile, forcing her into a vehicle.

Taking her.

"For days, he kept me locked up. I had no idea what he planned for me. I thought he was going to kill me." I make my voice shake and cling to Ethan, selling Violet's trauma.

Ethan covers my hand with his own. "You never have to fear that again. I promise I'll protect you." His voice rings with sincerity.

"How?"

"How, what?"

"How can you promise that? Unless you're always going to be around me, I don't see how you can make that promise."

Ethan meets my searching gaze. "I'll train you to defend yourself when I'm not around. Not just how to defend yourself but how to anticipate and read an environment. How to know when it's unsafe and when you need to leave."

I give him a brave smile. "Thank you. It means so much to have someone like you watching over me."

Seriously, his hero complex is too much. It's sickening, but—honestly?—a little part of me wants to believe men like him still exist. Sadly, most men are assholes or monsters.

Ethan pulls me into a gentle yet solid embrace. I hide my smile against the warm strength of his chest. His spicy scent lifts on the breeze and envelops me. He's slipping deeper into my trap with each tender gesture, but so am I. I'm falling for my gallant savior.

I would love to stay in his arms forever and live the future life he sees for me, but my path is a different, more treacherous one.

When we continue walking, I squeeze his hand as if cementing a hard truth. "There aren't many honorable men left. I'm glad you're one of them."

Ethan rubs his thumb over my knuckles, sending tingles up my arm. "Your trust is important to me."

I gaze up at him, knowing I need to keep this man close. "I feel safe with you, but don't let me down."

Ethan lifts my hand to his lips. "You have my word."

His breath warms my skin, sending a shiver down my spine. I have him right where I want him, which is perfect. I can reel him in further.

But is that what I want? To use and abuse him?

Truthfully, I wish I could spend more time with Ethan. He makes me want to believe in the goodness in others. Unfortunately, he's a rarity in life.

We wander across the rocky beach as the rays of the setting sun shine down through tufts of golden clouds. The thunderous roar of the ocean envelops us, matching the quickened beating of my heart.

I relish the sun's warmth kissing my skin and the crunch of small pebbles shifting under my feet. Gulls cry overhead, circling an untouched beach that seems made for romantic getaways.

I want this to be my life.

As for the beach? It's an amazing beach. A secluded beach. A perfect beach to seduce Ethan.

I slip my hand into his, savoring the contrast of his calloused palm against the softness of my skin. We're going to do a whole hell of a lot more down here than enjoy the beach.

We meander to the tide pools, the fresh salty air filling my lungs. I trace my toes through the frigid water, watching tiny crabs skitter away.

"It's beautiful here. Wild and untamed." I meet Ethan's conflicted gaze, feeling the heat building between us.

I point out crabs and anemones in the tide pools while subtly guiding us into a secluded nook away from prying eyes. Here, nestled between the craggy outcroppings, it feels like we have this stunning strip of coastline all to ourselves.

I take Ethan's hands, pulling him closer. "Kiss me." I gaze up at him invitingly.

Ethan inhales sharply, conflict plain on his face. "You're vulnerable, and it's not professional for me to take advantage of that." His protests sound feeble, and his gaze flicks down to my lips.

The air between us thickens with tension, a magnetic attraction that neither can deny. The heat of his gaze sears me, and I know what he's thinking. It's written in the intensity of his eyes, how he swallows hard, and the faint tremor in his hands.

I slowly close the gap between us. "Put me out of my misery. Ethan, kiss me." Each word drips with challenge and invitation, the tease making my heart race.

I slide my hands along his forearms, feeling the solid muscle rippling beneath my fingers, and continue up to the curve of his biceps. "We're alone. It's one stolen moment. One kiss…" I let the implication hang between us. "Where's the harm?"

Leaning in, I ghost my lips over his stubbled jaw, a feather-light fluttering, feeling the warmth of his skin and hearing his breaths quicken. His musky and inviting scent wraps around me, drawing me close.

The groan in the back of his throat is low and guttural. His hands instinctively find my hips, pulling me against him with a yank. The hardness of his body contrasts deliciously with the softness of his voice.

"This is unwise..." he murmurs, though the plea in his voice is more a wish than a warning. "You shouldn't tempt me."

With his resistance crumbling, I press my advantage. "One kiss." I drag my fingers from the corner of his ear, down the angle of his jaw, and press them lightly over his lips. My voice drips with seduction as I coax him to give in to his desire.

With a sound that's half sigh, half growl, his resistance finally shatters. His lips crash into mine, fervent and hungry. It's a mingling of breaths and souls, a frantic dance of lips and tongues, a blend of sweet surrender and powerful conquest. He grips me tighter, pulling me close as if trying to meld our bodies into one.

And just like that, the world fades away. The rhythm of our hearts, the heat of our bodies, the taste of him—everything converges into this one stolen moment.

This kiss, the melding of our bodies, is as inevitable as the tide and as relentless as the sea crashing against the shore. We are the primal dance of nature, lost in waves of sensation.

There's nothing else but him and how our bodies come together in a searing connection.

The intensity of the kiss escalates, and a mixture of pent-up longing and raw desire releases like a dam breaking. The world tilts and swirls around us, but all I'm truly aware of is Ethan.

The way his mouth moves against mine, gentle but demanding. It speaks to a depth of feeling he keeps buried.

His fingers splay across my lower back, anchoring me to him, and I sigh into his mouth, allowing myself to get lost in the sensation. His other hand slides up my spine, sending tiny electrical sparks dancing on my skin. When he buries his hand in the tangles of my hair, his possession turns primal.

The slight tug of my hair elicits a moan from me, which seems to fan the flames of his passion even more.

I loop my arms around his neck, pulling him impossibly closer. With our bodies flush against each other, every hard line of his frame, every rapid beat of his heart, is imprinted on mine. The heat between us escalates, a tangible force of nature threatening to consume us both.

His taste is intoxicating, a blend of warmth and a hint of the salty air. Each brush of his tongue against mine sends jolts of electricity through me, setting every nerve ending alight.

Talk about a great kisser.

Pulling back slightly, Ethan rests his forehead against mine, both of us panting, trying to catch our breath. His eyes, dark with desire, search mine, seeking and finding a reflection of his own passion.

It's a raw, unspoken acknowledgment of the connection between us.

"You undo me." His voice turns rough and ragged, filled with emotion he's still trying to process.

I smile, leaning in to steal another quick, soft kiss. "Likewise," I murmur against his lips, both of us still caught in the heady afterglow of our shared moment.

Ethan claims my mouth again. Our breaths mingle as we give in to desire. His strong hands grasp me fiercely even as his lips devour mine. I relish his struggle and the way his restraint snaps.

We come together like the sea meeting the shore—natural, primal, and destined. The crashing waves and crying gulls fade until only this man fills my senses, and I'm completely and utterly lost in him.

I never want this magical moment to end.

We break apart, panting, knowing we crossed a line. It's one I can't put back. I unlocked his passion, and he'll never be satisfied with just one taste.

I'll never be satisfied with just one taste.

The rough texture of his stubble grazes agonizingly against my skin, causing a tender and raw burn. Every slight movement of his lips down my neck ignites with promise, feeding a fire deep within me. My head tilts back, surrendering to the intoxicating trail of fervent kisses that blaze a path to my collarbone.

The warm gust of his breath teases the vulnerable hollow of my throat, and my skin erupts in a wave of goosebumps, each one a testament to the potency of his touch. Every cell in my body screams for more, craving more.

Needing more.

And then, his lips find mine again. The world blurs, the connection so electrifying that my knees buckle beneath me. Desperate for support, my fingers dig into the solid expanse of his shoulders, anchoring me to the tempest that is Ethan Blackwood.

The stroke of his tongue turns my heart into a raging beast, hammering against my ribcage like a caged animal taking flight for the first time.

I'm in trouble if a mere kiss can unravel me so completely. Pulling back, his gaze ensnares mine, revealing a vast and perilous landscape of emotions and desire he awakens in me. With nothing more than the press of his lips and the touch of his hands, he lights a fire in the deepest parts of me, eliciting desires I didn't even know existed.

This man poses a danger greater than any threat I've faced before.

I've played the seductress too many times to count, always with an armored heart and my emotions safely locked away, but one blistering kiss from this man and the impenetrable walls I've built around my heart show their first cracks. The foundation beneath me trembles.

For the first time, I stand on the brink of welcoming a stranger into the most vulnerable parts I've always kept hidden from the outside world. The thought of letting him in, of truly seeing me, absolutely terrifies me.

NINE

Ethan

REBEL IS INCREDIBLE. SHE FITS IN MY ARMS AS IF MADE FOR ME. HER luscious lips and tantalizing tongue stiffen my cock and make me ache in the best possible way.

Her sultry gaze does things to me, shattering the last vestiges of my restraint. A guttural groan escapes me. I'm too weak to fight this insane and crazy attraction. She's a visceral ache twisting my core.

I'm frozen in place, speechless before this mysterious siren who reduces me to sheer base instinct. In her arms, nothing exists but euphoria and an all-consuming hunger to dominate, claim, and control. Here, my principles turn to ash, burned up in blistering desire.

I'm lost.

Right or wrong no longer matters, only having her again. Tasting her…

Consequences be damned, I'm tired of resisting this attraction. I'm tired of fighting this raw need consuming me. I react on impulse alone, and that impulse urges me to rut and fuck.

When we part—both breathless—her burning eyes promise ecstasy.

I explore her feminine curves and run the pad of my thumb over her nipple. Rebel hisses and closes her eyes. She curls in her lower lip, and the tip of her tongue darts out.

"We can stop at any time." I provide her with an out.

"If you stop, I'm going to kill you. Fuck me like you mean it. Hard. Fast. Brutal. Soft. Slow. Sensual. Punish me, or don't. Force me, or not. However you want me, I don't care. All I ask is that you make me scream."

"You don't want me to lose control. I'm hanging on by a thread."

"That's exactly what I want." Her fingers curl around my hard length, stroking over the fabric of my jeans until my knees tremble and my breath catches. "Take what you need from me. Are you the kind of man who can?"

"That and more."

I want to possess her completely, make her surrender, and claim her as no other man has before. This isn't about sex anymore. I'm drunk on her whimpers of need. Craving control. Needing to rut and fuck and dominate.

"Then show me." She arches her back, thrusting her tits at me.

Her words are like crack to my cock. It's needy, hungry, and eager to get things started.

My cock throbs, begging to be satisfied. I press my body against hers. She gasps, her breathing becoming shallow. I capture her lips in a passionate kiss that leaves us both breathless. Our tongues dance together as I explore her mouth, tasting the sweetness of her lips.

My hands brand every curve possessively, roaming her body aggressively, divesting her of clothes until no barriers remain between our fevered flesh. The sea breeze whispers over her bare, sensitized skin, raising goosebumps as she shivers.

I break away from the kiss and grab hold of her wrists, pushing them above her head, pinning them against the rocks with one hand while my other slides down to cup her ass. She arches into me, turning my animalistic lust into something primal and unhinged.

I squeeze it tight and grind against her, letting my hard bulge press against her soft curves. She moans softly, sending shockwaves of pleasure through us both.

"Is this what you want?"

"Yes." Her breathy moan is divine. "And, Ethan…"

"Yes?"

"Don't hold back." Her voice trembles with raw need.

Holy shit, she's on fire, saying all the things that flip switches in my head that rarely get flipped. The kind of aggression I prefer during sex is seldom appropriate for most. Which means I often hold back.

But with Rebel?

It's as if she was made for me.

I claim her mouth in a searing kiss, sealing her surrender. She melts against me, pliant and willing as I brand her as mine. I'll give her the oblivion she craves, the freedom of belonging completely to me. When we come up for air, raw desire flames in her eyes.

My cock throbs, begging to be satisfied. I capture her lips in a passionate kiss that leaves us both breathless. Our tongues dance together as I explore her mouth, tasting the sweetness of her mouth.

Breaking off the kiss, I reach into my pocket and pull out a condom. "As requested." I can't help the smirk filling my face and love the eagerness in her eyes.

She takes the condom and swallows hard before dropping onto her knees before me. Her fingers deftly undo my belt before pushing my pants down my thighs. She takes her time, teasing me as she continues to slide my pants down inch by inch until they're around my ankles. My cock springs free, and she takes it in her hands, wrapping her fingers around it tightly.

My breathing deepens with the stimulation. Her touch is so much more than the desperation of my palm. When she looks up at me with an intensity that sets my heart racing, I understand this is exactly what she needs.

Rebel unwraps the foil packet with trembling fingers. Instead of using her hands to slide the condom over my turgid length, she places it in her mouth.

Holy fucking shit!

My toes curl as the warmth of her mouth wraps around my cock. Her deft tongue unrolls the condom as she takes me fully into her mouth, all the way to the back of her throat. My fingers curl in her hair, tightening as I brace against the pleasure coursing through me.

When she pulls back, she replaces her mouth with her hands, using both hands to tease and torment. She sits back on her heels and looks up at me expectantly.

I watch her, mesmerized by the sight of her kneeling at my feet, worshipping me with her eyes. I reach down and cup her chin, caressing it gently.

"Your hands, while amazing, are nothing compared to the feeling of your lips wrapped around me. Put me in your mouth again."

She takes me into her mouth, her tongue swirling around the tip of my shaft as she sucks and teases me.

I moan in pleasure, feeling my desire build to a fevered pitch. I grasp her head with both hands and thrust into her mouth with abandon. Each thrust is met with a gasp from Rebel that only serves to drive me wild.

I grip her hair tightly as I reach the brink of orgasm, my breathing coming out in ragged gasps. I try to hold back, but it's too much, and I groan loudly as pleasure courses through me. My grip on Rebel's hair tightens as my body quakes.

Rebel looks up at me with adoration in her eyes, and it's obvious she enjoyed every second as well. She stands slowly, her knees wobbling slightly, and wraps her arms around me, pressing her body into mine for support. I hold her close for a moment before stepping back to gaze into her beautiful eyes.

"You look pleased." I can't help but chuckle. It's rare for me to seek pleasure first. I prefer it when my partner comes before me. A second or third time is even better. With Rebel, however, this seems natural.

"I am." She curls into my embrace.

"Upset I went first?"

"Not at all."

Glancing around, I find a somewhat flat rock at the perfect height. Sweeping Rebel into my arms, I carry her over and deposit her ass on the rock. Spreading her legs, I allow myself full access to her body.

I start by tracing her curves with my hands, exploring every inch of her body. She shivers and moans as I make my way down to her legs, teasing and tantalizing until she begs for more.

Finally, I reach between her legs, cupping her pussy. My thumb finds her clit and, using a slow circular motion, I bring her up and over the edge, until her body convulses and she screams with pleasure with the waves of sensation rushing through her.

I keep up the rhythm, pushing her through several back-to-back orgasms until she cries out that she can take no more. I may have taken my pleasure first, but that doesn't mean I'm not interested in hers. Watching her come is intensely satisfying and arousing. It also gives me the time to prepare for round two.

Then, I'll show her what it means to get fucked by me. Hefting her into the air, I notch the tip of my cock against her folds and lower her down until I'm seated to the root. My eyes close with the sensation of being enveloped by her wet heat.

There's nothing she can do while I fuck her except hang on. Using my arms to lift her up and down, I drive deep into her pussy and fuck her until I'm almost ready to come.

Rebel's body trembles with pleasure, and she wraps her legs around my waist as I thrust into her, pushing us both ever closer to the edge. Finally, with one final thrust, we climax together.

I slowly lower her to the ground. Taking the blanket she brought, I lay it out on the rocky pebbles, and we both collapse on it.

We lay there for a few moments as we catch our breaths. Rebel looks up at me with a serene smile on her face, equally pleased with what happened as I am. I press a soft kiss to her lips.

"You look amazing, freshly fucked."

"Good to know." Her sultry laughter makes me smile. "That was..." She pauses for a moment before continuing, "Incredible."

I laugh softly before pressing another gentle kiss to her lips. "It was indeed, but we've only just begun."

"W-what?" Her eyes round, causing me to laugh.

My recovery time is fast, and it won't take long before I'm ready for another round, but I still need a bit of a breather before going again. I lay Rebel before me and take a moment to admire her body before I explore it again. This time, I take things slow, savoring every second as if it were our last.

I trace circles around her nipples with my tongue before gently biting down, making her moan with pleasure. Then, I move lower, licking a path from her navel to the crease between her leg and hip. Rebel squirms beneath me, trembling with anticipation.

Finally, when she can take no more teasing, I bury my face between her legs and use my tongue to bring her over the edge again. Her back arches off the pebbly beach as waves of pleasure wash over her, and she screams in ecstasy.

Once she's spent, I'm hard and ready again. I flip her to her knees and take her from behind. With one hand threaded through her hair, I arch her neck back as I thrust into her hard and fast, enough to bring another orgasm barreling through me.

Rebel whimpers with every movement. She arches her back and lowers her shoulders to the ground, creating the perfect angle for me to fuck. Soon, waves of pleasure course through me, and I collapse over her, exhausted but undoubtedly satisfied.

We lay there for a few moments, neither wanting to be the first to speak after such an incredible experience. Finally, it's Rebel who breaks the silence with a contented sigh.

"That was incredible." She turns until she faces me.

I run my fingertips lightly up and down her arm before gently kissing her lips. "You're amazing."

She lifts up enough to place a gentle kiss on my mouth. "I'm yours. Whatever you want."

With that, my exhaustion fades instantly, and I burst into laughter, happy with how this night turned out.

"I take it you're not ready to return to reality?"

"Reality sucks. I much prefer getting fucked and living out my fantasies." Her hand drifts down to my cock, and her fingertips dance down its length. "How do you feel about whips, ropes, and blindfolds?"

"Shouldn't that be my line?"

"I'm only making suggestions." That seductive grin is back, filling her face.

"My Rebel is quite the kinky girl."

"You have no idea..." She flips to her back and places her hands over her head.

"Is that so?" I roll over on top of her, my cock rested and ready for at least one more go. Taking hold of her hands, I grip them tight. Nudging her thighs apart, I settle between her legs. I'm nearly ready, but I need more time to recover.

She looks up at me with a satisfied smile on her face, and I can't help but grin in return. We lay in silence for a moment, our bodies intertwined in an intimate embrace.

"Tell me your darkest fantasies." I nibble along the sweep of her neck.

A soft smile fills her face before turning away. "My darkest fantasies will frighten you, Ethan Blackwood. They'll shock and alarm you."

"I doubt that," I whisper as my lips glide along the length of her neck. "Tell me."

"Later."

"Now," I demand, my voice firm and unwavering.

I won't allow her to dismiss my question. She must answer me.

Rebel turns back to look at me, surprise etched in her features.

"Answer the question."

"Control and dominance without consent."

"Non-con?" Now, that's a surprise. "What does that mean to you?"

Her answer should shock me, but I find it explains much. Nevertheless, I want to understand her desires. It's the only way I can give her what she wants.

"I don't want to discuss this." Rebel turns away from me.

"You have to answer." I cup her cheek and force her to look at me.

"And if I don't?" Resistance flashes in her eyes.

TEN

Ethan

Turning away, she refuses to look at me, but she does finally answer the question. "Does it surprise you that I like being overpowered?" She turns to me with anger rising in her voice. "Is that what you want to hear? From a woman rescued from human trafficking? Who faced the horrors of rape? Are you happy that my deepest, darkest fantasy is forced sex? Non-con? Rape fantasies?"

"Fantasies are a far cry from reality." With her most secret truth revealed, she's in a fragile state. "There's no shame in wanting what you want."

There's a dichotomy between her desires and what happened to her. I get it. It's something I understand well. Not only that, but as a dominant male who's spent time educating myself in the darker flavors of sexual desire, I have a deeper understanding of the differences between non-con and rape.

"Non-con and rape fantasies, although I don't like that word, are vastly different things. What I think is it all comes down to consent. One has it. The other does not."

"Isn't there? Are you going to run for the hills, thinking me a freak?"

"I'm not running."

"True, but…"

"Don't." I place more of my weight on her body, letting her feel the physicality of my size.

"Don't, what?"

"Don't negate what happened."

"What are you talking about?"

"When someone says something, then immediately says 'but' after it, it negates what they just said. I didn't run. I'm not going anywhere, and I think it's pretty clear I enjoyed myself. Full stop. I may not have used much force, but that can come with time if that's what we decide."

"You don't think it's weird after what happened to me that I…"

"I don't."

"I…" Rebel closes her eyes to think, and then her eyes slowly open. "I've always been wired this way. Sex is usually a lackluster experience for me."

"Lackluster?"

"Not what we just did. That was fabulous and intense. I lost count of the number of orgasms you gave me. Probably more than I've had in the past ten years put together."

"Good way to stroke my ego." I chuckle at that.

"I just mean, sex with boys and their fumbling never got me off. Then with other men…" She blows out a breath. "They're so cautious, asking over and over for consent, terrified of leaving a mark. Scared to death to fuck for the sake of fucking. As if every sexual encounter needs to be this soft, intimate, ethereal experience. Sometimes, I just want to get fucked."

"You definitely don't like it soft."

"Hate it. And I'm all for women's lib and equality between the sexes, but when it comes to sex…"

"You like your men to be men?"

"I like them to dominate. It's more than a man being a man."

I understand where she's coming from, although, in today's modern political climate, traditional roles have come under fire, and we're all doing our best to open our minds and adjust in all aspects of our lives.

As far as sex is concerned—in my mind—the only values that matter are those shared between the individuals engaging in sex with each other. There's no room for anyone else's opinion.

"Rebel, some women like to dominate during sex. Some like to submit. Some like to switch things up. Some are open and experimental. Some are polyamorous. Some are gay. Some are sexually repressed. The same goes for men. There's no shame in wanting what you want or expressing it to your lover. Sex should be fun."

"Yes, but I need it to be—more." Rebel's gaze drops, as does her voice. "I can't explain it more than that."

She continues on, revealing more and more of her specific fantasies, and as she does, I see deeper into this amazing woman's mind.

Contrary to what she said, she's not into rape fantasies or non-consent. It terrifies her, but she does enjoy surrendering control. Needs it. As she explains, I hold her in my arms as she bares her soul to me.

Despite what she may think, my desire doesn't fade after she tells me what she likes and doesn't like. It only grows stronger than before. That she trusts me with her dark truths makes me feel as if we've truly forged a connection.

Not as lovers. That's just sex. We're forging a connection as one.

We bridge many barriers when she entrusts me with her most personal self, and I will never abuse that trust. Reaching up, I brush a few strands of hair away from her face and kiss her lips softly. When she turns her head, I apply enough pressure to send a message.

It's not non-con, far from it. This is an expression of the deepest intimacy. It's me taking with respect and without judgment.

I want to show her how much I appreciate her trust. My hands roam her body with a sense of urgency, exploring every curve as if for the first time.

She resists at first, her body tightening in response to my touch, but I overpower her just enough to give her a taste without overwhelming her. My goal is to let her feel my aggression while letting her control how far she wants to go.

The more I think about taking care of her and not overstepping her boundaries, the more aroused I become. It's not long before my cock hardens again. The hungry fucker is eager tonight.

There's a wildness in her eyes, something dark and dangerous. Something needy and desperate. I shift, moving to my knees, and rise above her. With one hand gripping the base of my cock, I grab her roughly.

She struggles, but I'm too far gone to care. I barely know this beast within me. I rarely get to dominate a woman during sex. She's not the only one with darker cravings, and I'm eager to explore this part of myself with Rebel. I thread my fingers through her hair and yank her toward my cock.

"Suck me." The tone in my voice isn't one I recognize.

Her lips part, and that's all it takes. I force her to take me, gagging her on my cock. My fingers thread through her curly red hair, and I turn into something dark and dangerous.

Holy hell, the woman knows how to suck cock. My toes curl. My hips rock back and forth, speeding up until I thrust in and out of her mouth. Blood surges to my cock, stiffening it as heat coils at the base of my spine. It's not long before my balls tingle with my impending release.

Thinking to pull her off my dick and get her off before I come, she surprises me when she grips the back of my thighs. Her gaze tilts up, and our eyes meet. Her luscious lips wrap around my cock as she shakes her head, pleading.

At this moment, she is everything—my whole world condensed into flushed skin, ravenous lips, and the rasp of her tongue against my cock. I am utterly consumed, my senses over-whelmed, transformed beyond recognition into an untamed creature of raw lust.

This release takes me by surprise and comes powerfully, making my legs shake and knees tremble. I collapse beside her on the rocks, spent and soaked in sated bliss.

Tonight, I'm lost to wanton euphoria.

My restraint lies in tatters, burned away in blistering waves of heat. Only the beast remains, taking everything she offers again and again beneath the pounding surf. I reach for my belt and watch her eyes glaze over with lust.

It's a delicate balance, but one that ultimately pays off. Rebel relaxes and submits to my will. Her soft moans become louder as I claim more and more of her with each passing minute.

In moments like this, words are unnecessary—our bodies speak for us in ways that mere words cannot express.

After I'm done fucking her, I hold her close as our breathing returns to normal. At first, we revel in the afterglow of sex, but then she curls into my embrace, and I hold her through her soft sobs.

It's a dichotomy of emotions, forcing her, then holding her afterward. But I gave her exactly what she needed.

We rest for a while, each of us silent with our thoughts. In between waves of lust, we stare out at the ocean, listening to the crashing of the surf.

With her curled in my arms, she asks me about the Guardians and how I came to join them. What it is we do. How we plan and execute our missions.

With her opening up to me about her darkest secrets, I tell her everything about the four Guardian teams and the Guardian Protectors who provide personal protection detail to individual clients. I can't stop talking about Mitzy's amazing technical team and their incredible accomplishments.

Her questions are surprisingly astute, and I love that I can share something with her.

When the mood strikes, I take her hard and unapologetically. There's no asking. Her orgasms are notably longer and more intense the rougher I am with her. The more raw and feral, the more intense her pleasure.

I'll feed that beast all day long.

Or rather, all *night* long.

Nothing about this woman makes any sense. She seems too good to be true, and the two of us appear to be perfectly matched.

We simply—fit.

The first hints of dawn begin to creep over the horizon, signaling the end of our passionate night together. Rebel lays curled against me, skin glowing in the soft predawn twilight, our legs still tangled together.

I run my fingers idly along her arm, marveling again at how perfectly we fit, how in sync our bodies move. We've explored each other intimately—every sensitive spot investigated.

We also tested each other's boundaries, sharing fantasies in hushed whispers between heated kisses. She arched into my every caress, hungry and uninhibited. I've never met another woman as open and honest as Rebel.

Never experienced such an intense connection so quickly.

Stifling a jaw-cracking yawn, I drift off, lulled to sleep by the rhythmic pounding of the surf. Rebel nuzzles against my chest, her warm body pressed to mine. Safe and sated, I let sleep pull me under, content to hold her in my arms.

But when I later wake, I'm met with an emptiness that makes my heart drop. Rebel is gone. Only the imprint of her body beside me remains. I sit up in alarm, scanning the empty beach.

She's nowhere in sight.

A hollow ache settles in my chest at her absence. A sense of wrongness follows. I thought we forged a connection. One that went beyond physical attraction.

Was I wrong?

Dragging a hand through my hair, I stare at the endless ocean.

Confused.

An ominous foreboding fills me, like the first cracks of light exposing an illusion that can't survive the harsh glare of day. Jaw clenched; I rise to my feet.

The gray waves still crash against the rocks. The salty tang in the ocean still lingers in the air. The imprint of her body is still on the blanket beneath me.

Holding the ghost of her warmth.

But Rebel is nowhere to be found.

I scan the empty beach, my heart sinking. A hollow ache settles in my chest. I sit on a rock and stare out at the waves. As the rosy dawn light stretches across the rocky beach, memories from last night replay in my mind in a new, ominous light.

Things that seemed passionate at the moment now feel orchestrated and coldly calculated. The way she manipulated me into dominating her? Drawing out my deepest desires and secrets in the aftermath when my guard was down?

The intimacy that felt so real and vulnerable suddenly seems like a tool to serve her ends. She made herself into my perfect fantasy—attentive, submissive, uninhibited. Catering precisely to my wants and needs.

I should have seen it but was too spellbound to see the manipulation. She played me masterfully, luring me into revealing things about myself. About work. About the innermost workings of the Guardians.

Details no outsider should know.

The growing pit in my stomach tells me I've been played in the worst possible way. She saw a mark, not a kindred soul. Seduced and deceived me for her own agenda.

The beauty of what we shared disappears before my eyes. She sharpened her knife under the guise of submission, and I gave her the perfect opening to slide it between my ribs.

The ultimate betrayal.

Jaw clenched; I stand abruptly. I won't accept it until I hear the truth from her lips. I have to know if everything between us was an orchestrated lie or if some glimmer of genuine connection remains.

I leap to my feet and scan my surroundings, thinking she might be out looking at the tide pools, but it's high tide. The tide pools are buried beneath the surf, and there's no sign of the fiery redhead.

Anger comes swiftly, followed by rage. Not toward her, but directed at myself. I dress in haste and scramble up the cliffside path.

That sense of wrongness within me intensifies. My gut says she won't be found. Nevertheless, I search for her throughout The Facility.

No one has seen her since last night. A cold, leaden pit forms in my stomach. Alarm rises, then curdles to anger in my gut when I replay the events of the night.

What she shared.

What I shared…

The sensitive things I shared about the Guardians.

How could I be so stupid?

Teeth clenched, I yank out my phone and call my boss.

"What's up?" CJ answers on the first ring.

I palm my face, embarrassed, enraged, and horrifically compromised. In one night, everything is ruined—my principles, my career, and my heart.

"I fucked up." Those are perhaps the hardest three words I've ever had to say.

"Talk to me." CJ doesn't judge. He's honestly interested in the next words out of my mouth.

ELEVEN

Ethan

THE WEIGHT OF MY FAILURE SITS LIKE A ROT IN MY GUT AS I MAKE my way to CJ's office. Last night, I was on top of the world, drunk on passion and possibly love. Now, everything has turned to ash.

I fucked up—plain and simple. Broke every rule and protocol like a blind, infatuated fool.

There's no way to spin it. No way to lessen the bitter taste of betrayal. I got played, and now Guardian HRS is compromised because of my mistakes.

All that's left is to own up and accept the fallout. CJ's disappointment. The damage control we'll have to implement because I failed to guard what matters most—the secrecy and security of our organization.

I'm under no illusions. Careers have ended over less. I'll take my licks without complaint or excuses. I let passion blind me, and these are the consequences.

I don't know who said this first, but it's *Time to face the music.*

Squaring my shoulders, I ready myself to confess everything and take my licks because I forgot my duty in a heated moment of self-indulgence. However, I quickly sniff my pits and detour to my temporary quarters. I smell like sea, salt, sand, and sex. No way in hell am I facing CJ smelling like that.

I'm still new enough to Guardian HRS that I'm living in Guardian HQ dormitories. After showering and shaving, I make myself presentable, then head out with a heavy heart. By the end of this, Guardian HRS will be a footnote in my career, a massive black mark on my record.

Jaw clenched, I enter the briefing room to face the leaders who trusted me. They took Rex's word that I was qualified to lead Charlie team. Little did they know I would compromise everything.

Sam's steady eyes, CJ's scowl, and Mitzy's knowing gaze all focus on my failure.

"CJ briefed us, but I want to hear from you." Sam crosses his arms, a scowl firmly fixed on his face. He's not pleased. "What the fuck happened?"

I meet his stare and take in a steadying breath. "I allowed myself to be compromised by a survivor we rescued." As I recount meeting Rebel, Sam's expression darkens.

"What specifics did you disclose?" Sam's scowl nearly unmans me.

Every sordid detail shames me further, but I hide nothing.

Bile rises in my throat. I close my eyes, sifting through feverish memories. "Operational details. Training methods. Team compositions. Technical capabilities. Too much. I take full responsibility for my actions."

Mitzy leans forward. "Can you clarify the technical details?"

"I described our drones, embedded trackers, and surveillance systems." The leaders exchange concerned looks.

"This intel could be dangerous in the wrong hands, but it's not enough to undermine our security if used against us." CJ rubs his jaw. "We need to find this woman."

Sam runs a hand down his face, but his eyes never leave mine. "What's done is done. We control the damage. Recall everything you can about this woman."

I slump in my seat, the weight of my failure pressing down on me. "Of course, I resign as Charlie leader. My lapse in judgment has endangered everything."

Sam clasps my shoulder. "Ethan, you made a mistake but admitted it instead of hiding it. That shows courage. Your resignation isn't needed."

"But…" It's not like I'm not grateful, but this isn't the kind of dressing down I expected.

CJ nods. "Guardians take care of our own. We'll find Rebel and make it right."

Sam meets my eyes. "I believe you're the right man to lead Charlie team. One failure doesn't outweigh all the good you've done."

"Hell, we've all been young and stupid," CJ adds with a snort. "You owned up to it. Clean up your mess and move on."

The weight of their trust slams into me, almost buckling my knees. My chest tightens, air jammed in my lungs. I fight to keep my eyes dry, jaw clenching. I can't afford to crack. Not now. I vow to prove worthy of their trust and handle this crisis with decisive leadership, no matter what it takes.

However, days later, Mitzy enters the briefing room grim-faced. "I can't believe I'm saying this, but I've employed every tracking method imaginable. There's no sign of Rebel anywhere."

A chill sweeps through me at those ominous words. Rebel vanished off the face of the earth? If that was ever her real name. That woman holds dangerous knowledge that could bring down Guardian HRS.

All because of me.

———

Weeks later, my pulse spikes when CJ's name flashes on my phone.

The first thought in my mind is Mitzy's team finally located Rebel.

With a bitter sigh, I think back on how my emotions and physical desire for Rebel led me to abandon my discipline and leave my self-respect on that rocky beach.

She lied to me.

CJ and Sam assure me the things I told Rebel are nothing to worry about. They're all things easily discovered by a determined hacker; they're not worried about my ability to command Charlie team.

But me? I'm fucking pissed.

My cell phone rings, and I answer CJ's call.

"What's up?"

"New mission. Time-sensitive." CJ, as always, is brisk, business-like, and to the point. *"Meet in the admin offices ASAP."*

"Copy that." I place my phone down on the table with an odd look. Whenever my phone rings, I expect news about Rebel. Don't know why. In the weeks since her disappearance, there's been nothing.

Stone-cold nothingness.

I wish I could forget her, but thoughts of her continue to intrude on my daily life.

A new mission is exactly what I need—a reminder of why I'm here—something to take my mind off the woman who used sex to pump me for information about the Guardians. Every step I take, every decision I make, is stained by the bitter aftertaste of that failure. It would be great if I could wallow, but there's no room for such indulgences.

Not in this line of work.

Life moves on, and I have a new mission to focus on. What I need is to get my head screwed on straight about Rebel. She's nothing to me.

Nothing but a ghost, a mistake I need to let go of.

When I reach the briefing room, a hollow shell of a man sits across the table from CJ, Sam, and Mitzy. The client wrings his hands raw, eyes hollow from countless sleepless nights. The stinging stench of his despair—a raw, primal fear—permeates the room.

"Please…" His voice cracks. The man's shattered, and his word is a desperate plea for help.

I'm intrigued.

"Mr. Collins, this is Ethan Blackwood, head of Charlie team. His men will recover your daughter." CJ makes introductions and a promise.

"Please, you have to find Ally." Collins's voice cracks. "She's out there somewhere, terrified and alone..." His words turn into a choked sob that rattles in the back of his throat.

My chest tightens, thoughts flickering to another fiery woman who survived abduction, captivity, and worse, who also vanished. With a shake of my head, I jump into this mission to get rid of thoughts about Rebel.

"What can you tell us about when she vanished?" I pull back a chair and take a seat.

Across the table, I catch Sam's attention. He knows about my insecurities leading Charlie team after I allowed Rebel to compromise my values. His solid nod is a reminder of why we're here. Why we push through the punishing training, the endless nightmares, and the insurmountable odds.

Collins's shoulders slump. "Just bring my baby girl back to me." Raw with emotion, desperation punctuates his voice. He's living a parent's worst nightmare.

"The Guardians will find your daughter," I try to minimize his fears, but there's no easing this kind of terror. His daughter is missing, and he's lost all control.

"Mr. Collins," Sam's voice cuts through the oppressive air, his tone assertive yet comforting. "If you could tell us everything about the day your daughter disappeared." It's a delicate dance, extracting every detail while offering an empathetic ear, and Sam executes that task flawlessly.

"She was excited about a visiting lecturer. Someone speaking about cold fusion. She went to the lecture, then..." He looks up and chokes on another sob. "That was the last we saw of her."

"We? You mean her security detail?" It's hard to fathom a billionaire's offspring roaming free and unprotected.

"Yes."

"Why wait this long to contact us?"

"She often gave them the slip." His expression sours. "It's a sore subject."

"Ditched professional bodyguards?" The notion is almost comical. "She must be good at giving them *the slip*."

"Ally is good at everything she puts her mind to. They waited outside while she went to the ladies' room. She climbed out a second-story window."

"Why would she do that?" CJ asks.

"She wanted to party with her friends." Collins's shoulders slump. Clearly, he's at his wit's end trying to control his wayward daughter.

"Does she do that a lot?" I lean back and fold my arms across my chest.

"More often than I care to admit." His expression turns distant and haunted. "My daughter is a good girl, a bit wild, but that's to be expected at nineteen. I don't try to restrict what she does, but I do my best to keep her safe."

My instincts scream there's more going on here. This isn't a random kidnapping or an act of opportunity. It's cold and calculated.

A contract job.

"I'll dig into every corner of the web, analyze every byte. Someone always slips up." Mitzy pipes up, her fingers tapping her laptop like a seasoned pianist. "We'll find them. The digital breadcrumbs are there if you know how to find them."

"Anyone with a grudge?" I ask, my gaze doesn't waver.

"Against Ally?" Collins shakes his head, confusion flashing in his eyes. "No."

"It's college. Any chance of a sorority prank gone too far?" Sam asks, covering all bases.

"No, Ally isn't interested in the Greek life. She loves a good party, but she's a straight-A student. Heavily invested in her studies."

"You mentioned cold fusion. What is her major?" The more I know about Ally, the better. It'll make it easier to find her.

"Applied and Engineering Physics. She wants to study cold fusion. Her eyes are on a Ph.D. working in the field. She wants to bring clean energy to the world." Collins's pride in his daughter's aspirations is clearly not something he can suppress.

"Lofty goals." I tug at my ear. At first glance, this appears to be a simple missing person's case, but Collins is smart. Surely, he exhausted those options.

"She wouldn't disappear like this." He maintains his daughter's innocence in her disappearance.

I can almost see Ally in my mind: youthful defiance combined with a brilliant mind, thirsty for knowledge. She's like a mini-Mitzy.

"Does Ally have any enemies?" Sam's question remains soft and probing. It never ceases to amaze me how many times people lie to our faces, to the people they pay to rescue their loved ones.

"Ally?" Collins shakes his head. "Impossible. Everyone adores her."

"What about you?" I tilt my head slightly, a calculated movement. "Anyone want to hurt you?"

"I'm a rich, fat, white male with several billions to my name." His tone turns sarcastic and derisive. "Everybody hates me, and if they don't hate me, they despise me."

"But is there anyone with enough hatred to want to hurt you?" My eyes narrow. There's something in the way he hesitates which makes me think he's one of those clients holding back essential information.

"You think Ally's abduction is an attack on me?" His eyes widen, the thought dawning on him for the first time. "To hurt me?"

"It wouldn't be the first time wealth made someone a target. Has there been any ransom demands?" Sam taps his finger on the table.

"None." Mr. Collins exhales, the breath whistling through his teeth. His body sags with the weight of despair. "I initially thought she was partying, blowing off steam. When she didn't return by morning, her security detail alerted me. But we decided to wait. She's disappeared for entire weekends before. Girls' weekend is what she called it."

"You waited for two days?" Disbelief colors my tone.

"Ally is an adult, and I have my best people watching her. I want to keep her safe without smothering her." His eyes glaze, lost in regret. "But when she missed classes on Monday and an important exam on Tuesday, I knew something was dreadfully wrong."

It's Wednesday. Which means Collin's daughter has been missing for five days. Our task has just turned into a race against the clock, and we haven't even lined up at the starting block.

"Expect daily updates from us." Sam rises, his tone indicating this meeting is at its end. He extends a hand to Mr. Collins, and they shake.

"Thank you. Just—please, bring Ally back to me."

Collins's gratitude rings in my ears long after he's gone. His faith in us is a humbling reminder of the importance of our job.

Mitzy's team gets to work on the case immediately, but too many days bleed into too many nights. Three days later, I receive a call from CJ.

TWELVE

Ethan

"WE HAVE A LEAD ON ALLY COLLINS'S LOCATION," CJ SAYS. *"GATHER your team for a mission prep."* He never wastes time on pleasantries.

"Copy that." I send a group page to my team and double-time it to Command. I'm the first of my team to arrive, but soon the others trickle in. Once we're all present, Mitzy sweeps into the room in a whirlwind of energy.

Mitzy takes center stage with vibrant hair and eyes that spark with intelligence. "I traced back the security footage from the day. Not much to go on, but after looking at cellphone tracking and crowdsourcing, I matched up the phones in her vicinity before hers went dark. Ally was abducted."

"You did what?" Sometimes, Mitzy's mind boggles mine.

"You know?" She looks at me like I should understand. When I shake my head, she rolls her eyes. "It's how your phone knows when the traffic is good. Those green and red traffic zones are generated by crowdsourcing of GPS information transmitted by your phones. It's how you can see if traffic is flowing or at a standstill. How you search for restaurants near you?"

Her left brow lifts, daring me to admit I didn't know how that worked.

When I don't respond, she continues. "I tracked Ally's phone, tagged all cell phones in her vicinity, and then watched for the ones that followed her phone. It was simple, actually."

Simple? I bite my tongue, aware as the new guy, it's best to keep my thoughts to myself.

"After that, running the vehicle's license plates through every traffic database known to man was simple." She beams victorious. "They're taking her south, a snail's pace along the backroads. It's like they're trying to waste time. She's currently holed up in a rundown motel in Florida."

Damn. I can't help but shake my head. Her mind is on another level.

"Wheels up in twenty. We bring the girl home tonight." CJ's face hardens into a mask of determination, his soldier's instincts clicking into place.

Rebel's ghost comes to haunt me as we suit up. We've run several rescue missions since her rescue, but she embodies my last failure.

I need a better way to compartmentalize her betrayal.

My focus needs to be on saving lives.

This mission is about Ally. Not Rebel. It feels as if I need to say that over and over again, which is a very bad thing. It's not good for my mind to be focused on anything other than the mission.

As the jet roars down the runway, my team makes final weapons checks—the *click-clack* of ammunition feeding into chambers fills the jet with noise. There's no laughter. No banter. Just grim faces and absolute focus.

CJ and Mitzy join us on the flight. CJ's face is a hard mask of resolve. He's deployed countless missions, and my respect for him is immense. His gaze meets mine, and a shared understanding passes between us.

Despite my misstep and failure with Rebel, he trusts me to lead this mission. He trusts me not to fail. That faith sharpens my resolve to prove my worth.

"Ten minutes out." CJ's voice cuts through the silence. He gives us a brief pep talk, and I do mean brief. "Get the girl. Take down the hostiles."

"Understood."

On touchdown, we pile into two SUVs, faces set, eyes hard. Weapons ready. The darkness swallows us as we move out, predators sliding through the shadows.

"Room 212 at the Sunset Motel, off Highway 54," Mitzy provides the last piece of the puzzle, her voice crisp through our comms.

"Copy that." As long as the girl hasn't moved, this should be a walk in the park. I issue final orders to my team. "Hank, Walt—you take rear breach. Jeb, Blake, and Gabe—you're with me in the front." A chorus of affirmatives answers me, the rhythm of this deadly dance etched deep in our muscle memory.

As we roll to a silent stop, the world shrinks to the fifty-yard stretch between us and room 212. The motel light seeping through the curtains is a beacon drawing us forward. A beacon leading us to a scared, lonely girl who's about to be freed from this horror.

We move into position.

"Breach in 3... 2... 1..." My voice cuts through the silence, a whisper lost in the night. We move as one, a team honed into a deadly fighting force, and all hell breaks loose.

We split into two groups and surge forward as one. Hank and Walt circle around to the back, ensuring no one tries to move Ally out from under our noses. Jeb, Blake, Gabe, and I breach the front door with the force of a battering ram. A loud crack sounds as wood splinters and gives way. Two startled figures scramble from where they play cards at a small table, their hands reaching for holstered weapons.

They never stand a chance.

Shots rip through the air. One of them crumples to the ground, dead before he can pull his gun. The second man takes a bullet to the chest. I'd like to kill him, but we need him for interrogation.

As for Ally... She huddles in the corner, ropes biting into her wrists and binding her ankles. Metallic gray duct tape seals her lips; all we hear are her muffled cries.

"Ally, your father sent us." I squat next to the girl while Jeb and Gabe see to the wounded. Hank and Walt join us a few seconds later, standing guard by the shattered door.

Blake keeps watch over me as I slice through Ally's bindings.

"Can you walk?"

Her body shudders, but she nods. The ropes fall away, leaving angry red welts and bruised skin behind. She rips the duct tape off and works her mouth. Tears stream down her face, yet she whispers a shaky,

"Who are you?"

I help Ally to her feet, and she sags against me, her legs trembling and weak. Scooping her into my arms, I move through the room, headed to the first SUV.

Mission success.

Ally is free.

But our job is far from over.

Jeb and Gabe shove the surviving kidnapper into the second vehicle. Walt and Hank remain behind to deal with the authorities and the circus that will come.

It's not long before the plane comes into view. Ally stumbles out of the vehicle. She's somewhat steady on her feet but clings to me as we climb aboard.

She's in shock, unable to process what's happening.

I settle her in a seat, buckle her in, then drape a blanket around her fragile frame. Gradually, her shaking subsides, but she tenses when one of her abductors is dragged onto the plane.

"Don't worry about him." I shield her as Jeb and Gabe forcibly march the man to one of the rooms in the back of the plane. That's the last time she'll ever see that man's face.

Once we're in the air, I check in on our prisoner. Our medics treated the bullet wound to his chest. I watch the entire procedure with a hardened gaze, my mind already ticking with questions.

We did it.

We saved another innocent.

But satisfaction is fleeting when there's still a job to do.

We need information on who hired these men before Ally is

truly safe because whoever orchestrated the kidnapping is still out there.

We've saved the girl.

Now, we hunt the hunters.

Once the medic's done, I roll up my sleeves and get to work on our prisoner. In the back of my mind, however, are thoughts of Rebel.

THIRTEEN

Ethan

INSIDE THE JET, I SLIDE INTO THE SEAT OPPOSITE ALLY COLLINS. SHE huddles into herself, swaddled in a blanket, her fingers white-knuckled around a steaming mug of tea. A certain fragility about her triggers a protective instinct in me, but I can't afford to let that get in the way. We need answers, and she's the only one who can provide them.

"Ally," I start, my voice pitched low and gentle. "You holding up okay?"

She nods, a tiny bird-like movement, her gaze darting to meet mine before skittering away. Her eyes are still wide, a wild doe trapped in the headlights.

"Good. I've got a few questions. Only if you're up for it, though."

Another nod. A shaky breath followed by a gulp of her tea.

"All right." I clear my throat. "Do you know where they were taking you?"

"Florida." Her eyes shift to the floor. "I-I heard them saying Fort Lauderdale."

That's a wide net to cast, but it's a start.

"What else?" I ensure I give her plenty of space. I'm a big man;

the last thing she needs is me looming over her. "Anything else you can remember?"

She chews on her lower lip, brow tugging together. "They said other things." I lean in to hear her soft whisper, but she shies away.

"Words like what...?""Client. Pleased. An-and something about an auction?"

Auction?

That word hangs in the air like an ominous miasma. The implications are horrifying. This is officially a human trafficking case.

I grit my teeth, tasting bile creeping up the back of my throat.

"Was it just the two men?" I try to keep my voice as soft and supportive as possible, but I need to get this information out of her while it's still raw and fresh.

"Yes, just the two of them." She mumbles again, forcing me to lean down to hear. When her gaze meets mine, there's steel in her eyes, an alloy forged from fear and survival. "They were assigned to my protection detail a week ago."

"A week ago?"

Newly assigned?

I file away that fact for later. Security details have their influx of personnel. That, in and of itself, isn't significant, but a week before her abduction?

That smells like all kinds of shit.

I suck in a sharp breath, teeth gritting. Protectors turned traitors. My fists clench on instinct, knuckles whitening.

"Tell me again," I urge her to continue, my voice taut as the silence yawns wide. "What did they do? What did they say?"

It's not uncommon for victims to leave out important details. It's not that they try to hide the truth; they don't understand how the tiniest thread can often be the key to unraveling everything.

She flinches as if stung—as if I'm yelling at her or accusing her of something—but her strength returns. This young woman is strong. That resiliency will serve her well in the days to come as she recovers from this ordeal.

"They made calls, frequent ones." Her voice drops back to a whisper.

"Any names?" I press her for the smallest detail. "Did you catch any names?"

"Only one." Her gaze drops to the floor again. "K something. Like a cough drop." She shrugs and looks at me.

"A cough drop?"

"That's all I remember."

"Thank you, Ally." I keep my voice steady. "You've been incredibly helpful." I leave her with one of our team medics and stride toward the back of the plane. I reach the holding area where Jeb and Gabe stand guard over our prisoner.

With my arrival, the room becomes an interrogation cell, the stark white light illuminating the fear in our captive's eyes. One look at me, and he knows his secrets will unravel under my questions.

I take a seat.

I take my time.

I take an eternity before I address him.

"You have a problem." My voice remains deceptively soft.

"Fuck off," the kidnapper snaps at me, baring his teeth.

I ignore his outburst and continue. "I want to help you." I intend to drag every shred of truth from him, but first, I must convince him it's in his best interest to talk.

"Help?" he scoffs, and his gaze flickers toward my hands, then back up to my face, apprehension swirling in his eyes.

"I don't want to hurt you." It's the truth, and I'm honest to a fault.

"Fuck off." This guy's vocabulary must be exceptionally small. His eyes narrow, and a sheen of sweat on his forehead shimmers under the overhead lights.

Jeb and Gabe turned on the heat lamps, literally sweating the guy. It's hard to hold back a grin. It's the tiny things that make people crack under interrogation.

People think it's dismembering, disemboweling, and other egregious acts, but the truth is people hate being uncomfortable. Despite the sweat on his brow, the man shivers. His fingers curl into fists.

"Honestly, I'd prefer a simple chat. Tell me what I need and you'll be left with all your bits and pieces intact." I lean back, arms crossed. "Or we can do it the hard way. It's your choice."

There's a pause, one heavy with the weight of his decision. His eyes dart between Jeb and Gabe. "I'm not talking to you."

"It's your choice. Once we land, it'll be obvious you failed to deliver Ally Collins as contracted. I'm sure your employers will not like that. How do they react to failure?"

All the blood drains from his face.

"Right. That's what I thought." He's a dead man walking and knows it. I lean in, ready to peel back the layers of his lies, one truth at a time. "Now, what was the plan?"

This guy cares more about his hide than whatever he is being paid. It's sickening, actually, how easily he breaks.

"Get the girl," he snarls at me, clicking his teeth together, mimicking a bite.

"And do what with her? I'm sure a tour of sleazy motels in the south wasn't the goal." I pull out a pocketknife—a large pocketknife—and clean my nails, acting as if I have all the time in the world.

"I ain't telling you nothin'."

"I expect that sort of answer, but I want to let you in on a little secret." I pause, waiting to see if he'll respond. When he doesn't, I continue. "The way I see your problem—"

"Ain't got no problem." Again, he snaps at me.

"Your problem is you got caught. It means you're sloppy. I'm sure your employer doesn't reward sloppiness. In fact, I'm betting exactly the opposite."

"What's that?" The man's too stressed to know he should shut the fuck up.

He's more malleable than I thought.

"I think he'll march you out to a field with a shovel." No need to elaborate on what comes next—we all know—I just want to fuck with him. "Force you to dig your own grave. Lie down inside of it while he shovels dirt in your face.

He tries to swallow but gags instead.

"Whether you tell me anything or not, your life is over. At least as you know it." I point the tip of the knife toward him, emphasizing the point. "But I might be able to offer another solution."

"What?"

"Ah, see, this is where I must draw a line. I'll tell you what I can do to save your sorry ass, but only after you tell me what I need to know. Based on how useful that is—or isn't—kind of decides how well I can help you with your little problem."

"Doesn't matter. Like you said, I'm a dead man walking." He's not dumb, but it's taken this long for him to realize he's out of options.

"You could be walking on a beach in Costa Rica. New name. New—"

"A new name does me shit. Facial recognition these days is everywhere. You have shit to offer me." He leans back, crossing his arms, but his shoulders slump. He knows these are probably his last hours on earth."

"What if I could fix that?"

"Fix it?" He shakes his head, obviously not buying whatever I may have to offer him.

"Two words: facial reconstruction." I lean back, waiting for his bravado to disappear. When he says nothing, I know I've got him. "New name. New face. New life." I gesture with my hands as if offering him the world.

"You can do that?"

"Me?" I scoff and point to my chest. "Do I look like a doctor?" I make a show of shaking my head and rolling my eyes, then gesture again. This time, my gesture takes in everything around us. "The people who own this plane, the ones who employ me…" I press the pad of my index finger on the table. "Now, *they* can do that, but we're nowhere near talking about something like that unless your offer justifies the cost and their time."

"What do you want to know?"

"Everything." I lean back with a massive grin on my face. I've got this guy hook, line, and sinker. He knows it. I know it. There's no reason to gloat. We're at a point where our conversation can continue.

"They told me they had a job. Told me when and where." He shrugs as if handing over a sacred gem of knowledge.

"Don't waste my time. Any idiot could say that. I need details. If you won't share, I'm wasting precious time." I push back from the table as if getting ready to leave.

"How detailed do you need?" The man leans forward and practically leaps on top of the table. He can't get out of his way fast enough.

"Who. What. Where. When. And how."

"I got a call."

"A call? They just called you? How? How would they know to call *you?*"

"I responded to an ad."

"An ad?"

"On the deep web. I solicit jobs for people who need things done."

"Jobs?" I rock forward. "What kind of jobs?"

"Kidnappings. Hits. You know—jobs."

Shit, this man needs to be put six feet under, but I'm not here to judge. I need information.

"So you put out an ad for hire? People call, and you take the job?"

"Depends on what it pays. What's required."

"You can give us the details about that later. For this job, what were you told?"

"It was already planned out."

"You didn't have to plan it?"

"No. These guys…" He shakes his head. "They're crazy meticulous." He grunts, voice hoarse, then spills the details of the transaction and the instructions he received. I let him speak. The man is valuable as long as his lips are moving. The moment he feeds us shit for information, I have no problems expediting his death.

"And the girl? Was she a random grab?"

"Ain't no random grab." The guy leans back.

Now that he's talking, he's getting comfortable. Like we're old buddies sitting down for a beer and bragging about what we did that day. Yeah, his time on this earth is limited.

And as he talks, slow, icy dread coils in my stomach. His words chip at the veneer of what we initially thought was a simple case of abduction. The forethought. The intimate knowledge. Was Ally's personal protection detail compromised? A Judas in her midst.

"And where were you taking her?"

"There's an auction. Well, it's not an auction, seeing as money's already changed hands, but they put the girls on stage. Make them think they're being sold off, but it's just to fuck with their heads, make them malleable."

I'm ready to shove my knife into his chest and end him. What a fucking tool. Instead, I keep a smile on my face and the questions coming.

The edges of my vision tinge red. This is no mere job. It's a sickening 'boutique kidnapping,' designed like an obscene piece of art.

After hours of talking to the asshole, he clearly lacks one significant detail. He has no idea who wants Ally or who ordered her kidnapping.

My gaze hardens, locked onto the man across the table. No matter how deep we have to dig or the cost, we will unearth this entire operation, leaving no stone unturned.

FOURTEEN

Ethan

THE MOMENT MY BOOTS HIT THE TARMAC, MY MIND CHURNS
through the information I extracted. It feels good to be immersed in
a mission rather than wallowing over my regrets surrounding Rebel.
The world is reduced to white noise in the background, every ounce
of my focus already reassessing our situation and revising strategies.

At the edge of the landing strip, Forest Summers himself is there
to greet us. His silhouette is a monument of pure, raw power.
Towering nearly seven feet, he's one of the few men on the planet
who makes me feel small.

Recuperating after months of battling cancer, he's slowly recovering the muscle mass he lost. Still, he's a figure of strength. An
imposing presence that makes me want to do my best.

The walk to him is a series of snapshots—flashes of his tall,
imposing figure stark against the fading hues of the sunset, the
ripple of muscle under his fitted shirt, the quiet intensity of his ice-
blue gaze. The shock of white-blond hair crowning his head. This
man is a force of nature, steady as a mountain and unyielding as
the sea.

As I approach, he pushes off from where he leans against the
hangar wall, broad shoulders squaring off.

"Ally?" His concern fills in the air between us. I can't say I blame him. The sweet, vibrant young woman was cast into a world she was not equipped to understand.

"Minor cuts and bruising. She's shaken but coping."

"That's good. You got to her in time. Great job."

"That may be, but this is far from over." There's too much to debrief on the tarmac.

"How's that?"

"Until we put a lid on this, Ally's father can't whisk her away. He can't protect her. This is no simple kidnapping."

"Explain."

"It's a boutique kidnapping camouflaged as a human-trafficking ring complete with auction."

Forest's lids pull back in surprise, making his ice-blue eyes appear nearly as pale as the white of his eyes. He's silent, not because he's contemplating, but because he accepts what I say. I knew he would. Forest's the kind of man who would walk through fire for those who've been abducted and enslaved.

What follows next is the machine that is Guardian HRS springing into action. Ally is whisked off the plane to safety. She'll be reunited with her father and taken back under our care. Until Guardian HRS neutralizes the threat against her, her life remains at risk, and we will protect her.

I escort our guest to a holding cell where the real interrogation begins. Sam and CJ bring in Griff, a Guardian from Alpha team adept at advanced interrogation techniques.

With him on the job, I take my team for a debrief in our bullpen. The space is filled with lockers, cages, and bins, a utilitarian space of concrete and steel where the men of Charlie team gear up for missions.

Hank, Walt, Blake, Jeb, and Gabe are already there, moving through their post-mission actions with the steady rhythm of professionals. The hum of conversation falls silent as I stride into the room. I glance at each man as I pass.

Charlie team.

My team.

"Debrief." The single word commands their attention.

We gather in the center of our bullpen, a loose circle of hard bodies and harder eyes.

"Hank?" I turn to the former Green Beret. "Your assessment?"

"Target extraction went clean. We wasted time sending a team to the back as there was no egress out that way, but we didn't have that intel. Could have been smoother, but the rough edges weren't our fault and not a problem." Hank's voice rumbles, his words plain and blunt. A soldier's report.

"Walt?" He's one of the few who comes to the Guardians from the Air Force. An ex-para jumper, he's a skilled paramedic. He brushes his hand over his shaven head. "Medical assessment. Ally's stable, with no permanent damage. Other than a few cuts and bruises, she'll recover."

I nod, turning next to Blake. He's a solid wall of muscle, silent and watchful. "Tactical assessment?"

Blake raises a brow, a hint of amusement in his gaze. "We flew. We landed. We fought. She's here." His voice drips sarcasm, but that's Blake. He's a wiseass through and through.

I crack a smile. "Never change, Blake." The guys laugh, breaking the tension.

"Jeb?" I turn to our tech wizard. His fingers twitch as if itching for a keyboard.

"Secured their phones. The techies have them now. Should have full intel in a few hours." His voice is clipped and precise. Every syllable is a nugget of information.

"First thoughts?" No way in hell did Jeb not take a look inside those phones.

"Idiot never deleted his conversations. They're all on his phone. Mitzy and her team won't have any problem tracing those breadcrumbs."

Last is Gabe, a mountain of a man with a face as stern as an Easter Island statue.

"Nothing to add that hasn't been said." He's short on words, but I've learned not to discount his opinions.

"Well done. Another successful mission." I clap my hands, ending the debrief.

We break down our gear, and the room fills with the clatter of metal and lewd jokes between my men.

They are the best of the best. United under the Guardian banner, they are my brothers in arms. I've trusted them with my life, and they've trusted me with theirs. They're finally beginning to accept me as their team leader, and I value that trust.

They each bring unique skills and experiences to the table. Hank's strategic prowess. Walt's medical expertise. Blake's steady hand and eagle eye. His sniper skills are legendary. Jeb's a techno-logical genius, smart enough to be on Mitzy's team but stout enough to stand shoulder-to-shoulder with the Guardians. He may have a brilliant mind, but the man is a Guardian at heart. Then there's Gabe's raw strength and brilliance. He's a munitions expert and an all-around MacGyver when it comes to creativity and solving prob-lems in the field.

Each of them is crucial to the success of our team, and as I watch them, I can't help but feel a surge of pride.

"Just one more thing," I call out to my team, grabbing their attention. "Complacency kills. We stay sharp. We stay ready."

"Copy that." They respond as a collective, showing how deep our bond ties us together.

Brotherhood thrives in spaces like this—the bullpen, the show-ers, the common areas—where we eat, sleep, laugh, and bleed. This is where we train, where trust is earned, camaraderie is fostered, and bonds of the deepest friendship and respect are forged.

Hank's booming voice silences the room. "Pizza and beer tonight. Who's buying the first round?" He places his index finger on his nose, indicating it's not him.

A quick succession of nose-pointing follows. I find myself the last man, my finger not quite reaching my nose in time.

Walt grins. "Sorry, gotta be quicker on the draw, boss."

"Charlie-One is buying. *Whoop-whoop!*" Hank teases, a broad grin on his face.

"Fine, I see how it is. First round's on me then." The fact that they're picking on me and including me says I'm one of them now.

The laughter continues as we clean our gear. This is how we unwind and cope with the burden of our job. The weight of our responsibilities fades into the background for a moment, and we're just six guys looking forward to pizza and beer.

We descend on a local pizza joint, bringing the party with us. It's a hole-in-the-wall place known only to locals and is quickly becoming my favorite. The aroma of wood-fired pizza and hoppy beer fills the air as we lay claim to a large table.

As the evening progresses, we consume beer and devour pizza. Once that's done, the guys go on the hunt for their own conquests for the evening.

A gaggle of women surround Hank. He's a charmer and a favorite of the ladies. Walt, who's more reserved, finds himself a petite brunette to secret away in a private corner in the back.

"You got protection tonight?" Blake nudges Gabe, a cocky grin playing on his lips.

The table erupts in laughter at the pointed dig, recalling an unfortunate incident involving Gabe a few weeks back.

"Learned my lesson. I'm armed and dangerous now. You could say I'm ready for any—*mission*." He grins like a fool and holds up two fingers. "Got two on me right now."

"Only two? You're not very optimistic?" Blake chimes in, his deep voice laced with humor.

The table roars again, and Gabe's face turns beet red.

They're good men, and the women know it. They see past the rough and rugged edges to the honorable, dedicated men they truly are. Over another round of beer, I slowly lose Jeb, Gabe, and Hank until I'm the last man sitting at the table.

Watching my men pair off, it's natural for my thoughts to drift to a pair of emerald eyes, a fiery spirit, and a woman who captured my thoughts since the moment I saw her.

Rebel.

She's a constant presence in my mind, a flame that refuses to be extinguished.

Each of my teammates leaves with their chosen company for the night. I get stuck with the tab for the entire evening, which doesn't bother me. I'm happy to let them blow off a bit of steam. I'm all on board if that means paying for pizza and beer.

A part of me wishes I could cut loose like them. Lose myself in a woman for the night.

But I can't.

Following the success of our mission, the camaraderie, the jokes, the stories, and the tall tales all make for a good night, but it does nothing to alleviate the emptiness inside of me. I may not have a woman on my arm, but I have my brothers.

That's enough.

At least, that's the lie I tell myself.

After paying the bill, I hop on my Harley and ride down the dark, deserted highway. Not ready for the emptiness of my quarters, I drive to The Facility, the place that housed Rebel after I rescued her. The woman who plied me with her charm, stunned me with her beauty, and then captivated me with the warmth of her body.

The woman who betrayed me.

This late, The Facility is silent; its lights dimmed for the night. I spend the rest of the evening walking along the cliffs overlooking the rocky beach below. It's here where memories of Rebel are the strongest. Each wave that crashes against the rocks reminds me of the night we spent together.

The heat of our passion wasn't faked. I reject that thought. Despite her disappearance, what we shared was real.

I take a seat on the cliff edge, then lie back on the grass to stare at the stars. Each twinkling light reminds me of the laughter in her eyes. The gentle breeze blowing in off the water rustles through my hair; its touch is a pale imitation of the way her fingers combed through my hair.

I close my eyes, letting the sounds of the sea, the whispers of the wind, and the memories of her laughter fill the silence. She's a ghost, a phantom that haunts me.

And I can't get her out of my head.

How long has it been? Why do I still feel her so strongly?

Tonight, I cut loose with my men. We laughed, we joked, we lived. Just another day in the world of the Guardian Hostage Rescue Specialists. Tomorrow is another day, and there's no way to know what it will bring.

Is it foolish to hope it will magically bring Rebel back to me?

FIFTEEN

Ethan

THE SHRILL RING OF MY PHONE SHATTERS THE CALM OF THE NIGHT, spiraling through the quiet like a warning siren. The first thought that goes through my brain is always the same.

They found Rebel.

A quick glance at the screen reveals it's Mitzy. Her number lights up the display, and a jolt of adrenaline races through my veins.

Not one for idle chatter, her call carries weight. She found something. I answer, and her voice crackles through the speaker, urgent and tinged with the unique excitement only a breakthrough can elicit.

"Ethan, you need to hear this." Her voice comes through in a rush. *"I was combing through the phone you confiscated, and there's something here. Something big. I'm calling a meeting. Grab your team and meet in the Guardian briefing room in an hour."*

"Copy that. Can you tell me the highlights?"

"Not a kidnapping. Never a plan for ransom. This is brutal, cold revenge."

She spills the details, and each revelation forges a sickening picture in my mind. A connection between Ally's security detail and a man with a grudge against her father.

Not just any grudge—an ancient, festering wound begging to be avenged.

This is personal.

Vengeance served cold.

This complicates things because our enemy's motivations make him unpredictable and far more dangerous.

Ally's straightforward search and recovery is now a tangle of personal agendas, shadowed by a feud older and bitterer than the coldest winters.

The debriefing comes all too soon. Charlie team gathers around a large conference table that dominates the room. Sam, CJ, and Mitzy stand at the front of the room. Even Forest Summers is present.

An elemental power, he commands our attention without uttering a word. Just shy of a seven-foot titan, his Nordic features are an imposing blend of ice-blue eyes, winter-blond hair, and a face etched out of stone. He inspires awe and a deep-rooted desire to surpass our limitations, meet our challenges head-on, and win.

There's a godliness about him.

The man is a living testament to survival, as is his foster sister, Skye, aka Doc Summers. Her imposing brother may overshadow her diminutive height, but her gaze speaks to a quiet strength and unbending determination to survive and persevere. Yet the gentle tilt of her smile reveals a river of compassion miles wide.

Mitzy holds court at the end of the conference table. Behind her is a digital stage of a score of monitors mounted on the wall. Her vibrant, psychedelic hair sticks out in all directions, a halo of rebellion against authority. Her gaze never wavers from the screen as she scrolls through an endless stream of information.

Her voice, rushed with an urgent and methodical rhythm, lifts and rises over the clicking of her mouse and the steady tap-tap-tapping of keys. She's a maestro conducting an orchestra of data streams, bringing coherence to the madness.

Sam is a seasoned veteran and an impeccable leader. Exuding an aura of quiet authority, he commands the room without the need to raise his voice. There's an air of serenity forged in the fires of combat and polished in the aftermath of countless missions that define him. His demeanor might seem tranquil, but the undercurrent of razor-sharp focus reminds us of the soldier he once was and the powerful leader he has become.

Beside him, CJ carries a different brand of command. His broad shoulders, tempered by the rigors of special operations, bear the weight of responsibility with a warrior's grace. The battlefield may have honed his skills, but the heart beneath the hardened exterior gives him the courage to lead us into unknown territory.

"Collins and DuBois…" Mitzy begins the briefing and spits the names out as if their taste is repugnant. "I've been digging into Collins's past, exploring old connections, forgotten rivalries. The name DuBois kept coming up. A feud between them stretches back decades to a time when they were both climbing the corporate ladder. Collins allegedly stole patents from DuBois, siphoning off his success."

Forest's features harden. He's a warrior and businessman who understands the ramifications of corporate betrayals. "That's a significant motive for a grudge, but to kidnap Collins's daughter?"

"The corporate espionage is merely the beginning. Collins is no angel." Mitzy's lips press into a thin line, a signal she's about to drop a bombshell. "Dubois was married to a woman named Eleanor. Eleanor became Mrs. Eleanor Collins. She married Collins the day her divorce from Dubois was finalized, and her daughter, Ally, was delivered five months later."

"No shit." Hank runs his hand down his face. "That's cold. Affair aside, to marry Collins the same day her divorce was finalized? That's brutal."

"Yes, like a major kick in the ass." Gabe shares a look with Hank, and they both shake their heads."

"Kick in the ass. Slap to the face. She definitely sent a message." They say passion runs hot, but this is as cold as it gets. I shift in my seat, waiting for Mitzy to drop the real bombshell.

"I don't think *she* was sending any message. Collins did that." Mitzy purses her lips. "I dug a bit further into Dubois and Collins. They went to the same university, were in the same fraternity, and get this…" Mitzy glances around the room, letting the suspense build. We all lean forward, hanging on her every word.

"She dated Dubois during his freshman year. Collins took her from DuBois. She and Collins dated right up until graduation." Mitzy pops up pictures of college-aged Collins, Dubois, and Eleanor. The photos switch back and forth regarding which man's arm is draped across Eleanor's shoulders.

Hank's chair creaks as he leans back, a corner of his mouth twitching upwards. "I can see why they wanted her." His gaze flickers to the ceiling, a finger tracing the line of his jaw. "She's very attractive."

"Collins lost in the end. After graduation, Dubois proposed and married her within the month. I'll give you one guess who wasn't on the guest list."

"Collins." Not hard to figure that one out. I lean forward, elbows finding support on the hard tabletop. "We're dealing with a very twisted love triangle."

"One that Collins won in the end." Mitzy flashes images on a screen. The last one freezes the room—a funeral. Collins is a mournful statue next to a tearful eight-year-old girl. "Dubois tried to pay his respects, but Collins had him removed from the funeral."

"Heartless." Blake echoes my thoughts. He leans back; the casual nonchalance belies the thoughtfulness in his gaze.

DuBois lost everything to Collins. His livelihood. His wife. The love of his life.

A betrayal served not once but twice.

And Ally is the innocent collateral used in this vicious game. She's the flesh-and-blood symbol of DuBois's most profound loss.

An eye for an eye?

Walt's fingers drum on the table, and his steely gaze hardens. "Dubois retaliates by taking Collins's kid? Damn, that's dark."

Gabe's chair creaks as he shifts uncomfortably, his knuckles bone white against the table. "The guy's deranged. He's willing to destroy a young girl's life over a feud?"

"Not that it needs to be said, but it's even more vile." Mitzy rocks back in her chair. "He enlisted the services of an organization known as Haven."

"What's that?"

"A boutique operation involved in selective kidnappings." She glances around the room. "I wish I could say the next bit is a shock, but this is right up our alley. Haven promises to find the perfect slave for a price. DuBois hired them to groom Ally as his slave. Literally sticking it to Collins by taking his daughter and forcing her to..." Mitzy shrugs and leaves her words hanging in the air.

"That's some cold shit." I take in a breath and blow it out real slow. The depths of depravity in this world never cease to amaze me.

"How did you figure this out?" CJ, who's been quiet so far, swivels back and forth in his seat.

Mitzy doesn't blink, pushing forward with her revelation. "Our guest, one of Ally's security detail, is a DuBois employee. DuBois hired him to snatch Ally and deliver her to Haven. Griff got—*creative*—and the man sang like the proverbial canary. Once we involved witness protection, he opened up even more."

Blake's fist hits the table with a thud. "A scorned man playing monster, using his employee to snatch Ally. This isn't just some power play, it's..." He shakes his head, unable to find the words.

Every syllable is a punch to the gut. The ugly picture is complete —Collins's ruthless climb to the top, the stolen wife, a love child, and the kidnapping of a daughter to settle the score.

Definitely an eye for an eye.

"Mitzy," Sam clears his throat, gathering our attention as the heinous nature of DuBois's crime sinks in, "keep digging. We need everything, every scrap of detail."

"Already on it, boss." She winks and flashes a smile.

This revelation hangs heavy in the room, a monstrous tapestry of greed and revenge. It explains much, but some things still don't add up.

This mission is turning into something far more than what it initially appeared. It's a personal war, a dangerous game of chess with Ally as the innocent pawn. The implications for her are horrendous.

But we stopped Dubois. Unfortunately, she won't be safe until this issue of an auction is addressed. I run a hand through my hair, my mind reeling from Mitzy's revelations.

"Why would DuBois involve Haven? Why haul Ally to Florida when he lives in upstate New York? He could've just taken her. The Haven angle doesn't make sense."

Mitzy's expression shifts to one of strained concentration. "That's a good question, and it's been bugging me. I'm working on it, using information from the phone of the kidnapper we interrogated. I tracked his activity to Haven. Of course, it's not mentioned in any of their conversations, but enough threads point to a single entity. I found Haven and have a preliminary answer to your question."

"Please share."

"Haven's boutique services include training the girls before delivering them to their buyers."

"Haven?" Gabe murmurs, his brows knitting together. "It's not a haven. It's hell."

"Agree." Mitzy nods. "They're deeply rooted in the dark web and specialize in kidnappings-for-hire. The level of detail in their plans and the resources they provide their operatives is chilling. They turned abduction into an art form and are very good at it. The *training* comes at an extra charge. No need to guess, but Dubois paid for the supplemental fee."

"Then why use his own man?" My fists clench on the tabletop.

"Probably because he could. Or maybe it was a concession to afford Haven's *supplemental* fee." Mitzy uses air quotes for emphasis. "He paid not only to have Ally trained but to receive training himself."

"Himself?" Jeb looks up from cleaning his nails. "What the fuck does that mean?"

"They offer a service to train clients to master, subdue, and discipline their new property. That training is offered in week-long blocks of time. DuBois paid for a month."

"Shit." Forest's low whistle reverberates through the room. "So, we've got a shadow organization, a disgruntled millionaire with a vendetta, and an innocent girl caught in the crossfire. That's one hell of a mess."

It's more than a mess—it's a goddamn nightmare.

"What's next?" My voice comes out in a low growl. We're going to rain hell down on Haven. My gaze locks on Mitzy. "Any idea how to infiltrate Haven?"

She purses her lips, considering. "There's an auction scheduled two days from now. It's the one Ally was supposed to be in. They haven't given away the location yet, but I'm working on tracing it."

"We did something similar before," Sam speaks up. "Alpha-One went undercover as a buyer at an auction. He brought Eve back, and we rescued scores more. But two days?"

"Need I remind everyone that Max almost got himself killed?" The muscles of CJ's jaw bunch as he clenches his teeth. "No way am I sending in only two men like last time."

"Doesn't mean we shouldn't try it again." I tap my upper lip with my index finger, thinking. My mind races with options and variations. CJ's concerns are valid. Max got separated and nearly didn't make it out of his mission.

"Max had an in. We got him invited to that auction. But Haven? Seems to me, they operate differently." Forest's voice is thoughtful as he responds. "They're more cautious, more secretive. We don't have that this time."

"Then we make one." The spark of an idea flashes in my mind.

"How?" Forest turns his glacial gaze on me.

"First off, Ally's safe. We don't need to make that auction. And as for a way in, all we need is what Dubois had."

"What's that?" Forest's pale blue eyes sear into me.

"Dubois had a need—a want—and he didn't avail himself of their kidnapping options. He used his own men to grab her and deliver Ally to Haven."

"Where are you going with this?" Walt clears his throat and spins his chair to face me.

"We create the same thing. One of us poses as a man who wants a slave. We ID a woman and, just like DuBois, use our own men. Those men will have to know where to deliver the woman. Haven has to supply that information. We can also do what you did with that mission with Max."

"What's that?" CJ gestures for me to continue.

"We buy time to train as a master but insist on retaining our security escort. I can pose as the client. The rest of my team acts as my security detail."

"But you need someone to kidnap." Skye shakes her head. "Knowing what will happen to them while you infiltrate Haven isn't something I can ask any of our operatives to do."

A murmur of agreement echoes through the room. The plan is too rough, and the outcome too uncertain.

"Okay, what if we modify that a bit?" This is a good idea. I get Skye's hesitation, and there's no argument against it. "I see two ways in. One as a client and one as support for a client. How do we insert Charlie team?" My mind is a strange thing. The solution is coming to me; I just need to think out loud to get it to gel.

I tap my temple and continue thinking out loud. "We can't infiltrate Haven because that would raise too many red flags. We can only get in as a buyer or security detail to a buyer. I doubt we can insert ourselves into a potential client's security detail. Like Haven, too many red flags. But what if we return to the initial idea?"

"That's a hard no." Sam shakes his head and crosses his arms. "We're not putting one of our female operatives at risk."

"But what if we mitigate that risk?"

Everyone looks at me.

SIXTEEN

Ethan

———

WITH EVERYONE STARING AT ME, I CLEAR MY THROAT AND FINISH MY thoughts. "Let's say, for a moment, that we pose as a client and have one of our female operatives put herself up as the victim." I hold up my hand, forestalling the chorus of *Nos!* I'm about to receive.

"Let me continue. We bring the client, whichever of us is in that role, our kidnapping victim, and Charlie team as kidnappers and security. That gets us in the door."

"In the door, and it places one of our female operatives at risk for rape, torture, or worse." Sam's comment is dismissive, and he's moments from shutting me down.

"Not if we rescue her." I jump on Sam's comment.

"Rescue?" Mitzy's brows bunch together. "What does that get us?"

"Get another team to mount a rescue. Remove her from any threat. Our client will be pissed, make a scene…"

"And you're all tossed out on your asses." CJ shakes his head. "I don't see this helping."

"What if we become the solution to Haven's problem?" The final piece is coming to me. It's just out of reach, but all I have to do is keep talking. It'll come to me. "What if we offer a solution to a problem they don't know they have yet?"

Forest's gaze sharpens, his head tilting slightly. "You're suggesting we create a security breach for us to fix?"

Yes! It's like he's reading my mind.

"Exactly. That breach allows us to extract our operative. Get her out of there. The client will get pissed and demand answers. We will '*help*' Haven figure out what happened. Swoop in to save the day, as it were. Our client can insist we stay behind to fix the breach while he waits for another opportunity to kidnap his girl."

"Complicated." Mitzy's gaze practically bores a hole between my eyes, but her incredible mind is working on the problem. "But, if everything works, we could…" She turns to Forest. "What do you think?"

"It might work." Like Mitzy, Forest's brain is a modern marvel.

"I can engineer something they won't be able to ignore." Mitzy's eyes flicker with a spark of hope. "It'll take time to figure a way for Charlie team to solve it realistically."

"It's risky," Forest grunts, his eyes hard and assessing.

"Agreed. Too risky," Skye jumps in, the voice of reason.

"Everything we do carries inherent risk." My statement hangs in the room, but I'm right.

I feel it.

The determined faces of my men turn to me, each of them nodding in agreement. It is risky. No one debates this. There's no assurance of success, and if any of us is caught, it's a death sentence.

But we're Guardians.

We don't shy away from danger.

We charge headfirst into it.

"Not agreeing to anything, but let's see what we can come up with," Forest concedes, his voice confirming the resolve etched on his face. "We balance risks in favor of our personnel. I'm not exposing anyone to the risk of *rape*. Not without a solid plan and backups to that plan." His gaze shifts to Skye. "Lots of backups."

She returns a steady gaze.

The plan may be rough, the outcome uncertain, but one thing is clear. We're committed to taking Haven down.

As the meeting adjourns, the resolve in the room is palpable.

A MONTH LATER, WE'RE STILL NO CLOSER TO OUR GOAL.

Hours blend into days, and days blur into nights until they're nearly indistinguishable. We enter this vicious cycle of searching for any vulnerability we can exploit. When we think we've got it nailed down, someone invariably notices a critical flaw, and we start over from square one.

When not working the Haven case, Charlie team spends time on several hostage rescues in Cancun, reuniting families who lost loved ones to the kidnapping trade. When not on mission, we train, honing our skills in the field. In what free time we have leftover, we work with Mitzy and CJ to hammer out ways to attack the problem that is Haven.

Which is what we want. If there's a flaw, we want to discover it before our mission launches, not while Charlie team is in the trenches. But still, it's demoralizing. Each day we wait is another day another woman suffers a fate worse than death.

Restless energy fills the room during our weekly update. Mitzy outlines our next move, her image flickering on the screen as she dials in from her lab.

"Their digital fortress is a beast." Her tone conveys intense frustration. "Every angle we've tried has been shut down. They're cautious, meticulous... Paranoid."

"Keep at it, Mitz." Forest Summers provides what encouragement he can. "You'll figure it out."

"Easier said than done. If you think it's so damn easy, why don't you come in and help?"

"You don't need my help. You've got this." Forest's features remain stoic and firm. He's still in recovery following a life-threatening cancer scare he barely survived and is taking time off to heal.

One look at the man and it's clear he's regaining his strength, but he remains a shell of his former self.

"Whatever," she scoffs. "It's back to the drawing board. I don't have much more to report."

CJ wrangles back control of the meeting. "Do what you can, and we'll meet in a week for updates."

"I'm doing my best." Mitzy rolls her eyes and shakes her head in frustration.

"No one's saying you aren't. If it were easy, we wouldn't have a job."

In the long, tense weeks that follow, I find myself thrown back into the heart of what being a Guardian means—sleepless nights, meticulous planning, constant training, and fierce determination coursing through my veins.

It's a welcome distraction because—inevitably—when I'm not buried under work, thoughts of Rebel fill my mind. My body aches to hold, punish, and make love to her. The void she left behind is unending.

Honestly, I don't understand the hold this woman has over me. It doesn't make sense. However, with each passing day, week, and month, the hope of finding her grows fainter until it's no longer there.

Nothing but an echo.

As Charlie team rallies around this mission, and Mitzy's team immerses themselves in the world of Haven, the search for Rebel is no longer a priority. Eventually, Guardian HRS stops looking for her. This emptiness inside of me is something I resign myself to carry forever. A silent ghost that never leaves my side.

A WEEK PASSES, AND I FIND MYSELF AGAIN SUMMONED TO A BRIEFING. The tension in the room is palpable as I take a seat across from CJ and Mitzy.

"Mitzy, brief Ethan on where we are," CJ gets right to it.

"Sure thing." Mitzy taps rapidly on her keyboard, face illuminated by the glow of a dozen monitors. "Their deepest layers of encryption prevent outside access, but I can spoof an origin point from inside, make it look like there's a mole."

Mitzy straightens, her rainbow hair catching the light. "I built out backgrounds for each of your team members. Their aliases have thorough digital footprints as security professionals specializing in network encryption. Your team is now positioned as cutting-edge IT and security experts. All that's left is to make some noise and let Haven come calling."

Anticipation tingles through me. I flick through the dossiers on my tablet, marveling at the level of detail Mitzy put into each profile. We'll all need to be familiar with it, especially if Haven personnel start asking questions.

"That will get us in the front door." I set the tablet down and make a note to memorize the details later. "But, it's not much use going in if all we're going to do is hang out where they keep their servers. Gaining access to the entirety of the facility is going to require a more finessed approach."

CJ grunts in agreement. "Mitzy had a thought about that."

Mitzy continues, fingers still flying rapidly over the keys. "In addition to the system breach, I'm inserting strategically placed breadcrumbs."

"Breadcrumbs?" I ask, sipping my coffee.

"You mentioned you were concerned about bringing Charlie team to Haven. I'm giving you a reason to bring muscle." Mitzy's eyes remain glued to the screen. "Hints and whispers that there's a mole inside Haven passing information to outsiders."

"You think that will convince them to give us more access?" I like how her mind works.

"It should provide leverage. They'll want someone searching for the mole if they suspect information is leaking out of their facility." Mitzy flashes a grin. "I'm laying the groundwork across the digital sphere. Vague mentions in closed forums. Anonymous tips left on the dark web. Just enough to spark paranoia."

Her hands move adeptly over the keyboards, orchestrating her digital campaign. She spins in her chair, cracking her knuckles with a grin. "I'll monitor the chatter and make sure they're taking the bait. If needed, I can up the ante, stir more suspicions of a turncoat in their midst."

My respect for her deviousness grows. She thought of everything. I watch over her shoulder as she inserts carefully crafted misinformation across the web. Her ghost is everywhere yet nowhere, stoking paranoia inside Haven's ranks.

"That seems more IT-related. How does that spark suspicion of a mole?"

"It'll make it seem like a Haven employee is shopping information around. Nothing too obvious, but just suspicious enough activity to catch their eye if they go digging."

"Gotcha." I exhale, feeling the pieces slot into place. Between Mitzy's operations magic and our fieldwork, we might pull this off after all. "You're a genius. This is perfect."

Mitzy shrugs but looks pleased. "All in a day's work. Just make sure you sell the cover story, get them eating out of your hands."

I marvel at Mitzy's skill, conducting this intricate manipulation right under Haven's nose. Truly masterful.

"So, this justifies bringing in outside security specialists like yourselves to investigate a breach. You provide security for your IT specialists and outside support for Kaufman, who will be suspicious of his entire organization. He won't have anyone to trust but you."

"Kaufman?" I lean back. Ally's words return to me. *Something like a cough.* This must be who she meant.

"Yeah. Sorry, should've led with that. He runs Haven." Mitzy confirms, her voice even, factual.

"What do we know about Kaufman?"

"He's got his fingers in crime syndicates across the world, particularly in Eastern Europe. Wealthy, well-connected, and well-protected."

I nod, the pieces beginning to slot together.

"Haven is a relatively new venture for him. He calls it 'acquisitions management.'" Mitzy's lips form a straight line. "But we know what that means. He snatches women and sells them to the highest bidder. Kaufman's not just a criminal; he's a predator."

"And we're going to waltz into his hunting ground as tech specialists?" I glance around. "You realize we look nothing like geeks. No offense, but…" I gesture to my team.

"You're the muscle. Yeah, I've thought about that." She pauses, the air around her seeming to bristle with unspoken secrets. "You're security services."

"Security services?" I stroke my chin thoughtfully.

"We offer our IT services to fix the breach in their system, and our security services track down the imaginary mole. That gives you a reason to get out and about around Haven. Hopefully, it'll give you a reason to access sensitive areas under the pretext of your search. Although…" Her voice trails off, the word hanging tantalizingly as she shifts her weight. The creak of the chair fills the charged silence.

"Although, what?"

"From what I've seen so far, he's professionally paranoid. You might have to convince him to grant that access. All I can do is plant the seeds of a mole inside his organization."

"I can work with that. All I need is justification for an expanded presence inside Haven. Your idea of a mole gives me that. I'll have Kaufman ready and willing to give us the run of the place in no time."

This feels right. With Mitzy's narrative, we now have an airtight reason for Charlie team's presence. Not just the IT specialists but the whole crew.

"There is one problem." Mitzy surprises me.

"What's that?" I look up, a bit stunned.

"Charlie team can't pull off being IT experts," Mitzy continues. "No offense to your team, but this is complicated stuff."

I shrug. "None taken. Give us guns and combat, not geeky tech stuff. What about Jeb? He's our team geek?"

"This is beyond him. I'm concerned about that part of the plan the most. Technical training, especially dark web encryption, isn't something that can be faked."

"Can you '*prep*' him on what he needs?" I use air quotes to highlight my concerns, not at all sure I know what kind of training Jeb might require.

"Already on it. I asked Jeb to start shadowing my team." Mitzy looks up from her monitor. "He's adept, but he needs extra training. To be honest, Haven's security is too advanced for him." She tugs at her psychedelic hair. "That's why I'm sending one of my best with you."

"You're what?" I glance at CJ, who returns a shrug. "I'm not sure that's such a good idea."

"Why not?" She returns a steady stare.

"No offense, but a spindly, acne-faced geek barely out of high school is a liability."

"Stereotyping much?" Mitzy arches a brow, but then rolls on, not one bit put off by my comment. "Meet Stitch, not your average pimply-faced nerd."

"Stitch? What kind of name is that?" Once again, I look to CJ for support. He understands the unique dynamics of a team. The old saying, 'You're only as good as your weakest link' is there for a reason.

"Stitch was quite a mess when I found *her*," Mitzy says.

Her? I palm my face, realizing my error. I'm going to pay for my assumptions.

Mitzy shakes her head. "Bright teenager but channeling her skills where she shouldn't. NSA, major banks—you get the picture." She pulls up Stitch's file, photos flashing across the screen. "She got nabbed hacking into an NSA database and was facing serious jail time."

I whistle under my breath. This girl likes to play with fire.

"I saw her potential, stepped in, and made a deal to get the charges dropped if she joined Guardian HRS." Mitzy smiles. "Pulled a few strings, called in some favors. Next thing you know, Stitch is working for the good guys."

The door to the briefing room swings open, and a young twenty-something female saunters in, combat boots thudding on the tile. She wears a mismatched goth ensemble—a ratty black t-shirt, distressed jeans, and clunky boots.

Tossing her dark hair to the side, she surveys the room through heavily lined eyes, lips painted in black, and her mouth twisted into a wry grin. She leans against the wall, one ankle kicked casually over the other, looking every bit the rebel.

I hide a smile, used to her disregard for protocol and authority figures. Stitch will never officially join any organization, but she'll grudgingly collaborate when needed—giving me grief along the way.

Her raised eyebrow says she's waiting for me to speak. I say nothing, letting the silence grow, showing her that I'm not impressed by her goth persona. We have a lot to cover and not much time. No way am I spending any of that pandering to this societal rebel.

Finally, with a huff, she shifts her feet and speaks. "NSA security was pathetic." She blows a puff of air, moving hair out of her eyes.

"Yes, thank you for that colorful assessment." Mitzy sighs, but I can see the truth in her eyes. Stitch's goth persona is an absolute one-eighty from Mitzy's psychedelic quirkiness, but she sees a version of her younger self in the young hacker.

I chuckle under my breath. This girl has attitude to spare, and she's exactly what we need—someone unafraid to skirt rules and break barriers.

"Just point me to what you need hacked and I'll get it done." Stitch's unwavering gaze tells me she's ready for anything.

"If you're taking Jeb for additional training, I want Stitch to join Charlie team. I'm not taking along a young twenty-something female without basic self-defense skills."

"Who says I can't take care of myself?" Stitch scoffs. "Please. I think I can handle babysitting a few grunts."

I bristle slightly. "This is non-negotiable. You train with my team, or you're off the mission."

"There's no *mission* without me, dumbass." Stitch opens her mouth to say more but catches Mitzy's stern gaze. Stitch rolls her eyes dramatically. "Ugh, fine. Whatever. I'll train with the grunts."

"Glad that's settled." I hide a smile. This one has spirit, but she'll fall in line. "Report to the training room at 0600 hours."

Stitch gives a barely perceptible nod, her intense gaze taking my measure. She's ready to do whatever the job requires but can't help herself from grumbling under her breath.

She'll be a valuable asset with the right guidance. Haven's security doesn't stand a chance against someone who cracked the NSA's tight encryption and security protocols.

This mission just got a lot more interesting.

THE NEXT SIX WEEKS ARE A WHIRLWIND OF INTENSE TRAINING. Stitch surprises me, being well-versed in the art of self-defense. Only afterward do I find out she's been training with both Jeb and Jinx on the side. Jinx is one of Guardian HRS's newer female operatives, exceptionally adept at Brazilian fighting techniques. Stitch played me, knowing I would underestimate her skills.

I vow never to judge her abilities again.

Then Mitzy calls the team for another briefing.

"I created the security breach in Haven's network. Put in footprints for the mole. Guess who sent out inquiries, urgently seeking outside help?"

"Nice work." I can't help but admire her skill.

"If I do say so myself." Mitzy's not one to ignore praise. She's cocky and deserves all the praise in the world. I'm happy to supply a bit of an ego boost. "They *discreetly* reached out to our *experts.*" Mitzy switches the screen to show her monitor.

Urgent contract opportunity. Expertise required."

I'm exceptionally pleased. This may have started as my idea, but I didn't know if it would work.

"Here's my response. **Ready to assist. My team can be onsite within 24 hours.** We bickered back and forth over fees and the number of personnel I insisted on bringing. Unsurprisingly, they wanted to keep it at Jeb, Stitch, and one bodyguard. I talked them up to five bodyguards. You're taking your entire team."

"Mitzy, you are a miracle worker."

"I know." She flutters her lashes, looking impish and pleased, then her eyes gleam. "Haven won't know what hit them."

SEVENTEEN

Ethan

THE SHARP REPORT OF GUNFIRE CLEAVES THE AIR IN A RAPID *POP-pop-pop!* Charlie team trains in the kill house, prepping for our next mission. We don't know what Haven will throw at us, but we prepare, nonetheless. I give the technical team instructions on what scenarios to prep, then set my team loose in the kill house. They have no idea what scenario they face but execute brilliantly without hesitation or error.

Jeb and Gabe are up next. They move through the rooms quickly and efficiently, clearing each room in a blur of motion, leaving no corner unchecked and no enemy left standing.

Footfalls light yet precise, their motions are economical—the mark of true professionals. Jeb pivots, weapon raised, and fires three times in quick succession around a corner. His shots punch a tight group through his target's chest.

Gabe is on his six, steps up to clear the next room. Jeb drops back to cover the rear. After endless drills and years of fighting side-by-side, they operate like a well-oiled machine. They push forward. Focused. Methodical. They make it through the kill house in no time with a nearly perfect score.

When they emerge, I give an approving nod. "Outstanding work."

Jeb grins. He gives Gabe a fist bump.

I turn to their teammates. "Next."

Hank and Walt step up to run the course, but first, we debrief Jeb and Gabe's performance. This accomplishes two things. First, immediate feedback is the best feedback. Second, it allows the technical team to reset the scenario, changing it up for each run. This is our last run-through for the day. Blake and I went first. Jeb and Gabe were next. It's time for Hank and Walt to see if they can beat our times and accuracy.

I settle back to observe, pride welling in my chest. However dangerous this mission gets, my team has the skills to handle it.

Hank and Walt fly through their scenario with stellar marks, leaving the three two-man teams tied in the end.

After the kill house, we hit the sparring mats to unwind. Stitch, Charlie team's honorary member, steps into the fighting ring with Jeb. Stitch is a snit, hiding her proficiency in martial arts. Like a fool, I thought her skills began and ended in the technical realm. She's shown me how incredibly wrong it was to think that. The girl— young woman—is a firecracker.

The corner of my mouth bounces in a grin. After the first few times referring to her as a girl, she got up in my business, telling me she was a *grown-ass woman who could take care of herself.*

That little bounce at the corner of my mouth turns into a full grin when she faces off against Jeb. The two of them are dating. Jeb says it's casual, but I bet it's far more than that.

When Stitch sinks her claws into Jeb, he's not going to know what hit him. The two stare at each other for several long seconds as if to measure each other up, then Stitch suddenly launches at Jeb.

He meets her onslaught with skill, precision, and the professionalism of a trained warrior. He strikes back with a few well-timed jabs but doesn't go for the kill. Her lithe figure hides shocking strength as she launches a barrage of strikes—knees, elbows, fists— fast as a cobra.

It's almost a dance—the way they move around the ring—

throwing combinations and feints that neither of them land. Except Stitch manages to get around Jeb's defenses. She clips him on the chin with an uppercut, making him stumble. From the grin on his face, Jeb doesn't care. He's having the time of his life. Happy to take the hit.

The air thickens as they circle each other. Jeb holds his own, using his size to power through her offense. He groans as her blow lands hard, but then he counters with a sweeping kick that sends Stitch tumbling to the mat. As good as she is, Stitch is no match for a Guardian.

The air practically crackles with the tension vibrating between them.

They reset, eyes locked, then explode into motion again. They trade blows back and forth relentlessly until a sheen of sweat coats them both. Their competitive spark flames white hot. I feel the heat from there.

Too stubborn to tap out, they're driven by adrenaline and an undeniable chemistry burning between them.

Jeb grins like a fool, enjoying the challenge as the sparring session heats up. Sweat drips from his face as he trades blows back and forth. Every strike is like a caress, every clash of muscle and bone building up the tension between them until it's almost unbearable. But they're both too stubborn to give in, too driven by the adrenaline coursing through their veins. Finally, after what seems like hours, they collapse onto the mats, panting and exhausted.

"Nice workout." Jeb's grin is satisfied as he looks over at Stitch.

"That was fun." Stitch returns his grin, her sly smile tugging at the corners of her lips. "You definitely know how to make me sweat."

The tension between them is thick in the air as they look into each other's eyes. Jeb reaches out and strokes her cheek with his thumb, tracing it along her jawline.

With Charlie team at seven members, with the addition of Stitch, I'm the odd man out for this first round. The rest of the men pair off, fighting harder than usual, bleeding off excess tension.

Good-natured trash talk and roughhousing fill the air. The sharp echo of flesh striking flesh mingles with grunts of effort.

We cycle through several rounds, taking turns challenging each other and pushing our skills to the limit.

The mood is light, but there's an undercurrent of seriousness too. These men know the stakes and how deadly our mission could become. Training is as much psychological preparation as physical.

After training, we hit our favorite local pizza joint. Beers in hand, the mood grows celebratory as we reminisce over past missions. When we arrive, the bar is filled with locals celebrating the end of a long day. The delicious aroma of melted cheese and yeasty dough fills the air. After finding a table, we order several pizzas and plenty of beer.

We laugh hard and drink more. Moments like these bring us together and solidify our brotherly bond.

As the night winds down, the others break off to mingle with female patrons, their boisterous laughter fading into shadowy corners and out the back door. They're blowing off steam before we ship out. I watch the others pair off. Several female admirers inundate Jeb at the bar where he's picking up drinks for himself and Stitch. Although, he doesn't seem interested in anyone other than Stitch.

She notices the bevy of women vying for Jeb's attention, and her expression quickly sours. "Ugh, those skanks need to keep their paws off what's mine."

I can't help but chuckle at her jealous streak.

"Jeb's just being polite."

"He could be a little *less* polite and tell those bitches to back the fuck up."

"Don't worry about Jeb. He's not a player." I switch topics, asking Stich about her childhood and how she's feeling about her training.

"Why aren't you out there joining the fun? You don't hook up at these things? Are you gay?" She toys with the straw in her soda.

"Is that a problem? I'm not, but it shouldn't matter."

"Nah. I know you're not."

"Then why did you ask?"

"I dunno." She pulls at her hair, her irritation rising. "All the other guys are pairing off for the night. Several ladies are wiping drool from their mouths, staring you down, begging for a chance at you, but you're not biting. Why not?"

"Just not interested." I rub the back of my neck, irritation rising.

"It's Rebel, isn't it?"

I shouldn't be surprised she knows about Rebel, but it catches me off guard.

"I'm just not interested," I repeat myself, not interested in talking about Rebel with Stitch.

"Rebel's a ghost. No reason for you to sit on the sidelines."

"What if I like the sidelines?"

"You're a horrible liar." Her eyes glint with mischief. "But suit yourself."

This girl, barely a woman, knows how to push my buttons. Ignoring my silence, she stands and stretches her arms above her head. When I don't answer, she rolls her eyes at me.

"To each their own."

I pointedly ignore the dig, though her words hit their mark. My traitorous thoughts drift to memories of a passionate night on the beach so long ago. How can I be interested in bedding another woman with thoughts of Rebel filling my mind?

Stitch seems to read my mind, her gaze softening knowingly. Without another word, she pats my shoulder and turns her attention to Jeb.

"I'm not lonely," I defend myself, but even as I say the words, my thoughts drift to a pair of intelligent emerald eyes and a curtain of fiery red hair. My heart twists with a now familiar ache.

Rebel, where have you gone?

Stitch's knowing look tells me she senses where my thoughts go. She smiles at Jeb, but when he taps the back of his watch, she takes the last swallow of her drink and pats me on the arm.

"That's my cue. See you in the morning."

Soon, I'm alone with my memories and regrets. The ghost of Rebel still haunts me, no matter how I try to outrun her memory.

Some wounds take time to heal. With a sigh, I settle the tab, leave a generous tip, and head home to grab a few hours of sleep before wheels up.

The next morning, we gather at headquarters, boasting loud and proud to mask our pre-mission nerves. We bump fists, shoot the shit, and fill the air with bravado before loading up.

There's no fanfare. The jet engines rumble to life, and we roll out, headed toward Haven.

Let the games begin.

I take my seat and immediately lean back, close my eyes, and catch a few more Zzzz's.

EIGHTEEN

Ethan

AFTER ALLY'S RESCUE, I THOUGHT HAVEN WOULD BE IN FLORIDA, but it's hidden in the remote mountainous countryside of Montana. I take Charlie team, along with Stitch, our honorary member, and board a plane to Montana. Once we land, the mood shifts. The guys stretch and loosen up as I'm handed the keys to an SUV by a waiting attendant.

"Stitch, you're in front with Jeb and me. The rest of you..." I glance at the two rows of bench seats in the back. "Stow your shit and find your seats."

The guys unload their gear from the jet and transfer it to the SUV. I grip the wheel and settle in for the long drive ahead.

The Montana landscape rolls out before me, a tapestry of undulating grass beneath a wide-open sky. Where the plains give a silent nod to the sky, the Rockies rise like ancient guardians. These mountains know no allegiance; they stand proud, a fortress for all— whether saint or sinner, the wild or the haunted. Within their stony embrace lies Haven, a reminder that beneath beauty often lurks danger.

Hours bleed into each other as we abandon highways and plains for mountainous roads forgotten by time and care. The SUV bucks under my control as the rutted roads challenge our advance. The vehicle groans as we tackle a particularly nasty stretch: the remnants of a rockslide.

But we make it through.

Pines and spruces surround us, a dark audience to our ascent. We climb higher, spiraling up the mountain's spine, each turn drawing us closer to clouds that eventually engulf us. I barely see a few feet of the road in front of us for a time, but then, we breach the clouds and the world explodes in a canvas of brilliant blue.

Haven reveals itself.

A monolith of concrete and cold angles, it dares the wilderness to challenge its authority. Towers jut upwards, sparse windows glint like the eyes of predators, and fences crowned in barbed wire surround the perimeter. The signs screaming 'keep out' are as superfluous as they are clear.

Our SUV jostles over the deeply rutted road leading to a gate, spewing plumes of chalky dust. Loose gravel pings against the undercarriage and sets my teeth on edge.

Evil festers within those imposing walls, but it feels as if there's *more*. What that *more* might be is beyond me. It's one of those gut instincts no one understands. But I trust my gut and prepare for the worst.

Stitch is jammed tight between me and Jeb in the front seat. Her slight frame dwarfed by our much larger ones. She meets my gaze, eyes grimly determined, and nods. She understands the risks of this infiltration, as we all do. It's her first mission as an operator rather than tech support, and I've asked Jeb to keep an eye out and protect her if need be.

Failure is not an option.

I meet Jeb's steely gaze beside me, exchanging a terse nod, then scan the faces of my team wedged into the back seats—Hank, Gabe, Walt, and Blake. With their jaw muscles clenched tight, eyes hooded and alert, they look like coiled springs ready to unleash calculated violence.

Good.

We need that edge.

The SUV lurches over the last rut, and the gate looms before us. Two armed guards emerge, their boredom evident as they check our forged credentials. We have no illusions about what goes on inside those fences, but the bland mannerisms of the guard checking our IDs grates, betraying no hint of the vile enterprise lurking within.

His gaze pauses on Stitch's credentials, thick brow furrowing. "We don't allow—her kind here." His meaning is clear as his gaze sweeps lewdly over her.

My jaw clenches, but I keep my tone bored, almost annoyed. "Stitch is one of my most valuable assets. I was assured having a female on my team wouldn't be an issue. If that's a problem, we'll take our business elsewhere."

The guard's eyes flick uncertainly between Stitch's stony face and mine. She stares straight ahead, refusing to be cowed. After an interminable pause, he recovers and hands back the IDs with a smirk. "Of course, sir. My apologies. Right this way."

As the gate screeches open, I meet Jeb's satisfied gaze. First obstacle down. Ten thousand more to go.

Haven's fortress sprawls before us, a hulking windowless structure hewn from cold gray stone. Guards with automatic rifles patrol along high fences topped with coils of razor wire. More are stationed at regular intervals on the roof, scouring the compound below.

Our SUV crawls across the central courtyard, the only sound the crunch of gravel under our vehicle tires. The blank facade reveals nothing of the secrets within.

We stop outside a fortified entrance flanked by more armed guards. Their assessing gazes sweep over Stitch as we exit the vehicle. Stitch will attract unwanted attention, but we can't do this without her. Mitzy was clear about that. Jeb's computer skills may be phenomenal in the field, but he can't hold a candle to what Stitch can do.

We proceed with caution.

I angle my body into a subtle, threatening posture, staring them down. My hardened gaze also sends a message. She's with us, and no one is to touch her.

After an uneasy beat, their eyes skitter away.

We're greeted by a stone-faced man who introduces himself only as Kaufman. "Ethan Blackwood, welcome to Haven."

"Thank you." I quickly introduce my team.

His calculating gaze sweeps over me while my team lines up behind me. When his gaze pauses on Stitch, his mouth tightens ever so slightly. Jeb closes the distance, standing closer to Stitch.

Protecting her.

I level a steady look at Kaufman. "We can handle any job discreetly, regardless of team composition, but it is *my* team." My meaning is clear.

"Good." He stands straight as a rod, practically clicking his heels as he comes to attention. "Discretion is paramount for the job ahead." He motions us down a stark hallway. "Come. We have much to discuss."

I step closer, invading his space. When I speak, my voice is low, laced with subtle menace.

"Let's be clear. My teammates will not be touched, sampled, or breathed on." I hold his hooded gaze. "The women inside might be your playthings, but mine is off-limits. Are we clear?"

Kaufman's eyes widen briefly in surprise before his expression shutters. "You seem remarkably well-informed about certain aspects of our operations." His hand drifts toward his waistband. The guards around us tense, hands poised to draw their weapons.

I stare Kaufman down, utterly unruffled by the silent threat. "As I said, discretion is paramount in my work. I make it my business to know everything about a client before engaging." My voice hardens with steel. "Now, do we have an understanding regarding my team?"

A charged beat passes where violence hangs in the air. Then Kaufman relaxes subtly, hand moving away from his gun. "Of course. You have my word; your people will remain untouched." He motions briskly down the hall. "Come. We have much to discuss." But as we turn to follow, his calculating gaze lingers on Stitch for a beat too long.

He's suspicious but doesn't know why he should be.

The game is on now, and he has no idea of the ruin that awaits inside his precious walls.

He speaks to me over his shoulder nonchalantly, as if he owns me.

"You come highly recommended for matters requiring—discretion." His English is precise, with only a hint of an Eastern European accent.

I meet his gaze steadily. "You'll find we can be very discrete, no matter the nature of the job."

Kaufman's mouth tightens, eyes narrowing slightly at the implication. But he doesn't comment on it.

"Our systems were impenetrable until a few days ago." Kaufman's voice drips disdain. "This breach must be contained quickly and quietly."

He leads us to Haven's control room, where Haven's IT guys try in vain to trace the hacker's digital footprints. The rapid clicks of typing and the low murmur of strained voices create a chaotic backdrop.

"Looks like you've got a problem." I make a show of studying the data, hands clasped behind my back. Kaufman's presence beside me is a constant threat, his interest as welcome as a spider evaluating its next kill.

When Jeb asks a pointed question, Kaufman's initial flash of suspicion quickly morphs into a ticking in his jaw and an appreciative nod. This man is suspicious by nature and knows enough to recognize when someone's trying to fool him. We have to be careful not to overplay our hand.

I turn to Kaufman, injecting authority into my tone. He needs to know I run my team. "To locate the origin of this breach, we need full access to your systems, surveillance feeds going back six months, and the physical servers, including all monitoring devices installed on the premises."

Stitch quietly elbows her way to a keyboard, hip-checking one of Kaufman's men out of his chair. Her fingers hit the keys and begin to dance.

"You won't be able to access our systems without the passcode."

Kaufman stiffens beside me. He's not wrong about that. I have to get him to open up his kingdom, as the saying goes, and give us a full run of the place.

But suddenly, the monitor in front of Stitch comes to life, data streaming across its display. "No need. I'm already in." The look she gives me is cocky as shit. "Your system was easy to hack. Someone installed a back door, but they weren't very creative. Juvenile at best. Looks like you've got someone working from the inside to sell Haven's secrets. I've got my work cut out for me to fix this shit." She cracks her knuckles and turns her back to Kaufman.

"What does that mean?" Instead of asking Stitch, his question is aimed at me.

But I'm not the one who answers. Stitch keeps her back to Kaufman and gives a flippant answer. "I've got to install basic security protocols. Your system is woefully outdated and inept. It's going to require a whole system upgrade."

Kaufman's eyes narrow. "I don't know if I like a…"

"A what?" Stitch spins around and bats her eyelashes. "A computer expert? Is it my age that concerns you, or the fact I'm female? Because your system is shit, ripe for anyone with the right skills to waltz right in under your nose."

Kaufman's IT guys scramble to trace the hack.

"Your people are running into dead ends because they're working with limited data," I say. "To connect the dots, my team needs unrestricted access. The full picture, as it were."

Kaufman's jaw ticks, eyes calculating. "And what guarantees do I have you won't abuse this access for your own purposes?"

I meet his gaze levelly. "Our reputation is built on discretion. Short story, you have no assurances. Longer answer: You decide whether finding the source is worth the risk of giving my people the access they need to do the job you're hiring us to do." I pause for effect.

A charged silence follows. Kaufman's need to control wars with his distrust of outsiders. Finally, he gives a curt nod. "Very well. But know that we will be monitoring closely. Any suspicious actions will be dealt with accordingly."

I dip my head in acquiescence. We've cleared the first hurdle, but the mission is just beginning.

"We need space to work," I tell the armed men gruffly. "We'll call if we require assistance."

With wary glances, the men retreat and close the door, leaving us alone. My team sets up a disruption field. Another one of Mitzy's technological wonders, it provides us the freedom to speak openly.

After we're all set, I rock back on my heels and contemplate my next move. "I'm going to make a quick circuit of the halls. See what I can find."

"Want company?" Walt turns to look at me.

"No. I just want to get a quick lay of the land and see what we're up against. Also, I want to see how closely Kaufman's men are watching us. Best you stay here."

We're not ready to map out the interior of Haven, but restlessness simmers within me. I've got nervous energy to shed, and a quick exploration of Haven is perfect for getting rid of my nerves.

Alone at last, I slip into the hallway. The sound of my shoes on the polished floor feels thunderous in the empty passageways. There's literally no one wandering about.

I pass closed doors with muted voices and ringing phones behind them. There are signs of life, but I'm otherwise alone.

I wander down a dimly lit hall, senses on high alert. The overhead lights flicker and hum. What secrets hide behind these ominous steel doors? I creep forward, listening intently for any clues.

Hushed voices murmur behind one door. I pause, pulse racing. A woman's low laugh, then a man's anxious tone. My blood turns to ice—I know that voice.

Hand trembling, I crack open the door. There, across the shadowy room, stands the woman who has haunted my dreams for months.

Rebel.

NINETEEN

Ethan

BLOOD ROARS AS IT RUSHES PAST MY EARS; THE SOUND OF IT NEARLY deafens me as I watch the unfathomable. The unthinkable.

Rebel works the room. She's draped in a slinky red silk dress that hugs every curve. Blood-red lips smile coldly, matching red lacquered nails. My gut twists. This polished predator is far from the woman I rescued from a cage.

The scent of cigar smoke and alcohol rolls out into the hall, a thick, disgusting miasma clotting the air.

She stalks between the captives in stiletto heels, clicking a staccato rhythm on the grimy concrete floor. The women gathered in a straight line before her shrink under her assessing gaze, arms crossed over their bruised and broken bodies. Rebel tilts their chins with one manicured finger, clucking her tongue at swollen lips and blackened eyes.

"Poor, darling, those animals roughed you up a bit, didn't they?" Her voice drips false sympathy as the girl flinches. Rebel *tsks* and moves on, heels clicking.

She stops at a slight blonde with haunted eyes. Running a nail down the girl's cheek, she muses aloud. "Pretty face, nice shape. You'll fetch a good price." The blonde squeezes her eyes shut, and tears streak her grimy cheeks. Rebel grabs her jaw, nails biting in. "But we'll have to fix this skin. No man wants to fuck a girl with blemishes."

The blonde chokes back a sob.

Grinning, Rebel releases her and steps back. "You're the elite now, ladies. The best of our stock. You should be grateful you'll be auctioned to gentlemen rather than whored out on the streets."

Their despair hangs thick in the rancid air. Bile burns my throat. I know depravity, but never like this. And the woman I once cared for is somehow at the heart of it?

What happened to her?

What happened to the Rebel who clung to me as I carried her to safety? This polished monster is a stranger to me.

I still remember how she looked at me with relief swirling in her emerald eyes. I'll never forget the brush of her fingertips as I draped a blanket over her shaking shoulders, whispering over and over, "You're safe now."

As the shock of her abduction and imprisonment faded at The Facility, I swore I'd protect her. Cradling her outside under the stars, her tears of gratitude dampened my shirt; I promised she'd never suffer again.

I was her salvation. Or so I thought.

But the woman I hold in my memories bears no resemblance to the monster crossing the room in scarlet stilettos. This ruthless woman holds no warmth as she condemns innocents to unspeakable fates. The sweetness of her body wrapped around mine now tastes like bitter, acrid bile.

I should roar out in rage, make her sorry she ever crossed my path. I should feel disgusted at how she strokes their hair and whispers false comfort to the condemned. But as she passes by my shadowed alcove, a hint of lavender trailing in her wake, my gut churns with something far more shameful.

Hunger.

She is poison incarnate, but that doesn't stop my damned foolish heart from wanting her still. Lust wars with rage until I choke on the bile rising in my throat.

Rebel, what have you become?

And why can't I stop wanting her?

Once, she was locked in a rust-streaked cage. Now, she cups each girl's face with false warmth? Whispering empty reassurances as she coolly selects which poor soul to condemn. It makes no sense.

I've stared true evil in the eyes, but this cruelty unnerves me.

I watch her trail one long, red nail down another girl's cheek and my fist clenches. In Nicaragua, I stroked those same tears from her face and promised to protect her. Promised she'd never suffer again in this rotten underworld that deals in the destruction of innocence.

Yet here she is, multiplying the pain.

Bile scorches my throat as she laughs breezily and condemns another. I want to believe this is an act. That the woman who clung to me still lives inside somewhere, but the cool efficiency in those emerald eyes, as she sentences them to hell, chills me to the core.

What twisted lies did they poison her mind with to turn her into the thing she fears most? I search her painted face for any shred of the woman I saved, looking for a crack in this polished new facade.

But I find nothing.

"Ready when you are, boss." Hank's gravelly voice in my ear comm yanks me back from the edge of despair. My teammate knows nothing of the ghost from my past taunting me from across the room. To him, this is just another mission, another horror show we're here to shut down. For me, it's turned personal.

"Stand by," I grate out, clenching my jaw so hard my teeth ache.

"You see something?" Hank presses. *"Want Charlie team to engage?"*

I should give the order and put an end to this depraved scene. Take Rebel down. She's the enemy. A traitor. It's what Hank would do if he were here, seeing what I'm seeing.

"Boss?" Hank's voice buzzes impatiently as I hesitate.

What do I do when the woman who haunts my dreams reappears as a nightmare in the flesh? When the lips that once begged for rescue now drip contempt and death sentences?

I harden my heart. "Stand down. I need more intel."

"Copy that. We await your signal."

I mute Hank's mic, cutting off his squawk of surprise. This confrontation with my personal ghost will happen on my terms.

I march into the room, pulse thundering in my ears, and approach Rebel.

She doesn't notice me or glance up when my fingers close around her elbow. Her muscles flex instinctively, then go still. It's almost as if she expects such rough treatment.

When she does look up, her eyes flare with surprise. Her mouth gapes when I steer her away from the other women. I usher her into the empty hall and close the door to the room behind us.

"What the hell?" She snarls and snaps at me, wrenching her arm from my grasp. "Who do you think you—"

"Cut the act. Surprised to see me?" I can't keep the bitterness from my voice.

She recovers quickly, eyes flashing dangerously. "I don't know who you think I am, but—"

I slam my hand against the wall beside her head, causing her to flinch. "I've been balls deep inside your worthless cunt. You *know* me."

Her eyelids widen in shock, but a tiny flicker of relief is there as well. But it's gone so fast that I'm not sure it was ever there to begin with.

Her entire face turns into a hardened, stone-cold mask.

Up close, her floral perfume competes with the stench of alcohol and cigars infusing the air of the room. The rapid flutter of her pulse in her neck belies the icy glare she levels at me.

And fuck me.

Despite everything, my body responds.

To her.

"Tell me this is a lie," I demand through gritted teeth. "That you aren't one of *them*." I can't keep the disgust and derision out of my tone.

"I don't know who the hell you are, but get the hell out of my face." Her jaw clenches and she vocalizes without moving her lips. "There are cameras everywhere."

It's a message, but not one I'm ready to process. When it's clear

I won't let her go, she tries to shoulder past me, but I drive her back against the cold concrete wall. Leaning in, my face is inches from hers.

"What the fuck are you doing here?"

"That's none of your business." Her voice suddenly lowers to a whisper I barely hear, and that catch in her throat is one of fear. Not anger. "Are you on a mission? Is your team…" What she was about to say is lost when her eyes flick down the hall.

I turn to look, but we're alone. There's no one around.

"What the fuck is going on?"

"There are cameras everywhere. You can't be here." Rebel places her hands on my biceps. "You'll ruin everything." Her eyes flash dangerously. "You have to leave."

"You said that already, but why would I leave?"

"It's not safe for you to be here."

"Because you're going to run to Kaufman?"

"No." She shakes her head frantically. "I'd never do that, but you can't be here."

The cloying scent of alcohol and stale cigarettes seeps from her pores, mingling with the floral perfume I once gifted her. I shove her roughly against the concrete wall, forearm pressed against her delicate throat.

This woman is a threat to my team. With one word, she could blow our cover. That's not going to happen. I'll kill her if I have to.

She gasps, more in shock than pain. The pulse in her neck flutters like a trapped bird desperately trying to fly away. Up close, telltale dark circles ring her bloodshot eyes. She's just as on edge as I am, this nightmare taking its toll on us both.

This feels all kinds of wrong.

"Was this your plan all along?" I snarl through gritted teeth. "Seduce me, gather Guardian secrets, then disappear? Have you been working for Haven all along?"

"You know nothing about me or my reasons for being here, but you must leave." She chokes out the words, clawing at my arm. There's real panic in her voice.

True fear in her eyes.

I release pressure on her throat and allow her to take a strangled breath.

She's been in worse spots than this. I should know, considering I freed her from the inside of a cell.

"Then explain it to me," I demand, putting more pressure on her windpipe. She grimaces but stays defiantly silent. There's a weariness in her eyes; a flicker of doubt flares within me.

With effort, I ease the pressure on her throat. She massages it gingerly but doesn't break my gaze.

"Talk to me," I rasp. "Make me understand. What are you doing here?" I sweep my arm out, gesturing toward the door. I expect fiery denial, reflexive anger—anything but the hollow laugh that falls from her ruby lips.

"You have to leave."

"You're a broken record, Rebel, but I'm not leaving until you answer my questions."

"You don't get it, do you?" She shakes her head, an undercurrent of bitterness in her voice. "This is so much bigger than you can imagine."

"Bigger?" The color red creeps into the edges of my vision. Anger burns in my veins. I slam her against the wall again. Only, this time, my fingers tighten around her delicate throat. "Help me understand." I clench my jaw and grit my teeth. "Make me see how the innocent woman I pulled out of a filthy cell became this monster."

My gut twists even as I spit the words at her. Because despite the truth standing in front of me, a part of me still clings to the memory of that night we spent on the beach.

Her emerald eyes flash, but she says nothing. The pulse in her throat taps rapidly under my fingertips.

"Talk to me, damn it." I slam my other fist against the wall by her head.

She flinches but lifts her chin. "You think you know me, but the woman you're looking for died long ago. I don't owe you an explanation except to say this: you ruined things for me once. That's not happening again. You need to leave. Leave before I force the issue."

Her words land like physical blows, but under the bitterness lies a current of deep sorrow that gives me hope. Something shifts in her gaze. For a fleeting moment, the hard mask slips, and a glimmer of the Rebel I know—the one who trusted me, needed me—still remains.

Then, she viciously slams the tip of her stiletto on my foot. I recoil with a pained grunt, grip loosening. In a heartbeat, she spins me and slams me roughly to the wall, arm barred tight across my shoulders.

Her warm breath feathers across my ear as she pins me in place. "You judge without knowing who I am or why I'm here. Is your team with you?"

I don't answer, but there's no need. She reads my answer easily enough.

"Shit, you have to get them out of here. It's not safe." Her words sink like stones in my gut.

"What the hell have you gotten into? I can help." Despite everything, my innate need to protect and defend runs too deep. "Talk to me." I shift against her hold, but she's like steel. "Tell me what's going on. Why are you here?"

"You want the truth?" Her voice trembles with barely repressed emotion. "I'm in too deep to be saved. Do yourself a favor and walk away."

There's an unspoken plea behind the bitterness, and then footsteps sound down the hall.

Anger roars through me. I pivot swiftly, reversing our positions, pinning her body against the rough concrete wall. My hand fists tightly in her hair, eliciting a wince.

My lips crush desperately against hers before she can respond, seeking answers, seeking the woman I thought I knew.

I expect her to slap me. To shove me away in disgust. Instead, her mouth melts into mine for one searing moment, returning the kiss with an intensity that ignites every nerve in my body. In that electrified instant, nothing exists but the two of us tangled together in the dark, breaths quickening, heartbeats syncing as one.

But just as quickly, she turns her face away, breaking the spell.

We stand frozen for a suspended moment, shaken to our cores. Her curves press tightly against me, warm and vital, as my pulse hammers deafeningly loud in my ears.

The Rebel I care about still lives inside this callous exterior she portrays.

"Let me go," she says.

I don't budge. "You can't fake that kind of heat, sweetheart. Tell me I'm wrong."

Voices sound from down the hall. She shoves me, eyes panicked, moments before two armed guards round the corner. Their hands drift toward their holstered guns.

"Get this trash away from me," Rebel snaps, adjusting her dress with feigned annoyance, but her hands tremble.

The guards grab my arms, and I let them steer me down the hall, but when I glance back, Rebel stands alone, looking small and shaken. Whatever her reasons, this is taking a toll on her.

I'll uncover the truth. The real Rebel is still in there somewhere, and I'll do whatever it takes to find her again before this nightmare kills us both.

TWENTY

Ethan
___

I SLIDE INTO THE CHAIR IN THE SECURED COMMS ROOM, THE DOOR hissing closed behind me to seal out any chance of eavesdropping. The guys on my team shuffle around, dropping gear and watching the screens intently.

"What's going on?" Gabe gives me a look.

"I just ran into Rebel." My teeth grind together.

"Rebel?" Hank glances at Gabe, eyes widening. "I'm sorry, we're talking Rebel? From Nicaragua? Your Rebel?"

"Yes." I lean back and blow out a breath.

"Red hair, green eyes? That Rebel?" Jeb glances at Hank and mouths *No-fucking-way*.

My heart hammers as I key in the encryption code to connect with CJ back at headquarters. The guys gather close, listening in. We take no chances communicating from within these walls.

CJ's craggy face flickers onto the screen. "Status update?"

I take a bracing breath. No way to ease into this. "Rebel is here."

"Come again?"

"Rebel. She's here."

"We're not prepped for a hostage rescue."

"She's not a captive."

"What?" CJ's brow furrows. "Impossible. Why would she..." He blows out a slow breath, eyes sharpening. "Explain everything."

I recount the details, ignoring my team's suggestive grins and elbow jabs. I mention Rebel orchestrating operations.

When I finish, Hank whistles low. "Daaayumn, didn't see that coming."

"She's the single greatest risk to your safety. One word from her and this whole op gets shot to hell." His expression hardens. "But you said she didn't expose you to the guards. I want to know why."

I brace myself. "We should abort."

CJ is silent for a moment, considering. "Something doesn't add up."

"How's that?"

"Like I said… The guards. She didn't expose you, and I want to know why."

"The risk to my team…"

"Is calculated. I'm going with my gut here. Her rescue in Nicaragua doesn't match up to her being on the other side now. What if she's hiding something? We planned too long for this shot at Haven. Figure out what she's doing and keep her from exposing your team."

"Easier said than done."

"The only easy day was—"

"Yesterday. Yeah, I get it." I run a hand through my hair.

'The only easy day was yesterday' is a saying that comes from our days as US Navy SEALs. It means every day is a new day, and it's going to suck harder than the day before.

"She protected you from the guards, kept quiet that she knew you." CJ's tone turns thoughtful. "It could mean she has her own reasons for being there."

"Mutually Assured Destruction?" My palms sweat at the thought of confronting her again. "Although, I wouldn't say she protected me. She handed me over fast enough."

"But that's it. If she turned you in, we wouldn't be having this conversation. You'd already be—"

"Dead. Yeah, don't tell me." I nod slowly, mind spinning at the implications.

"Tread carefully, but find her angle. Get her to keep your covers intact, at least for now." His voice hardens. "Finish this mission. Get out."

I swallow hard. "Understood."

"Watch yourself with Rebel. Don't get played this time." His blunt words twist like a knife to the gut.

"I learned that lesson last time." I spit out the bitter words. The shame of how she duped me still gnaws at me.

"We all make mistakes when emotions are involved, but you're wiser now. Hardened. You've earned your place leading this team."

I release a slow breath, letting his trust temper my churning emotions. I won't fail him, or my men, again.

"Dig quietly into Rebel's motives. Keep it professional," CJ advises, more gently than before.

"Copy that. I'll report back when I know more."

"Take no prisoners. CJ out."

Rebel's presence changes everything, but CJ is right. Something doesn't add up.

"Boss?" Walt speaks for the rest of the team. "What's the play?"

"We stay the course for now. Too much depends on the intel we can rip from Haven's grasp." My fists clench involuntarily. After months of questions, she's within reach. Every instinct screams to confront her and demand answers. Yet, one misstep could ruin everything.

Discovering why Rebel is here, while important, is not my mission. Eyes on the prize, I have to stick to the mission. Yet even as I make that promise, traitorous memories of emerald eyes, fiery hair, and searing kisses threaten my composure.

CJ's final words linger. This mission calls for ruthlessness and clarity; I thought I possessed that focus until Rebel returned to blur the lines.

The door to the comms room crashes open. Slowly, I turn to face the phantom from my past.

Rebel.

Her emerald eyes blaze with cold fury, jaw clenched so tight the delicate cord in her neck pulses. Her floral perfume curls insidiously around me, pulling up memories better left buried.

She stalks closer, lithe as a panther, until we're nearly chest to chest.

My team tenses, ready to back me if needed.

"What the hell are you doing here?" Her voice is razor-sharp and scrapes against my nerves. Her gaze flicks to my teammates, pauses on Stitch, then returns to me with emerald fire burning in the depths of her eyes.

I cross my arms, pulse racing. "I could ask you the same thing."

We trade bitter words. With each verbal jab, the guys shift restlessly, eager to jump in. I catch Hank's eye and shake my head, holding them back. This is between me and her.

Her eyes flash. "You're going to ruin everything."

When she surges against me, fury radiating off her slight frame, Blake steps forward instinctively. I halt him with a raised palm.

My gut twists even as bitterness wells up. "What exactly am I going to ruin?" I step closer, looming over her. "Helping monsters profit off innocence? Luring girls into slavery? Didn't you get enough of that in Nicaragua?"

"That's a low blow."

"I call it how I see it. What did you do? Fuck Kaufman's brains out? Did he remove the chains as long as you worked for him?"

"You sanctimonious bastard!" She surges up against me, eyes flashing emerald knives. "You know nothing about what I've sacrificed."

"You're right. I don't know, but I do know this…"

All the old hunger and hurt I've tried to bury comes roaring back up my throat. Without thinking, I crush my mouth to hers, kissing her fiercely.

For one electrifying instant, she returns it with a passion that steals my breath. Then her teeth sink into my bottom lip, hard. I rear back with a curse, tasting blood, as she slaps me viciously across the face.

The guys let out low murmurs of protest but hold their positions.

We stand frozen, panting, poised on the brink of violence or something far more dangerous.

"Get out now, and we can both pretend this never happened." Her voice wavers almost imperceptibly. She backs away slowly toward the door, eyes pleading with what her mouth can't say.

I should stop her. Should rage or threaten to get the answers I crave. Instead, I wipe the blood from my mouth and nod tiredly.

"You could always tell the truth." I grab her wrist before she can disappear. "Why are you here? I'm owed that much." My voice drops to a dangerous whisper. "Unless you want me revealing who you are to your new friends."

"You don't have the balls to do that." She wrenches her wrist out of my grip, but the unsteadiness in her voice reveals true fear.

I step close, crowding her. My tone turns deadly calm. "If you expose my team, I'll tell Kaufman *how* we know each other. Consider it Mutually Assured Destruction."

For a second, her steely facade cracks. Fear and desperation flash in her eyes. "Ethan, please..." she whispers urgently. "You have to trust me. It's not what it looks like." She swallows hard. Her mask slips for a fleeting moment, revealing a torrent of emotions, but it's back in place.

"Trust you the way you trust me?" I'm not giving her an inch.

"At least we agree on one thing." Her tone holds an undercurrent of regret.

"What's that?"

"You expose me, and I won't hesitate to tell Kaufman about the Guardians. I'm sure he'll be pleased as piss that a bunch of hostage rescuers are digging around inside Haven." Without another word, she turns and is gone, leaving even more questions swirling in her wake.

At least I learned one thing from that horrible exchange. I let out a calm breath as Rebel disappears down the hall.

The team relaxes fractionally as the confrontation ends.

"You alright, boss?" Jeb asks, eyeing the blood on my mouth.

"I'm good." I wipe it away.

This isn't over yet. Not by a long shot.

TWENTY-ONE

Rebel

————————

I SHOULDN'T HAVE DONE IT. I SHOULDN'T HAVE TRACKED ETHAN down. On the way to the control room, hands balled into fists, heart hammering wildly, I kept telling myself: *'Turn around. Turn around and run away.'*

Yet, I kept moving.

I wish I were noble enough to say I want to protect him, but the honest truth is I need him to leave.

The moment I barged into the control room, however, the words died in my throat. All I saw was *him*. The man I ran away from. When I realized Guardian HRS was *not* the kind of organization that could help me, I cut ties and ran.

Went back to square one.

How can I explain my presence at Haven? How do I explain what was happening in that room? How do I explain to a man like Ethan, a pure, noble soul, that I'm a monster?

Yes, those young women will be auctioned off. I can't save them from that fate, but I can make their misery a little less horrifying. Not to mention, getting in on Kaufman's good graces might lead me to answers myself.

My feet move quickly, placing as much distance between me and

Ethan as possible. A finger confirms the thrumming pulse in my neck. A hand over my belly calms the fluttering nerves there.

But none of it helps.

Ethan's searing kiss shocked me.

I press trembling fingers to my lips, cursing this desire awakened by his presence.

It was a bad idea to confront him. I walk faster, heels clicking loudly on the concrete floor. After all this time, I thought I was immune to his pull, but the heat of his mouth on mine rekindled a fire I believed I extinguished.

I take a deep breath, willing my racing heart to slow down.

But it's no use.

Ethan's kiss lingers on my lips, echoing a promise... Or maybe it's a threat?

Desperately, I push away thoughts of him and refocus on why I'm here.

With my pulse racing, I pause and lean my arm and forehead against the cold concrete wall. Its chill leaches the heat from my body, letting doubt and self-loathing boil to the surface.

I've sacrificed too much to fail.

But what do I do?

If I reveal Ethan's identity, it will result in not only my death but his and those of his teammates. Kaufman is a ruthless man with no pity, no remorse, and no morals.

If Ethan discovers why I'm here, he'll try to stop me. Or worse, he'll try to help me. He's too honorable and protective to let me do this alone.

Dammit, he's going to ruin everything—again.

With an agonized groan, I push off from the wall and force myself down the hall.

"Rebel," Kaufman calls out to me. His oily voice lifts the hairs on the back of my neck. The man's a snake charmer, smooth as silk but rotten to the core. "I heard there was an— altercation?"

He approaches as if he cares what happens to me. Immediately, I school my features and smile pleasantly. My stomach clenches as

Kaufman's gaze rakes down my body. He wants me but has yet to force the issue. It's coming, but he enjoys the chase. Loves the kill.

For now, I'm safe, but I'm no different than those women back in that room. Like them, I've chosen one hell over another.

"It's nothing to worry about." Tension spikes in the air between us, and for a moment, I fear he can see right through me. When his expression hardens, my muscles tense.

His eyes narrow as he studies me. I hate when he does that. It's as if he's trying to climb inside my head and figure out whether or not I'm lying to him. He steps back, and it feels like he sucks all of my breath out of my lungs.

"If he laid hands on you, that won't be tolerated."

It takes everything within me to maintain my smile and gaze up at him with adoration and worse—gratitude.

I hate Kaufman. Despise him with the entirety of my being.

But I smile graciously and dip my head in deference to him.

"No need." I use my most convincing voice. "I put him in his place. Who is he anyway? Surely not a buyer. The auction's not for a few days."

"A few weeks."

"What?"

"I pushed back the date."

"May I ask why?"

"Issues with our security systems. His team is here to fix it."

Ah, that explains why Ethan's here. Not really, but he's obviously undercover, which makes things all the more complicated.

"I see." I pull in the corner of my lip and gently nibble on it, knowing Kaufman will eat it up. But I can't avoid his gaze for too long. There's a fine line between deference and avoidance. Slowly, I lift my gaze to meet his eyes.

Kaufman's gaze bores into me, probing for cracks. He's not buying it. There's too much suspicion on his face. I have to think fast and come up with something that will satisfy him without giving away Ethan's secret.

An idea forms in my mind. It's a bit of a long shot, but it might work. "He probably thought I was one of the merchandise and was trying to see what he could get away with." I put on a coy smile.

My plan works better than expected; rather than hostility, boredom appears on Kaufman's face. The man feeds off my adoration for him. He's a twisted, ugly soul, but nothing I can't handle.

"I could dismiss them and bring in another team."

"That's not necessary. I made things very clear, and your men backed me up. That man won't touch me again. Besides, I'm going to be busy training your Angels."

Kaufman rubs his chin, eyes calculating. "Well, if he gives you any trouble..."

"I'll let you know. Thank you." I dip my head demurely, playing to Kaufman's inflated ego.

"Speaking of, how are my new Angels coming along?" Kaufman's face softens almost imperceptibly.

My heart sinks a little at his words, and I swallow the bile rising in my throat. "Your new Angels are coming along nicely. Honestly, they're not ready. I'm thankful to have a few more weeks. There's still resistance in some. Not that a security issue is a good thing, but I'll have them auction-ready." My skin crawls at the words coming out of my mouth. "I apologize for underestimating the time it would take to pacify them."

"I thought your timeline overly ambitious."

"I'm sorry. I thought they would be more grateful. I don't think they understand how things could've gone for them. The surgeries are a bit of a sticking point."

"How's that?"

"Honestly, I think when I mentioned it, they finally understood what they agreed to when they volunteered to be an Angel."

"Hope is a hard demon to crush. You're doing admirably with my Angels."

"Thank you." Once again, I duck my head like a dog begging for its master's praise. I hate myself and loathe what I've become.

I try not to think too much about it because that's me trying to rationalize the evil I'm putting into this world. They're captives, abducted and held against their will. I give them the illusion of choice, and a little bit more of me dies each day. My goal is to brainwash these women until they forget how it feels to be free. Until they accept their fate with gratitude.

My stomach churns as acid burns the back of my throat.

I'm a monster. I'm not Kaufman, but what I'm doing is reprehensible.

Kaufman stares into space as if lost in thought before looking me dead in the eyes. "Your progress with those women is remarkable." His voice is laced with admiration, making me squirm uncomfortably. "You'll accomplish great things in the weeks to come, which will make the auction all the more profitable."

He reaches out and places one hand on my shoulder in what can only be described as an intimate gesture, but his fingers press hard enough to leave marks. It's his way of reminding me why I'm here and why I'm the only woman allowed to roam freely within these walls.

I exist to serve Kaufman's desires no matter how corrupt they may be.

"Thank you." I return exactly what he expects. My gaze dips to the floor, just like a submissive.

"Buyers are eagerly adding their names to the list. They await your Angels with great excitement." My heart sinks as Kaufman preens about his new product line.

"I'm happy to hear the response is good." My response is rote and automatic, not daring to show any hint of pleasure at my accomplishment. "I will ensure your Angels do not disappoint." Revulsion burbles inside me at what I'm forced to do.

Kaufman gives me some much-needed personal space. "You believe they will adhere to the conditions placed upon them?" His voice is soft but stern; there's no denying the underlying threat in his words.

I swallow hard before answering him. "They are grateful for this —this opportunity. They're hesitant but willing to please." My thoughts flash to the terrified young women I'm grooming to become his bevy of willing slaves.

I'm a monster.

"They know what will happen if I'm not pleased?" His gaze narrows.

"Yes." My throat tightens as a chill creeps down my spine. "They know the punishment for disobedience."

Revulsion surges within me, but I choke it down, burying my outrage deep. It's becoming harder and harder to stomach the moral atrocity I commit on a daily basis.

Kaufman takes my chin in his hand, forcing me to meet his gaze. His icy cold stare sends a shiver down my spine. "You've been gifted a few extra weeks. See that their training continues. I expect nothing but success. Failure is not an option." He releases me abruptly, his demand for perfection ringing loud and clear in my ears.

"Understood." My heart sinks, but I reply without hesitation. I dip my head demurely, seething inwardly at this monster.

"Rebel…"

"Yes?"

He watches me for a few moments before speaking again. "I find your devotion—refreshing." His lips twitch into a wolfish smile. My pulse pounds in my ears as I swallow against the lump in my throat. Kaufman claps suddenly. The sound cracks through the empty hallway. "Enough chatter. I'm hosting dinner for our guests. Your presence is required."

"Of course." Bile scorches my throat.

I have to attend dinner with Kaufman while Ethan watches.

Just kill me now.

"Dress nicely for me. I wish to make a point." Kaufman's smile turns predatory, eyes raking down my body. His fingertips graze my cheek, and revulsion slithers within me.

Flaunting me before Ethan, like a trophy, is meant as a vulgar display of power. Kaufman may not know the history I share with Ethan, but he's no fool. He senses something, and that's too much.

Tonight, I must smother my emotions and play the role I created willingly.

"I look forward to it." My pulse thunders, and my breath quickens. I will play my part.

Smile coyly. Laugh lightly. I'll pretend I belong to Kaufman.

I'll do it all in front of Ethan while watching the betrayal and pain in his eyes swell. I'd say it'll break his heart, but I did that when I walked away.

If he doesn't hate me for that, he will after this dinner.

Finally, Kaufman appears satisfied with this display of power over me. He turns without another word and strides out of sight, leaving me standing in that cold hallway, feeling violated and thankful it wasn't worse than it could have been.

Perspiration beads across my brow. The thought of being paraded before Ethan is unbearable, but I have no choice. Kaufman holds all the cards, and I'm barely playing his twisted game. I run to my quarters, slam the door behind me, and lean against it, hyper-ventilating.

That's when I feel it.

A presence in my room.

TWENTY-TWO

Rebel

———

SLOWLY, I MAKE MY WAY ACROSS THE ROOM, SCANNING EVERY corner for any sign of danger. Then, I catch a whiff of something familiar that sends a shiver down my spine.

I turn around, and there he is, standing in the shadows like a ghost.

"Ethan?" My pulse spikes. My breath hitches. "You can't be here."

His eyes blaze with fierce intensity, and the heat of his gaze scorches my skin. I'm frozen in place, barely able to move or speak. Then he steps forward, hand outstretched. Like a moth drawn to a flame, my feet move of their own volition. My hand lifts. Our fingers touch.

The connection is electric, sending pulses of desire coursing through my body. I want him more than anything in the world, but I can't have him. Not now, not ever.

Certainly not with Kaufman watching my every move, waiting for me to slip up. "You have to leave." I pull away.

"I'm not leaving until we talk."

Storms brew in his blazing blue eyes, radiating fury. His cedar scent assaults me, unlocking memories I tried hard to bury. We spent weeks tempting, teasing, flirting, and connecting.

Something like that *should* be easy to walk away from. One night of passion shouldn't leave this kind of ache behind. I thought I was over him. Convinced myself a thousand times that I made the right decision to leave. Buried his memory and told myself I didn't care.

"You don't understand. You can't be here." I grab his arm and try to push him toward the door.

"I'm not leaving until we talk." His voice grates down my spine.

"Are you insane? Kaufman's guards could have seen you come in here." I peek out to scan the empty hallway.

Ethan grabs my wrist, spinning me back around. He places his palm on the door and slams it shut. "I don't give a damn about Kaufman. You owe me an explanation."

His fingers dig into my wrist, firm and unyielding. He's so close his earthy scent threatens to unravel me. I harden my voice, though it trembles. "You don't understand. Kaufman will kill you if he catches you in my room."

"Why? Are you fucking him?"

"Does it matter?" I rip out of his grip and point to the door. "You have to leave. Being here puts everything at risk."

"I'm not going anywhere until you tell me what you're doing here. Out of all the places on Earth, why are you at Haven? Why are you working for him? Tell the truth, Rebel, because I'll know if it's a lie."

His eyes pin me as effectively as his hands, twin blue flames searing away my defenses. I want to cling to him and confess everything—how much our night together meant, how it broke me to walk away.

The impossible situation that forced my hand.

But I stay silent. He can never know my burden and the lives hanging in the balance.

"You need to leave. Please. Before it's too late..." My voice cracks on the last word.

He crowds me against the back of the door, broad shoulders caging me in. His carotid artery pulses with rage. Worst of all, the heat radiating off his body makes me want to fall into his arms and bury myself in his embrace.

"Why are you here?" His breath heats my cheek, sending traitorous shivers racing through me. "In bed with Kaufman?"

I shove back, my own anger rising. "Don't judge me. You need to back off."

He slams his palm against the door right next to my head. I flinch before I can stop myself, pulse jackhammering.

"You played me for a fool that night on the beach. Made me think you wanted me, all while you fucked me, mining me for intel." His eyes bore into mine, sparking with betrayal. "Is my team safe? Or have you already revealed who we really are?"

My cheeks flame with shame. "If I'd done that, you'd already be dead."

"Explain this to me." He grips my shoulders, giving me a shake. "Explain why you seduced me. Why you disappeared the next morning after everything we shared? And how it is that I find you in bed with a human trafficker?"

I squeeze my eyes shut as memories of that night flood through me. The balmy ocean breeze caressed my skin as we stripped under the stars. The surf crashed against the rocks as our bodies came together. The way the moon gave just enough light was ethereal. The way his rough hands explored with reverence, wringing gasps of pleasure from my lips, is something I'll never forget.

I never felt anything like the tenderness in his eyes when he gazed down at me, or the exquisite care he took pleasuring my body. He worshipped me until I was breathless, lost to everything but his touch, his taste—his love.

Afterward, we lay spent in each other's arms, legs intertwined. I rested my head on his chest, listening to his heartbeat, more content than I'd ever felt in my life. Nothing in my chaotic existence ever felt as right as that night.

I could've stayed there, with him, forever. I would have if I could, but then that text came, shattering the perfect illusion.

New intel. Timetable moved up.

The cruel claws of reality ripped me from his side. I disappeared, but my heart never left that beach or the man I walked away from.

"I never meant to hurt you." Tears spill down my cheeks. "Please believe that, if you believe nothing else. That night was real for me."

His Adam's apple bobs and his grip loosens. The anger in his eyes wavers, warring with doubt. Will he understand? I can only pray this is enough of the truth to redeem me in some small way. To prove that what we shared still lives inside me. He's the eye of the storm raging all around me. A beacon of hope I cling to in my darkest moments.

He should be my north star guiding me home. Instead, he may very well bring devastation to everything I hold dear. I avert my eyes, throat tightening. I want to defend myself, to make him understand, but the words stick in my throat.

"I opened myself up to you, held nothing back. Then you vanished. It led me to believe it was all a lie. You used me." He grabs my chin roughly, forcing me to meet his blistering gaze. I avert my eyes, too cowardly to face him. "Give me one reason I should trust a word you say now."

Tears prick hotly behind my eyes, but I blink them back. "I never meant to hurt you," I choke out. "You have every right to hate me, but what we shared was real to me."

"You don't walk away if it was *real*." His derisive tone makes me flinch. He releases me with a snarl, raking both hands through his hair. "You haven't answered me. What the hell are you doing here? I saw you with those girls. I don't even know who you are. If I ever knew you at all. What was Nicaragua? A trap for the Guardians? Is that what you are? Bait?" His chest heaves, eyes wild with anger and remnants of the agony I caused him.

"Nicaragua was real. What we shared was real." I hug my arms around my midsection, feeling ill. "There are things I can't tell you. Reasons I had to leave, reasons to keep my distance after..." I close my eyes, shuddering. "Just know I never stopped thinking of you. As for leaving, I had no choice."

"Because Kaufman called you back?"

"No. It's not like that. I didn't have a choice."

He turns his back to me, hands braced on the wall. We stand frozen, the gulf of misunderstanding still gaping wide between us. When he finally looks at me again, his eyes are filled with fresh hurt and bitterness I deserve in spades.

"You always have a choice." His words blast through my heart like bullets. He pinches the bridge of his nose and then punches the wall beside my head. I jump in surprise. I've never seen him so angry and raw.

"If you trusted me, you could have confided in me. We could have figured something out." His voice strains with frustration. "Didn't you learn anything that night on the beach? I would have walked through Hell to protect you. I would still do that today if you gave me the chance."

His words strike deep. He's right—if only I had faith in him, everything could be different, but the life at risk tied my hands.

"Some things I have to do alone." I meet his searching gaze defiantly, even as tears threaten. If I reach out to anyone and involve anyone, I lose everything.

But there's no way to explain that to a man like Ethan. He's a Guardian. He does whatever it takes to save those in need. He'll do whatever it takes to help me, and that's the one thing I can't allow. I have to do this alone.

As I try to slip away, his fingers dig into my wrist. He pulls me roughly against him. "Was it all a game to you? Making me believe you cared?" His voice drips bitter poison.

Being so close cracks my composure. My heartbeat quickly matches his as I fight the urge to melt against him.

My voice comes out choked. "Walking away was the hardest thing I've ever done. You shouldn't be here. I can't protect you or your team. Kaufman will know there's something between us, and trust me, you don't want him digging for answers. You need to take your team and leave. Leave before it's too late."

"Are you going to tell him?" His eyes blaze into mine, probing deep. Then, some of the hardness leaves his face. His hand comes up to cup my cheek with exquisite gentleness at odds with his rage just moments before. "Do you know what Haven is about?" His eyes close, and disgust fills his face. "Of course, you know. I heard…" His eyes open. "How can you work for him?"

"Ethan…" I grab at him. "I need you to trust me."

"Trust you?" he whispers urgently. "How can I trust you when everything you've done is a lie? You want me to trust you? Tell me everything."

I nearly break down and confess it all, but then I remember the lives hanging by a thread.

The life I'll do anything to protect.

"I can't." I pull away. The loss of contact leaves me cold and bereft, but I force myself to turn my back to him. "And I can't tell you why. I just need you to trust me. I won't tell Kaufman who you are or who your team works for, but if you're here to rescue these women, it's not going to happen."

"Why?"

"Because they want to be here."

"Bullshit."

"It's not bullshit. It's the truth."

"Those women want to be sold and traded like chattel?"

"You wouldn't understand." I make it one step before his iron grip wraps around my arm. He pulls me to him. This close, his heat and scent envelop me. "It's better than the alternative."

"Fuck, Rebel, why won't you talk to me?"

"Because…"

His mouth crashes down on mine, angry and hungry all at once. Shock explodes through me, immediately replaced by blistering heat as our lips clash and our tongues tangle. He kisses fiercely, all tongue and teeth, like he wants to devour me.

I try to twist away, to resist the molten desire rising to meet his savage kiss, but my traitorous body disobeys. My mouth moves rhythmically under his, soft and pliant despite my anger. I kiss him back with a ferocity that shakes me to my core.

His stubble scrapes my skin as his mouth slants over mine, again and again, relentless and demanding. I'm lost in his flavor and the scorching pressure of his lips possessing mine, claiming them completely. I nip his bottom lip, and he growls into my mouth, low and feral.

His hands grasp at me greedily, hauling me tighter against him. The hard planes of his body pin me to the wall, muscles coiled and quivering with restraint. Heat engulfs every point we connect—chests crushed together, hips fused in delicious friction, thighs interlocked in a tangle of need.

I'm dizzy, senseless, and shattering.

Consumed by a desire transcending anger, betrayal, bitterness, and self-preservation. In this searing suspended moment, there is only Ethan—his blistering kiss staking an irrefutable claim, hands branding my body, his heart hammering wildly against my own.

A red haze of passion clouds my vision when we finally break apart, gasping raggedly for air. I'm untethered and dangerously adrift. I press shaking palms against his chest, pushing him back by inches. He releases me slowly, eyes scorched by the same inner fire that rages through my veins.

"You have to stay away from me." My voice trembles with the effort of denial, even as my body screams otherwise. "Please. Kaufman will know, and he will kill you."

"Your words say one thing, but your body says another. Which one is the lie?" His eyes blaze into mine, refusing to release me from his simmering gaze. "You want me to trust you, yet you give me no reason to do so."

"It's complicated."

His thumb brushes my bottom lip, still tender and swollen from the blistering kiss. At his touch, desire shudders through me, traitorous and undeniable.

"You can't fight this." His voice is a gravelly whisper meant only for me. "We're inevitable. Written in the stars. Tell me what's going on. Give me a reason not to hate you."

I clench my fists against the urge to grasp him and drown myself in his heat and intensity. With monumental effort, I gather the tattered remnants of my will.

"You're right about one thing," I say.

"What's that?"

"I'm not who you think I am." The words come out choked and clogged with remorse. "Whatever we had? It's nothing but ash."

"You don't believe that." His eyes blaze, refusal etched on every taut line of his body. "I lost you once—it won't happen again."

"You want the truth?" Even as the words tumble from my mouth, I regret them, but I have to cut Ethan loose.

"Yes."

"We shared one night on the beach. It meant nothing to me. As for Kaufman and why I'm here…" These are the hardest words I've ever had to say, but I grit my teeth. "I came to him."

"Th-that's not true."

"It's true. It's one hundred percent true. I came to him with a business proposal. A way to turn the women he kidnapped into willing, eager, and fiercely loyal slaves. That's the truth."

For a suspended moment, his eyes blaze, probing for the truth. When he sees the truth shining in my eyes, his shoulders slump.

"I won't expose you, or your team, to Kaufman, but you can't be here. You have to pack up and leave. Leave before something horrible happens."

The look of betrayal on his face is enough to shatter my heart. He turns without another word, yanks on the door, and leaves my room. The echo of his footsteps reverberates through my hollow chest.

Alone, I press trembling fingers to my lips.

An undeniable truth haunts me—some fires, once ignited, can never be quenched.

TWENTY-THREE

Rebel

LATER THAT NIGHT, I PRESENT MYSELF FOR KAUFMAN'S INSPECTION. With a lurid stare, I apparently pass because he grips my arm like a vice and yanks me into the opulent dining hall. Haven is a place of great beauty amidst gripping evil, and the grand ballroom is where that beauty and evil collide.

Gentle candlelight illuminates crystal glasses and makes the silver cutlery shine. My pulse spikes as I spot Ethan seated across from my chair. Next to him, his team lines the long table. They all give me weighty, judgmental stares, and there's a woman with them. Young and fierce. Does she understand what this place does to women? Why would Ethan risk her safety, bringing her here?

Kaufman's oily voice drips false charm as he introduces each man, his grip tightening when Ethan's icy stare meets mine. Suspicion smolders in Kaufman's gaze. I'm his prized possession, and he's a jealous man. I pray he never discovers the ties linking Ethan and me together.

Kaufman seats me with a rough shove, pushing me into my chair, displaying his dominance and my submission. It's one of many ways he stakes his claim and tells others he's in charge.

He immediately rounds on Ethan. "What progress have you made tracing the breach?"

"We're investigating several potentials. It's a tedious process, but I expect results soon." Ethan meets Kaufman's gaze coolly, unfazed by Kaufman's rough treatment of me. It's like I don't exist, which hurts the most.

But isn't that what I asked for?

Kaufman's fist clenches, knuckles whitening. "I dislike disruptions in my business, and I have an auction slated for the end of the month." His smile doesn't reach his flinty eyes.

Too risky to look at Ethan directly, I feign boredom and disinterest. Why is he here? Why is Charlie team with him? Who is the goth girl sitting at the far end of the table?

There are too many questions. None that I can ask. To show interest is to arouse suspicion. My job here is singular and focused. I'm arm candy to Kaufman and nothing more.

Ethan's much better at this game than I am. His stoic mask reveals nothing. My nerves fray as Kaufman's possessive hand settles on my thigh under the table.

My thoughts churn as Ethan and Kaufman force idle small talk between them. Kaufman's suspicion toward Ethan compounds the danger we're both in. One misstep, and we're done.

"I heard you met Rebel in the halls?" Kaufman's gaze bores into Ethan as his grip on my thigh turns punishing, nails digging into my flesh.

"I did." Ethan leans back, completely at ease. "I did not know she belonged to you."

How does he maintain his composure like that?

"I don't like others putting their hands on what's mine." Kaufman's rancid breath invades my nostrils as he stakes his claim. "You'd be wise to keep your distance."

"Didn't know she was taken." Ethan's gaze flicks over to me. He cants his head to the side, then turns back to Kaufman. "Apologies. Your woman made it abundantly clear my attention was unwanted."

Ethan's words hit me with the weight of a sledgehammer, knocking the breath out of my lungs. It's over. Not that there was ever a future between us, but Ethan just hammered the last nail into the coffin of our very brief relationship. My heart splinters and breaks into a million pieces because there's no coming back from this.

I have to accept the truth.

It's over.

"See that it doesn't happen again." Kaufman's jaw ticks, the muscle pulsing erratically. He refuses to let his dominance go unchallenged.

"It won't." Ethan inclines his head slightly, but his stormy eyes flick to me, piercing in their intensity. "I have no interest in what is clearly not mine."

I sit immobilized, scarcely daring to breathe, hyperaware of Kaufman's bruising hold and the violent tension in his body coiled tighter than a viper ready to strike. He's threatened by Ethan and desperate to establish his supremacy, no matter how petty the matter.

Kaufman's cologne makes me wrinkle my nose. He leans in, moist lips grazing my ear. "You belong to me. Never forget your place." His stare dares me to defy his claim, but his words aren't for me.

They're meant for Ethan.

I meet Kaufman's gaze, my polished mask never slipping. "Of course." The lies taste like a bitter pill on my tongue.

Inwardly, I seethe. Does Ethan know I'm trapped? Even now, I'm desperately fighting to find a way out, battling to make things right between us. I ache for him and miss how he cradled me under the stars.

I hold Ethan's ocean-blue eyes for a suspended heartbeat, wishing he could read the thoughts etched on my soul, but Kaufman's grip forces me to turn away. I retreat behind my mask, frantically planning my next move in my deadly game of lies.

Tension crackles in the air as the first course is served. Kaufman taps his gaudy rings on the table, the sharp clicks piercing the uneasy silence. "Exactly what headway have you made tracing the breach?"

"These things require finesse and care." Ethan meets Kaufman's probing stare, his face an impenetrable mask. "All indications are the attack likely originated from inside your own walls."

Kaufman's meaty hand stills, the sterling silver knife frozen halfway to his sneering mouth. "You believe one of my own people is responsible?" His eyes slit in suspicion.

Ethan spreads his hands neutrally. "It's far too premature to say. We need full system access to track the digital trail accurately."

Kaufman's jaw ticks, the muscle pulsing erratically. Unease and distrust flicker across his blunt features. "Do what you must quickly. I want this matter resolved."

The grating scrape of cutlery on china fills the uneasy void as servants in crisp white uniforms whisk away our half-finished plates and present the main course. The tang of fear on my tongue mingles with the cloying remnants of roasted meat and heavy wine.

Kaufman's gaudy rings rap the table sharply, the shrill sound piercing the heavy silence. "Enough with business. Let's enjoy some entertainment before dessert is served." His thin lips peel back to reveal teeth in a predatory approximation of a smile. "A preview of my latest business venture."

At his lecherous signal, the ornate double doors sweep open. Ethereal visions of beauty glide into the candlelit hall.

Kaufman's Angels.

The women I've both saved and condemned.

TWENTY-FOUR

Rebel

DIAPHANOUS GOWNS CLING TO THE WOMEN'S BODIES, SHIMMERING with every subtle movement, leaving the hidden secrets of their figures merely a breath away from revelation. The sultry strains of a lute weave through the room, its minor chords embracing the dancers as their bare feet caress the cool marble, each step a sensual whisper, a delicate kiss.

With exquisite grace, they undulate their bodies, making the flowing fabric ripple like the surface of a tranquil pond disturbed by a gentle breeze. The fabric clings lovingly to every curve, becoming a second skin that reveals and conceals in a tantalizing play of shadow and light.

As the Angels dance, they tease the eye with flashes of bare skin, the seductive contour of a hip, the inviting valley between breasts, and the dark triangle between their legs. Each movement is designed for grace and seduction.

The air grows thick with the suffocating stench of objectification, at least for me. It invades my nostrils, assaults my taste buds, and causes my tongue to stick to the roof of my mouth. Only years of mastering my reactions keep my mask of indifference intact.

The haunting melody of the lute is a masterful blend of desire and lust. The women sway and twirl, each movement flowing into the next perfectly in time with the music. Their diaphanous silks float like wind-touched petals of a flower, each sensual movement a hypnotic vision of grace that ensnares the eyes and the soul.

The room itself seems to hold its breath, captivated by the sensual elegance of the dance. It transcends the physical world and becomes an embodiment of raw emotion and carnal desire.

When the dancers approach the men, they pull back. Hank's knuckles pale where they grip his armrests, accentuating the corded muscles in his forearms. Gabe shifts to the side in his seat, tension radiating from his hulking frame. Beside him, Walt's lips thin into a hard line, while Blake's stony expression betrays none of his thoughts. But color rises on Jeb's cheeks as he shifts in growing agitation, darting glances at the dancers.

Stitch curls into herself, arms crossed protectively over her chest. Jaw clenched, she refuses to look at the dancers. Throughout the entire dinner, she's been ignored.

But she's female. In Haven, women are to be seen and admired. Rarely heard. Kaufman didn't even introduce her when we sat at the table.

Ethan's hard gaze bears down on me, a turbulent storm contained behind his stoic facade. He thinks he knows why I'm here and what I'm doing.

Does he realize what's at stake?

These women's lives hang by the thinnest threads that can be severed instantly.

Only I can save them from a lingering death preceded by endless torture and rape.

His men stir, besieged by unwanted lust. Their honor wars with their baser instincts, helpless against the intoxicating sight of the dancers and mortified to take pleasure in this perverse entertainment.

Only Ethan remains unaffected.

Oblivious to the churning undercurrents, Kaufman toys with his signet ring, supremely satisfied. My emotions find a mirror in

Ethan's stormy gaze. However, Kaufman's proprietary hand on my knee forces me to turn away from Ethan.

If Kaufman only knew the forces in this room will one day take all this away from him, he wouldn't be so smug. Ethan won't tell me why he's here with his team, but they are Guardians, and Guardians do only one thing.

And they're experts at their job.

"Behold my latest inspiration. An elite class of willing Angels gentled into an eagerness to please." Kaufman's signet ring glints as he gestures toward the dancing Angels.

"I would think men with the ability to pay would find willing women on their own without difficulty." Ethan's eyes harden, jaw clenching.

Kaufman's laughter grates harshly. "I simply provide a service to discerning clients. Some prefer more—spirited conquests." His smile sharpens. "Others prefer them already broken. All of them wish to own them. A willing woman hanging on your arm must be bought and paid for day after day. Plying her with trinkets for her continued interest. That is not what my clients crave."

Ethan tenses but betrays nothing. "I understood your clients sought more—aggressive services." His tone drips contempt.

Kaufman bristles slightly but smooths his expression. "Indeed, the auction offerings attract those with particular proclivities. Prime specimens for clients with particular tastes. Men who value discretion aren't afraid to take what they desire." He runs a proprietary hand along my bare arm. "But Rebel convinced me an untapped market existed for more refined sensibilities. Men who don't stomach the fine art of breaking a woman, but desire a willing, devoted—companion."

"Is that what we're calling slaves these days? Willing companions?"

"Only the Angels," Kaufman smirks, then laughs as he pats my knee. "I still have many who relish that initial breaking-in period."

I force myself to lean into Kaufman's touch, suppressing a shudder of revulsion as I play my part.

Ethan bristles but betrays nothing.

Pride warms Kaufman's eyes as he turns his attention to me. "Rebel screens new acquisitions, then takes only the most promising prospects. She then gentles them into willing pets. Eager to serve their new masters. Women who only need to be *bought* one time." His chest swells. "It was her brilliant idea."

Bile scorches my throat at his twisted words. I demurely lower my gaze, the ultimate picture of compliant consent. Yet inwardly, I seethe, my fury a caged beast desperate to sink its teeth into Kaufman's neck.

Soon, I silently vow. *Soon, your fortress will fall.*

Ethan inclines his head slightly. "Your business is yours. Forgive any bluntness or disinterest from my men. After yesterday's incident, I've instructed them not to touch your offerings. Tracing your security breach is our sole focus."

"I appreciate that, and this display is to demonstrate the quality of our offerings."

"They are exquisite." Storm clouds swirl in Ethan's eyes.

Kaufman turns to me. "Rebel has become invaluable to me."

I force myself to meet his gaze and smile.

"I'm sure she has." Ethan's eyes bore into mine across the table.

Kaufman misses the tense undercurrent. "Indeed. She is indispensable for transforming our more reluctant acquisitions." His possessive hand on my knee makes me sick, but I know how to hide my revulsion and remain outwardly compliant.

Kaufman's rings flash as he claps sharply, echoing through the room. "As a token of my thanks, you and your men should indulge in my hospitality." He snaps his fingers, and Angels glide to the men, draping themselves over tense shoulders.

"Tempting as your gift may be, we're here to work. My men must remain focused on the task at hand. Regrettably, we must graciously decline."

Jeb shifts away from the dancer's seeking hands, his cheeks flaming. Gabe stands abruptly, nearly toppling the petite blonde, pawing at his arm.

Kaufman pins Ethan with a look, his grip on my knee tightening until his rings bite into my flesh. "Enjoy the rest of your evening.

Use the Angels as you wish, or don't." Kaufman rises, hauling me to my feet with him. "Good night, gentlemen."

The Angels retreat, but Ethan's stormy gaze follows me.

Does he know that behind my demure smile, fury smolders at the beasts who seek to control and possess me?

Our silent battle of wills continues, but deception cannot thrive in this place. I need to come clean with Ethan, but to do that, we need to be alone.

And that is something Kaufman will never allow.

TWENTY-FIVE

Ethan

DAYS PASS SINCE THAT DINNER WHEN MY TEAMMATES AND I WERE honored guests at Kaufman's table, where the horrible truth was revealed.

Rebel's working with Kaufman. Selling innocence to the highest bidder. Ever since that night, my dreams have become nightmares.

Those nightmares always start the same, playing out in slow motion. A macabre dance that twists my guts and sets my heart racing. A flash of fiery red hair. Her voice is distant and cold. Then, there's Kaufman leering at Rebel, who stands beside him.

I wake with a start, drenched in sweat, the image of Rebel's betrayal fresh and raw, her association with Kaufman gnawing at my soul. The threat she presents to me and my men is significant.

We're undercover, pretending to be something we're not. She knows who we are. What we are. And what we do. At any moment, she could blow our cover.

It's the worst time to be distracted.

Her eyes pierce me even in sleep.

Her betrayal remains a deep, raw, and angry, festering wound.

For now, we're safe, and I'm on task.

Why hasn't she betrayed us?

That's the one question that keeps spinning in my head, going round and round, without any answer that makes sense.

Today, I'm out investigating Kaufman's peripheral security systems. I patrol the halls, catalog monitoring devices, and dutifully match them against Kaufman's list. It's my job to uncover discrepancies. After telling him there may be a mole in his organization, he's much more forthcoming with information—and access.

It's an opportunity my team takes full advantage of. Over the past few days, we've nearly mapped out the entirety of Haven, personally walking the halls, cataloging server locations, video cameras, and sweeping for listening devices. You name it, we're looking for it.

Looking for '*anomalies*.' Anomalies that don't exist. But Kaufman doesn't know that. He's a paranoid motherfucker and desperately wants to find the breach, seal it, and make whoever created it pay.

That's where my focus should be.

But all I can think about is Rebel.

When I glance up from my musings, I see fiery red hair turning a corner down the hall.

Could it be?

Rebel?

The vacant corridors and a bit of Mitzy Magic to block any surveillance of my actions offer an opportunity I can't refuse.

With a sharp intake of breath, a reaction I can't control, my legs move of their own accord, lengthening my stride. Before she can slip away, I catch up to her and block her path.

"We need to talk. Now."

Her emerald eyes, those stunning jewels that once drew me in, flash dangerously. They've changed and hardened over the months since we last saw each other.

Since we had sex on the beach.

Since she disappeared from my life, taking the Guardians' secrets I spilled to her—with her.

"I have nothing to say to you." Her voice is cold and distant.

She tries to shove past me, a forceful push aimed at my chest, but my hands find her shoulders, and I hold her in place. The warmth of her body radiates through my palms, and I can't help but notice how right it feels to hold her, even now.

Even here.

I spin her to face me, desperation clawing at my insides. "Why are you here?"

Her lips, once soft and inviting, press into a hard line. She refuses to meet my eyes. Instead, she fixates on something beyond me. Up close, I'm once again struck by her beauty. Beauty marred by dark shadows under her eyes.

They hint at secrets and pain, things she's not telling me.

What have you been through, my dearest Rebel?

Frustration bubbles up within me until it suddenly boils over. I give her a little shake, my hands trembling with anger. "Are you one of them now?" My voice breaks on the last word.

I have to know the truth. The uncertainty of not knowing feels like having a knife stabbed in my chest, twisting with every heartbeat.

"Believe what you want, but stay out of my way." Her words are a slap to my face, stinging and unexpected. She shoves me back.

Viciously.

The force of her aggression leaves me staggering.

Her eyes blaze with a fire I've never seen before, filled with contempt and something else—something like sorrow. "For my safety and yours, we have no past. You're nobody to me."

"Nobody?"

"Yes. Nobody."

"Tell me why you're here."

"No."

Her words hang in the air like a heavy, suffocating weight. My chest aches. It's that knife twisting. Sharp, physical pain causes a hitch in my breath.

"No?"

"That's what I said."

"No, as in you can't? Or won't?"

"Does it matter?" She lets out a deep sigh and glances down the hall as if expecting someone to appear at any moment.

The sweet smell of her perfume, once so comforting, mocks me, a reminder of what I lost when she walked out of my life.

"Of course, it matters."

"I don't have time for this. Please—just leave me alone."

She can't be here of her own free will. I refuse to believe she would do such a thing.

We stand there, two people who once meant everything to each other, now complete strangers. The only thing hanging in the crushing silence between us is the sound of my ragged breaths.

"I can help you." She turns to storm away, but I grab her wrist, stopping her. "Don't shut me out."

Rebel halts, eyes downcast. Slowly, she turns back, unshed tears glistening. Gently, she reaches up to caress my cheek. Her touch is electric, sending desire burning through my veins. I close my eyes, leaning into her palm, covering her delicate hand with mine. We reconnect for a suspended moment, and the rest of the world disappears.

When I meet her gaze again, her pupils are blown wide. She feels this. I brush my thumb over her parted lips. Her breath catches, and she sways closer. We're two magnets drawn by an irresistible force.

"Rebel..." I whisper her name like a prayer, overcome with longing. "You must trust me."

"I wish it were that easy." Her entire body trembles.

Unable to resist, I pull her into my arms. She comes willingly, melting against me. Her body is soft and warm, so achingly familiar. I bury my face in her fiery locks, breathing her in. The floral scent brings back vivid memories of our passion. She clings to me tightly, our hearts hammering in tandem.

When we finally pull back, her face is just inches from mine. A single movement would bring our lips together. Her eyes keep darting to my mouth. I trace her lower lip with my thumb, desire raging through me. She leans into my touch, eyes fluttering closed.

Unable to stop myself, I brush a feather-light kiss to her lips. It's the softest caress, but electricity jolts through me. She makes a faint sound, swaying into me.

I pull back just enough to meet her dazed gaze. Cupping her cheek, I brush my knuckles along her jaw, tilting her face to mine.

"I've missed you so much."

Emotion wars on her face. Slowly, she turns her cheek into my palm, pressing a fervent kiss there. My knees go weak at the contact. Unable to stop myself, I lean in, our breaths mingling...

Abruptly, she turns away. My kiss lands on her hair instead. Gently but firmly, she pushes me back. The wall slams down between us once more.

"Don't," is all she says, eyes squeezed shut against temptation. "I can't..."

My fingers flex helplessly, aching to pull her back into my arms. To crush her lips with mine until we're both senseless with need. But I restrain myself through sheer force of will.

"Meet me later. Please," I beg quietly.

She hesitates, conflict clear on her face. For a long moment, I think she'll refuse. Then slowly, she gives a single nod before fleeing down the hall.

I watch her go, desire and hope swirling inside me. Our passion still smolders. I will stoke those embers into flames once more. I yearn to kiss away the shadows in her eyes and feel her come undone in my arms.

I sag back against the concrete wall, chest heaving. Being near her again ignites a fire inside me, hot and consuming. One I thought long extinguished. I press my fingertips to my tingling lips, craving her taste, her touch.

This changes everything. Despite her cold facade, an ember of our passion remains. If I stoke that spark carefully, we could rekindle what we once had.

But I must be cautious. Kaufman watches Rebel's every move. If he discovered the fire smoldering between us, it would ruin everything. We're playing a dangerous game here at Haven. I'll have to be patient. Earn her trust one stolen moment at a time. It felt, for a moment, that she was almost ready to confide in me. Fear held her back, and I understand and respect her fear. If our positions were reversed, I'd probably do the same. But there's still no explanation as to why she's here.

Knowing our love is not completely lost will have to be enough for now. I cling to that fragile hope as I turn in the opposite direction from Rebel and slowly return to my teammates.

After our brief encounter, I admit to being more confused than anything else. I still need answers she refuses to give.

The woman I loved, the woman I thought I knew, is gone.

With the bitter taste of rejection on my tongue, my world shifts fundamentally.

What hold does Kaufman have over you?

What are you hiding?

Seconds tick by, and the emptiness of the hallway expands around me. Losing Rebel like this, for a second time, is an agony I can't articulate. Finally, a growl of frustration escapes my lips, and I turn away, my mind in turmoil.

There's no way I can let this go, but I'm not going to solve anything standing here. I won't give up. It's not in my nature. The Rebel I know is still in there, buried deep by the imposter she's become. I complete my segment of Haven, cataloging this and that, then return to our base of operations, the comms suite, where Kaufman gave us room to work.

I find Hank, Walt, and the others gathered, their voices low and deep in discussion, planning our next move, but my entrance halts their conversation. My expression must expose my inner turmoil because Hank grasps my shoulder and gives me a reassuring shake.

"Everything good, boss?"

I rake an agitated hand through my hair, my heart still hammering from my confrontation with Rebel. "I ran into Rebel. She shut me down when I confronted her."

"Does that surprise you? She joined these bastards." Blake's lips curl in disgust, one fist smacking his palm. "I can't believe she's working with him."

"If she were working for him, she would've turned us in. That she hasn't says something else is going on. She was terrified when I confronted her."

"Then why is she here?" Walt leans back in his chair, arms crossed over his chest.

"I don't know. Kaufman couldn't help but preen at that dinner we were forced to choke down. He loves that she's working for him and wants me to know it, but I don't believe it. If she is, it can't be willingly. There's more going on, and I want to know what that is." I pound my fist against the rough concrete wall in frustration, the impact jarring but centering.

"But if she's not talking, she's not talking." Stitch, who rarely engages in conversation, speaks up. "Whatever her reasons, they're her own. If she wanted our help, she would have it. She knows this. Since she keeps pushing you off, whatever reason she's here, it's sensitive enough that she's keeping it from us and from Kaufman. Her secrets are her own. Pushing her to reveal them is only going to make things worse."

"How?" I stare at Stitch, not liking her assessment.

"If you push too hard, she might do exactly what we can't afford and tell Kaufman who we really are. My opinion, not that anyone's asking, is to let Rebel do her thing while we do ours. Don't poke the bear. It never turns out well."

The room fills with my team's uneasy breaths. They exchange worried glances, uncertainty in their eyes. They trust and follow me but can't understand the depth of my connection with Rebel and my desperation to save her.

"I agree with Stitch." Walt's steady baritone flows like smooth whiskey, calming the churn of my gut. "You'll figure out her secrets soon enough." He leans against the cool concrete wall, arms crossed over his broad chest, a tower of composed strength.

Jeb swivels his chair around, the worn leather creaking beneath him. His fingers twitch with anticipation, like a conductor before the first note. "On a separate note, we're making progress. Stitch created a worm, and it's tunneling through their encryption layers as we speak." His eyes glitter with excitement and obsession, a hunter zeroing in on his prey. "Mitzy sends an attack every now and again for us to discover and close down. That way, we can show Kaufman we're really working, and he's getting his money's worth hiring us. Basically, we're just wasting time and dragging our feet.

"We're using those breaches to funnel data to Mitzy." Stitch's voice is soft amongst the deeper voices of my men. "Kaufman's men are wholly inept and have no clue what's really happening. At least I look good when he comes around—the misogynistic bastard."

Like Mitzy, she doesn't look up from her rapid typing. The constant clatter creates a rhythmic undercurrent to our conversation. Strands of black hair fall across her pale face, shadowing her intense concentration.

I pivot to Gabe and refocus my efforts. I'm Charlie team leader, not some love-struck idiot who's forgotten why I'm here. "What about physical security?" My voice is low and controlled. Gabe's stern face, etched with lines of wisdom and warfare, gives nothing away. "Notice any weaknesses we can exploit?"

Gabe slowly shakes his head. His arms cross over a chest that's seen its share of battles. "Armed guards everywhere, patrols covering every inch. They're always watching. We'd need a damn army for any kind of frontal assault on this place." His voice is flat, unyielding, like a wall you'd never dare to scale. "But we're mapping out their patrol routes and when they change shifts. It's slow going but coming together nicely."

Hank grunts in agreement. "These bastards are paranoid, but we knew that going in." His voice rumbles, a storm contained. "We'll find a way."

Infiltrating Haven is merely the first step of a multi-phased attack. The ultimate goal is to tear it down, but certain things must come first, which is why we have Stitch on loan from Mitzy.

No need to lead a full-frontal assault when you can sneak in through the back doors. Stitch's computer worm will give us that access.

"Good." My voice cuts through the room. "Keep at it. The rest of us will keep walking the halls, learning the patterns of their security personnel."

That's the true reason behind cataloging security devices. We're using that excuse to map out the halls and determine the guards' rotation schedules, looking for gaps in their physical security measures and technical security protocols.

"Rebel can do her thing. We'll do ours." I meet each man's gaze in turn, setting the tone from this point out. Not that they need to hear it. They're not the ones obsessed with Rebel. Those words are solely meant for me.

No more obsessing over Rebel.

TWENTY-SIX

Ethan

THE SUFFOCATING LABYRINTH OF HAVEN'S CONCRETE HALLWAYS twists around me as I venture deeper into the complex. This place hides a network of dark corridors laden with secrets and corruption, and a damp chill clings to the air, echoing the pain of previous victims.

For days, I've been lost in this warren, cataloging surveillance gear, validating server locations, and looking for hidden access points, hunting for the weakness we've been hired to discover and eliminate.

A weakness we created in the first place, thanks to a bit of Mitzy Magic.

Kaufman's restricting our access, although I can't prove it. His paranoia is evident in every guarded glance, every camera watching from shadowed corners.

His security is nearly impenetrable, a maze of encrypted channels and well-placed sentinels. Even as I pretend to bolster the walls of this hellhole, I can't help but be amazed by how impenetrable Haven is.

We're looking for cracks, chinks in Haven's defenses, where

Mitzy's phenomenal technical team can destroy this place from the inside out, and that's proving to be exceptionally difficult.

The depressing atmosphere clings to me, oppressive and chilling, as if the very walls watch me, waiting for me to slip up, but my job is all for show. With the exception of Stitch and Jeb, the rest of the team must appear as if we're working to find the mole in Kaufman's organization.

All the while, Stitch and Jeb are at it nonstop, inserting layer upon layer of Trojan horses into the very base code of this hellacious place. While the rest of us might seem superfluous in this operation, we're nearly finished tracking the movement of guards through this place.

That kind of intel can only be obtained with boots on the ground.

It still leaves me feeling like I'm walking in circles, wandering the halls, pretending to be hard at work.

A soft scuffle of movement breaks through my thoughts. I pause as a slight figure emerges ahead of me in the dim hallway.

One of the Angels wandering unaccompanied?

She freezes at the sight of me, eyes wide and frightened. She's like a deer caught in headlights, stunned and unmoving.

"It's okay. I won't hurt you." I keep my voice low and comforting.

The girl hesitates, her small body poised to flee, but unable. She's a bundle of nerves and clutches a book to her chest.

A book?

"What are you doing wandering alone?" I ask gently.

"I've done nothing wrong. I have library privileges and can move about some now that I'm an Angel. It's better than..." Her voice trails off, a tremor of fear rippling through her words.

"Better than what?" I prod, my gut twisting with what she'll say next.

The girl shivers, hugging the book tightly. "The—the cages below." She points toward the floor. "Rebel said becoming an Angel was my best chance to avoid being sold to awful men." The words spill out, tinged with horror.

My pulse quickens, the world narrowing to this moment. "Rebel recruited you to be an Angel?" It's the confirmation of Kaufman's words I never wanted to hear.

"She saved me." Defiance enters the girl's eyes, a spark of something unbreakable. "I chose to live rather than die like that. If I work really hard, apply myself, and draw the eye of a buyer—"

"That doesn't sound like she's saving you." None of what this girl says makes sense.

She lets out a deep sigh. "It's better than the alternative."

The machinery of my mind whirs, pieces clicking into place. Rebel hasn't fully turned against us. I still don't know what she's doing here, but she's *saving* at least some of the trafficked women from a fate worse than death. I have to believe she's resisting the evil infecting this place.

Resisting Kaufman.

A faint glimmer of hope stirs within me.

"You shouldn't be out walking alone." As far as I know, women aren't allowed the freedom to wander. I gesture down the long hall, my voice gentle but firm.

She tries to scurry away, her footsteps a soft patter against the unforgiving floor, but the abrupt clatter of heavy footsteps freezes her in place.

The girl's fear lingers in the air, a tangible cloud of despair. When Kaufman appears around the corner, his eyes narrow, and a deep scowl takes over his hardened face.

The girl cowers under Kaufman's baleful stare, her body shrinking back as if trying to become invisible.

"Library privileges are granted to get a book and return to your quarters, not to linger in the halls talking to my men. Go. And tell Rebel your privileges have been revoked." He dismisses her with a sharp clap.

"Yes, sir." She flees down the hall, tears streaming down her cheeks, her hurried steps echoing the rhythm of a terrified heart.

Kaufman turns to me. "Why are you speaking to that girl?" His demand cuts through the air, sharp and cold.

I spread my hands, the very picture of innocence, my voice

smooth and controlled. "My mistake, idle curiosity. I was unaware Angels had privileges to roam freely."

Kaufman's eyes bore into mine, suspicion sparking in their dark depths. "They earn certain rewards through proper training and demonstrating impeccable behavior." His words twine through the air like serpents, sinister and smooth. "Iris just lost those hard-earned privileges."

"Because she was talking to me?"

"Because she *stopped* to talk to you."

"What's the difference?"

"They are to go and return. Stopping is not permitted."

"Wish I'd known. I wouldn't have stopped her."

"She knows the rules. It's none of your concern."

"As that may be, I have other concerns."

"What concerns?"

I bite down the bile rising in my throat. "There are areas of Haven we have not seen. My team can't secure your facility when you restrict our access. There are levels below us we haven't been granted access to."

Kaufman's face tightens, the skin around his eyes stretching taut. "The lower levels are not your concern."

I meet his stare evenly, but my face remains a calm mask. The silence between us grows heavy, but I'm not interested in engaging in a pissing match with Kaufman. I'm happy to blink first.

"My team can't do our job without full knowledge of the grounds. You hamstring our ability, but I defer to your judgment. We can leave if you're not serious about finding the breach in your system."

Putting that out there is a risk, but Kaufman is the kind of man who only responds to strength.

Kaufman's eyes hold mine in a taut silence, considering, weighing, judging. I can almost see the gears turning in his mind, the calculations and machinations churning behind his discerning gaze. Finally, he nods sharply, a quick jerk of his head, conceding and warning all at once.

"Focus on the task at hand." His words are a dismissal, a closing of doors.

"My team will be packed within the hour and depart." I'm all on board if he wants to play games with me.

"That is not—"

"Look, I don't respond to threats and dislike my team being cut off at the knees. I'm not a dog you can snap your fingers at and order me to focus on the *task at hand*. What you do here is none of our business. As I've mentioned time and time again, we're discreet. I won't jeopardize our reputation by working for a client who refuses to allow us to do our job. Open access to the entirety of your operation, or we leave within the hour. You've got a mole in your organization. I leave you with that much knowledge. Hire another outfit if that's your wish, but if you want us to stay, I need full access."

The air between us crackles with spoken and unspoken threats. Kaufman's face goes rigid, his eyes narrowing into dangerous slits. The silence in the hallway becomes thick, charged with the tension of a gathering storm. The only sound is the distant hum of machinery and the muffled voices of guards.

It's just him and me, two adversaries locked in a battle of wills.

Kaufman finally cuts through the tense silence, his voice icy and controlled, each word carefully measured. "You are playing a dangerous game."

"I play to win and don't gamble with my team's integrity." I hold his gaze, refusing to back down. My resolve is as solid as the concrete walls surrounding us. "You hired us to do a job. We're wasting our time if you don't allow us to accomplish that job."

"And what makes you think you can speak to me like this?" He steps closer, and the heavy weight of his cologne slaps me in the face, a sharp, metallic scent that matches his personality. His eyes bore into mine, probing, searching for any crack in my armor.

"Because you called us. You know our reputation, our expertise. You have a problem, and we're the best at solving it." I let a small smile play on my lips, a challenge and a promise all at once.

His jaw tightens. He needs us and knows it, but his pride stands in his way. This isn't a man who backs down, but this security threat is too important for him to ignore.

"You will have the access you need." His voice grates like stone against stone. "But be warned. There are things here, things best left undisturbed. Your men have access. Your woman does not. Understood."

"Understood."

"Tread carefully."

I nod, acknowledging his warning, but remain undeterred. "We'll take it from here."

Kaufman clicks his heels, executes a precise left face, and then retreats down the hall without another word.

There's darkness in Haven, a web of secrets and lies that goes deeper than I feared. I return to my team, my mind racing, cataloging the new information and recalculating our strategy. We've gained access, but at what cost? As I return to my duties, cataloging the intricate web of surveillance and security systems, my thoughts circle back to Iris's frightened eyes, Rebel's hidden agenda, and Kaufman's threat.

What am I missing?

TWENTY-SEVEN

Ethan

HANK, WALT, AND I NAVIGATE THE TWISTED LABYRINTH BENEATH Haven. Old fluorescent bulbs flicker and buzz, making our shadows dance on the walls. Today, we explore corridors once forbidden to us.

Walt's voice breaks the silence, a whisper barely audible over the distant hum of machinery. "It's like something out of a nightmare."

"We know what Kaufman does within these walls." I glance at Walt, whose heavy gaze takes in the grim surroundings. "Nightmare for sure."

"It's more than that. Kaufman's hiding something here." Walt places his hand over his stomach. "Something worse. Can't describe it more than that."

"Worse than kidnapping and trafficking women? Selling them to be sex slaves?" Hank shakes his head. Like me, he believes there's nothing worse than trafficking women.

"Something—more." Walt's voice is tinged with disgust. "Can't say what, just that this…" He spins in a slow circle, extending his arms to encompass all of Haven. "This place feels off."

I nod, feeling the chill in the air, a warrior's awareness sharpening my senses. "We agree on one thing. Whatever's going on in this place, it's dark and twisted."

Hank's hand drifts to his side, to where his gun would be if we were allowed to carry weapons. "The deeper we go, the more depraved it gets. I've seen some sick stuff in my time, but this—this is something else."

I meet his eyes, understanding the horror he's feeling.

The weight of our mission hangs heavy on my shoulders, the walls seeming to close in on us. With every step, we descend further into madness, and the echoes of our footsteps serve as haunting reminders of the darkness we're facing.

The hallway seems to stretch forever, a gloomy abyss that the dim light barely reaches. As Hank, Walt, and I press on, my skin prickles with anticipation. We've reached the bowels of Haven, where no semblance of humanity remains.

As we round a corner, a heavy iron door looms before us. I enter the access codes Kaufman reluctantly handed over, and the lock disengages. Hank attaches a device Stitch created on the fly to insert a code that will allow us to unlock the door if Kaufman changes the code.

When he changes the code, the man is a paranoid bastard.

Walt checks the door, his hand hesitating for a fraction of a second before he nudges it open. We step into a chamber filled with rows of holding cells. Thin mattresses line the floor, and rusty chains hang from the walls. The distant *drip, drip, drip* of water echoes through the room. My heart pounds in my chest, a revulsion building deep in my gut.

"Jesus," Walt murmurs, his voice a hoarse whisper. "This is where they keep them?"

I swallow hard, feeling the bile rise again. The terror that permeates these walls is almost tangible. "Let's keep moving." I keep my voice barely above a whisper.

Next, we come across a group shower facility. The room is bathed in a nauseating fluorescent light, revealing tiles stained with god-knows-what. My eyes are drawn to the chains affixed to the walls, rusted and worn. It doesn't take much to imagine the bodies that have been bound here, the hollow eyes staring out in desperation and terror.

Hank's breath catches as he examines the drainage grates, clogged with clumps of hair and unidentifiable matter.

Walt turns away, covering his mouth, his face a sickly shade of green. "What kind of people do this?" His voice breaks as he chokes on the words.

My throat is tight, my words struggling to find their way out. "Monsters," I reply, my voice devoid of emotion. "Only monsters do this."

The air is heavy with the residue of human fear, suffering, and humiliation. The water-streaked mirrors reflect a twisted reality where innocence is lost and cruelty reigns.

I move to a row of sinks, grimacing at the brown stains splattered across the porcelain. The faucets are caked with grime, and the handles are polished by regular use. Everything is a testament to the depravity of this place.

We stand in silence, the only sound the distant drip of a leaky pipe, each drop a reminder of the tears shed within these walls. The echoes of anguished cries seem to reverberate in the tiles beneath our feet, the memories of countless victims forever etched into the very fabric of this hellish room.

No one speaks as we exit the wash facility. Our minds are unable to fully grasp the atrocities that have occurred here.

The weight of our mission has never felt heavier, and as we press on, I can't shake the feeling that we've barely begun to scratch the surface of the darkness that awaits us.

Those chains, those stains, that room will forever be etched in my mind, a haunting reminder of the inhumanity that exists in the shadows, hidden away from the world, but all too real for those trapped within the atrocity.

The nausea is almost overwhelming, but we press on. The deeper we go, the worse it gets: a twisting, gnawing realization that the darkness we uncover is far more malignant than we could have imagined.

More rooms filled with cells. More wash facilities. It's a never-ending horror show.

Finally, we reach a door marked "CLINIC." I push it open, and we enter a pristine, sterile room, starkly contrasting the grime and decay outside. Everything is white and gleaming, with shelves lined with medical supplies.

"What is this place?" Hank asks, his voice trembling.

I look to Walt. "I think we've found what was twisting your gut." I stand outside another door. This one is marked "OR."

I open it, and we're met with a sight that freezes us all in our tracks. It's an operating room, state-of-the-art, equipped with everything needed for complex surgeries.

The operating room is a pristine, sterile environment, filled with the sharp tang of antiseptics and the cold gleam of metal. Every surface is spotless, reflecting our stunned expressions back at us. I move further into the room, the dread growing in the pit of my stomach.

Hank's voice breaks the silence, his tone flat and grim. "Look at this." He holds up a medical chart with photographs, his hand trembling. "These records detail extensive surgeries. Faces, fingerprints, dental records... All altered."

It's the photographs that chill me to the bone. Photographs of girls and women, before and after surgery, their faces altered and identities erased.

The room grows colder as I take in the full scope of the operation. Not only are they trafficking humans, but they're turning them into untraceable ghosts.

"What else is going on here?" Walt's face is ashen as he examines the instruments. "These aren't just regular surgical tools."

"They're not just trafficking them; they're changing them. Making them disappear completely. Erasing them from existence," I state the obvious and shake my head, the pieces coming together in a horrifying puzzle.

A shiver runs down my spine as the magnitude of the situation hits me.

The room spins, and I grip the edge of a table to steady myself. This is bigger and more insidious than we ever thought.

Hank, voice filled with urgency, says, "We have to stop this."

I nod, feeling the weight of our discovery. This isn't just a mission anymore. It's a crusade, a fight for the very soul of humanity.

But our grim discoveries don't end there.

We stumble upon another room adjacent to the OR, which stops us dead in our tracks. It's filled with small, empty, sterile basins, each meticulously cleaned and arranged in a neat row.

"What are these?" Walt asks, his voice catching. Stamped imprints on each basin offer an answer. There's a heart, a liver, kidneys—one left, one right.

I can't find the words to answer. My mind reels, trying to make sense of what we're seeing, but the truth is too horrifying to comprehend.

Hank's face is a mask of revulsion. He's thinking the same thing as me. The implications are too terrible to put into words.

We leave the room, the door closing with a soft, ominous click, but the image of those basins lingers, haunting our every step.

The deeper we explore, the more monstrous the truth becomes. The shadows hold more grotesque and terrifying secrets than we ever imagined, and the nightmare has just begun.

Those empty basins will haunt me.

And then, as if in answer to our unspoken fears, agonized screams pierce the air. My blood runs cold, and bile rises in the back of my throat.

The three of us creep down a dingy hallway, searching for the origin of the terrified cries.

We pause outside a room with its door ajar. My heart pounds in my chest, every instinct screaming to rush in to protect and defend. I push on the door, just enough to peer through the narrow gap. Bile rises in my throat at what's within.

Kaufman stalks between rows of blank-eyed girls, holding a long whip in his hand. He's a predator among his prey. The women bear evidence of the abuse designed to break them; their clothes, torn and filthy, hang loosely from emaciated frames.

Faces smeared with grime, they bear masks of despair, but it's their eyes that haunt me most. Hollow, defeated, robbed of all humanity, their gazes are filled with unimaginable terror.

They cower at his approach, some trembling with fear, others frozen in a submission borne from endless terror. They kneel on the cold, hard floor. Knees bruised and bloody, hands clasped tightly in a futile attempt to ward off the blows that inevitably come.

A few of the women clutch at the remnants of dresses, garments once colorful and bright but now reduced to tatters. Their hair hangs limp and matted, tangled with sweat and pain. The air is thick with the stench of hopelessness, a tangible cloud that hangs heavy over the room.

Kaufman moves with the certainty of his power over these women, and his lips twist as he surveys his handiwork. Each step is a calculated assault, each word a weapon wielded with cruel precision. He pauses before a petite brunette, her eyes wide and filled with a terror that cuts me to the core.

"Pathetic," he sneers, his voice dripping with contempt. "You call yourself worthy? You are nothing. Less than nothing."

Her response is a feeble attempt to defend herself, but her plea for mercy only fuels his rage. With a swift, brutal movement, he backhands her to the floor. She crumples like a broken doll, her sobs echoing through the room.

My vision reddens, and rage builds within me, a fury that threatens to consume all reason. Every fiber of my being screams to intervene, to end this monstrous display. To act now, however, would be to risk everything.

The room falls into silence. The only sound is the ragged breathing of the women and the relentless ticking of a clock on the wall. Time seems to stand still as Kaufman continues his slow, methodical assault on their dignity, stripping them of their humanity, their very souls.

My eyes pan across the room, sweeping past the rows of terrified women, and then my blood runs cold.

Rebel.

She stands apart from the others, dressed impeccably in a red silk dress that clings to her curves and shimmers with a life of its own. Her hair is a cascade of fiery waves, her makeup flawless, her stance proud and defiant. Yet despite her outer composure, there's strain in her eyes, belying the effort it takes to keep her face a mask of indifference.

She's definitely a player in this twisted game, but not by choice.

Kaufman turns to address the room, his voice cold and unyielding. "Rebel offered you the chance to become Angels." He sneers, gesturing grandly toward her. "And yet, you refuse this gift. Your defiance will be the death of you. We offer that, too, just so you know. Your death bartered and sold. Is that what you want? To die before an audience?" He scans the terrified women. "Or will you become Angels? Docile, obedient slaves with the chance to live?"

His words are weapons cutting through the room, silencing any protest before it forms. The women's faces blanch, eyes widening with terror as the true weight of his threat sinks in.

"You see," Kaufman's voice drips with malice, "to be an Angel demands absolute obedience. Anything less, and you are useless to me. Useless to anyone. I can crush you as easily as I can elevate you. Remember that."

He pauses, letting his words sink in, and his gaze flicks to each woman. Then his sight settles on Rebel. A slow, wicked smile spreads across his face. "Isn't that right, my dear?"

Rebel's eyes meet his, and for a moment, something raw and primal flashes in her gaze, but then it's gone, replaced by a cool, calculated determination.

"Yes, sir." Her voice is rock steady, betraying none of the turmoil I know she must feel. I refuse to believe she does this by choice. Kaufman has some hold over her.

I watch from the shadows of the hall, my heart pounding in my chest. Beside me, Hank and Walt are as still as statues, their faces set in grim lines.

We're all aware of the danger we're in, of how easily we could be discovered, but I can't look away. The scene unfolding before me speaks to the twisted world we've stumbled into.

And Rebel's role within it.

As Kaufman speaks, his threats become more and more explicit.

It's all I can do not to burst in and end the vile spectacle, but that would doom the mission and forfeit countless more lives. With one last look at Rebel, her face a study of controlled grace, I pull myself away from the door, my mind racing ahead to our next move.

I turn my back on the victims inside. With Walt and Hank by my side, we continue the pretense of why we're here, stopping to check, log, and test every piece of electronic equipment we find. None of us say a word.

We're too choked up by what we've seen.

The scene inside that room is seared into my mind.

The sobs of the terrified women are a haunting refrain that propels me forward. Behind me, Hank and Walt are silent shadows, their faces pale, eyes wide with shock. We move as one, driven by a purpose greater than ourselves, but the horror of what we've witnessed lingers, a stain that can never be washed away.

TWENTY-EIGHT

Rebel

EXHAUSTION DRAGS AT MY LIMBS AS I MAKE MY WAY DOWN THE LONG hallway to my quarters after another grueling day playing the part of Kaufman's prized Angel. My cheeks hurt from all the demure smiles.

The door opens, and I step inside, barely making it two steps before collapsing back against the wall in sobs. These sessions with the new captives are draining in every way. The things Kaufman forces me to do…

I slide down the wall, curling into the fetal position and hiding my face as gut-wrenching sobs overcome me. I cry until I have no tears left.

I wish I could scrub the images from my mind—the blank terror in their eyes. The bruises blossoming on their pale skin with each blow. And my voice, cold and taunting, telling them this is their only path to survival.

It's the only way, I repeat to myself. If I can convince them to become Angels, Kaufman will protect them. I can teach them how to endure. They'll live as pampered pets rather than chattel sold to the highest bidder. It's the devil's logic, but the only way out I can ease their suffering.

Still, it shreds my soul to break them like this. I cling to the hope that in doing this, I'm giving them the tools to someday be free of their masters. The fighting techniques I teach under the guise of *"poise and grace."* The lock-picking skills hidden in lessons about manners and etiquette. It's all I can do to arm them for escape—one day.

I barely register the creak of the doorway over my cries. I bolt to my feet, thinking it's Kaufman, but it's Ethan instead.

And rage burns in his gaze.

"What are you doing here?" I press back against the wall. His unexpected presence sends adrenaline surging through my veins.

"I saw you today." Ethan closes the door behind him with an ominous click. "With them. With him." His voice is tight and controlled. His rage simmers beneath the surface.

My stomach drops. He must have witnessed the training session with the new captives. Bile rises in my throat at the thought of how it looked—me poised and beautiful amid their suffering, seemingly allied with their tormentor.

"You don't understand—" I begin weakly.

"You're right. I don't understand. Explain it to me." Ethan stalks toward me, eyes blazing. "Explain the exam room. The OR. Those goddamn collection trays." His voice rises with each question until he's nearly shouting.

I flinch, shrinking away from his fury. "I can't…"

"Dammit, Rebel!" He slams his fist against the wall in frustration. I flinch as he looms over me. Then he steps back, raking a hand through his hair. When he meets my gaze again, his eyes are pleading. "Whatever hold Kaufman has on you, I can help. Just let me in. Tell me why you're here."

"The truth is too dangerous." I look away, blinking back tears. I wish desperately I could confide in him, but to involve Ethan would make him complicit in my crimes.

"I can't." I infuse steel into my tone. "It's necessary. The only way—"

"Like hell." Ethan grabs my shoulders, voice breaking. "This goes way beyond trafficking. What you're doing—it's inhuman." His voice cracks on the last word.

My soul shrivels at his damming words. I squeeze my eyes shut, willing my composure to hold. "It's the only way."

Ethan makes a low sound of frustration. His fingertips dig into my arms, then slowly loosen. When I open my eyes again, he stares at me.

"Rebel, look at me." He tilts my chin up, forcing me to meet his piercing gaze. "This isn't you. Let me help before you're in too deep."

Being this close to him ignites a longing inside me, an ache to cling to him and leave this nightmare behind, but my mission comes first. Ethan can't know. Kaufman can't discover my true purpose. I'm all alone in this.

I shake my head mutely.

We argue in circles, Ethan begging me to let him help, to turn from this dark path. But I refuse, terrified of implicating him in my crimes. After a weighted moment, Ethan releases me with a ragged sigh. He turns toward the door, but hesitates, one hand on the knob.

My soul is already lost. Ethan's right. I'm a monster, just like Kaufman.

At last, he leaves, casting me one final anguished look. The chasm between us brings me to my knees, sobs wracking my frame. I don't know how long I cry on the floor, but a knock at the door stirs me from my bleak thoughts.

Has Ethan returned? Fresh tears spring to my eyes at the prospect. I need so badly to unburden myself to him, to feel his strong arms around me again.

But Ethan wouldn't knock.

A hulking guard enters when I take too long to respond. His smile is a lewd and heartless thing. He looks at my tear-streaked face and snarls, upper lip curling in disgust. "Time to get prettied up. Boss wants his favorite Angel to look nice and sweet."

Revulsion twists my gut, but I keep my face impassive as I dress and follow him down the hall. The farce continues, even as my spirit fractures.

Soon, I stand polished and perfected before Kaufman's scrutiny. The gleam in his eyes turns my blood to ice, but I incline my head submissively.

"You look exquisite as always," he purrs, trailing one finger down my bare arm. It takes all my willpower not to shudder at his touch. Tonight will push me to new depths, but I must play my part.

Kaufman takes my elbow, leading me to the grand dining room where his "client" awaits. I steel myself as we approach the doors, donning the mask of Kaufman's Angel once more. The horrors I've endured fade into the background, overshadowed by my single driving purpose: my vow to Violet. If I can dismantle this monstrous regime from within, while I fulfill her dying wish, then so be it.

Whatever Kaufman and his cronies do to me along the way doesn't matter, so long as my efforts bring Haven crashing down. If my soul is forfeited in the process, so be it. My life is already stained beyond redemption.

The double doors swing open, revealing the luxurious dining room where unspeakable deals are made. Candlelight glimmers off crystal glasses, silver cutlery, and the cold smile of Kaufman's guest. I bow my head demurely at the introduction.

Inside, I'm screaming.

Another night of degradation in exchange for the chance to strike a fatal blow against Haven. I cling to that thought as Kaufman presents me to his leering guest, Mr. Crawford.

Let the performance begin.

Squaring my shoulders, I turn to greet our *guest*, a coy smile arranged on my lips. Another layer of my innocence is lost tonight.

"Rebel is my finest Angel," Kaufman says, giving me an approving once-over. "Aren't you, my dear?"

"Yes, sir," I reply demurely, keeping my eyes downcast.

"She trained the latest group of recruits herself. They're coming along beautifully thanks to her guidance and firm hand." Kaufman chuckles while I fight to keep my smile intact.

"I must say, she looks too spirited to be so obedient," Crawford comments doubtfully.

"And there is where perfection lies," Kaufman preens. He

reaches over, grasping my hand. "The thrill lies in owning a willful yet obedient slave. Killing their spirit is easy. Any slob can do that. I offer something different. Something unique." Kaufman's eyes harden, and panic lances through me, but I speak up in a sweet, deferential tone.

"What Kaufman is trying to say is that it's my pleasure to serve his wishes, as your Angel will take pleasure in serving yours. This is what Haven offers to the discerning client. To you…"

Kaufman relaxes, patting my hand indulgently. "You see? Utterly devoted. My training methods are most effective."

"Indeed. I'm impressed." Crawford takes a sip of wine. "Tell me, my dear, what methods do you employ to tame such strong-willed fillies?"

I swallow hard but launch into the rehearsed speech, detailing our process of breaking and conditioning the women into obedient pets. Crawford listens avidly, hunger in his eyes.

Kaufman loves my performance, patting my hand with affection. "He has a certain woman in mind to train as his personal Angel."

"And you can ensure she'll be completely devoted to me?"

"Yes, sir." My reply is a dull and listless thing. "The training eliminates any sense of self. An Angel's sole purpose is serving her owner's needs."

Kaufman beams with pride as though I'm a prized horse performing tricks on command.

The darkness in this place runs deep, but I'll continue to choke down my revulsion to become what they want. If playing my part convinces these women to become Angels, it will have been worthwhile. It will have been worth it if I can plant the seeds that someday lead to Haven's destruction.

The night drags on in a blur of forced smiles and veiled humiliation. I feel Kaufman's eyes on me the entire time, glinting with sick satisfaction at his control over me.

After an eternity, I'm permitted to leave. In the hall, I once again pass Ethan speaking with the guards. These random encounters are too frequent as if he stalks me through the halls of Haven.

His eyes bore into mine at my approach, forcing me to confront the stranger I've become. My steps falter at the strained distance between us, but I continue on, hugging my arms around myself.

I duck my head and hurry, disgusted with myself.

Alone in my room, I scrub my skin raw, trying to remove the shame of this place. A sob hitches in my throat as I wrap my arms around myself. I want to claw my way out of this vile place.

The door to my room creaks as it opens. It's Ethan again. He steps inside, features etched with grim purpose. My shoulders slump, and I brace for another round of interrogation about my role here and Haven's depraved practices.

"Please," I beg, throat raw. "I can't…" Truthfully, I'm tired. I'm tired of pretending—of surviving—of lying.

A broken sound escapes me. Before I can stop myself, I lurch forward, clutching at his shirt as sobs wrack my frame. The emotions I've been choking down release in a flood of tears and gut-wrenching sobs. I cling to Ethan, tears spilling down my cheeks.

His arms wrap around me, surrounding me in his warmth and strength.

I wish I could confide in him.

One of his hands strokes my hair while the other rubs soothing circles on my back. I bury my face in his chest, breathing him in, letting the steady thump of his heart ground me. We stand entwined for long moments as my sobs gradually subside.

"I've got you," Ethan murmurs. "You're safe."

He's wrong, but I allow myself a moment to believe his quiet reassurances. It loosens the tight knot inside my chest. For now, his arms are refuge enough. I cry until no tears remain, soaking the front of his shirt. He continues holding me, cheek pressed to my hair, as my breathing gradually calms.

Exhausted, I sag against him, soaking up his strength. There are no simple fixes here, no easy choices, but letting him comfort me eases the bleakness inside, if only for a moment.

"You don't have to bear this alone," Ethan whispers. "I see good in you. Don't let this place extinguish your light." His voice is thick with emotion. "I can help you."

"I'm beyond redemption." I shake my head, too spent to argue anymore. Whatever comes next, just having him here gives me the courage to continue.

For now, this is enough.

As my sobs subside, he guides us gently to the edge of the bed. He sits, drawing me onto his lap, and wraps his arms around me. I nestle against his broad chest, eyes closed, focusing only on the comfort of his embrace. His hand smooths my hair back from my damp cheeks. I feel his lips press softly to my temple.

"I'm here," he murmurs. "I'm not going anywhere."

My eyes fill with fresh tears at his quiet promise. After everything I've done, all the secrets and lies between us, he still reaffirms his loyalty.

"Talk to me," Ethan implores, his voice achingly gentle. "Don't carry this alone."

"Just hold me." I burrow closer with a shattered sigh, soaking up his warmth. "Please, just hold me."

Ethan presses his cheek to my hair, pulling me tight against his chest. "Always," he vows.

We stay entwined as the minutes tick by in silence. The demons can't reach me in his arms. I know this is only temporary, but feeling his steadfast heartbeat renews my fraying strength.

Tomorrow, I'll don my cloak of lies, but tonight, I cling to Ethan. It's time to confess my sins and tell him the horrible truth. I push away from his embrace and meet his gaze, determined to get through what I must say.

He'll hate me.

He'll despise me.

He's likely to walk away from me.

I try to convince myself that the ends justify the means, but I know it's a filthy lie.

The truth is, I'm selfish.

I've hurt others.

And I'll continue to hurt them to achieve my goal.

"I'm looking for Violet." My voice rasps now that I'm sharing my terrible secret.

"Who's Violet?" His brows furrow.

"She's my sister. *Was* my sister." I watch him closely, gauging his reaction.

It takes a moment before understanding dawns in his eyes.

Taking his silence as encouragement, I continue, bracing for the moment when the love in his eyes turns to disgust.

"That story I told you about my abduction. It wasn't mine. It was hers. Violet was taken years ago. Almost ten years. She was bought and sold and forced to be a surrogate, but she escaped in the chaos following the birth." I have to look away. The pain is still too raw. "They caught her. Then, they killed her, but I never stopped searching.

"Searching?"

"Her child is out there, in the hands of madmen."

"Rebel…"

I place a hand on his chest. "Don't speak. Let me get this off my chest. My sister is gone. When she escaped, she called me, terrified and so alone. She told me what happened, but they found her before she could tell me *who* had her."

My hands fist as old anger surges through me. "I didn't know where to begin hunting for her, but I put my ear to the ground, looking for organizations that trafficked women."

Ethan absorbs this, though some confusion lingers on his face. "Is that how you wound up in Nicaragua?"

I grimace. The bitter taste of failure is still fresh.

"I was desperate, arrogant, and incredibly naïve back then. A lead pointed me to Nicaragua, to a man named Artemus Gonzales. I believed he was someone who might have information about Violet. I thought I could use him as an influential trafficker in my search."

I take a shaky breath. "I approached him with a proposal, a way I could make myself useful. I told him I could train and groom captive women to be more docile and compliant. Make them obedient companions instead of unwilling slaves."

Understanding dawns in Ethan's steady gaze. "You were trying to work your way into his inner circle."

"I thought if I could prove my worth and gain his trust, he would give me access to records that might hold clues about Violet. But..." She looks away, pained. "Artemus saw more value in selling my body than using my skills. Your team found me before... Suffice it to say Nicaragua didn't go as planned."

Shame twists my gut.

"I don't understand why you left us. You knew our capabilities." Ethan chooses his words carefully. "Why didn't you ask us for help?"

I close my eyes against the surge of emotion. "Because I didn't need that kind of rescue. I needed access to records over a decade old, a chance to follow the trail myself. If I involved the Guardians, you'd shut down Haven before I could get the answers I needed. After you rescued me, all those years of work gaining contacts and intel were lost. So I disappeared. I was determined to start over, work my way up again in a different network." Her jaw sets stubbornly. "That's how I ended up with Kaufman. Before Artemus Gonzales threw me in that cell, I was able to find out that while his group abducted Violet, he traded her to another organization."

"Why was that?"

"There's a network of *clearing houses*, for lack of a better name. These places talk to one another. They share unique finds and buyers who might be interested. I kept following the breadcrumbs until it led me to Haven." I search Ethan's face, willing him to comprehend. To stay by my side despite the blood on my hands.

It's cost me so much to come this far; still, the search drags on. Ethan reaches out to squeeze my hand, a silent comfort.

"Violet's gone," I whisper, tears slipping free. "But, she made me promise to save her baby. That's all that matters now. It's why I couldn't ask for help from the Guardians."

"We would've helped."

"I didn't need *that* kind of help." I close my eyes. "I've done horrible things in trying to find my niece or nephew. If I asked for your help, Guardian HRS would've mounted a rescue and taken down Haven before I had the chance to get in and find any record of my sister."

"Tell me about these clearing houses."

"It's founded on the premise that each operation has a unique offering of product and access to its unique pool of clients. It's not uncommon to exhaust your client base or to have a client interested in a particular acquisition and not be able to fulfill that client's needs. It's kind of like a matching service."

"You have to talk to our leadership about this. I don't think we've considered such a thing. If you want help finding your niece or nephew, you have it." He brushes a tear from my cheek. "But what you're doing here… It's wrong." He brushes my hair off my face. "I can't condone your methods. Forcing these women to embrace slavery? I can help you, but only if you stop what you're doing here."

I absorb this new knowledge, keeping my face carefully neutral.

"I swore to my sister I would find her child. There's information here that can help me. I'm not stopping, but there's more you should know…"

TWENTY-NINE

Ethan

_____

DAYS AFTER WITNESSING KAUFMAN'S DEPRAVITY IN THE BOWELS OF Haven, unease gnaws at me. We're running out of time before our cover is blown. I stand with my team in the control center with the tapping of keyboards filling the room as my team works.

Kaufman enters unexpectedly to check our progress. "Any issues to report?" he asks, scrutinizing our busy activity.

Stitch surreptitiously notifies Mitzy, who then launches a well-timed cyber-attack against Haven.

"Smooth sailing so far," I assure him. "My team has everything under control."

Kaufman nods, prowling behind Stitch and Jeb's chairs. "Let's hope so."

Suddenly, alarm klaxons blare, and red lights flash. Jeb's monitor shows a spike in activity.

"Here we go again." Stitch leans back and cracks her knuckles. She turns to Kaufman. "This is what a mess your security protocols are. You're being attacked daily. It's relentless."

"We've got incoming. DDoS attack attempting system overload." Jeb's fingers fly across the keyboard as he works to counteract the distributed denial-of-service attack overwhelming Haven's servers.

Stitch jumps in to assist, firewalls and safeguards popping up on her monitors.

I watch the inbound traffic spike on Stitch's screen as Mitzy's bot hammers Haven's systems.

"East wing servers are wavering," Stitch reports. "Rerouting traffic to shore them up."

"Initiating lockdown protocols." Jeb is right on her heels.

Kaufman's eyes narrow, watching intently as Jeb and Stitch work to counter the cyber assault.

The room becomes a hive of activity as Stitch and Jeb contain the attack. No words are wasted; they know the drill and perform flawlessly beneath Kaufman's critical eye.

Finally, the attack slows to a trickle and then stops entirely. The oppressive tension in the room eases as we verify all systems are secure once more.

"Nice work." Our presence here hinges on these demonstrations of our usefulness. As long as Mitzy keeps the attacks coming, our sham can continue. "Let's tighten up those firewalls," I direct my team.

Mouths set in determined lines, Stitch and Jeb turn back to their keyboards.

The alarms go silent. Kaufman turns to me with an appraising look. "Well done."

"We're nowhere near done." Stitch spins to face Kaufman. "Dealing with an attack isn't what you want. We're here to prevent them from ever reaching your system, and your system is so messed up we're relegated to going to the base code and fixing it line by line. It's going to take time."

Once again, Kaufman completely ignores Stitch. He clasps my shoulder firmly. "It seems I was wise to enlist your team's services."

After Kaufman departs, I exchange subtle nods with my team. Mitzy's test went perfectly. She keeps our charade alive while we chip away at Kaufman's inner sanctum.

I leave my teammates to their jobs and wander Haven's halls. Memories of the horrors we unearthed play before my eyes like a grotesque slideshow in my mind. The holding cells, the chains on the walls, the empty sterile basins, and the operating room. Images of the women, their hollow eyes, and how they cowered and knelt before Kaufman.

Sometimes, this job feels never-ending. We take down one monster, and ten more pop up in its place. It's hard not to feel our purpose is futile on days like today.

Shouting erupts from behind a closed door. There's the unmistakable sound of an open-handed slap. Red creeps into my vision, hands reflexively clenching, nails digging into my palms because I know the owner of that voice.

Kaufman's tirade continues, vitriolic and crude, his voice a whip that lashes and scars. Then comes a thud and a pained cry in another voice I know too well—Rebel.

In an instant, every protective instinct within me roars to life, a primal urge that drowns out all reason. I have to stop myself from kicking down the door and tearing the monster limb from limb, but Rebel would never forgive me for exposing us both.

I find myself frozen outside the door, every muscle tensed, ears straining to catch every word of Kaufman's tirade. His voice is a poisoned dagger, laced with fury and contempt, slashing through the air ruthlessly.

"What is this pathetic display?" he screams, his voice cracking with rage. "These new Angels are useless, utterly worthless. They're weak, pitiful, and defiant. You promised they'd be ready, and this is what you bring me?"

I can almost see him now, eyes blazing, face contorted with anger, standing over Rebel, a predator ready to strike. The thought of him hurting her, of his hands on her, twists my gut, but I force myself to remain still, to listen.

Rebel's voice is softer and measured, starkly contrasting Kaufman's fury. I can sense the fear in her voice and the effort it takes for her to maintain her composure.

"I'm doing everything I can." Her voice trembles ever so slightly. "They need more time. They're still adapting and learning. Please, give me a chance to—"

"No more chances!" Kaufman roars, cutting her off. "I have

clients stacking up, eager to taste this new offering, and you're failing me. Failing me at every turn."

There's a pause, the silence heavy. Suffocating. I can almost feel Rebel's desperation and struggle to find the words to appease the monster before her.

"I'll fix it," she finally whispers, her voice full of resolve yet laced with vulnerability. "I'll make them ready. Just give me a little more time, please."

Time. The word echoes in my mind, a cruel reminder of our own desperate race against the clock. Time is running out for all of us, and every second counts.

Kaufman's response is a low growl, a threat veiled in a promise. "You have one week. One week to make them into Angels or face the consequences."

"That's not enough—"

"One week." His words are final.

My heart pounds in my chest as Kaufman's heavy step nears the door.

In a flash, I'm around the corner, hidden in a shadowy recess, my back pressed against the cold wall. I hold my breath, listening as the door creaks open, followed by the muted rustle of Kaufman's expensive suit as he exits the room.

His anger is a wild thing, a force that leaves destruction in its wake. I peek around the corner, watching as he retreats down the hall, his fury a palpable force that seems to echo off the walls.

When he's out of sight, I move.

I cross the cold, dimly lit room, the air heavy with the lingering scent of terror and violence. Rebel's back is to me, her shoulders slumped, her dress torn, her very being radiating defeat. The weight of what she's been forced to do, the guilt and shame, clings to her like a shadow.

Quietly, I come up behind her, my heart pounding, my throat tight with emotion.

I wrap my arms around her, feeling her body tense before a shudder runs through her. She knows it's me. Of course, she knows.

Our connection runs too deep and strong for her not to recognize my touch.

"I'm here," I whisper into her ear, my voice cracking with emotion.

She whirls around, her face pale, eyes haunted, lips trembling. No words are needed. We've shared too much pain for words.

Her arms go around me, holding tight as if I might disappear, then she breaks down, sobs wracking her body. "I'm sorry. I'm so sorry. What I've done—it's unforgivable… Reprehensible… I can't bear it."

I hold her, rocking her gently. While I remain steadfast in not condoning what she's doing here, I take some comfort that she's not here by her own choosing. She opened up and told me the truth, but demons still drive her. She won't leave until she's found what she needs.

"I've become something I despise." Her eyes search mine, desperate for reassurance, desperate for forgiveness. I see the battle within her, the self-loathing warring with the need to believe in herself again.

I lift her chin to look into her eyes. "I may not agree with what you've done or understand why you're here, but I love you, and nothing changes that."

"How can you love me after what I've done?"

"Because I believe in us." I wipe away her tears. "You're a victim, not a villain, and when you're ready to let me in, I'll stand beside you."

She clings to me, her body wracked with sobs, her soul bared, and I realize that this moment, this raw and vulnerable connection, is the truest expression of our love. It's messy and painful, filled with doubts and fears, but it's real.

Slowly, her sobs subside, and she looks up at me, her eyes filled with a fragile hope, a tentative trust. I kiss her forehead, promising her that I'll never let her down and that we'll face this together.

Whatever *this* is.

Because that's what love is. It's messy and raw. Beautiful and fierce. It's as much joy and passion as it is pain and struggle. The good with the bad. It's standing together, even when the world is falling apart around you.

The room seems to contract around us, the walls bearing witness to our shared pain and connection. We stand there, locked in an embrace that's about much more than physical touch. It's a lifeline, a promise, a bond that transcends all the horror surrounding us.

Finally, after what feels like an eternity, Rebel's breathing steadies, and she steps back, wiping her eyes. The vulnerability is still there, but so is a spark of determination, a flicker of the fire that I know burns within her.

I watch her carefully, sensing the darkness she's not yet ready to share, but I have to ask, even if it means unearthing more pain.

"When we talked, you told me why you're here. You mentioned there was something else. Does Kaufman have some hold over you?" I ask softly, my eyes locked on hers.

She looks away, her face tightening, and I see her battling with herself, torn between wanting to tell me and fearing what the truth might do to us.

"It's complicated," she finally whispers, her voice trembling.

"Trust me." A simple request, but one that carries so much weight. I want to trust her, but doubt gnaws at me, the fear that something she's hiding could ruin us. "I need to understand."

She shakes her head, tears welling in her eyes again. "It's not about me. It's bigger than that. There are lives at stake, secrets I can't share."

"You can share them with me." I pull her close again, feeling the desperation in her voice, knowing that whatever she's hiding, it's tearing her apart.

She buries her face in my neck, her body shaking. "I wish I could tell you everything, but I can't. Not now. He's always watching." The sorrow in her voice chills me to the bone.

I hold her tight, fear settling in my stomach, a premonition that whatever she's hiding will change everything, but I push it aside, focusing on the here and now, on the woman I love and the battle we're fighting.

"You're not alone anymore. I'm here. Let me in. Let me help you."

Deep within me, I rejoice. I rejoice because the real Rebel is still there. The woman I fell in love with, the fighter, the survivor, she's still here, beneath the layers of pain and fear. I feel her, and that gives me hope.

My gut twists imagining what she must have endured alone all those months. If only she had trusted me.

But the past can't be changed.

Rebel searches my face anxiously. "At Haven..." her voice breaks, "training those girls, I know it seems horrible, but I'm teaching them skills. Ways to escape if the chance ever comes."

My eyes widen as understanding hits me. "In marketing them as willing and obedient, the men who buy them are lulled into a false sense of security. The guard they place on their *acquisition* is less than it would be otherwise."

"Precisely." She nods, fresh tears welling up. "I know you don't condone it, but I'm trying to give them hope. It may take months, or a year, before the opportunity to escape occurs, but it's better than the alternative." Her voice trembles with emotion. "I should have come to you. I'm sorry I didn't. I was desperate and traumatized after what happened in Nicaragua, and the last thing I expected was to fall for you in ways I didn't understand. It terrified me."

"Why?"

"Because I wanted to stay with you. Be with you. Choose you. But I couldn't abandon my sister's dying wish. I have to find her child and save it. I couldn't let anything get in my way. I had to leave. I regret leaving the way I did, but how could I explain what I was planning to the man who rescued me from captivity? That I was willing to do horrible things to women I didn't know to save a child I may never find?"

I gather her into my arms, holding her close as she cries. "Shh. It's okay now. We're together." I stroke her hair, forgiving her completely.

She clings to me. At last, all the missing pieces fall into place between us. No more secrets remain. I don't agree with what she did. That's her cross to bear, but I love her enough to forgive her actions and move forward from here.

I search her eyes and see a plea for understanding and forgiveness. Perhaps that should be enough. For now, it has to be.

"I forgive you." My voice is steady and firm, my conviction unwavering. "And I love you."

But I won't allow her to use these women.

That's my line in the sand.

THIRTY

Ethan
———

Rebel's eyes well with tears as she clings to me, her body trembling. I cradle her head against my chest, my cheek pressed to her hair.

Eventually, her shaking subsides. She pulls back just enough to meet my gaze, her eyes two shimmering pools of anguish. I smooth back her hair, letting my fingers linger, tracing the delicate lines of her face like a blind man seeing the sun again.

Her lips part as if to speak, but no words form. Instead, she turns into my palm, pressing a feather-light kiss there. My breath catches at the contact.

Slowly, almost tentatively, she reaches up to caress my cheek. I close my eyes, covering her hand with mine, letting her relearn the shape of my face. Her touch travels downward, grazing my jaw, tentative brushes mapping the contours of my lips.

When I open my eyes again, her face is just inches away, eyes searching mine. I see the question there, the silent request hovering between us.

In answer, I lean in. Our lips meet, the contact ghostly at first—more breath than touch. Then I capture her mouth. The tentative kiss shifts into something deeper, fueled by months of pent-up longing. I kiss her with abandon, leaving no doubt that she still holds my shattered heart.

Before she can pull away, I cup her face in my hands, holding her there. Our foreheads touch as we share a shuddering breath.

I capture her lips again, unable to resist. The spark ignites into an inferno. I kiss her deeply, urgently, blazing a trail to her soul. She responds in kind, mouth opening eagerly to mine.

Our kiss turns hungry, almost bruising in intensity. It's a kiss that erases months of separation, a desire denied too long. Her fingers twist in my shirt, mine tangle in her hair. We're lost in relearning each other.

We kiss until we're forced to break for air.

Rebel clings to me, fresh tears spilling over. "I never stopped loving you," she confesses in a broken whisper. "Not for one second."

Those words heal a wound inside me I thought would never go away. Her mouth opens, and I taste her, the unique flavor that's all her own, a blend of sweetness and strength I've missed more than words can express. I pull her closer, my hands sliding down her back, feeling the curve of her body against mine.

We lose ourselves in each other, the kiss deepening, becoming a dance of desire and devotion. The beating of her heart flutters against my chest, the rapid rhythm matching my own, two hearts in perfect sync.

The taste of her lips, the smell of her hair, the sound of her soft moans as she clings to me—they're all a symphony of sensation that fills me with a raw, visceral emotion that's almost overwhelming.

This is love in its purest form, without reservation or condition, and it burns with a fire that will never be extinguished. I hate that I doubted her. That I lost faith. I still don't condone what she's done, but I understand.

Her hands move to my face, her fingers tracing the lines and contours, reacquainting herself with the man she loves. And I do the same. My hands explore her, relearning her, rediscovering the woman who has always been my other half.

Our eyes lock, understanding passing between us without the need for words.

I break the kiss, holding her face in my hands, looking into her eyes, knowing that I have to be strong for both of us.

"I have work to do." My voice remains gentle but firm.

"And what is that?"

Desire rises within me to answer her, but caution remains. She used me once. Whatever her motives, I won't let it happen again.

"Do you trust me?"

"I do." She nods, her eyes filled with a determination that matches my own.

We step away from each other, a silent pact sealed.

The door closes behind me with a soft click, and I'm back in Haven's cold, sterile world. Only this time, I carry her warmth, her strength, and her love with me.

I make my way down the twisting hallways of Haven, the kiss still lingering on my lips, Rebel's warmth still wrapped around me, but I push those emotions aside. This mission is far from over, and time is running out.

My footsteps lead me to the control room, where my team is entrenched, eyes glued to monitors, earphones in place. The air hangs thick with tension, the silence broken only by the occasional murmur of voices and the clacking of keys. We are all aware of the stakes, the eyes of Kaufman ever-watchful, ever-judging.

"Updates." My voice cuts through the silence. I need to focus, to be present, but my mind is elsewhere, a part of me still in that room with Rebel.

Hank answers, his face drawn but determined. "We've created enough noise and false leads. They think we're chasing a mole, just as planned."

I absorb the information. "Jeb, status on Mitzy's code?"

"Inserted and dormant," Jeb responds. "No signs of detection. Once activated, it should cripple Haven's security systems."

"Good. And escape routes?" I turn to Blake.

"Taken care of. Guards' rotation schedules are mapped. Escape routes identified. We'll be ghosts." A hint of mischief flashes in his eyes.

"Cyber security?" I look to Stitch.

"Firewalls are down. Haven's mainframe is under control." A spark of excitement flashes in her eyes.

Walt chimes in, "Secondary systems are also in our hands."

"Gabe, anything to add?"

"All quiet on the western front," Gabe replies, his expression serious. "We're ready."

I can't help my thoughts from drifting back to Rebel and the pain she carries. I'm about ready to share with my team when the door to the control room bursts open. Kaufman strides in, his presence like a dark storm cloud, his eyes sharp, his voice cutting through the room like a knife. His gaze locks onto mine with challenge and threats. He knows something. Senses something.

But he's not sure what it is.

"I'm getting pressure from my clients. How soon until your team is done?"

I hold his gaze, refusing to back down. "If this were easy, you wouldn't have hired us, but if you want…" I gesture toward Stitch, knowing Kaufman will snub her. "Love, show him what we've found so far."

"Sure, boss." She opens several screens. "It's tech-heavy, but I'm sure I can break it down so he can understand." Without waiting for his response, she launches into a rapid-fire, tech-heavy explanation of various encryption algorithms and computer coding that makes my head hurt.

Before she gets too far, Kaufman raises a dismissive hand. "Don't bother me with the details. I want to know whether I proceed with the auction as planned or push it back?"

We're running on borrowed time, and Kaufman's demands are only escalating. I wish we had more time, but we'll make do with the time we have.

"We'll be done in a week at most." I glance at Stitch and wait for her to confirm.

Ignoring Stitch completely, Kaufman studies me for a long time before turning to leave. The door slams shut, and we're left in silence, the tension lingering, the threat hanging heavy in the air.

"What the hell was all that about?" Stitch props her hands on her hips, her eyes narrowing as she studies me, expecting an answer.

"With Kaufman?" I respond, casually leaning against the wall, trying to shake the tension that still lingers in the room. "Thought it was pretty obvious. He wants results."

"I know that, but what was all that?"

"All, what?"

"That macho pissing contest?" She's not good at hiding her irritation.

"It's a guy thing." I shrug, dismissing her question as trivial. I sigh, pushing away from the wall.

"A guy thing? Seriously? That's your explanation?" Her voice rises, and it's clear she's not going to let this go.

"When two men have a disagreement, they don't exactly sit down with tea and crumpets to discuss their feelings."

"Are you saying women do?" Her eyes narrow further.

I shrug, playing it cool. "I'm not saying anything about women. I'm explaining how men communicate. Sometimes, words are unnecessary. A glance, a gesture, a posture—it all conveys meaning. Men understand each other that way. It's primal, instinctual." I keep my tone patronizing, knowing it will get under her skin.

"Primal, huh? Like cavemen grunting at each other?" Stitch crosses her arms, clearly unimpressed.

"Exactly," I exclaim, feeling like I'm making progress. "Like cavemen. It's a way to establish dominance, to feel each other out without having to say a word."

"Oh, please." She rolls her eyes. "That's the biggest load of crap I've ever heard. You're telling me that grown men can't have a civil conversation without resorting to caveman tactics?"

"It's not that simple."

She's not buying it.

"And did you establish dominance with Kaufman?" Stitch's lips twitch, fighting a smile.

"Of course." I puff out my chest, then laugh at her irritation.

"Okay, maybe not dominance, but I let him know I'm not backing down. That's important. That's how men negotiate."

She shakes her head, amusement dancing in her eyes. "You men and your games. You do realize it's all a little ridiculous, right?"

"Maybe to you." I give her a wink. "But it works for us."

Stitch rolls her eyes, but I see the hint of a smile tugging at the corner of her mouth. "Whatever you say, Charlie-One."

"It's the truth."

"Men." She snorts, shaking her head, her eyes gleaming with something that looks suspiciously like amusement. "Always trying to out-macho each other. Puffing chests, flashing glares. You might as well whip out a ruler and measure."

"I'd win," I counter, grinning, knowing full well the direction she's taking the conversation. I laugh, feeling the tension lift. "Trust me, it's all under control."

"Is it?" Her eyes meet mine, a knowing glint in them. "Is it really *all under control*, Charlie-One?" She rolls her eyes, crossing her arms. "All that macho bullshit isn't about dominance. The two of you are fighting over a woman."

"What?" I feign innocence, though I feel a small knot of apprehension in my stomach.

"Don't play dumb with me." Her gaze narrows, probing, searching.

"That's not what that was about."

"You saw her again, didn't you?" She jabs a finger at me.

"I can't avoid a chance encounter."

"You kissed her, didn't you?"

"Did not."

Stitch laughs, then points at me. "Dude, you totally kissed her."

"I don't know what you're talking about," I say, but my voice lacks conviction.

"You're a lousy liar, Ethan Blackwood. We all know what's at stake here, and you're out there playing kissing games and pissing off Kaufman."

"I'm not compromising the mission," I snap back, feeling a

sudden surge of anger. "And he has no idea Rebel and I know each other."

"Could've fooled me." She meets my glare with one of her own. "Don't think I didn't see how distracted you were earlier? And Kaufman? He may not know why he hates you, but his inner caveman senses something."

I look at her, and I see the worry in her eyes. She's not attacking me; she's afraid. Afraid for me, for all of us.

"I've got it handled." I meet her gaze. "Trust me."

She looks at me for a long moment, then nods, a reluctant acceptance in her eyes. "I do. But be careful. Please."

I nod, understanding the unspoken warning, feeling the weight of her trust and the responsibility it carries.

"I will. I promise."

And I mean it.

THIRTY-ONE

Rebel

THE WALLS SEEM TO CREEP CLOSER WITH EACH PASSING DAY, THE twisting corridors of Haven becoming more claustrophobic than ever before. I wander aimlessly, my mind churning, my heart heavy with regret and doubt about what I'm doing and why.

Ethan's kiss still lingers on my lips. His touch still tingles on my skin. The comfort it brought, however, was fleeting. Now, only emptiness and questions claw at me from the inside.

What have I become? Do the ends justify my means? Am I a monster?

I pause outside the Angels' training room, peering through the small window at the blank faces of the recruits—the latest group of kidnapped girls I'm meant to twist into Angels. Their wills are still strong. Their eyes still hold defiance. They've yet to accept their fate, and I haven't had time to motivate them properly. To train them to bide their time and escape only when they're absolutely certain they'll get away.

They're far from ready.

Kaufman demands they be auction-ready within a week. An impossible task. He'll hurt them for my failure. Then he'll kill them;

it won't be an easy or quick death either. It'll be a lesson for those who remain.

And me.

He'll make a spectacle of it, auctioning off the rights in a macabre twist. This is what I need these girls to understand.

There are only two paths out of this place. The first comes at the end of a leash, shackled to a man willing to pay for an obedient and pliable female. The other is to be disposed of in a mass, unmarked grave.

My hand goes to my bruised cheek, the swollen flesh a visible reminder of Kaufman's rage. His visits have become more frequent, his moods darker, and his words crueler. I bear the brunt of his displeasure because I embody his precious Angels.

I'm the first Angel.

It was my idea, a desperate gamble that hasn't failed me yet.

His control is slipping. I sense his growing madness and the instability that simmers beneath the surface. He is a predator who enjoys the hunt, and the game grows boring when the prey is cowed.

That's me. I'm the prey, and he tamed me.

Or rather, I tamed myself.

Because I'm desperate.

So now, he inflicts pain to provoke a response. To feel alive. To feel strong.

Somehow, men think hitting a woman makes them more of a man. There's no reasoning with men who believe that. It's baked into their psyche and what makes them who they are.

But I dare not show weakness. That only fans his cruelty into an inferno.

I force strength into my voice when I want to weep and meet his gaze with defiance when I want to crumble. I maintain the facade for both our sakes—his and mine.

But it's a taxing performance behind which the real me withers more each day. I'm a ghost of my former self, full of self-loathing for what I've done.

I lean my head against the cool glass, releasing a slow breath.

On the other side, a petite brunette meets my gaze, her eyes wide and frightened. Her face is a mass of bruising and swollen flesh.

Iris.

The girl whose library privileges were *revoked* for speaking with Ethan.

She should hate me for that, for enforcing Kaufman's cruel dictates. Instead, her eyes shine with a tentative trust. I've truly broken the poor creature. She trusts me because I'm the only one who's shown her any scrap of kindness in this hell.

It's more than I deserve.

I turn from the window and head into the training room, bracing myself for another brutal session. The recruits are lined up already, their bruises visible beneath their thin shirts and dresses. Their wide, frightened eyes follow my every movement.

I pause before a shaking blonde girl. Her lip is freshly split. She can't seem to stop tugging on a lock of stringy hair.

"What's your name?" I ask gently.

She blinks rapidly. "Leah."

"That's a lovely name." I tilt her chin up. "You have such potential, Leah. You all do. Becoming an Angel is your only chance to avoid an even worse fate."

I move down the line, meeting each girl's gaze. "I know it seems bleak now, but you've endured the worst of it already. The horrors below are behind you." I sweep my arm toward the floor. "Never again will you be caged, beaten, or sold off to awful men."

That last part isn't true. They will be sold, but only to one man. Not several. And *not* to those who broker in torture for the sake of gratuitous pleasure. That's what I'm saving these women from.

A few girls shudder, eyes growing misty. I continue, voice low and urgent. "You have a real opportunity here. Take hold of it. Dedicate yourself to becoming an Angel, and you'll want for nothing. Fine clothes, gourmet meals, your every whim catered to."

I stop before Iris, offering an encouraging smile. "It won't be easy. You'll have to work hard and be obedient. But you can do this. I believe in each of you."

Iris nods, eyes glinting with that burgeoning trust I don't deserve.

It buoys me, bolstering my fading spirit. Then the guilt crashes into me, sucking the breath from my lungs.

I resume pacing before them. "You know what will happen if you don't succeed, don't you?" I let coldness creep into my tone. "Kaufman's patience is at an end. If you can't become Angels…"

I trail off meaningfully. Some girls turn pale, fresh tears spilling down their cheeks. Others set their jaws, defiance in their eyes. Those are the ones most at risk. That defiance is a walking death sentence. I need to convince them this is the only way.

I feel a pang at having to be so harsh, but it's the only way to reach them.

I go to Iris again, tilting her chin up. "You don't want to end up back in those cells, do you?" I murmur so everyone can hear but let it seem like I speak directly to Iris. "You're better than that. Smarter. Don't let fear hold you back."

I release her and step away. "No more coddling now. The real training begins." I clap my hands sharply, making them jump. "Line up! We have a lot of work to do."

The Angels scramble to obey as I force authority into my demeanor. The persona of trainer comes more naturally each time I wear it. Beneath the facade, I cling to the truth—I'm still helping them in the only way left.

By making them Angels, I save them from fates far darker.

Training lasts several hours, and by the end, I'm as wrung out as the women I prepare to survive what's coming.

With a final glance at the broken souls I'm molding into Angels, I continue down the hallway. There's somewhere I need to be and only a sliver of time to get there and back before I'm missed.

The air grows colder as I descend into the lower levels of Haven, the lighting dim and ominous. Down here are the true horrors, rooms that froze my blood when I was first granted limited access.

The holding cells. The showers. The operating room. The bins…

I suppress a shudder, moving quietly. There's one final place down here I have yet to explore. The records room beside the OR has been locked to me. Hopefully, this room holds details about my sister.

The sister whose ghost drives my every action.

I pause outside the locked door, its dark wood faded but still imposing. My pulse thrums as I retrieve the ring of stolen keys from my pocket—keys lifted from a careless guard whose eyes lingered too long on my body. Men are easily fooled when they think with the wrong head.

The key slips soundlessly into the lock, and breath hisses between my teeth as the tumblers align. The knob turns under my hand, and I'm inside, pushing the door closed behind me.

THIRTY-TWO

Rebel

My heart skips a beat. No one has entered this room in ages. Thick layers of dust coat the rows of metal filing cabinets lining the walls. The air is heavy with the musty scent of old paper soaked into the walls.

Kaufman puts nothing in electronic form if he can avoid it. Paper can't be traced. It exists in this room, and only in this room, with no copies ever made. I've learned that much when asking about the procedures the Angels will endure after they've been sold.

I suppress a shudder, squaring my shoulders. No time for hesitation.

Methodically, I begin working through the files, scanning the names and dates. Most of the records are appallingly detailed—photos, medical charts, and client forms. All chronicling the misery inflicted within Haven's walls. All documenting the monsters who keep this place churning.

All documenting *who* each woman was sold to. That's what I need. Who bought my sister? I'll figure out the rest after that.

My eyes blur, bile rising in my throat as the minutes stretch by. So many broken souls are reduced to data and photographs. But there are too many files. Rows of filing cabinets stretch before me, hundreds upon hundreds of medical records.

How am I going to find Violet's record in all of this? It's like searching for a needle in a haystack; I only have seven minutes.

Seven minutes before I need to head back.

My mind begins calculations, and I stop that before it gets too far. It's too much. Too hard. Impossible even.

But I'll take seven minutes over never having this chance.

The sound of approaching voices slices through my churning emotions.

No, not yet!

No time to hide before the heavy tread of boots stops outside the door.

I cross the small room in a flash, flicking off the light and pressing into the corner, praying the darkness hides me. Not a breath stirs the air as the knob turns, and three hulking guards step inside, sweeping flashlight beams over the dusty cabinets.

"Thought I heard something," one of the men mutters, his pockmarked face creased in suspicion as he peers into the gloom.

I sink deeper into the darkness, my pounding heart surely loud enough to give me away. The guards merely grunt, make a cursory sweep, and then leave, securing the door behind them.

I dare to exhale only after their footsteps fade, gulping air into my starved lungs. That was too close. I won't get lucky again.

Still reeling from my discovery, I make my way back through the bowels of Haven, mind churning over how to find one record out of hundreds.

I wish I could tell Ethan. I long to rush to him, to unburden myself of the dangerous knowledge now burning a hole inside me, but I can't be so selfish. His mission must come first. If my Angels have any hope of rescue, it'll be because of him and his team. I trust him implicitly, but involving him now in my search could distract him from why he's here.

By the time I reach the upper levels, I'm composed and don the mask of a cold-blooded trainer once more. Straightening my shoulders, I push open the training room door, readying myself for another brutal session of crushing souls.

But the room is empty, the Angels nowhere to be seen. Before panic can set in, the door opens again behind me.

"Looking for something, my dear?"

Kaufman.

I turn slowly, pulse raging. He stands far too close, crowding me with his imposing bulk, a cruel smile twisting his lips.

"I sent the Angels back to their cells to—reflect on their choices." He closes in, eyes burning with malevolence. "Their progress remains unacceptable. Where were you? I would've expected you to double down on their training." He reaches out, deceptively gentle, and grasps my chin between his thumb and forefinger. "I warned you there would be consequences for failure."

I jerk my head back, anger overriding fear. "You've given me an impossible task. It's not enough time to undo the trauma they've endured. I've barely been able to get half of them to trust me. I need more time." I stand boldly in place, refusing to cower and show weakness.

The sharp crack of his palm against my cheek whips my head to the side. I gasp at the explosive pain and stagger back.

"You dare take that tone with me?" Kaufman roars, bearing down on me. I retreat until my back hits the wall, nowhere left to go as his bulk traps me in place. His hand clasps my throat, squeezing just shy of cutting off my breath completely.

"Please..." I choke out, clawing at his iron grip. His eyes are wild, pupils dilated with rage. He's lost all control, driven by impulse and whatever sick hunger drives him.

The pressure increases, and dark spots swim across my vision. This is it. He's finally going to kill me.

Just then, the door bursts open, and Ethan strolls in, flanked by Hank and Gabe. Kaufman's grip on my throat loosens in surprise.

"Oh, sorry to interrupt," Ethan says casually as if he doesn't notice Kaufman assaulting me. "We're just checking security systems in this sector."

Ethan's gaze sweeps to me for a brief moment before he turns away, feigning disinterest, but I see the fury burning beneath his calm facade.

Kaufman roughly releases me. I slide down the wall, gasping for breath as oxygen floods my starved lungs. My fingers probe the tender flesh of my throat, surely already darkening with bruises from Kaufman's vice-like grip.

"We can come back later if this is a bad time," Ethan says mildly, not a trace of confrontation in his easy tone. His face is placid, almost bored, as his eyes sweep the room.

Kaufman bristles at Ethan's flippant suggestion, straightening his suit jacket and smoothing back his hair. "No need. I was having a—disciplinary meeting with my trainer." His dark gaze cuts to me, naked warning in his eyes. "Isn't that right, Rebel?"

I give the barest hint of a nod, not trusting my voice. Speaking now, with my throat raw and lungs still heaving for air, might provoke more of Kaufman's volatile temper.

As I avoid his piercing stare, my eyes drift over Ethan, Hank, and Gabe. They stand in casual formation. Shoulders relaxed. Mouths neutral. Masculine tension hums just below the surface. They're coiled springs, ready to unleash calculated aggression at the slightest provocation.

Ethan meets my gaze, and though his face remains impassive, a blaze of fury burns in his eyes. It lasts only a heartbeat before he notices the marks on my throat and the handprint on my cheek. His jaw clenches almost imperceptibly as he buries his rage.

Kaufman turns his attention back to Ethan. "Carry on with your security checks." His voice snaps with a warning.

He moves past Ethan and his men, attempting to intimidate them with his size. Ethan deftly sidesteps into his path, casual but deliberate. Kaufman pulls up short, brows lowering at this obstacle in his way.

"Of course," Ethan replies easily, infuriatingly polite. "But since we're here, maybe you could clarify some questions I had about the restricted areas…"

He continues talking about security protocols, his tone light, as if unaware he's infuriated Kaufman twice over already. I marvel at his composure. If I didn't know him, I'd think this meeting was of little consequence to him.

But I do know Ethan, know the iron willpower he possesses beneath that relaxed facade. I recognize the subtle signs of his restraint as he engages Kaufman—the barest tightening along his jawline, the way he allows no hint of confrontation to enter his voice or eyes.

This mastery of self-control is an amazing weapon in Ethan's arsenal, and right now, it's the only one he can safely deploy.

Kaufman's massive shoulders bunch, cornered-animal tension radiating off him in waves. His hands open and close at his sides, but Ethan remains maddeningly polite. After a silent battle of wills, Kaufman responds gruffly, "Fine. Walk with me."

He turns on his heel, expecting Ethan to step behind him in a show of submission, but Ethan glides smoothly to Kaufman's side, an equal keeping pace with an equal.

If this insolence bothers Kaufman, he gives no outward reaction as they exit the room, already conversing about off-limit sectors and camera blind spots.

Hank pauses in the doorway, meeting my eyes just long enough to give an almost imperceptible nod. It lasts only a second but carries a wealth of meaning. They have my back, and I'm not alone, even if it feels that way.

His eyes reflect understanding and kindness. Empathy even, although I don't deserve any of it. He nods subtly, as if saying he understands, and then follows after the others.

The door eases shut, leaving me alone in the room that seems to press in from all sides. I draw a shaky breath, rolling my tender shoulders, regaining my equilibrium after the shock of Ethan's timely intervention and the pain throbbing in my cheek and neck.

However calmly Ethan concealed it, seeing Kaufman's hands on me triggered animalistic rage. I pray he restrains the impulse to tear Kaufman apart long enough to complete his mission.

Then fear grabs a hold of me. When his mission is complete, I'll be left alone with Kaufman. This is no surprise. I knew the risks and accepted them when I began my search for Violet. It's too late to back out now. Not when I finally located the records room.

The thought of finding my sister's killer fortifies me as I draw myself up, steadying my shaking limbs. Squaring my shoulders, I take five deep breaths and squash my fear.

No matter Kaufman's violence, I will survive.

THIRTY-THREE

Ethan

Kaufman stalks ahead of me down the hallway, radiating irritation. His broad shoulders are tense, hands clenching and unclenching at his sides. Our conversation about security protocols is an unwelcome distraction to whatever is on his mind.

At least his hands aren't wrapped around Rebel's throat any longer.

I keep pace beside him, my tone polite but persisting with questions, subtly needling him for reactions. After seeing his hands around Rebel's throat, it's all I can do to maintain this civil facade. The urge to slam Kaufman's head into the unforgiving wall simmers below my calm exterior.

"So, the lower levels? Are they restricted for all staff?" I continue conversationally. "Is your trainer barred from certain sectors?"

"That's what restricted means." Kaufman cuts me a sharp look. "The product housed below requires careful handling and privacy."

Product.

The word curdles my gut, but I keep my voice level.

"Of course, I'm just clarifying because it appears there are still areas restricted for my staff. I thought we were in agreement my team needs full access?" I scratch my jaw, feigning contemplation. "Without knowing the full layout of your facility, ensuring a comprehensive security sweep down there is impossible."

Kaufman stops abruptly, fists clenching as he turns on me. "I've given you enough access. Only my most trusted men have access to those areas. I trust them implicitly."

"Yeah, I get that. Sadly, that's exactly what your mole would do."

"What does that mean?"

"To bring down Haven, your most trusted associate would need unlimited access to the entirety of your operation. The labyrinth you have is complex enough, but if you're certain none of those men could be a traitor, then there's no reason to send my team in." I try to push his buttons by backing off and pray my gamble works.

His eyes bore into mine, searching for any hidden agenda. I widen my eyes innocently.

"Fair enough." I raise my hands in acquiescence. "Your operation, your rules. My only aim is to provide quality service."

Kaufman studies me a moment longer before resuming his brisk pace. "See that you continue to do so," he warns.

Up ahead, the hallway intersects with a larger corridor. Kaufman slows, and I detect a shift in his demeanor. The subtle tells are all there—tightened jaw, accelerated blink rate, fingers twitching at his sides. He's made a decision I instinctively know I won't like.

"Your team needs to step up the pace."

"We're working as fast as we can. Your operation is complex and highly decentralized. Which is why we need full access to your facility." I keep my tone neutral.

Kaufman clasps his hands behind his back. "The needs of my clients come first. As such, I am moving the auction up to this Friday."

Careful to betray no reaction, I nod slowly as if this is reasonable. Inside, my mind spins scenarios on how to salvage the operation. We're not prepared to move on the women.

Kaufman plants his feet firmly on the cold floor, every vertebra in his back aligning in a defiant rod of steel. The corner of his mouth quivers upward in a smirk, the epitome of condescension.

"Therefore, your team must accelerate its efforts to ensure the proceedings go smoothly." His mouth curves into a parody of a smile, cold and reptilian. "And I would like you to attend the auction as my guest."

Bile rises in my throat at the thought of standing idle during this horrific slave trade. I swallow my disgust and nod. "I appreciate the invitation."

The harsh glint in his eyes sharpens, his smirk deepening. Every inch of him radiates conceit, an unmistakable aura of a man who believes he's invincible. "Excellent."

With that, he turns abruptly and stalks off down the corridor, disappearing into the bowels of Haven. I stand a moment, hands clenched, wrestling murderous fury back under control.

Attending the auction complicates matters tremendously, but also presents an opportunity. I can gather last-minute intel and help coordinate the timing of the operation. And when the chaos unfolds, I'll be positioned to reach Rebel quickly.

I just have to play nice with the devil in the meantime.

Adrenaline courses through me as I reach the secured communications room, our makeshift command center within Haven. My team is on high alert, senses primal and focused.

I gather my men. Their faces are grim, sensing this impromptu meeting signals a call to action. "Kaufman's pushed the auction to this Friday."

"Fuck." Jeb whistles. "We're close, but not that close."

"I know this adds a wrinkle, but it doesn't alter our goal." I outline the new developments tersely. "We adapt and make it work."

A chorus of muttered curses answers me. Hank's massive fists clench, corded veins standing out in his forearms. Gabe's stern face sets in implacable lines while Blake grinds his jaw, a storm brewing beneath his stony exterior.

"I'm open to suggestions."

Jeb, ever the pragmatist, speaks first. "Getting the women out won't be easy. We can disable security systems, but we're not able to deal with armed resistance." His fingers twitch as if typing on an imaginary keyboard. "I'm not excited about taking on Kaufman's men with just my fists, and I'm not sure we can sneak out with that many women."

Hank crosses his bulging arms. "These bastards watch us like hawks. Stealth won't work. We need a distraction if we're getting those women out." His gruff voice leaves no room for doubt—he's ready to bring the pain.

"Agreed. Hitting them hard is our best option." Blake shrugs. "Fewer moving parts to screw the op. We need weapons and explosives, though. Something to lay down suppressing fire, blow some doors, grab the women, and exfil as fast as possible."

Walt shakes his head. "Getting out won't be easy even with a distraction. This place is a fortress."

"We need exit strategies and alternate routes planned out in advance." Gabe's deep voice rumbles with authority. "It's a lot to risk without the right gear. There will be casualties among the women if we fuck this up."

A hush falls as we absorb Gabe's words. He's right—lives will be lost once we cross this line, but weighed against the innocent suffering here, we must be willing to pay that price.

"After that auction, they're dead already." I hate saying it, but it's the truth.

"I might know a way." All eyes turn to Stitch. For her part, she seems deep in contemplation. "A remote overload of the main generator would cause system disruptions. Under cover of darkness, I could guide you to the women undetected through maintenance tunnels. There are *other* exits from this place."

"Other? Where?" I'm curious.

"Old drainage ditches in the sub-basement to remove waste."

"Sounds wonderful." I scrunch my nose at the thought of wading through old waste tunnels.

"Haven was built on the bones of a much older structure. That's why there are so many sub-levels. I don't think those ditches have been used since this place was overhauled and modernized plumbing installed."

I consider this carefully. Stitch is brilliant.

"That might just work." Combined with guerilla-force distraction tactics proposed by my men, we have the kernels of a workable plan.

It's not an easy choice, but it's our only choice.

I meet each man's gaze again, seeing my steely resolve reflected back.

One by one, they nod, a wordless promise passing between us.

"Then it's decided. "With steady fingers, I input the 25-digit encryption code for the secured line to Guardian HRS Stitch set up the first day we arrived. It has yet to be used. The line crackles to life, and CJ's craggy face appears on the screen.

"Ethan, what's the status?" His gruff voice is all business.

"Kaufman moved up the next auction to Friday." I keep my voice low but crisp. These walls have ears. "Request permission to execute a rescue."

CJ leans forward, interest sparking in his eyes. "We're not prepped for a rescue, let alone one by week's end."

"We've mapped Haven's layout, and Stitch found an unmonitored extraction route through old drainage tunnels."

"What numbers are we looking at for hostiles and rescues?" CJ's tactical brain is already synthesizing the operational details.

"Two dozen women held captive. As for hostiles…" I tick through our estimates in my head. "At least thirty armed guards, plus administrative staff with military backgrounds."

CJ blows out a breath, scrubbing a hand over his stubble-shadowed jaw. "It's doable, but you need weapons and one hell of a distraction."

Before I can respond, Mitzy nudges her way into view of the camera, psychedelic neon hair framing her youthful face.

"I've got this. We can weaponize the Rufi. Send them via HALO jump." Her words come rapid-fire in her signature style. "They'll carry weapons, explosives, and supplies."

CJ nods approvingly. "Solid start, but Charlie needs more than the Rufi for extraction."

An anticipatory grin splits Mitzy's face.

Stitch pipes up. "I'll disable power to critical systems. With comms and surveillance down, Charlie team can grab the women in the chaos."

"Sounds solid," I agree without hesitation. This might be our only shot to cripple Kaufman's operation and save those women.

CJ's mouth twitches, a ghost of a smile. "How about this? Alpha and Bravo teams HALO in with the Rufi. The Rufi peel off to supply your team while Alpha and Bravo prep for a diversion outside Haven's walls. That should give your team the cover you need." His eyes gleam. "Time to pull the trigger on Operation Exodus."

"Exodus?"

"Sounds like it needs a catchy name." CJ doesn't apologize for naming my Op.

"Copy that." I glance at my team, happy to see nods all around. They're tired of playing pretend security experts and are ready for action.

Mitzy cracks her knuckles, already immersed in planning her technological ambush. "Stitch, stay in contact with me. I don't want any hiccups. We'll initiate when you signal. I'll get creative and see what else we can develop from this end." She winks before moving offscreen, fingers flying over keyboards.

CJ meets my gaze through the monitor. "Stay sharp down there. Bring those women home."

"Will do."

CJ's face splits into a fierce grin. "See you topside, Charlie-One."

The screen goes dark, and I turn to my men. "Kaufman invited me to the auction. That takes me out of the prep work with the Rufi. Once the diversion starts, I'll grab Rebel and meet at the tunnel." At least, I hope Rebel will let me grab her. I don't know that she will, and it's slowly killing me.

"The Rufi are an awesome bonus. Did she say fully weaponized?" Gabe punches his fist in his hand. "A real mission with weaponized Rufi. About damn time."

I couldn't agree more. Mitzy's combat robots will provide critical support during our escape.

"Let's work on our part." It's time to run through timelines and positioning. We run through several scenarios, picking each apart. We'll continue to refine our plans until the mission's over.

Because the best-laid plans always go to shit during combat.

THIRTY-FOUR

Ethan

LATER THAT NIGHT, I'M SUMMONED TO DINNER WITH KAUFMAN. THE candlelit dining hall is hushed, filled only with the soft clinks of fine china and silverware. Crystal glasses of crimson wine sparkle under the warm glow. The tantalizing aromas of roast beef, buttery potatoes, and fresh greens fill the air, at odds with the tension palpable between us. It smells amazing and would be a great dinner if not for the host.

I take my seat across from Kaufman, hyperaware of Rebel's presence by his side.

Kaufman eyes me over his glass, swirling the wine before taking a leisurely sip. "Tell me, how goes the hunt for our little security breach?"

I cut into the tender steak, keeping my tone casual. "I expect definitive answers before the auction."

"I should hope so. Your team is cutting it close." Kaufman drags his fork through the drizzle of sauce on his plate. "The systems must be secure for my clients. The auction must proceed without issue." His tone brooks no uncertainty.

"We've traced the breach and are locking it down tight." I infuse confidence into the lie and swallow the last of the excellent Pinot

Noir in my glass. It's exquisite, which irks me. Degenerate scum like Kaufman don't deserve such fineries. "You have my word."

The moment I set my wine glass down, one of the servers fills it.

"Excellent. I expect perfection, as always." He smiles, satisfied, then turns his attention to Rebel.

She keeps her gaze demurely lowered as he reaches out to stroke her neck in a vulgar display of possession. His fingers wrap around her throat, precisely over the bruising he put there.

"And your Angels?" His eyes leer at Rebel. "They will be ready?"

"They're motivated to please." Rebel's composure never cracks, but I sense something simmering beneath the surface. Her gaze remains fixed on her plate.

Her posture is rigid.

Rage simmers in my gut at what awaits those terrified girls.

"Marvelous." Kaufman's eyes remain calculating as they shift between Rebel and me.

He and I may be seated across the table, but there's no doubt we're warily circling the other.

Kaufman dabs his mouth with an embroidered napkin. "I'm curious what your plans are once you're finished here." He arches an eyebrow. "Your talents could be leveraged for more—sensitive matters."

I swirl the wine before taking a sip, buying time. Kaufman is fishing for something, but I can't let my cover slip.

"We go where the business takes us and prefer short-term clients." My meaning is clear. I intend for there to be no long-term business here.

Kaufman's chuckle is low and grating. "Loyalty can be a fleeting thing in your profession."

I incline my head in concession. "Trust is built over time. But you're correct; loyalty is only as strong as the incentive behind it." I keep my tone neutral, giving nothing away.

His lips twist as he slices into a pear. "In my experience, fear is the greatest motivator." He pops the pear slice between his lips, eyes glinting.

"Fear has its uses, but also its limits." I drag a bite of tender steak through the savory sauce. "Inspiring loyalty earns more dividends than fear ever will."

Kaufman's gaze turns thoughtful at my subtle challenge. He dabs his mouth again before speaking. "Perhaps you're right." His hungry gaze lingers on Rebel.

I barely suppress a shudder of revulsion. Glancing at Rebel, I try to discern her thoughts, but her polished mask reveals nothing. Still, the tension in her spine speaks volumes.

For now, I merely smile and take another sip of wine, playing my role. In a few nights, the women of Haven will reclaim their lives, and his entire sadistic enterprise will come crashing down.

Until then, my team and I will continue as we have. I'll drink Kaufman's fine wine, make small talk, and pretend my purpose here aligns with his evil ends.

My thoughts drift to Rebel.

I replay our last conversation and the desperation in her eyes. If there's a way to extract her, I have to try. Whether she'll come is another matter.

Dinner ends without overt confrontation, but it's clear Kaufman senses something's off.

Hours pass at a snail's pace.

One day turns into two.

We continue on, pretending we're bolstering Haven's defenses. I can't have Kaufman kick us out before we have a chance to save the women.

I put the team on a strict schedule and rouse Hank for his watch, then try to rest, knowing I'll need all my strength. Sleep eludes me, however, because my thoughts churn with our plans.

Finally, the time comes. It's auction night, and we're as ready as possible. I send the men out in pairs to make their way through the twisting tunnels toward the drainage grate, where the Rufi will arrive with our supplies. From there, they'll move the supplies in, hiding them until Operation Exodus begins.

When I rise from an unsettling nap, I make my way down to the tunnels to see what we have. The tunnels are dark, dank, and reek of things I don't want to identify. I make my way to the grate at the end, where a single shaft of moonlight spills through the rusted bars above the drainage ditch. This will be our exfil point once the women are secure. Now, to retrieve the Rufi and weapons Mitzy is sending.

We halt before the pale light filtering in through the grate. Breaths held, pulses racing, we wait for any indication the drop has begun. This gear will arm us for war—we can't begin without it.

Suddenly, six gleaming black metallic forms appear outside the grate, blocking the moon's light.

"What the hell?" Hank rears back. "Glad they're on our side. They're silent as fuck."

Indeed, the Rufi have arrived, lean robotic canines created for combat. Jet metal black, they're impossible to make out against the background sky. With weapon mounts and armored chassis, they're beyond state-of-the-art. This is truly cutting-edge technology.

One of the Rufi extends its neck, an ingenious combination of a head and an arm appendage. It swivels with precision, its eyes glowing with an eerie mechanical intelligence. A torch at the end of its head/arm flickers to life, casting a searing blue flame.

We shield our eyes from the intense light, the air thickening with the smell of burning ozone. The Rufi's torch hits the rusted metal and liquefies on the spot. Hissing metal turns to slag, accompanied by pops and crackles as molten iron shoots through the air. Sparks fly in all directions, hot and angry, as we step back to avoid the dripping slag.

The grate groans, surrendering to the Rufi's relentless assault. But it's not free. It still needs a bit of muscle to wrench it out of place.

"Grab the grate." I nod to Gabe and Hank, our heaviest hitters.

They yank on the weathered metal with raw, unbridled force, their muscles straining as beads of sweat gather on their foreheads.

Gabe's face twists in determination, his jaw clenched, eyes narrowed, as he grips the grate with hands that have known labor and struggle. Hank's biceps bulge, the veins in his arms a vivid roadmap of his strength.

The grate resists at first, but they pull harder. The acrid stench of molten metal, rich and metallic, mingles with the sharp tang of sweat and the bitterness of ozone.

The grate breaks free with a tortured scream, a sound that sends shivers down my spine. It clatters to the ground, and we're greeted with a gust of cold, dank air from the darkness beyond.

The Rufi's torch flickers out, leaving us bathed in the unsettling afterglow, our chests heaving.

With their compact bodies, the six Rufi leap effortlessly into the drainage tunnel, landing with a mechanical grace that belies their deadly purpose. I expect to hear their hydraulic limbs, but the Rufi are deathly quiet, a cold reminder of their artificial nature. They line up, standing at attention as we approach.

We crowd around the first of the six Rufi. Assault rifles, ammo, flashbangs, and other weapons are strapped to its back. Each Rufi carries gear for each man on my team, their metal bodies laden with the tools of our trade.

Stitch's gear, a mishmash of technology and weaponry, is interspersed between them all. Mitzy provided her with a pistol, vest, and a HUD.

As I power on my HUD, anticipation charges the air. The optics flicker to life with an electric blue glow. Lifelike hydraulic movements ripple through the Rufi as they shake out their limbs and await further commands.

Hank reaches for his gear, his hand steady, his eyes never leaving the Rufi. Walt and Blake move in sync, grabbing their weapons, their faces masks of intense concentration. Jeb's fingers brush over his gear with a quiet reverence in his touch. Gabe's movements are efficient, with no wasted motion as he secures his equipment.

Stitch, the outlier in our crew, looks at her gear with curiosity and determination. Her fingers, more accustomed to keyboards, hesitantly reach for the pistol. She glances at me with fire in her eyes, a promise she won't be the weak link.

"Drop successful. Dogs are online," I murmur into my comm, my voice as cold as the damp walls surrounding us. "Geared up.

Oscar Mike." I notify Command that the Rufi arrived, and we're officially *On Mission*.

"Copy that." CJ's voice returns through the headset. "What's the play, Charlie-One?"

I kneel before the Rufi. Intelligent machines, tonight, they hunt with us.

"Hold here and stand guard." I point toward the tunnel mouth. The Rufi dutifully blend into the shadows. "Status of Alpha and Bravo?"

A soft buzz of acknowledgment comes through the earpiece. The Rufis' blue eyes dim as they switch to standby mode. The silence that follows is heavy with the weight of what's to come.

"Holding position outside the walls. Ready to launch a frontal assault on your mark."

"Kaufman invited me to the auction. Blake and Gabe will stay here. Jeb and Stitch will wrap things up in the communication suite. Hank and Walt, I need the two of you to come up and keep appearances normal. When I head to the auction, you'll excuse yourselves. No need for Kaufman's men to get suspicious. Head down and kit up. When I give the signal, you rescue the women. Jeb and Stitch, you must make your way down here unobserved."

"And what about you?" Gabe gives me a stern look.

"Once Alpha and Bravo engage, I'll use the chaos to rescue Rebel."

Jeb looks to Stitch with a smirk on his face. No need to guess what he's thinking. I stayed up long after my watch last night, trying to figure out how to get my men to the lower levels of Haven without raising an alarm. Pretending Jeb and Stitch are an item, slinking off for a bit of fun, was the easy part. Sending the others below is more problematic, but Stitch figured that out for me.

"Any questions?" After checking out my gear, I remove it and methodically place each piece back on the Rufi's frame.

My men follow suit, their movements crisp and practiced. I pull out a small earpiece, almost invisible in its design, and place it discreetly behind my ear. This connection to my team is my lifeline tonight, a thread of communication that must remain unbroken.

"None, boss." Hank's voice is steady, his eyes locked on mine. Deadly determination radiates from him and the others. They know the stakes, and they're ready.

The musty dampness of the tunnel fills my nostrils as I take a deep breath. The unspoken resolve of my team never fails to astound me. They've trained for this, and now that it's time to execute, there's a shift in the air. An unspoken urgency.

Leaving Blake and Gabe behind, the rest of us head back upstairs, our footsteps echoing in the confined space. The main parts of Haven loom ahead, a maze of opulence and decadence masking the dark underbelly of this place.

Reaching the control room Kaufman gave us during our stay at Haven, we disperse to our assigned tasks. Jeb and Stitch get to work on the systems, their fingers dancing over keyboards. The others head off, their faces masks of casual indifference, but their eyes remain hard with purpose.

I take a moment, standing alone, the room filled with the hum of technology. The auction is tonight, a grotesque spectacle I must participate in. My stomach churns at the thought, but I push it aside. Those women are depending on us, and we can't fail them.

I prepare for the evening, changing into the attire befitting one of Kaufman's guests. My reflection in the mirror is a stranger, a facade I must endure to navigate this world.

THIRTY-FIVE

Rebel

THE DAYS DRAG BY IN A HAZE OF ENDLESS TRAINING SESSIONS AS I push the Angels to their breaking point, desperately trying to hammer them into auction-ready condition. Despite the long hours and grueling demands I place on them, the girls remain hollow-eyed and fearful, shells of their former selves filled with trauma.

I pause the training and approach Leah, placing a hand gently on her shoulder. "I know this is difficult," I say softly. "But it's the only way. Becoming an Angel will spare you an even worse fate."

Leah blinks back tears, unconvinced. "How can being forced to obey some man be better than this?" she asks tremulously.

I tilt her chin up. "You will want for nothing as an Angel. Fine clothes, gardens to wander, your every whim catered to."

Leah searches my face. "It doesn't sound like freedom."

"It's the only freedom left to us," I reply. "And far better than the misery below. You're stronger than Kaufman knows. Endure this training, and you'll have an easy life pampered and protected. This life is better than the alternative."

Leah absorbs this quietly. "Is he—kind to you?"

I consider the bruises hidden under my sleeves. "Kaufman can be difficult," I admit. "But I want for very little. I have a comfortable

262 • ELLIE MASTERS

room, leisure time, and access to grounds and gardens." I smooth a hand over Leah's hair. "The life ahead may not be what you wished, but it holds potential. With care, you can cultivate happiness even in captivity, perhaps even freedom."

Leah listens intently, taking some solace in my experience. If framing it as us being in this together gives her strength, then so be it. I've carried darker deceptions than white lies meant to help these girls survive.

She hesitates, conflicted, but wants to believe me. I offer an encouraging smile before moving on, hoping my words sway her. She is bright and might understand in time. I pray I can convince them all before it's too late.

"It's not ideal, I know," I say gently. "But you can make the best of it. You have some control over who buys you."

Leah looks skeptical. I lean in close. "Be strategic—catch the eye of men you find appealing. You can ensure you end up with someone young and handsome, not old and fat."

I squeeze her hand. "An Angel's life can be quite luxurious with the right man, but you must be proactive and seduce the bidder you want."

Leah considers this, holding onto a shred of agency in her fate. "So, I'm not powerless?" she asks hesitantly.

"Not completely. It's a game of influence," I reply. "Play it well, and you may find contentment."

Leah nods slowly, seeing a glimmer of hope. I pray my advice gives her the will to endure the trials ahead and guide her future.

Leah hesitates, then asks quietly, "Is Kaufman why you're our trainer?"

I nod slowly. "Yes. He let me choose my role here, and I perform it willingly. It keeps my own life relatively pain-free."

Leah absorbs this, reading the truth in my eyes. "I'm sorry," she says softly. "That you had no choice either."

Her empathy brings a lump to my throat. I have to turn away under the pretense of retrieving training equipment, not wanting her to see the sheen of tears in my eyes. She may retain her kind heart, even once it's all beaten out. That innocent part of Leah gives me hope—that maybe, just maybe, some flicker of their souls can survive this place unchanged.

I turn to address all the Angels. "I know you despise me for what I do." The words come with the pain of my heart breaking for these women. "I regret every cruelty, but preparing you for what's to come is necessary."

I meet each girl's eyes. "But, I'm saving you from fates infinitely more horrific. The misery you've endured is nothing compared to where these men would send you without my intervention. Dark places fueled by sadism, where pain and degradation have no limits. Where death comes slowly, and part of you prays for its bitter release."

The girls go still, faces draining of color. I continue more gently, "As Angels, you will know a far kinder life. What I do, I do to spare you indescribable suffering and keep you from the deepest pits of hell this world contains."

My voice hardens. "So you will endure the training. You will break and let yourselves be remade because the alternative is death. My cruelty is kindness compared to what awaits you otherwise."

I stop before Iris, who bears fresh bruises. "I wish I could spare you pain," I murmur. "But you must prove you're ready. Take each blow silently and with thanks. It will serve you well with future masters."

Iris's eyes well with tears. "I don't know how much more I can take."

I tilt her chin up. "You can endure this. And more. You have that strength in you, Iris, even if you doubt it."

She searches my face, wanting to believe.

"True Angels require steel spines and resilient hearts." I take Iris's hands gently. "I tell you such harsh truths because failure to become an Angel brings fates far darker." Iris's eyes widen as I continue. "Make no mistake, you will be sent away from this place if deemed unready. Kaufman will wash his hands of you. There are those who would take full advantage of your vulnerability for their own purposes."

I let that sink in before going on. "You will know suffering and cruelty far beyond what you feel now. There are evil men in this world who revel in inflicting pain and anguish. With none to protect you, that agony could go on for years before you're of no further use. Your life cut short." Iris trembles, but I need her to understand. "However difficult this may be, being made an Angel will spare you infinite misery."

Iris searches my face and finally nods, resolve strengthening in her eyes. My methods are harsh but necessary for their survival. Hopefully, it's enough to prepare them for what is to come.

Iris sets her jaw and nods. I squeeze her shoulder.

"No more tears. You are an Angel. Each lesson is a badge of honor, proving you will make a fine Angel."

Iris stands a little taller. As training resumes, she accepts each strike mutely. I pray my words help strengthen her for what lies ahead. She shows promising signs of having that inner resilience all Angels need.

Iris nods, eyes welling, but sets her jaw in resolution. I squeeze her shoulder, wishing I did not have to break these girls' spirits to save them.

Another piece of my soul shrivels and dies with each crack of the whip. This brutal conditioning goes against my very nature. I was never meant to be warped into such a monster.

Yet, I tell myself it's necessary. I'm saving them from abyssal suffering and agony compared to what Kaufman would unleash upon them.

The justification sounds hollow, even in my own mind.

It's the lie I tell myself so I can sleep at night.

Am I truly saving them or merely exchanging one trauma for another? Carving away pieces of their souls and humanity as Kaufman did to me?

I hate myself more with each despairing tear I force them to shed. Each timid voice I silence and defiant glare I crush. I'm slowly killing everything good and pure within them, just as it was dismantled within me.

My humanity is gone.

Stolen by Kaufman.

When we finally finish each day, I wander Haven's twisting halls aimlessly, unable to quiet the doubts churning within me. My thoughts inevitably turn to Ethan.

After unburdening myself and confiding my dangerous truths, we remain at odds. He loves me, and I love him, but he doesn't condone my actions. He wants me to stop, but I can't. I won't. I made a promise to my sister on her dying breath, and that is my priority.

No matter how isolated I feel, I won't compromise his team's mission. So, I weather each day alone, slipping away during brief recesses to comb the records room, still seeking some clue about my lost sister. I search more frantically each time, sifting through endless accounts of cruelty and exploitation, but find nothing.

Still, I cling to the hope that if I'm thorough enough, some small detail about Violet will emerge. Her ghost drives me relentlessly onward each and every day.

Too soon, it's auction day, and Violet's records remain maddeningly elusive. Meanwhile, Kaufman's temper grows increasingly volatile as the Angels' conditioning falls short of perfection. My body bears the bruises of his displeasure beneath concealing garments.

During Kaufman's absences, I feel the heat of Ethan's watchful gaze follow me through the halls, alert and protective from a careful distance. Our eyes occasionally meet, an unspoken longing passing between us, filled with words we cannot say.

I ache to hear his voice and feel the strength of his presence, but the gulf between us is too wide.

One restless evening after curfew, I slip outside to clear my head, wandering beneath a sky salted with stars. Their remote pinpricks of light mock me, oblivious to the suffering transpiring below.

With my arms wrapped around myself to stave off the chilly air, I meander aimlessly, filled with churning doubts I can't voice. My breath plumes before me in the silence.

I've never felt so alone.

A shadow suddenly detaches from the darkness up ahead. Fear

stabs through me before it steps into a swath of moonlight, becoming a familiar broad-shouldered form.

Ethan.

Even at a distance, he radiates a formidable, commanding power. The moonlight glints off his hair, throwing his rugged features into sharp relief. He moves with the power and lethality of a warrior.

A protector.

A Guardian.

We stare wordlessly across the span for endless racing heartbeats. Propriety and caution scream at me to turn away and retreat to my rooms, but I find myself helpless to move as Ethan approaches with firm strides. His presence envelopes me, radiating strength, protection, and empathy that pierces my soul.

He stops beyond arm's reach, searching my face in the pale illumination. "Rebel," he murmurs, my chosen name intimate on his lips. "Are you okay?"

I open my mouth but can't find any words. It's been too long since someone asked about my well-being. Am I okay? I can't remember the last time that was true. I nod in a mute reply.

Ethan's gaze traces the lurid bruise on my cheek, visible even in the silvered moonlight. His jaw tightens, old fury simmering beneath his controlled exterior. Slowly, giving me time to pull away, he extends a hand.

When I don't retreat, his fingers graze my skin with a feather-light caress, his touch impossibly gentle on the tender bruise. I don't deserve such tenderness, but a shaky exhale escapes me at this caring contact—the first I've known in ages.

My eyes close, a lump rising in my throat. Ethan steps nearer, his presence enveloping me in familiar warmth and strength. For a fleeting moment, the icy chill of my isolation melts away.

"You don't have to serve him." Ethan's hushed words are heavy with empathy. He searches my downcast face. "Let me help." His voice catches with emotion.

I shake my head, unable to meet his eyes. "It's too late," I whisper. "Just finish your mission and forget me. Please."

Ethan cups my cheek, thumb gently tracing the ugly bruise marring my skin. "I will never abandon you here." He swallows hard. "You deserve better than this."

"I deserve to burn in hell." Overcome, I briefly cover his hand with my own, clinging to this lifeline of selfless devotion, but reality intrudes. With deep regret, I step back out of his sheltering embrace. "Go," I plead raggedly. "Before we're seen."

Ethan searches my face, tormented, but he respects my choice, hand falling away with reluctance. My skin instantly misses his warmth. We stand frozen, drowning in an ocean of unsaid words that fills the space between us.

At last, Ethan melts back into the shadows, the darkness closing around him until he's gone from sight. The imprint of his tender touch remains, a bittersweet reminder that I'm not forgotten.

Someone still cares.

It is enough, barely, to sustain me through the deepening isolation.

I shake my head, a lump rising in my throat. I want to accept the refuge he offers, but my secrets run too deep. Kaufman would sooner kill me than let me go. Not that I can think of escape until I find something that will lead me to Violet's trail.

I remain frozen long after Ethan's gone, wrapped in an aching hollowness. His compassion leaves me more gutted than Kaufman's cruelty ever could because Ethan offers what I crave most.

He offers me a way out of this nightmare.

During a short reprieve the next day, I steal away to the records room again, combing through the endless files, but like all the other times, my visit proves fruitless. Violet remains lost to me.

Utterly disheartened, I make my way back upstairs.

As auction day looms, Kaufman's temper builds. Yet, I still search. When I can't slip away to the records room, I wander the halls, feeling the heat of Ethan's watchful gaze, taking what solace I can in our wordless kinship.

THIRTY-SIX

Ethan

THE OPULENT BALLROOM OOZES WITH DEPRAVITY, MASQUERADING AS civility. The soft murmurs of polished men mingle around me as they await the auction, sipping aged scotch and smoking cigars. Their wingtips glint under the chandeliers as they move between groups, voices low and eager.

I stand apart from the men, jaw clenched, maintaining a polite veneer while disgust twists my gut. These men have come to purchase captive girls forced into slavery, the Angels. Conditioned into obedience, they will be sold as fantasy pets.

I must play along a little longer before Alpha and Bravo teams are in position. Kaufman sidles up to me, oozing smugness. "Quite a turnout, wouldn't you say?"

"Your clients seem eager," I reply neutrally, bitterness on my tongue.

He chuckles greasily. "Oh yes, they're salivating for this offering. Only the finest wares." His hands rub together greedily. "It will be a night to remember."

The lights dim, and the men take their seats, hungry with anticipation. Kaufman guides me to the back row. Jaw clamped shut in disgust, I sit and wait.

"Bring them out!" Kaufman calls out.

The double doors swing open, and a hush falls over the crowded ballroom. I sit rigidly in my chair, braced for the depraved spectacle about to unfold.

A live string quartet in the corner strikes up a lilting melody, the notes dripping with sensuality. The men lean forward in their seats, mouths parted, eyes glinting with ill-concealed excitement. Low murmurs and eager whispers fill the room.

The Angels drift in like ethereal creatures in fluttering white gowns that leave little to the imagination. Their heads are bowed, eyes downcast in conditioned submission. Bare feet glide soundlessly across the polished floor. They move in perfect synchrony, limbs unfolding in lithe, sensuous motions honed through coercion and manipulation.

The men devour the vulnerable forms with rapturous eyes. Wet lips part, hands grip chair arms, pulses visibly quicken—the room thrums with restless desire.

The quartet's melody swells as the Angels turn in graceful pirou-ettes, diaphanous fabric floating around supple curves and long, unblemished legs. A few men can stand it no longer, gasps and moans escaping them as composure breaks.

My jaw aches from clenching as I stare straight ahead. Rage simmers beneath my impassive facade as this dehumanizing spec-tacle continues. The things I would do to these leering lowlifes…

But I must maintain appearances.

My team awaits my signal, ready to strike. So I sit motionless, hearing the eager whispers, inhaling the perfume-laced air, feeling the writhing depravity pulsating around me—and I wait.

Kaufman leans in, gloating. "Exquisite, aren't they? The finest stock."

I force a smile. "You have an eye for quality." My hollow compli-ment nearly chokes me.

Kaufman preens under the perceived compliment. "Yes, I leave their training to someone with a special touch. Ah, speaking of…"

His reptilian gaze fixes on Rebel as she enters, stunning in a tight ruby gown. Our eyes lock briefly before she glides smoothly to

Kaufman's side. His possessive grip on her wrist makes fury boil in my veins.

"Rebel has done wonders training these girls, gentling them into the most sublime obedience." Kaufman's eyes caress Rebel's body greedily as she forces a thin smile.

He turns and has a quick, hushed conversation with her. Rebel's face pales, but she nods reluctantly. Kaufman smiles and taps his champagne flute, calling for attention.

"Before we present tonight's offerings, the talented woman who so perfectly prepared them will say a few words."

He indicates Rebel with a flourish. She glides to the front on trembling legs. I sit tensely, unsure what Kaufman is playing at.

Rebel's voice wavers slightly before she steels herself. "Each of the Angels you will meet tonight represents countless hours of dedication and training. Everything about them, from their movement to their thoughts, has been gently guided into creating the most pleasurable companion imaginable."

Murmurs of eager anticipation ripple through the room. I feel sick at her forced words.

"Training is a delicate art," Rebel continues, staring straight ahead. "First, we must peel back the layers of individual identity and willfulness, persuading a subject that her deepest fulfillment lies in obedience to another. This reframing takes time, but the results are exquisite—a lovely flower unfurling to offer its petals for your pleasure."

The men smile and nod, enthralled. Kaufman looks immensely pleased at this endorsement of his vile work. I yearn to strangle him with my bare hands.

Rebel concludes, "It has been my privilege to prepare these Angels for your enjoyment. I hope what you find tonight exceeds your most imaginative fantasies."

She returns to Kaufman's side with her head bowed. He kisses her cheek indulgently before turning back to me.

"Rebel has done wonders training the girls, gentling them to obedience." His eyes caress her hungrily as she gives a thin smile. Kaufman turns from me for a quiet conversation with Rebel.

Discreetly, I touch my earpiece and subvocalize my request. "Status?"

"In position. On your signal." The terse reply comes from CJ, who will coordinate the combined activities of Alpha, Bravo, and Charlie teams.

Kaufman drones on as I nod politely, every nerve coiled tight. My moment approaches. With a subtle look to Rebel, I rise, adjusting my cuffs. "Please excuse me a moment. Nature calls."

I stride smoothly from the ballroom, the noise fading behind me. Alone in the corridor, I touch my earpiece. "Execute Operation Exodus. I repeat, Exodus is a go."

"Roger that. Initiating attack in ten," CJ fires back in snappy tones.

Adrenaline floods my system. Alpha and Bravo teams will strike the external gates as a diversion while I secure Rebel and the Angels. I return to the ballroom, mind racing. The plan hinges on perfect timing to get the women out during the chaos.

When I re-enter the ballroom, my senses are heightened. Across the room, Rebel stands frozen. The Angels twist and pivot to the swelling music.

Several minutes pass, and then precisely ten minutes after I spoke to CJ, a deep, resonant boom shakes the room, halting the Angels' performance. The women scream in fear as cracks spiderweb up the far wall and plumes of dust drift down from the rafters. Another concussive blast rocks the building. The explosions continue, approaching closer.

Panicked patrons leap up, drinks spilling. They swarm toward the exits as the room quakes. The string quartet screeches into chaotic notes, the musicians white-faced. Clouds of acrid smoke wind between the stampeding men.

The Angels clutch each other, wailing in terror. The floor pitches violently. Across the room, I glimpse the massive double doors blown inward, flames licking beyond. The far wall crumbles, exposing the night sky.

Kaufman draws a pistol with a crazed look. Before he can fire into the crowd, I grab a bottle and smash it across his temple. He collapses, knocked out cold.

I sprint through falling debris toward Rebel, who tries to corral the hysterical Angels. My earpiece crackles to life.

"Charlie team, we're outside making noise." Brady Malone, Bravo-One, reports on their progress. "Diversion underway."

I almost laugh in disbelief. Against the odds, Alpha and Bravo have breached Haven's formidable defenses. Now, to fulfill my mission—get the women out of here alive.

The explosions thunder ever closer as I reach Rebel across the crumbling ballroom. "Come with me," I yell over the deafening destruction and grasp her arm, ready to haul her to safety.

Rebel wrenches her arm free. "I'm not leaving."

I stare at her in bewilderment as debris rains down around us. "What are you talking about? This whole place is imploding. I need to get you out of here."

"Take them to safety." Rebel's face is resolute. "I can't leave until I find…" She shakes her head. "Save the Angels. There's something I must do."

"Rebel, please—" I grab her again, desperate to understand. "It's not worth your life."

She twists sharply out of my grasp. "Get the Angels out of here." She points toward guards ushering the Angels out of the ballroom to safety.

I'm immobilized by shock and incomprehension. Rebel remains an enigma. I thought she would escape with us now that we're finally bringing his operation down, but she refuses to leave. I search her face desperately, trying to understand, but her jaw is set, eyes ablaze with resolve I can't comprehend.

She's made her choice, and it's not escaping with me. That realization cuts deeply.

I plead with her to reconsider, but she only pushes me to save the others. With a heavy heart, I turn to do just that. I can only pray this isn't the last time I'll see the mysterious woman I care for so deeply.

THIRTY-SEVEN

Ethan

"STATUS, CHARLIE TEAM?" CJ'S VOICE CRACKLES URGENTLY through my earpiece.

"Working on it," I reply tersely, squinting through the swirling dust and smoke filling the disintegrating ballroom. "Stand by."

I'm vulnerable, unarmed, and exposed. I need my team.

As if summoned by my thoughts, the ballroom doors crash open. Hank and Walt stride in wearing full tactical gear, heavy rifles at the ready. Their faces are obscured by HUD helmets with optics displays glowing electric green in the haze. Eyes sweeping the chaotic scene, they spot me and make their way over.

"Fuck me, you don't do anything small, do you, boss?" Hank has to shout to be heard over the ongoing explosions pummeling the upper levels. He passes me my own helmet and my weapons.

"Subtlety's overrated." I grin fiercely, relieved at the sight of them. "Where are Jeb and Stitch?"

"Wreaking havoc in the security center," Walt yells back. "We locked it down to protect them when all hell broke loose."

I nod, clasping their shoulders in thanks. We may just pull this off.

A sudden movement catches my eye—across the ballroom, two

guards force a group of Angels through a side door at gunpoint. The girls shriek and resist until the guards fire warning shots into the ceiling. The Angels quickly subside, terrified into obedience again.

"They're taking them back to the cells," I snap, "We have to stop them."

"Ready when you are, boss." Hank's voice comes steely and cold through the helmet's modulator. The optics lock onto the retreating forms, tracking their progress.

We surge forward, weapons raised. The guards notice us when we're halfway across the open space. Their own guns swing up. Adrenaline spikes through me.

"Down!" I roar. We dive behind overturned tables as a hailstorm of bullets peppers our previous location. The Angels scream and cower as wood splinters explode around us.

"Suppressing fire!" At my command, Hank and Walt rise up and unleash a barrage from their weapons. The heavy caliber rounds chew through the guards' cover, driving them back. They retreat through the door, pulling the hostages with them.

"Don't let them get away." I break cover and sprint after them. Hank and Walt are right on my heels. We charge through the door, weapons ready, but the corridor is eerily empty. Muted gunfire and faint screams echo from up ahead.

"Ambush," Walt warns tersely.

We advance swiftly, covering each other through intersections, checking our six. The low ceiling and bare concrete walls seem to press in. Industrial lighting flickers erratically, throwing ominous moving shadows.

Up ahead, I hear a girl's pleading whimper followed by a harsh male voice. We stack up on a closed door labeled "Holding Area 6" from which faint sounds emanate. I nod to Hank, who rips it open, sweeping inside with his weapon. Walt and I rush in behind him.

The scene within makes my blood boil. Five Angels cower against the far wall, bloody and bruised. Before them stand six guards, two with pistols aimed at the girls, the rest training rifles on us. The hostages' wide eyes flip between us and their captors, terrified.

"Well, looks like we've got ourselves a standoff," one guard sneers. "Guns down, or these bitches get it." He jabs his pistol at a girl who sobs hysterically.

"How about you let them go, and we leave you breathing." I adjust my aim. Walt and Hank stand rock steady at my flank.

The guard's eyes narrow. "Drop your weapons unless you want to see their brains splat—"

His word cuts off mid-syllable, replaced by a strangled gurgle as Hank's rifle barks, dropping him with a gaping neck wound. Before the other guards react, Walt and I open fire. The corridor fills with deafening reports. Two more go down instantly in sprays of blood. The remaining three dive for cover, firing wildly back at us.

"Get the girls clear." I point Walt toward the cowering group. He nods and lays down suppressive fire while circling around. Hank and I drive the guards back down the hall until they duck through a doorway.

Fucking cowards.

I signal a halt, not wanting to charge blindly after them. "Walt, status?"

"Hostages secured. No injuries, but they're scared shitless."

"Take them to the extraction point, we'll handle these assholes."

"Copy that." Walt gathers the Angels and heads out.

I tap my comms. "Walt's headed your way with five hostages. Gabe, meet up with him to assist."

"On my way." Gabe's clipped reply crackles through my headset.

"Watch your six." I jerk my head at the doorway and look at Hank.

Walt escorts the whimpering Angels back the way we came while Hank and I stack up again. We breach the room in unison, sweeping with rifles ready. It appears to be a barracks, with triple-decker bunks lining the walls. The guards are nowhere to be seen.

I'm about to move deeper when a barrage of fire drives us back into the hall. These bastards are putting up a vicious fight. Hank tosses a flash-bang through the doorway to clear the room. It detonates with an earsplitting *bang*. We rush in while they're still stunned, laying down relentless fire.

Two guards pop up from behind a bunk, pistols blazing. My rifle punches them back down, howling and bleeding. Hank eliminates another trying to flank us. I press forward, sights hunting the final target.

There's a flicker of movement between some lockers. I empty a burst, and a scream rings out as the guard crumbles, clutching his shredded leg. Hank kicks away his fallen weapon while I cover him.

"Please, no more." The guard crawls back, whimpering, hands raised in submission. "I give up."

"Where are the other Angels?" There are twenty in total. Walt has five. I need to know where the others went.

Hank grinds the heel of his boot into the guard's mutilated leg while I question the motherfucker, demanding answers.

Rage courses through me at how easily he surrenders the information. "Should've let the girls go when you had the chance." I slam my rifle stock into his face, knocking him out cold.

Adrenaline still surges in my blood, we do a final sweep to confirm all targets are neutralized. My earpiece crackles as we head upstairs.

"Status, Charlie team?" CJ demands impatiently.

"Five targets secured, en route with Walt to rally point," I report, relief flooding through me. "We've got fifteen more to locate."

"Hurry it up. Alpha and Bravo are taking a beating out there." CJ's comment makes sense, considering the resistance we've encountered inside Haven has been relatively light so far.

We swiftly descend into the windowless sub-levels, our senses hyper-alert. Jeb feeds navigation directions through my HUD as we methodically clear each room.

Fighting intensifies the lower we go, contrary to expectations. The remaining guards are hardened, disciplined, cornered rats willing to fight to the death to protect their secrets. They establish kill zones at choke points and inside rooms, pinning us down with coordinated interlocking fields of fire.

Hank and I quickly burn through ammo, taking cover as we try to break their ranks. We score hits, taking down a few defenders, but more appear from hidden alcoves, driving us back and flanking our sides.

I slam a new magazine into my smoking rifle and peer around the corner, only to jerk back as blistering fire peppers my position. My HUD shows our ammo reserves dipping critically low. Hank meets my eyes and shakes his head—he's nearly out, too.

These fanatical bastards mean to entomb us down here. We must break their ranks soon, or we'll never reach the hostages.

I signal Hank with a feral grin. He nods back in agreement. Time to take the fight to them and save precious ammo.

We stop firing and switch to knives. In the lull, they think we're falling back. When they rush us, we carve into them like the angels of death we are.

Arterial blood sprays hot across my neck as I slash throats and drive my blade into chests, puncturing lungs. They fall, gurgling and thrashing at my feet. Hank moves methodically, plunging his knife through ears, eyes, and hearts—whatever kills quickest and quietest.

We leave none alive, a trail of mangled corpses marking our descent into the bowels of Haven. The coppery tang of blood mixes with acrid smoke, filling my nostrils. Rivulets of sweat cut through the grime on my face. My shoulder aches from recoil, and my muscles burn with fatigue, but we push on.

More resistance awaits. We take them apart piece by piece until finally, muffled cries draw us to a large metal door labeled "Processing."

Hank and I stack up and breach the door on my signal. Inside, seven Angels huddle as three guards hold guns to their heads.

"Drop your weapons," the leader yells. The girls whimper, eyes scrunched closed, preparing to die.

My knife flies through the air and takes the leader mid-sentence, opening his throat in a wet gush. Hank's blades drop the other two before they can pull their triggers.

280 • ELLIE MASTERS

It's over in seconds.

Makes me appreciate all those hours working on my knife skills.

I rush to free the hostages. Tear-streaked faces look up at me with awe, relief, and hope as if they can't believe we're real. They're no longer Angels.

We are.

Blood-soaked angels, delivering them from evil, but guardian angels nonetheless.

But this shit isn't over. Not yet.

"There are others." One of the girls whispers. It's Iris, the girl I met in the hall. "Through there." She points to a heavily locked door.

I make the call. Hank and I can't afford to split our forces. "Stay close," I urge them.

We breach the next room and find nothing.

"Iris, where else would they have taken them?"

"There's a holding room down two levels. It's secure." She shivers violently. I can't tell if it's from fear or trauma from that holding room. From the way her voice shakes, I'm guessing the latter.

We press deeper into the maze with seven former Angels in tow.

A final locked room labeled simply "Holding" echoes with muffled pounding and cries. I blow the door, and the panicked cries of the last eight girls sound out in a rush. Relief washes over me— we found them all.

These Angels, however, are unguarded and chained to the back wall, wrists raw and bleeding. Their wide, streaming eyes flip between us and the open door, certain their tormentors will return any second.

An uneasy silence fills the small room. Hank and I take a moment to slam our last mags home. Locked and loaded, but dangerously low on ammo.

"Let's move quickly." Hank nods, face grim. This detour has already cost us too much time.

I step toward the first girl to free her. It's a simple lock. Pulling out my multitool, I find what I need and get to work. Iris stands beside me, watching, When the world erupts in a rain of gunfire, I leap back to defend.

"I'll free them." Her voice shakes and is low enough I strain to hear what she says.

"How?"

She reaches for my hand and her tiny fingers wrap around the multitool.

"Do you know how to use that?"

With a jerk of her chin, Iris steps up to free the women. Her courage allows me to defend us all.

While deafening gunfire hammers beyond the doorway, she frees the remaining girls. A squad of guards pins us down. Hank and I flatten against the walls while waves of bullets chew the room to shreds between us.

The Angels who are free plaster up against the wall. Only Iris stands in front of the deadly rain of lead. She stays there until the last Angel is free from her chains. The two of them dive for the floor and roll to the walls. It's the best cover they have.

The Angels scream and sob.

Hank and I exchange fire with the guards, ruthlessly dropping targets. But it's never enough. For each we kill, more arrive.

Soon, my rifle coughs on an empty chamber. Hank is down to his sidearm. Our position rapidly deteriorates under the endless assault.

We're caught in a kill-box, outgunned and outmanned. Still, the girls cry for salvation behind us.

"Gabe…" I yell desperately into comms. "We need you now."

"On our way." His terse reply sounds in my ears, but relief is too far off. We're going to get eaten alive under the barrage of bullets.

Hank meets my eyes across the devastated room, blood and sweat mixing on his grim face. We're going to lose this battle and the mission with it. All I can do now is buy the Angels a few more seconds.

With a roar, I draw my pistol and charge into the fatal corridor, determined to meet my end on my feet with bullets flying.

An unearthly shriek joins me. It rises rapidly, hurting my ears.

The guards scream and fire wildly as five sleek metal forms burst into the room—the Rufi have arrived. One of them stops by my side, delivering a fresh supply of ammunition.

Lord, I love the Rufi.

Mitzy's Rufi unleash a savage assault with integrated guns instead of "jaws." Their black metal armor bristles with weapons, bullets shredding concrete and bodies. The Rufi carve through the panicked defenders with precise robotic execution.

When the deafening chaos ceases, Gabe and Blake follow them in. I shake my head in awe at the carnage. "Remind me not to piss off Mitzy."

Gabe grins tightly. "Robots don't leave witnesses."

"You're supposed to be with Walt." I glance at Blake.

"And miss all the fun?" Blake grins. "Left a Rufi with Walt. He's good. You, however…"

"Needed the assist." I incline my head in a mock salute.

The Rufi stand guard in the hall, heads swiveling, optics glowing blue. Artificial intelligence stares back at me through those eyes. I thank Mitzy's ingenuity, but the gleam in the dogs' gazes leaves me unsettled.

"Let's move before more guards arrive," Gabe urges. We form a protective ring around the girls and head toward our exfil point's drainage tunnels. The Rufi take point and rear, eliminating any resistance.

Floor by floor, we fight down to our rally point. The sound of battle intensifies. Suddenly, the stairwell explodes with gunfire, cutting us off. "No way we're getting down there," Gabe yells.

Desperate, I hail CJ, but get only static. "We need alternate exfil, third sublevel."

"I can direct the Rufi to create a distraction." Hank has an idea. "It's risky…"

I don't like it, but we're trapped. "Do it."

At Hank's command, two Rufi detach and lope into the stairway, sleek metal forms on a suicide mission. Their integrated guns scythe into the ambushers until a massive explosion silences them.

"Move." We rush the stairs during the chaos. The remaining

Rufi carve our escape route. We reach the tunnels just as CJ's voice crackles through comms.

"The tunnels are collapsing. Get out!"

No time to think. We spin on our heels and sprint back the way we came, dragging the Angels with us.

As the adrenaline fades, my thoughts turn to one person, her fate unknown. Did you escape, Rebel? I cling to the frail hope that she found a way out—that I'll see her face again someday.

THIRTY-EIGHT

Rebel

_____

THE WORLD IS COMING DOWN AROUND ME, BUT I BARELY NOTICE THE flaming debris and crumbling walls. All I can think about is the records room in the basement—my last desperate hope of finding Violet.

When Ethan came for me, begging me to escape with him, my heart shattered into a thousand pieces. But I had to refuse. As long as there is the slightest chance a record still exists, I must find it or die trying. Violet deserves that much.

Ethan's eyes pleaded with me to go with him, but I didn't.

I couldn't.

And he couldn't help me. He has others to save.

I pray he makes it out of here. That he saves the women. I hope he lives to fight another day. The world needs more heroes like him. As for me, I forge ahead alone into the flames and smoke, willing to sacrifice everything for just one scrap of hope.

The air grows choked and acrid the lower I descend into Haven's bowels. Muted gunfire and unearthly shrieks echo from distant battles. Blood smears the walls where bodies have already been dragged away. The Guardians brought hell with them.

A squad of guards pounds past, decked in full tactical gear. His radio squawks. *"All personnel to Sectors 3 and 7 immediately."* They're so focused on the incursion that they barely glance at me hurrying by.

I overhear them mention a breach in the northwest quadrant. That must be where Ethan's team broke in. May fortune favor them. They provided the perfect diversion for me.

Reaching the final sublevel, I find the corridors deserted. The records room sits at the end behind an unmarked steel door. Please let something remain intact. I can't come this close only for everything to turn to ash now.

The heavy door groans on its hinges as I shove inside. My heart sinks. The entire ceiling collapsed, leaving mounds of smoking debris. Cabinets lie crushed and overturned. Acrid dust coats my throat, leaving me coughing.

It's hopeless. Whatever paper trail existed is buried forever now. I squeeze my eyes shut against bitter tears.

Violet slips further away with each dead end I meet.

But her memory won't let me walk away that easily.

Climbing over the wreckage, I dig through the piles. The debris cuts my fingers, and smoke stings my eyes, but I keep clawing relentlessly. For Violet, I have to try.

My hands close around a charred file box, its contents still intact. With trembling fingers, I pry off the melted lid and leaf through the files inside, squinting to make out the words. Records, intake forms, status updates—but nothing about Violet. I hurl the useless box away in frustration.

A loud groan shudders through the room as part of the remaining ceiling gives way. I barely throw myself clear as it crashes down, plunging the room into flickering darkness.

I lie there coughing, ears ringing in the sudden silence. Through the noise, a faint buzzing reaches me. One of the industrial lights dangling from the rafters still has power, its bulb blinking erratically.

The light sways, and sparks fly from the wires. It casts a flickering beam across the wreckage. Long shadows dance over the debris. The buzzing and strobing light feel suited to this nightmare.

Crawling on my knees, I comb over every inch, pulling aside boards and chunks of plaster. My nails split, my muscles scream, and dust chokes my lungs. None of it matters. I only stop when the room starts to spin, gulping down air that can scarcely be called oxygen anymore.

When my head clears enough, I resume my desperate search. The bulb dims dangerously, threatening to plunge me into darkness. So I talk to keep it glowing, babbling to Violet as if she can hear me.

"I'm trying, Vi, I swear I'm still trying." My raw throat scratches out the words. "I know you'd keep going if you were me. You always were the tough one, Vi."

I imagine her voice urges me on. Each new discovery brings hope, but it's always followed by crushing disappointment. The light flickers faster, its death imminent.

"Just a little longer, hang in there," I plead with the failing bulb, shaking it as if that will keep its electricity flowing. The room plunges into momentary darkness again and again, each time staying dark longer than the last time.

The buzzing takes on an urgent cadence as if warning me it's about to die. When it clicks off again, I know in my gut this is the last time. "No, no, no!" I cry hoarsely into the sudden void. "Please, not yet." Deep sobs wrack me.

My hope of finding some trace of Violet is buried beneath my feet. I release the dead bulb and double over with an anguished sob.

It was all for nothing.

Exhausted tears stream down my smoke-stained face. My hands are shredded, and my body is pushed far past its limits. But my spirit hurts most of all. I scream Violet's name until I have no voice in the lightless room.

Spent, I slump atop the debris pile that entombed my hopes. Above me, the facility groans and trembles as the Guardians' assault continues. Fiery oblivion creeps closer by the second, but I can't bring myself to rise, to seek escape or shelter.

What reason do I have left to keep going through this life alone? Everyone who ever mattered is gone—my parents, my sister, my reason for living. The final card I pinned my last hopes on proved worthless.

A heavy darkness swallows Haven, the silence of it seeping into my bones. Maybe it's fitting, a shadowy end in a place that's forgotten the sun. I can already feel the cool embrace, ready to take me to wherever Violet is.

The end feels close, a silent companion in the dark, until a sudden crash, deafening, roars through the silence, vibrating the ground under me. I don't budge, letting the dust cloak me, my breaths as shallow as the grave I'm expecting to join.

Silence again, but not for long. It's broken by a distinct crunching, a steady, purposeful rhythm.

Footsteps.

They're moving through the wreckage with intent, each step an echo in the hollow of Haven's broken heart. The sound grows closer, the cadence of someone not lost in the chaos but master of it.

A flicker of light cuts through the darkness, bobbing with the rhythm of the steps. My heavy eyelids fight against the grit and the sudden invasion of light. Boots, black as the void I'm sinking into, halt in front of me. There's a sudden vice on my jaw, a force pulling my face up to meet the eyes of the intruder. Kaufman's wild eyes bore into mine. Gone is the composed, cultured businessman—now, only the feral madness remains. The attack has stripped him down to primal savagery.

His fingers dig painfully into my cheeks as he jerks my face close to his. Flecks of spittle fly from his bared teeth. Blood mars his face where Ethan broke his nose.

"What the hell are you doing here?" He yanks my roughly. "The place is coming down, and you're crawling around a bunch of records?"

When I don't respond, he shakes me violently. "Answer me!"

Through the ringing in my ears, I rasp the bitter truth that brought me crawling back into this collapsing hellhole. It doesn't matter what he thinks or what he'll do to me. I'm already dead inside.

"I was looking for records."

"Records?" He scowls in incomprehension. "What records could possibly be worth your pathetic life?"

I swallow, throat raw and scraped. "Records of my sister. You sold her years ago. Forced her to carry a child." My voice rasps with smoke and grief and simmering rage.

Confusion flickers across Kaufman's face. For a moment, he seems truly perplexed, struggling to place this sister I speak of. So many captive girls have passed through his twisted hands over the years. It's no surprise their faces and stories blur together for him.

But then a slow, awful grin spreads over his face. The devil remembers an old sin. "Ah, the surrogacy project. Not as profitable as I had hoped. Closed that down years ago. Destroyed all the records. All the product." His chuckle sends chills down my spine. "I bet she was a pretty young thing. Brilliant genetics always fetch a great price."

His grin widens as understanding hits him. "You used me, you deceitful little cunt. Embedded in my operation, spying and feeding my enemies intel, all to find your beloved sister?" He throws his head back and cackles with wild abandon when I don't deny it. The sound echoes through the ruined space.

I stare numbly past him, too hollow to feel anything at his taunting.

"Oh, my savage little Rebel." He grasps my shoulders almost tenderly. "Did you really think you could use me and walk away?" His fingers dig in cruelly, making me gasp. "I own you, forever and completely. You'll never be free."

With that, he hauls me to my feet. When I stumble, he simply drags me along through Haven's wreckage.

We pass flickering scenes of chaos. Blood smears on the walls, lifeless bodies sprawled around each corner. Kaufman pays them no mind, maniacally focused on one goal—staking his claim on me.

I drift in a daze, one foot stumbling in front of the other. What does it matter where he takes me? Kaufman's path takes me to a place I never knew existed. This hall is unfamiliar to me.

I crane my neck as we stagger past several doors. Kaufman yanks me along heedlessly, but I manage to glimpse a faded plaque by the entrance to one of those doors: *Surrogacy Intake & Assessment.*

He notices the direction of my gaze.

"Hah, I may have kept some. Sadly, you looked in the wrong place, my savage Rebel."

My heart leaps. He wouldn't taunt me without reason.

New strength surges into my limbs. I stop resisting Kaufman's pull, playing the exhausted, compliant captive again, but my mind spins with possibilities. I know where I must look for Violet's trail. All I need is a chance to slip away and get inside that room.

Kaufman hauls me onward through the groaning facility. I can't let him remove me from this place. Not until I search that room. Despair no longer weighs down my feet. I move with purpose. The next opportunity Kaufman gives me might be my last, but I will seize it without hesitation.

For you, Violet. No matter the cost, I will find out where they took your baby. Kaufman continues dragging me through Haven's wreckage, but I'm done being led by him. Kaufman's distracted. His guard is down, thinking I'm a broken doll.

That mistake will cost him.

When we reach a deserted corridor, I make my move. With a feral cry, I whirl and launch myself at Kaufman, fingers clawing for his eyes. He shouts in surprise and anger as I rake bloody furrows across his face. We crash to the floor, kicking and thrashing violently.

"You bitch!" he roars.

I go for his throat, but he catches my hands, flips me to my back, and pins me beneath his greater weight. His bloodied face twists in rage and madness.

"Still have some fight left? Good." His grin chills my soul. "I'll enjoy breaking you all over again."

He wraps his hands around my throat, squeezing mercilessly. Darkness creeps across my vision as I gasp uselessly for air. This is it. After everything, I'm going to die here at Kaufman's hands.

A gunshot splits the air. Kaufman pitches to the side with a scream, freeing me. I roll away, choking violently as air floods my starving lungs. Against the far wall, Kaufman clutches a mangled leg, howling in agony. I lift my blurry gaze to my savior.

Ethan strides forward, face carved from stone, pistol leveled at

Kaufman's head. He flips up the visor on his helmet and our eyes meet across the space, a hundred unspoken words passing between us.

He came back for me.

But then I see the Angels.

He's not here for me. He's saving *them*.

Did I expect anything else? Isn't that exactly what I told him to do?

My gaze lands on Iris, and she returns a soft smile. Despite everything I did to her and the others, she offers kindness. With ruthless efficiency, Ethan knocks Kaufman out with the pistol grip.

"Come with me. You can't stay here."

I swallow through my raw throat and shake my head. "The assessment room. I need to get there."

Ethan turns to me, brow furrowed in confusion. "We need to get to the extraction point before this place collapses around us."

He reaches for my hand to lead me away, but I stand firm. "You don't understand. That room holds records of where they took her." I meet his conflicted gaze steadily. "I can't leave until I check. I may never get another chance to find her."

Ethan hesitates, urgency warring with sympathy in his expression. He turns to his men. "Get the Angels out of here."

"Boss?" Walt hesitates. "We have to get to exfil."

"Take the Angels. I'm going with Rebel."

"Copy that." Walt ushers the Angels down the hall toward freedom while I scurry to my feet.

"Lead the way. Quickly." With a terse nod, Ethan gestures down the hall.

Relief sweeps through me. I take off with Ethan close behind me. After years of searching, Violet's trail is finally within reach.

I hope.

Rooms blur past until we finally reach *Surrogacy Intake & Assessment*. The door hangs drunkenly off one hinge. Inside, file cabinets lay strewn everywhere.

Ethan stands guard at the door while I dig through the mess, shoving heavy cabinets aside and clawing through scattered papers.

I don't deserve his compassion, but I've never needed it more than I do now.

I scramble through the overturned file cabinets, tossing drawers and rifling through the jumbled papers. Most are burned or water-damaged beyond recognition. The room spins as panic rises in my throat.

It has to be here.

Frantically, I claw across the floor, shards of glass and metal cut into my palms and knees. Ethan calls my name, voice taut with urgency, but I barely hear him over the roaring in my ears. Only one thing matters now.

When I'm ready to scream with frustration, my fingers close around a partially charred folder, edges curled from a nearby fire. With trembling hands, I pry it open, hardly daring to breathe.

The top page is intact enough to make out key details.

Intake assessment...Violet.

"Oh, thank god," I gasp raggedly. The rest is burned away, denying me answers about where exactly she was taken, but this crumpled, smoldering page is tangible proof that Violet once walked these wretched halls.

My vision blurs with tears. After years of tormenting dead ends, I hold a piece of my sister in my hands. I press the precious, fragile page to my heart with shaking hands.

"We have to go. Now." Ethan's hand on my shoulder pulls me back. His voice holds deep empathy, but rings with urgency.

Blinking away tears, I tuck the file inside my dress and let Ethan pull me to my feet. His hand on my shoulder grounds me through the dizzying storm of emotion. He pulls me up and toward the exit. Toward a future Violet might be proud of.

Toward her child, my niece, or nephew.

THIRTY-NINE

Rebel

THE WALLS PRESS IN ON ALL SIDES AS ETHAN AND I RACE THROUGH the maze of Haven's lower levels. It's a terrifying labyrinth down here—cold concrete corridors with endless identical doors. The air hangs heavy with the metallic tang of blood and the acrid sting of gunpowder.

Up ahead, the muffled sounds of battle echo through the twisting passageways. Ethan's team must still be embroiled in fierce fighting, judging by the cacophony of automatic fire, screams, and explosions reaching us.

Ethan moves with confident familiarity through the sterile halls, hyper-alert and scanning continuously for threats. I trust him to guide us—he knows Haven's layout just as well, if not better than I do. Wherever the fighting rages fiercest above, he steers us away into safer territory.

We round a corner, and the overhead lights flicker wildly, threatening to plunge us into darkness. The sounds of slaughter seem to grow louder, creeping closer. My heart hammers against my ribs.

Sensing my fear, Ethan touches my shoulder. "Stay close. I'll get us out of here." His steady voice calms my racing pulse. However chaotic the world becomes, Ethan remains unshakeable beside me.

He's *with* me.

He *chose* me.

We continue downward, through corroding passages into older, more dilapidated sectors beneath Haven's sleeker facades. Here, the walls exude menace, stained with dark splotches that look suspiciously like old blood.

A thunderous boom shakes the ground beneath our feet. Cracks race along the grimy surfaces. The stale air fills with smoke and the acrid tang of explosives. Sounds of a raging firefight filter down through the aging concrete above us as if it's seeping steadily downward.

"They're bringing this whole place down around the bastard's ears," Ethan mutters. "If we don't hurry, we'll be buried down here too."

At last, we reach a sagging metal door secured by a rusty padlock. Ethan shoots it off and yanks the screeching door open, gesturing for me to proceed. "Old drainage tunnels," he says tersely. "They'll take us out of here."

We rush through, away from the stench of blood. Dim emergency lighting guides us along crumbling brickwork that predates the rest of Haven's structures. The fighting seems muted down here.

"Watch your step." Ethan's voice echoes through the cramped corridor. We pick our way over stagnant water and foul odors, past dripping pipes and piles of sludge.

Ethan continues through the crumbling maintenance tunnels. I follow close behind, trusting him to guide me to safety.

During a lull in our frantic flight, Ethan touches his earpiece. "Charlie-One to Charlie team. Report." His brow furrows as his team reports in. I can't hear what they say but follow the one-sided conversation, watching Ethan's reactions as his team reports in.

He pauses for a moment, waiting, then speaks again to his team. "Charlie-Five, status report?" Ethan repeats the hail, tone tightening with urgency. His face falls, and dread flickers through me.

"Who's Charlie-Five?" I hate to ask, but the expression on his face tells me something's horribly wrong.

"Jeb and Stitch." His eyes reflect grief that pierces my heart.

"Are they okay?" I reach for his hand, wishing I could ease this fresh pain, but Haven burns and collapses around us.

"We have to keep moving." Eyes hardening, Ethan gives my hand one brief squeeze. His tone brokers no argument, so I don't ask again.

Rounding a tight corner, the passage ends abruptly in a wall of collapsed rubble. Ethan swears. "Cave-in. We have to double back."

Turning in the narrow space proves difficult. A deafening groan shudders through the confined tunnel as I try to squeeze past Ethan. We freeze as dust rains down on us and cracks spiderweb across the ceiling. A support beam crashes a few feet away, punching through weakened brick beside us, creating an opening outside Haven.

"Go!" Ethan shoves me through the jagged gap. No time for stealth now—we scramble over debris, racing the destruction behind the facility.

I crawl up a banked slope, ready to crest the brink, but Ethan grabs me by the waist and yanks me down as bullets pepper the ground where I would have been exposed.

I sag against the slope, exhaustion and relief hitting me at once. We finally made it out of that hellhole.

"Charlie-One, over." Ethan touches his earpiece, eyes scanning our surroundings. He pauses to listen, then speaks again. "We're out, pinned down by sniper fire. No visual on transport. Request direction to rally point."

There's another pause while he cocks his head, listening to whoever's at the other end of his radio. "Wilco. Any word on Charlie-Five? Has Jeb checked in?" Another long pause. Ethan's expression darkens. He signs off and catches my gaze. Then he points down the ditch. "Time to move."

We run hunched over. Mud sucks at my feet with each frantic step, hampering my steps.

"This way," Ethan urges, splashing through the filthy water. I follow without question, trusting him to lead us back to safety.

Bullets dig into the dirt above us, reminding us we're not free yet.

But we're close.

So close.

In the distance, a transport waits under heavy guard. It's one of those big military transport trucks with an open bed in the back.

Ethan's grip steadies me. "When I say run, you run with everything you've got." His eyes are hard but determined. "Don't stop. Don't look back. Just run."

I nod, bracing myself.

Ethan's hand tightens on mine. He says something I can't hear. From how he tilts his head, I figure he's waiting for a signal from his team.

Suddenly, he pushes me up the bank and shouts. "Run!"

I sprint forward, expecting bullets to punch into me at any second.

Gunfire rips through the blackness right in front of us. Ethan tackles me down as bullets whiz through the air. I struggle to control my panicked breathing, ears ringing.

Hot shell casings rain onto my neck as he returns fire at the unseen threat. Squeezing my eyes shut, I make myself as small as possible. My heart hammers wildly against the ground. I'm helpless like this, a liability, and unable to do anything to help.

All I can do is trust Ethan will shield me.

When I dare to peek, something glossy and jet-black rushes past. I blink as another, and then another glossy black shape races past us. Gunfire rips through the air. Not aimed at us but coming from those stealthy shapes.

Aimed toward Kaufman's men.

Ethan rolls off of me and ejects a spent mag.

"You good?" His cool professionalism would be unnerving if it wasn't keeping us alive. "Can you run?"

"Yes."

He practically hauls me off the ground and tosses me forward where my feet contact the ground. I'm off and running again. This time, Ethan holds my hand, urging me forward.

We race toward the transport. Bullets pepper the dirt around us, but none find their mark. We're almost there. My heart pounds; freedom is so close now.

The other Angels huddle inside the back of the truck, their

exhausted forms slumped together. When they see us sprinting toward them, they shout encouragement. Leah, Iris, Gwen, and Elinda wave their arms, urging me to run faster.

Suddenly, a searing pain rips through my thigh. My leg buckles as I cry out and crash face-first to the ground. Grit fills my mouth, and blinding agony radiates from my leg.

This is it, I'm dead.

Ethan yanks me off the ground, hauls me into the air, and drapes me over his shoulder, never breaking his stride. "I've got you." His arm tightens over the backs of my thighs as I bounce like a ragdoll hanging over his shoulder. Something warm and sticky runs down my leg.

When I look behind us, I blink, not believing my eyes. Four robots, the size of a fair-sized dog, fire bullets from what look like mouths. They raze the ground, taking down dozens of guards chasing us.

Ethan reaches the truck. It's stuffed with Angels and men dressed in black tactical gear—Charlie team.

But there are only four men. Five with Ethan.

No sign of Jeb or Stitch.

Men reach down, pulling me out of Ethan's arms. Ethan turns around to lay down covering fire as I'm dragged into the bed of the truck. His men lay me flat on the hard metal, and the engine roars as Ethan leaps on board.

"Any word from Jeb?" he asks his teammates, but they all shake their heads.

"They're not here and aren't responding to comms." Hank's lips set into a grim line.

"We have to go." I watch him lock down his emotions and reach for his hand, trying to say what words can't. For men like Ethan, leaving men behind goes against their core values, but I understand his dilemma. He can't return to find Jeb and Stitch and rescue the Angels. This whole place is a hot zone with active fire all around us.

"We have to go." Ethan looks at his men. As a unit, they return the same sharp jerk of their chins. He barks an order to the driver.

With a lurch, the tires spin, and we surge away amidst peppering gunfire.

He stands at the rear, his gaze fixed on the smoking rubble that used to be Haven. Though his stoic expression reveals nothing, it's clear his thoughts remain with his missing teammate and Stitch.

The searing agony in my thigh returns as the adrenaline surging in my blood runs its course. I grip my thigh, feeling a sticky wetness, then glance down at the dark blood pooling beneath me.

Lots of blood.

My head swims, consciousness threatening to slip away.

"Rebel's hit," Walt calls out, snagging Ethan's attention. "Shit, that's a lot of blood."

"She needs a tourniquet." Ethan's strained face comes into focus above me. "I told you not to look back," he says, but there's no heat behind it. His eyes reflect only bone-deep relief as he helps me sit.

"What were those things?" I have no idea why I ask about the black shapes that saved us. I suppose it's better than thinking about what's going on with my leg. The world spins around me as the truck jostles over the uneven ground, and blackness creeps in on me.

"Rufi."

"What?" I shake my head, pushing the blackness away.

"Mechanized mayhem." Ethan laughs when my brows bunch together. "Robotic Ultra Functional Utility Specialists. Rufus, or Rufi when plural."

A tearful, delirious laugh escapes me. Dizzy from blood loss and the magnitude of what we survived, a rush of euphoria overwhelms me as Ethan's teammates crouch around me.

Ethan's steady hands apply a tourniquet to my injured leg, causing white-hot pain to momentarily blind me. But through it all, his face remains my anchor. As hard as I tried to shut him out, I couldn't sever something that ran soul deep.

Ethan grasps my face, his rough palms so impossibly gentle. Our eyes lock, speaking a language only we understand. No more holding back.

He crushes his lips to mine and pours every bottled-up longing, fear, and devotion into this imperfect moment of hard-won joy.

This is different than our first kiss.

We share breath, tears, the taste of grit, smoke, and abiding love. Our past suffering fades away until only this exquisite sense of rightness remains.

When we finally break apart, the promise of a future shines through the trauma and exhaustion shrouding us. The other Angels huddle together for comfort, but Ethan and I only have eyes for each other. We need no words to express what our hearts have always known.

I cling to Ethan, dizzy with adrenaline and overwhelming love. My fingers trace his beloved face, needing the tactile proof that he's real. That we made it out together against impossible odds. Exhaustion pulls at me and darkness rushes toward me. My thoughts drift as I reach down and tap my chest.

The file's safe.

Vi, the file's safe.

With that, I succumb to the pull of unconsciousness and let it take me under.

FORTY

Ethan

I SLUMP BACK AGAINST THE REAR GATE OF THE DEUCE, ADRENALINE fading. Haven is burning. The women are safe. I look at Rebel tucked in my arms and feel a surge of rightness filling me from the inside out.

The transport bounces through the woods until finally turning onto a paved road. The bumpy ride smooths out from there as we escape.

The jarring ride should be unbearably painful for Rebel with the bullet wound to her leg. Maybe it is? Fortunately, she slips in and out of consciousness. That's both good and bad. I don't want her to endure the added pain, but she lost a lot of blood. I worry she's in shock, but there's little we can do other than place the tourniquet and put her in a recovery position.

The back of the truck is cramped, but we rescued all twenty women. Twenty-one counting Rebel. The women huddle together, some crying softly, others staring numbly ahead. The emotions coursing through them overwhelming—the trauma of captivity, the sudden violence of the rescue, and the spark of hope kindled inside them.

My team comforts the rescued women as best they can, speaking in low, soothing voices. The others cast frequent glances into the dark, alert for any sign of pursuit.

The Rufi disappeared; I assume they altered course to assist Alpha and Bravo team in evacuating from this hellish place. Several times, I try to contact Jeb over my comms.

Nothing but silence returns. I hope he's with Alpha or Bravo. "Charlie-One to Alpha-One."

"Max here. What's up?"

"Did you happen to run across Jeb and Stitch?"

"We have not."

"He's not answering his comms. I'll call Bravo and see if they have them."

"Copy that. Want us to circle back?" Max is always ready to lend a hand.

"Are you able?"

"We're several clicks out, but I've got Rufi we can send."

"Thanks." I pinch the bridge of my nose and send out a silent prayer that Jeb and Stitch are with Bravo. "Charlie-One to Bravo-One."

"Brady here. What's up?"

"Is Jeb with you? He's not answering comms."

"Negative."

"We got all the women out but are missing Jeb and Stitch. Max is standing ready to send the Rufi back to look."

"We'll meet up with Alpha team and problem-solve from there."

"Thanks. Appreciate you."

"Back at you. Get those women to safety. We'll find your teammate."

"Copy that."

I wrap my arms around Rebel, feeling tremors coursing through her slender frame. She leans her head against my chest and sits in the cradle of my legs, where I protect her injured leg. I stroke her hair, murmuring soft words of comfort.

So much remains unspoken between us, but I hold her for now, letting my presence anchor her. Soon, we'll be safe. Soon, we can begin unwinding the tangled threads between us—if she's ready to let me in.

Violet.

I don't think I really understood what her sister means to her. Rebel was willing to risk her life to find whatever was on that paper. She never lost her grip on it. Not when she stumbled. Not when she fell. Not even when I lifted her over my shoulder and carried her to safety. She clutches it even now as if it means the world to her.

The trip to the airfield seems endless, but we finally arrive where Guardian HRS's jet waits on the tarmac, engines rumbling in anticipation of our arrival.

When we pull up next to the airplane, Walt and Gabe climb out of the back of the truck. Hank and Blake stay where they are. They help Rebel stand on her good leg while I jump to the ground.

Gently, they lower her injured form into my arms. Cradling her, I take off for the airstairs while my teammates help the women climb down from the tall truck.

CJ's craggy face greets me at the top of the airstairs. Beside him, Doc Summers is there with her medical team. Fortunately, our injuries are light.

Except for Rebel.

"Any word on Jeb?" I ask.

"Not yet." CJ ushers me into the plane, where Doc Summers greets me. She takes one look at the tourniquet on Rebel's leg and immediately directs me to the in-flight medical suite, where I place Rebel on an operating table.

With practiced efficiency, they inspect the damage and jump right in. The CRNA, Tia, places an IV in Rebel's arm while the Respiratory Therapist, Ryker, preps his airway equipment for surgery.

I take that as my cue. Her injury is not only serious, but life-threatening.

Knowing that whatever's on that paper is precious to Rebel, I gently extricate it from her arms and keep it safe.

"We need to operate." Doc Summers places a hand on my chest, the gentle pressure pushing me back from Rebel's side. "That bullet hit an artery. Smart move with the tourniquet, but we have to operate now if we're going to save her leg." She excuses me from the in-flight surgical suite, leaving me to join my teammates and help settle our newest rescues.

CJ clasps my arm. "Damn fine work down there."

"Thanks, but I'm missing Jeb and Stitch."

"Mitzy's already on it. She activated his trackers, and Alpha and Bravo stayed behind to find them. Right now, let's get you home."

"I should stay."

"Normally, I'd agree, but we can't afford the distraction." CJ glances toward where Rebel is getting prepped for emergency surgery. It's his way of telling me to take a step back from my responsibilities as team leader. He knows what Rebel means to me.

"Understood." I give a tired nod, unwilling to argue the point when I know he's right.

A flash of memory strikes me, returning me to months ago when we pulled Rebel out of Nicaragua.

A fiery-haired woman who stood out from the others. Defiance blazing in her eyes, her spirit unbroken despite the condition we find her in.

From the instant we met, I knew there was something different about this woman. I have questions, but they'll have to wait until after Rebel emerges from surgery.

The flight back passes in a blur. We offload the women, taking them directly to the medical facilities at Guardian HQ. When I'm not hovering outside the surgical suite, I drift in and out of sleep, thoughts churning.

Debriefings follow, a hazy recounting of the events leading up to the rescue. CJ and the others listen intently, probing for details, analyzing where we succeeded and where we can improve.

Finally, my team is released from duty with orders to rest and recover. I make my way to Medical and check in on Rebel. Doc Summers catches me and tells me Rebel's still recovering and under heavy sedation following the surgery.

"Come back in the morning."

I want to sit by her side, but Doc Summers politely tells me to leave.

Exhaustion bears down on me as I make my way through Guardian headquarters. The successful rescue leaves my spirits soaring, but my body feels like it went twelve rounds with a heavyweight boxer. I'm operating on fumes at this point.

But sleep remains elusive and out of reach. Too many questions churn through my mind, and every single one is centered around the mysterious woman now recovering from surgery.

Rebel risked everything for the charred papers I carry. She was willing to die for the secrets they contain. Well, I can help with that. I take the papers to our technical expert, Mitzy, and see if she can recover anything useful. Going behind Rebel's back this way feels invasive, but my need to understand her outweighs those hesitations.

I find Mitzy hunkered down in her technical kingdom, surrounded by an orchestra of beeping CPUs and glowing displays. She glances up, fingers tapping away at three different keyboards simultaneously.

"Ethan, shouldn't you be in bed?"

"Shouldn't you?"

"Too much work to do." She gestures to the monitors. "We've got weeks, if not months, of data to comb through. Hopefully, we'll be able to find the records of previous women sold through Haven. No rest for the weary."

"Ain't that the truth."

"So…" She taps her fingers. "Why are you up at Oh-dark-thirty?" Her psychedelic hair sparkles in the low light.

"Couldn't sleep and holding these for Rebel." I pass the folded papers to Mitzy. "I'm hoping you can work some magic on these. They're damaged, but important to her."

"Important?" Her brows pinch together. "How?"

"I'm hoping you can answer that for me. I know her sister was taken ten years ago, impregnated for a *client*, and escaped just after the birth."

"Wow, that's a lot to process."

"There's more. Violet called Rebel. Violet was caught and killed during that call, but not before telling Rebel about the baby. She's hoping something on those papers will tell her where that child wound up."

"Damn. When I think I've heard and seen it all."

"I'm hoping you can find something. It was important enough for Rebel to brave fire, smoke, and the building nearly coming down around her ears."

"I'll see what I can do." Mitzy spreads the charred documents on the table. Her brow furrows. She turns on an overhead camera and magnifying lens. "Well, this is a mess."

"I can't make out anything. Is it a total loss?" I admit to being somewhat conflicted. Part of me wants to find nothing on these documents. Part of me hopes there's something there. Something worth Rebel risking her life.

"Let me see what I can do." She looks up from the papers.

For the next half hour, I watch her manipulate the pages under different light spectrums, run chemical tests, and try various imaging techniques to draw out faint impressions.

Aside from a partial logo, the papers remain stubbornly illegible.

"Ugh, stupid, stupid paper," Mitzy mutters, taking the failure personally. "It's almost as if it was engineered to self-destruct if tampered with. I'm wringing every trick out of my bag here."

"Those documents have been through hell." I squeeze her shoulder. "I appreciate you trying." When I lean in to take back the documents, Mitzy places a hand on my arm.

"Do you mind leaving it with me?"

"Not at all."

She's got a better chance of figuring out whatever's on the paper than I do. I take my leave, discouraged but unsurprised. Nothing's ever easy.

FORTY-ONE

Ethan

THE NEXT DAY, MY FEET CARRY ME TO MEDICAL ON AUTOPILOT. I pause outside Rebel's room, peering through the narrow glass pane. She looks small and pale amidst the tubes and wires, but her chest rises and falls steadily. Just knowing she's alive sends relief flooding through me.

I press a hand to the glass, aching to go to her, but unwilling to disturb her recovery.

"You care about her." A soft voice startles me.

I turn to see Iris hovering timidly behind me. She survived Haven along with the other Angels, but trauma haunts her eyes.

I've rescued countless individuals, yet I still struggle to comprehend the horrors they've endured. I find them the strongest people alive; for some reason, Iris makes me feel comfortable opening up to her.

"We have a—complicated history," I hedge. Even I don't fully understand what binds me to Rebel.

Iris nods. "She talked about you sometimes. When it was just us." She risks meeting my gaze. "You were the only thing that gave her hope."

"That surprises me."

"You think Rebel is horrible for grooming the rest of us to be Kaufman's Angels. I see the judgment in your eyes and the confusion."

"It doesn't make sense."

"She did us a favor, and we're grateful for the chance she gave us."

"She offered you slavery. How could that be—"

"Our options were limited. Escape was impossible. Rescue…" She makes a gesture toward me. "Well, rescue seemed even more impossible. Faced with two evils, she gave us an opportunity to pick the lesser evil. I don't know if I can explain it better than that. Except when she was alone, working with us, convincing us to do the unthinkable and accept our fate, she always talked about the man she met, fell in love with, and left."

"She did what?" I'm struck speechless. Even after we parted ways, Rebel still thought of me as she endured Kaufman's world alone? It shakes something loose inside me, making me see our connection in a new light.

"She said few people ever meet their soul mate. That she met hers, but duty and obligation forced her away. Forced her to do the unthinkable and become Kaufman's Angel. She told us life wouldn't be easy, but we would have a life to live." Iris shrugs.

"How are you doing?" As much as I could talk about Rebel all day, Iris is still recovering from her trauma. I don't want to be insensitive to her needs.

"Evidently, the same as you." Her warm gaze is like a balm that soothes my soul. Iris would make a good healer. She has that magical touch.

"Huh?"

"Not sleeping." She wraps her arms around herself and blows out a deep breath. "The people here are amazing. Your organization—its mission—is incredible. They patched those of us that needed patching up and let us take these amazing hot showers. For the first time in months, I feel somewhat human." Iris draws back apologetically. "Take care of Rebel. She needs someone who can forgive her. The choices she made are some I hope never to be forced to make. Be that person for her. The one who loves her unconditionally and despite her faults."

Over the next few days, I split my time between checking in on Rebel's recovery and undergoing debriefings about the Haven rescue. The whole team walks around, high on adrenaline, exhausted but satisfied. We accomplished what we came to do, though at a cost.

Jeb and Stitch finally reported in; thank God. Buried in the rubble that was Haven, it took two days for Mitzy's Rufi to dig them out. They rented a van to bring the Rufi back and are somewhere between the mountains of Montana and the rugged coastline of California.

A cheeky grin fills my face. I'd love to be a fly on that wall.

At last, Doc Summers gives me the green light to visit Rebel. I enter her room quietly, not wanting to wake her, but her eyes crack open when I sit beside her. Relief floods me at that small response until her eyes pinch with pain, and she turns away.

"Welcome back to the land of the living. You had me worried." I keep my tone light, but emotion thickens my voice. "Doc Summers had to operate on your leg in the plane. You lost a lot of blood and nearly didn't make it."

Rebel's face spasms with some internal struggle. She avoids my searching gaze, fingers gripping the sheets. The yawning silence expands between us. I don't push, sensing she's working up to speaking.

But a knock at the door shatters the moment. Doc Summers bustles in to check vitals, and Rebel shuts down, avoiding my gaze once more. The wall is back up, at least for now. I bite back my frustration.

Over the next few days, Rebel gradually regains strength. Her leg keeps her confined to Medical, and the forced immobility visibly grates at her.

"You need to give your leg time to heal. Focus on getting stronger. The rest will come in time." I do my best to encourage her.

"I don't have that luxury." Rebel just gives me a cryptic look.

Her restless obsession with the past worries me, but perhaps one

310 • ELLIE MASTERS

thing can provide solace. I visit Mitzy and collect the damaged records the day before Rebel is discharged.

When I enter Rebel's room, she greets me as guardedly as ever. Wordlessly, I pass her the folded paper. Confusion knits her brow until she unfolds it.

"Sentinel?" Rebel frowns. "I don't know what that means."

"We don't either." I squeeze her hand. "But we'll keep digging, see if it leads anywhere."

Rebel nods, but the hope in her eyes fizzles out.

"I know how much it means for you to find Violet's child. Guardian HRS will do everything possible to uncover leads on your niece or nephew."

"You would do that? After everything I did?" Tears shine in Rebel's eyes.

"Hey, look at me." I tilt her chin up. "You've been fighting this battle alone for so long. You don't have to carry this burden yourself anymore. Let me—let the Guardians—help shoulder it now."

Rebel searches my face through her tears. Slowly, she nods, lips trembling but resolute.

I kiss her knuckles softly. "We're going to find your family." It's the least we can do after all Rebel has sacrificed.

She grips my hand tightly, wordlessly at first. At last, she whispers roughly, "Thank you. For not giving up on me."

I gently brush a tear from her cheek. "Never."

"I don't deserve you."

"You deserve me more than you know."

"Thank you," she rasps. "Thank you for understanding and for forgiving me. What I did...leaving you..." Her eyes tear up. "It was the hardest thing I've ever done. I never knew you'd find me and rescue me again."

No other words are needed.

FORTY-TWO

Ethan

Several Weeks Later

THE SETTING SUN CASTS A MUTED CURTAIN OF FIRE ACROSS THE SKY as it sinks into the ocean. I make my way up the coastal road toward my new quarters. It's been another long day of training drills and tactical meetings at Guardian headquarters. My muscles ache pleasantly from being pushed hard.

Less than a week ago, I signed on the dotted line, making this place mine. My life with the Guardians has given me purpose, and sharing this space with Rebel makes it feel complete.

Stepping inside, I pause to take in the cozy interior. Late afternoon light slants through the windows, casting a warm, soothing glow. The faint scent of Jasmine tickles my nose—Rebel's favorite soap.

A smile tugs my lips, and need stirs my cock to life.

Curled up on the sofa, her nose is buried in a book. An oversized sweater slips off one creamy shoulder, revealing the distinct absence of a bra.

I like that.

The dying light softens her features and sets her fiery curls ablaze. She looks up at my entrance, a pencil tucked behind her ear, and her face melts into a smile. In the warm light, she seems fragile, strung out by exhaustion and emotion.

I'm across the room in two strides and scoop her eagerly into my arms. She comes willingly, legs wrapping around my waist as our mouths find each other. We kiss hungrily, reuniting after a day apart. My pulse quickens, feeling her curves press against me.

"Welcome home," she murmurs, nuzzling my jaw.

"God, I missed you." I breathe her in, overwhelmed with gratitude that she's safe. After everything, having this chance to build a life together feels like a gift.

Our kisses begin lazy and unhurried, a reminder we have all the time in the world, but as desire rushes through us, our kisses grow rougher and more passionate.

We struggle with our clothing, tearing it away in our frantic rush to divest ourselves of any barrier between us. Running rough with desire, I yank off her shirt and smirk at the widening of her lids. I pull her roughly against me, claiming her mouth with mine, loving the way she trembles for me with a raw mixture of fear and pleasure.

She surprises me when she goes to her knees. My cock twitches eagerly, anticipating the heat of her mouth and the rough rasp of her tongue. My heart thunders as I reach for her hair and wrap it around my wrist. A primal and fierce need for her roars within me.

The air crackles with raw sexual desire, and my muscles quiver with the need to possess her in every way. My free hand finds her throat, and I trace the delicate line where her pulse thrums with desire. With her hair wrapped around my wrist and my hand guiding the back of her head, I pull her to my eager cock.

"Open." It's a single word but filled with male dominance.

That subtle shift in our power dynamic is a heady aphrodisiac, and Rebel responds. She opens her mouth and takes me in, licking and sucking as I press into her.

The pleasure is intense, and I groan, urging her to take more of me. I move my hand to guide her movements, loving how she uses her mouth and tongue to pleasure me. I thrust deeper, feeling a wave of pleasure building within me, but before I come, I need to be inside her.

I pull away, quickly lifting her onto the couch. Then it's me who goes to my knees. Rebel's entire body trembles, her eyes dark with desire as I notch the flare of my cock between her folds. She knows what's coming and shifts her hips to welcome me.

I plunge into her, and her gasp of pleasure shoots through me like a liquid bolt of lightning. We move together, our bodies finding the perfect rhythm. Her tight heat wraps me in a blissful cocoon, and I thrust deeper and harder, loving how my cock slides in and out of her body.

I love watching her come. Love the way her face morphs as pleasure races through her body. Love how her eyes roll back as the pleasure builds. How her inner walls grip me with delicious, sweet heat.

With each thrust, I sink deeper and deeper into her, joining us together as one. The tension in her body builds as I bring her closer and closer to the edge.

"Come for me," I urge her in a voice filled with raw, desperate need.

Her entire body clenches around me, her body shuddering in pleasure as she cries out my name. Her orgasm triggers mine, and I bury my face in the crook of her neck, breathing in her scent and feeling her body arch beneath me.

I groan with my release, barely able to stand the sensations rushing through me. Our moans mingle together, a unique symphony that is just us.

I collapse onto her, feeling the warmth of her skin against mine. We stay like that for a while, with me still buried deep inside her, both of us panting and locked in the perfect embrace until my breathing slows and the last of the tension leaves my body. I run my hand over her back, feeling the warmth of her body against mine.

"I love you," I murmur, pressing a kiss to her forehead.

"I love you too," she whispers, her voice still husky with desire. "And I love it when you get bossy during sex."

"I aim to please." I smile and pull her closer, grateful to finally have her beside me and happy I have a home to come home to. "You make it fun coming home after a long day."

"Then it's me who aims to please." She cups my face and pulls me in for a kiss.

Once is not enough. It's merely the beginning, and I shamelessly take everything she offers again and again.

Unbound by rules or reason, we chase euphoria as our bodies join together over and over again. The primal rhythm of our movements turns frenzied and raw, building anticipation until neither of us can take it any longer.

I take her on her knees, bend her over the couch, fuck her on the kitchen counter and against the far wall. If it's a flat surface, vertical or horizontal, I make good use of it. That includes the shower. Our cries harmonize with the pounding surf below as pleasure crests and rushes over us in waves.

Her breathy moans fuel my hunger. Lost in her, nothing exists except skin on skin. Her gasps and my grunts. We're consumed by rapture as pleasure courses through us both.

I move my lips against her skin, tasting the salt on her neck as her hands run through my hair. My heart skips a beat as I realize this is what it means to be truly alive.

I trace my tongue along her shoulder as our breathing slows.

My hands slide up her body, and I flip her onto her knees, pushing into her deeply from behind. Her muscles flex as she pushes back against me, moaning deeply. The softness of her skin intoxicates me. The silky grip of her walls wrapping around my cock drives me insane.

My hands slide from her hips up her sweaty skin, tracing the shape of her rib cage and the swell of her breasts until they gather at her nape. Here, I fist her hair and draw her head back.

With each thrust, I force her head to turn, demanding access to her mouth. My hips move in time with hers as our sweat-slickened skin glides together. I slow the pace, working us closer to climax but also enjoying the path getting there.

The feral sounds of our passion, and the slapping of our bodies against each other, grow louder and higher pitched with each stroke of my cock.

I thrust harder into her depths, pushing us both into a wild frenzy of pleasure. She screams as I drive into her, our pleasure cresting and exploding together. We cling to each other, lost in a moment of bliss, until our breathing slows, and we drift back down to earth.

We collapse in a tangled heap of limbs on the floor, breaths coming hard and fast, yet somehow intertwined. A comfortable silence falls over us as our bodies slowly cool down from our passion-fueled exertion.

I pull out and draw her against my chest, wrapping my arms around her protectively. A satisfied smile tugs at my lips as I trace circles on her back.

"Mmm," Rebel sighs contentedly against my chest, "I love when you come home eager to fuck."

We make love until the sun has long set, and the night is filled with nothing but the two of us tangled together, breathless and sated, our hearts beating in unison.

"I love you," I whisper, my lips brushing her ear.

She sighs contentedly and snuggles closer, smiling as she murmurs, "I love you too."

Later, tangled in the sheets, Rebel traces lazy patterns on my chest as I run my fingers through her hair. No words are needed in this perfect moment. She's in my arms, and I'll never let anything take her away again. This is home.

"How are you holding up?" I take her hand in mine.

She attempts a shaky smile. "I'm not sure. It's like I'm caught in a dream." She searches my face. "Thank you for coming after me. For believing in me."

"I'll always come for you." I kiss her forehead, a silent promise. She sighs, leaning her head on my shoulder. We sit like that as the sky darkens outside, drawing comfort from each other.

I stroke Rebel's hair until her tears subside. Exhaustion claims us, and I curl around her, keeping the nightmares at bay. She's safe in my arms, and I'll die before I let anyone hurt her again. That's a vow carved into my soul.

In the dark, she whispers, "Promise you don't hate me."

"I promise." I kiss the top of her head, breathing in the floral scent of her hair. "I'm here. Always."

THE NEXT MORNING, THE POUNDING WAVES CRASHING ON THE ROCKS below stir me awake. I stretch and smile, hardly believing this cozy cottage overlooking the Pacific is mine. After nearly a year of bunking in Guardian HRS temporary housing, having a private space to call home feels like a luxury.

Early morning sun filters through the gauzy curtains. The first rays of sunlight fall over Rebel's silhouette curled against me, casting her in a warm glow. I brush a stray copper curl from her face, struck again by her beauty. Her chest's peaceful rise and fall soothes my soul.

I never imagined sharing my personal space so intimately with another person, but waking up with her feels natural. She belongs here.

Rebel stirs, nuzzling into the crook of my shoulder with a contented sigh. Her slender arm drapes over my bare chest. I continue stroking her fiery locks, letting her wake slowly.

At last, her sea-green eyes blink open to meet mine. Those eyes pierced my heart the first time our paths crossed. Now, I get lost in them each morning.

"Good morning, beautiful," I murmur.

She gives me that smile that makes my heart skip a beat, fluttering like a fool in love. "Mmm—morning."

Her voice is still husky with sleep. I can't resist leaning in to kiss her parted lips. She responds eagerly, hands coming up to cradle my jaw as we exchange lazy, unhurried kisses.

Sunlight spills over our entwined bodies while our passion ignites. I trail kisses down her graceful neck, along her collarbone, and across the swell of her breasts, taking my time to relearn every sensitive spot. She arches into my caresses, hands grasping at my back.

I kiss lower, over her taut stomach, along her inner thighs. When I finally taste her slick folds, her back bows off the bed. I lick and suck until she is trembling on the edge, then slide back up to enter her slowly.

We move together, wrapped in each other's arms. The rhythm builds gradually until we crest as one, sighing into a deep kiss. Rebel completes me in ways I'm still discovering.

After, we lay tangled in the rumpled sheets, trading lingering kisses. The only sounds are our breathing and the steady crash of waves outside. I could stay like this all morning, but a growl from Rebel's stomach makes me chuckle.

"I guess we need to feed you, beautiful."

I roll out of bed and pull on boxer shorts. Rebel doesn't bother dressing, stretching cat-like and unabashedly nude. I can't tear my eyes from her as I head to the kitchen.

While whisking eggs for an omelet, I call over my shoulder, "You know, I meant to ask how you got so good at hand-to-hand combat."

Rebel glances up from where she's slicing fruit on the counter. "When I went underground, I knew the kind of dark world I was entering. I started training in Brazilian jiu-jitsu, Krav Maga, anything I could pick up. Street fighting, too."

I flip the omelet, fascinated by this glimpse into her mysterious past. "So you were preparing yourself in case things got rough?"

She nods, bringing the fruit platter over. "I had to be ready for anything. Same with learning to shoot. I needed to be able to defend myself."

I kiss her temple. "Remind me not to get on your bad side."

She smirks. "I could take you."

"Is that a challenge?" I pinch her backside playfully, making her yelp. Chuckling, I plate our breakfast. We sit down on the sunny patio overlooking the cliffs and dig in. Rebel closes her eyes blissfully at her first bite.

"So good. Thank you for cooking." She leans over to kiss my cheek. Having someone to cook for makes the cottage feel even more like home.

We chat comfortably between bites about nothing in particular. For the first time in ages, Rebel looks unburdened, the ghosts of her past kept at bay for now. Seeing her like this, I'm overwhelmed with gratitude that she's safe with me.

But unrest stirs within her. That vow to her sister remains.

After clearing the dishes, I pull Rebel close for a slow dance in the kitchen, swaying to music only we can hear. She rests her head on my chest with a contented hum that vibrates through me. I don't ever want to let her go.

My laptop chimes with an incoming video call, interrupting our idyllic moment. Keeping one arm around Rebel's waist, I cross over to punch the button. CJ's grinning face pops up on the screen.

"Morning, lovebirds," he says jovially.

I roll my eyes but can't help smiling. He knows me well. "What's the word?"

Before he can reply, Rebel squeaks, having just realized she's naked and in full view of the camera. She dives out of frame.

CJ just chuckles. "Glad to see you two are enjoying yourselves."

I feel my ears burning but have to laugh. "Sorry about that. What were you saying?"

CJ's expression turns serious again. "We got a lead on Sentinel. Mitzy dug up an old case file connecting it to a fertility clinic in Marin. It looks like Rebel's sister was a patient there."

I glance toward the bedroom where Rebel is hastily dressing. "That's huge. We'll head in as soon as possible."

"No need to rush," he assures me. "Just wanted to update you. Give Rebel a hug from all of us. Let her know we're working on it."

"Will do." I manage a tight smile before ending the call.

Rebel emerges fully dressed, and I brief her on the new lead.

"This could be it." Her green eyes shine with hope. After years of searching, answers about her sister's fate may soon be within reach.

I brush my lips over her knuckles. "We're going to get to the truth. I promise."

She moves into my arms. I hold her close, burying my face in her fiery curls. "You don't have to face your demons alone anymore."

"Because I have you." She loops her arms over my shoulders.

"And I have you." I close my eyes, envisioning the day she gets to hug her niece or nephew for the first time.

Soon, my love. Soon, your family will be whole again.

Until then, she has me to help shoulder her burdens, and I will be there, standing by her side, from today to tomorrow and all the days that follow.

Dear Reader,

Your journey through the thrills and passion of "Rescuing Rebel" may have reached its pulse-pounding conclusion, but I'm inviting you to delve deeper into Ethan and Rebel's romance with an exclusive bonus scene.

Witness Ethan and Rebel in a moment of raw vulnerability and fierce intimacy. This scene is a hidden chapter that will give you insider access to their tumultuous love story.

Grab Ethan and Rebel's Bonus scene HERE.
elliemasters.com/RescuingRebelBonusScene

Craving more of the Guardians' heart-racing heroism?

Are you ready to see if the Guardians can unravel the mystery and bring Rebel's niece or nephew home?

Don't miss out on the adrenaline-fueled exploits of CHARLIE Team.

RESCUING STITCH is the next book in the series. Grab your copy HERE.
(EllieMasters.com/RescuingStitch)

Dive back into the world where danger is matched only by desire, and the promise of a happy-ever-after is earned, not given.

These former military special ops soldiers turned hostage rescue specialists are not just saviors; they're the ultimate protectors.

The stakes have never been higher, and the Guardians are ready to risk it all.

They're not just fighting for justice—they're battling for family.

xoxo,

Ellie Masters

THE ADVENTURE CONTINUES in Rescuing Stitch Jeb and Stitch's powerful story of love and survival. Grab your copy of Rescuing Stitch HERE.
(EllieMasters.com/RescuingStitch)

ELLZ BELLZ

ELLIE'S FACEBOOK READER GROUP

If you are interested in joining the ELLZ BELLZ, Ellie's Facebook reader group, we'd love to have you.

Join the ELLZ BELLZ Facebook Reader Group
elliemasters.com/EllzBellz

Sign up for Ellie's Newsletter.
Elliemasters.com/newslettersignup

Also by Ellie Masters

The LIGHTER SIDE

Ellie Masters is the lighter side of the Jet & Ellie Masters writing duo! You will find Contemporary Romance, Military Romance, Romantic Suspense, Billionaire Romance, and Rock Star Romance in Ellie's Works.

YOU CAN FIND ELLIE'S BOOKS HERE:

ELLIEMASTERS.COM/BOOKS

Military Romance

Guardian Hostage Rescue Specialists

Rescuing Melissa

(Get a FREE copy of Rescuing Melissa

when you join Ellie's Newsletter)

Alpha Team

Rescuing Zoe

Rescuing Moira

Rescuing Eve

Rescuing Lily

Rescuing Jinx

Rescuing Maria

Bravo Team

Rescuing Angie

Rescuing Isabelle

Rescuing Carmen

Rescuing Rosalie

Rescuing Kaye

Cara's Protector

Rescuing Barbi

Charlie Team

Rescuing Rebel

Rescuing Stitch

Military Romance
Guardian Personal Protection Specialists

Sybil's Protector

Lyra's Protector

The One I Want Series
(Small Town, Military Heroes)
By Jet & Ellie Masters

EACH BOOK IN THIS SERIES CAN BE READ AS A STANDALONE AND IS ABOUT A DIFFERENT COUPLE WITH AN HEA.

Saving Abby

Saving Ariel

Saving Brie

Saving Cate

Saving Dani

Saving Jen

Rockstar Romance
The Angel Fire Rock Romance Series

EACH BOOK IN THIS SERIES CAN BE READ AS A STANDALONE AND IS ABOUT A DIFFERENT COUPLE WITH AN HEA. IT IS RECOMMENDED THEY ARE READ IN ORDER.

Ashes to New (prequel)

Heart's Insanity (book 1)

Heart's Desire (book 2)

Heart's Collide (book 3)

Hearts Divided (book 4)

Hearts Entwined (book5)

Forest's FALL (book 6)

Hearts The Last Beat (book7)

Contemporary Romance

Firestorm

(Kristy Bromberg's Everyday Heroes World)

Billionaire Romance
Billionaire Boys Club

Hawke

Richard

Brody

Contemporary Romance

Cocky Captain

(Vi Keeland & Penelope Ward's Cocky Hero World)

Romantic Suspense

EACH BOOK IS A STANDALONE NOVEL.

The Starling

~AND~

Science Fiction

Ellie Masters writing as L.A. Warren

Vendel Rising: a Science Fiction Serialized Novel

Books by Jet Masters

If you enjoyed this book by Ellie Masters, the LIGHTER SIDE of the Jet & Ellie writing duo, and aren't afraid of edgier writing, you might enjoy reading BDSM themed books written by Jet, the DARKER SIDE of the Masters' Writing Team.

The DARKER SIDE
Jet Masters is the darker side of the Jet & Ellie writing duo!

Romantic Suspense
Changing Roles Series:
THIS SERIES MUST BE READ IN ORDER.
Book 1: Command Me
Book 2: Control Me
Book 3: Collar Me
Book 4: Embracing FATE
Book 5: Seizing FATE
Book 6: Accepting FATE

HOT READS
A STANDALONE NOVEL.

Down the Rabbit Hole

Light BDSM Romance
The Ties that Bind

EACH BOOK IN THIS SERIES CAN BE READ AS A STANDALONE AND IS ABOUT A DIFFERENT COUPLE WITH AN HEA.

Alexa
Penny
Michelle
Ivy

HOT READS
Becoming His Series

THIS SERIES MUST BE READ IN ORDER.

Book 1: The Ballet
Book 2: Learning to Breathe
Book 3: Becoming His

Dark Captive Romance

A STANDALONE NOVEL.

She's MINE

About the Author

Ellie Masters is a USA Today Bestselling author and Amazon Top 15 Author who writes Angsty, Steamy, Heart-Stopping, Pulse-Pounding, Can't-Stop-Reading Romantic Suspense. In addition, she's a wife, military mom, doctor, and retired Colonel. She writes romantic suspense filled with all your sexy, swoon-worthy alpha men. Her writing will tug at your heartstrings and leave your heart racing.

Born in the South, raised under the Hawaiian sun, Ellie has traveled the globe while in service to her country. The love of her life, her amazing husband, is her number one fan and biggest supporter. And yes! He's read every word she's written.

She has lived all over the United States—east, west, north, south and central—but grew up under the Hawaiian sun. She's also been privileged to have lived overseas, experiencing other cultures and making lifelong friends. Now, Ellie is proud to call herself a Southern transplant, learning to say y'all and "bless her heart" with the best of them.

Ellie's favorite way to spend an evening is curled up on a couch, laptop in place, watching a fire, drinking a good wine, and bringing forth all the characters from her mind to the page and hopefully into the hearts of her readers.

FOR MORE INFORMATION
elliemasters.com

facebook.com/elliemastersromance

x.com/Ellie__Masters

instagram.com/ellie_masters

bookbub.com/authors/ellie-masters

goodreads.com/Ellie_Masters

Connect with Ellie Masters

Website:
elliemasters.com
Amazon Author Page:
elliemasters.com/amazon
Facebook:
elliemasters.com/Facebook
Goodreads:
elliemasters.com/Goodreads
Instagram:
elliemasters.com/Instagram

Final Thoughts

I hope you enjoyed this book as much as I enjoyed writing it. If you enjoyed reading this story, please consider leaving a review on Amazon and Goodreads, and please let other people know. A sentence is all it takes. Friend recommendations are the strongest catalyst for readers' purchase decisions! And I'd love to be able to continue bringing the characters and stories from My-Mind-to-the-Page.

Second, call or e-mail a friend and tell them about this book. If you really want them to read it, gift it to them. If you prefer digital friends, please use the "Recommend" feature of Goodreads to spread the word.

Or visit my blog https://elliemasters.com, where you can find out more about my writing process and personal life.

Come visit The EDGE: Dark Discussions where we'll have a chance to talk about my works, their creation, and maybe what the future has in store for my writing.

Facebook Reader Group: Ellz Bellz

Thank you so much for your support!

Love,

Ellie

Dedication

This book is dedicated to you, my reader. Thank you for spending a few hours of your time with me. I wouldn't be able to write without you to cheer me on. Your wonderful words, your support, and your willingness to join me on this journey is a gift beyond measure.

Whether this is the first book of mine you've read, or if you've been with me since the very beginning, thank you for believing in me as I bring these characters 'from my mind to the page and into your hearts.'

Love,
Ellie

THE END

Made in the USA
Coppell, TX
27 April 2024